By Ian Slater:

FIRESPILL
SEA GOLD
AIR GLOW RED
ORWELL: THE ROAD TO AIRSTRIP ONE
STORM
DEEP CHILL
FORBIDDEN ZONE*
MACARTHUR MUST DIE
WW III*
WW III: RAGE OF BATTLE*
WW III: WORLD IN FLAMES*
WW III: ARCTIC FRONT*
WW III: WARSHOT*
WW III: ASIAN FRONT*
WW III: FORCE OF ARMS*
WW III: SOUTH CHINA SEA*
SHOWDOWN: USA vs. Militia*
BATTLE FRONT: USA vs. Militia*
MANHUNT: USA vs. Militia*

*Published by Fawcett Books

MANHUNT
USA vs. Militia

Ian Slater

FAWCETT GOLD MEDAL • NEW YORK

A Fawcett Gold Medal Book
Published by The Ballantine Publishing Group
Copyright © 1999 by Bunyip Enterprises, Inc.

All rights reserved under International and Pan-American Copyright Conventions. Published in the United States by The Ballantine Publishing Group, a division of Random House, Inc., New York, and simultaneously in Canada by Random House of Canada Limited, Toronto.

Fawcett is a registered trademark and Fawcett Gold Medal and the Fawcett colophon are trademarks of Random House, Inc.

www.randomhouse.com/BB/

Library of Congress Catalog Card Number: 99-90161

ISBN 0-449-15046-1

Manufactured in the United States of America

First Edition: August 1999

10 9 8 7 6 5 4 3 2 1

For Marian, Serena, and Blair

I am indebted to my wife, Marian, whose patience, typing,
and editorial skills continue to give me invaluable support
in my work

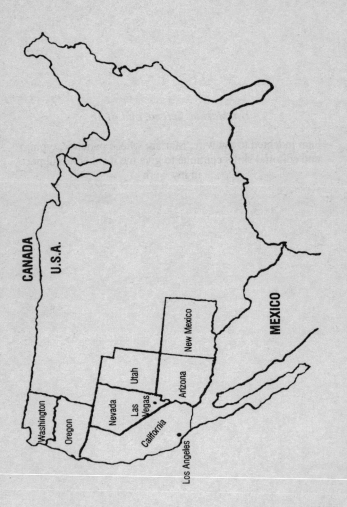

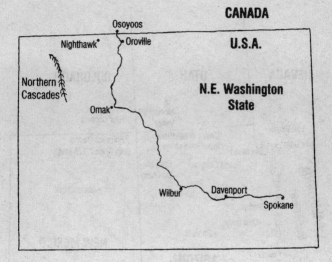

CANADA

U.S.A.

Osoyoos

Nighthawk•   •Oroville

Northern
Cascades

N.E. Washington
State

Omak•

Wilbur•   Davenport•   •Spokane

NEVADA

UTAH

COLORADO

Monument
Valley
Four Corners

Las Vegas

Chinle Wash (Navajo
Indian Reservation)

Shiprock (town)
Ship Rock 7,178 feet

Hoover Dam

Lake Mead

Grand Canyon

Canyon
De Chelly

CALIFORNIA

Mojave Desert

Colorado River

Albuquerque

Parker

Quartzsite

Phoenix

NEW MEXICO

Yuma

ARIZONA

Sonoran Desert

MEXICO

MANHUNT

PROLOGUE

WASHINGTON, July 1—Federal authorities today arrested twelve people it said were members of an Arizona paramilitary group. . . . The authorities said that those arrested called themselves the Viper Militia and trained in the desert with explosives for what one member said was an "upcoming war" with the federal government.

—*The New York Times*

CHAPTER ONE

Phoenix

The panicky call came into Holy Rosary during rush hour, shortly after five. The shaky voice informed the hospital's emergency room that there'd been another clash between federal authorities and Arizona's Scorpion Militia north of the city. Ambulances were already en route to Holy Rosary, where casualties from earlier confrontations between federal troops and the USMC—United States Militia Corps—were now receiving medical treatment under a twenty-four-hour police guard. On Interstate 10 some cars managed to pull over to the shoulder; others, unable to change lanes, simply stopped where they were as the five wailing ambulances, preceded by two motorcycle policemen, wove their way through heavy traffic.

At the hospital, reflections of the flashing lights of the police outriders and ambulances danced madly in the emergency ward's sliding glass doors. The staff had been alerted and was waiting, ready to perform triage the moment the stretchers were wheeled in. The first ambulance's doors opened, the two motorcycle policemen waving onlookers aside as a stretcher bearing a man with bloodied, matted hair sticking to his forehead and breathing laboriously through an oxygen mask was quickly wheeled in.

With this first arrival, a warm push of air invaded the antiseptic smell of the emergency room. A security guard watched as the man was wheeled inside. "It's okay!" one of the motorcycle cops told him, booting his kickstand down. The guard nodded self-importantly, eyeing the interested onlookers outside, determined not to let any unauthorized personnel through the doors, especially the press. Since the federal-militia flare-up in Washington State, some of the wounded militia leaders, like Colonel Vance and Captain Lucky McBride, had been moved here to Phoenix, to stand trial by juries who weren't from the Northwest. But nosy tabloid and even mainstream press types would occasionally try to sneak in to interview anyone, including the police guards posted outside the rooms of Vance and McBride.

A trim intern in her mid-twenties, her emerald-green eyes conveying a no-nonsense air, immediately took over as the resident was called to the phone. As the two ambulance attendants wheeled the patient in, the young intern indicated the nearest bay to a nurse. The intern, whose name tag identified her as Dr. D. Teer, moved inside with the patient and the two ambulance men, the nurse entering last and drawing the yellow modesty curtains. Dr. Teer felt the man's pulse as the two ambulance men undid the stretcher's restraining straps, reaching under the patient's blanket and withdrawing two nine-millimeter Sig/Sauer machine pistols and pushing the two women up against the wall.

Dr. Teer's pager started beeping.

"Turn that off," the taller of the two ambulance imposters ordered quietly.

The third man, the "patient," sat up, holding a .44 Magnum.

"Listen carefully," the ambulance man continued, "You're to tell whoever's in charge on floors two and four that you're being held hostage by the militia, that they're to go get Colonel Vance and Captain McBride and bring them down here—*now*! Any screwing around and you get it right between the eyes. You understand?"

Dr. Teer nodded and Nurse Beverly Malkin tried to speak but couldn't, the gun of the smaller, stockier man against her jugular.

"Then do it," said the tall one, a lean man in his late twenties. "And punch the right fucking numbers. No 911."

The doctor lifted the phone from its wall bracket and pushed the five digits of Holy Rosary's internal emergency number. "It's Dr. Teer here," she said. "Nurse Malkin and I are being held hostage. Bring Colonel Vance and Captain McBride down to Emergency now." There was a pause, then, "Don't argue with me. I said *now*. And alert security that they're to stand aside. I repeat, we are being held hostage. Bring them down now."

"Good girl, Dana," the tall man said. "Now I want you to order whatever you and Beverly here need to take care of Colonel Vance and Captain McBride. We're going on a little trip."

The "patient," a short, red-haired man still sitting on the gurney, retrieved a walkie-talkie from under the blanket. He winked at Teer. "How you doin'?"

She ignored him and told the tall one, "Colonel Vance and Captain McBride are too wounded to be moved."

"Don't con me," he replied. "They're over the worst. We know when they can be moved. All you have to do is call up the dispensary and get the stuff you need. Don't forget anything. And keep your voice down."

She called the pharmacy. The line was busy. She was still in shock. How did he know her first name was Dana? It could only mean that these men had planned it carefully, even knowing who would be on shift. She now recognized Michael Hearn's face from TV's *America's Most Wanted*. He was one of the militiamen who'd escaped from federal custody at Camp Fairchild up in Washington State. She'd never seen a harder face. She called the pharmacy again and told them what she wanted. Replacing the phone in its cradle, she said, "You know you won't get away with it."

"You may be right," Hearn replied, surprisingly calm. "But we're gonna give it the ol' American try. And if we go down, honey, you and Florence Nightingale here—"

The curtain moved. The smaller militiaman glimpsed a face through the slit, whirled about, and fired at the same time as the security guard. The dark-haired militiaman was dead before he hit the floor, and the security guard was writhing and screaming in a pool of blood.

The "patient" held the .44 Magnum on the two women as Hearn yelled into the walkie-talkie, *"Foxtrot go!"*

Dana Teer and Beverly Malkin, the nurse's face drained of color, stood frozen in front of the phony patient. He jammed the Magnum's huge barrel into Dr. Teer's back, the air thick with the odor of blood from the security guard and the dead militiaman.

Seconds later Teer and Malkin heard a soft rush of feet as the Vibram-soled boots of twenty militia assault troops in full desert camouflage uniforms poured in from the other four ambulances. There was a cry for them to stop, a thud, and the crack of broken bone on the hard, polished floor. Half the militiamen stormed the stairwell then, several steps at a time. They were heading for the second floor and McBride. The other ten men commandeered the elevator for the fourth floor, where Colonel Vance could be found.

CHAPTER TWO

General Douglas Freeman was astonished. With over thirty years in the military—from 'Nam, the Gulf, to Bosnia and beyond, and then called out of retirement by the White House because of the increasing militia threat—he had assumed he'd seen it all. Known as George C. Scott among his Special Operations forces because of his striking physical

resemblance to the movie actor who'd played the role of legendary General George Patton, Freeman was now learning
something more. Here, in California's Mojave Desert, his
steel-blue eyes had witnessed something that not even his
fecund imagination had thought possible.

"Most amazing damn thing I've ever seen," he told
Colonel Norton, his second in command.

"Ditto for me," Norton replied, both men's faces, despite
their sunglasses, creased by the hard glare of the Mojave's
sun-bleached sky.

"American know-how," Freeman said. "By God, Norton,
you can't beat it."

At times the general's chauvinism, like that of George
Patton, could be embarrassing, especially during joint exer-
cises with allies. But at this moment on the hard-baked earth
of the artillery range, Norton too took pride in his country's
technological genius—its love affair with gadgets, with the
machine, with everything from electric toothbrushes to the
Mars lander.

"This shell," Freeman told Norton, indicating the nearby
pile of neatly stacked 155mm artillery rounds, "with its
ability to carry either cargo or a high explosive warhead,
will revolutionize warfare." He was talking about the revolutionary Savage system, named after Master Sergeant Ernie
Savage. Packed with munitions instead of high explosive,
Savage rounds could deliver two hundred 5.56mm M-16
rounds for every combat soldier in a six-hundred-man bat-
talion in less than thirteen minutes. The payload of each
155mm shell, the liaison artillery officer explained to Freeman, drifted earthward via a drogue chute deployed by a
small explosive charge in the nose of the shell. The main
chute deployed a short time later, the shell maintaining its
flight path until falling to earth about a half mile beyond the
first-aid target or the combat area target.

"At present," the liaison artillery officer added, "we're working on a high-capacity projectile that will have a longer range
and will house antitank rocket launchers and grenades—both
hand and rifle grenades."

"How about more medical supplies?" Freeman asked.

Another artillery officer came up and tapped Norton on the shoulder. "Phone, sir."

As Norton excused himself, Freeman, staring grimly into the desert, said to the liaison officer, "I was thinking of our Rangers in Somalia. In 'ninety-three. Fighting one of the battles in that godforsaken capital—Mogadishu. Our medics had exhausted all their intravenous supplies. Some of 'em were crying as they carried out triage—forced to decide who needed what the most. Had to rip IV drips out of some boys to put in others." The general was shaking his head. "For the American army to run out of supplies like that, goddamn—"

"Sir," the liaison officer hurried to assure him, "with Savage, we can supply frontline medics with all kinds of stuff—not just blood and plasma. We can shoot in everything from Band-Aids to bone saws, electric monitors, urgently needed drugs, IV drips. More hypodermics, morphine, surgical instruments—you name it."

"Good," Freeman said. "You know, eighty percent of all deaths caused by battle wounds occur in the first hour." It was more a statement than a question.

"Yes, sir."

"Well, Captain, let's hope we don't have to use it."

"Amen to that, General."

Norton returned to inform Freeman that the news media was reporting a militia attack of some kind in Arizona.

CHAPTER THREE

The first of the ten militiamen to reach the second floor of Holy Rosary jerked back the hydraulically hinged door, the nine men behind him streaming into the highly polished corridor. A nurse's aide in a crisp blue uniform saw them, dropped a tray of juice containers, and ran back into the nurse's station. The cop sitting on a chair outside Room 201 saw her flee and looked down to the other end of the corridor. There, he glimpsed the banana-shaped mag of a Kalashnikov, and jumped to his feet, drawing his weapon. He was flung back, dead, before his .38 cleared the holster, the forward militiaman's AK-47 burst punching the policeman up against the wall, where he slid down, his blood smearing the wall, before he collapsed in front of 201.

By now a male nurse's aide in Emergency had phoned the fourth floor, and the policeman and three other security guards guarding Vance were waiting, two on either side of the elevator. It didn't stop on four, as they'd expected, but kept going up to the fifth floor. But no shots were heard on the fifth.

Not sure what to do, the policemen and security guards decided to split up, two outside the elevator, two to cover the stair door, as the elevator came back down. None of the four had pressed the button, but it stopped nevertheless. As the doors opened, the two hospital security men began firing, their shots echoing loudly in the elevator shaft. When the smoke cleared, two nurses lay dead in a pool of blood on the elevator floor.

The stairway door to the right splintered then, the stairwell resounding with gunfire as four militiamen opened up before reaching the door, bullets passing through it and killing one of its two defenders; the other security guard, badly wounded, was finished off by a vicious kick that snapped his neck. The two guards by the elevator threw down their weapons, raised their hands, and were used as hostages to assure the safe passage of Vance and McBride in the militiamen's ambulance motorcade. The leader of the storm troopers' rescue/attack against Holy Rosary, Lieutenant Hearn, a neo-Nazi murderer of Pacific Northwest fame, told the federals—by which militiamen meant all U.S. state and federal authorities—that he would release the hostages when he was ready. Which meant when he felt safe.

Phoenix homicide detectives discovered that the two nurses in the elevator were already dead when the elevator doors opened. Hearn's storm troopers had killed them in cold blood on the fifth floor, slitting their throats, before blazing their way down the stairwell to the fourth floor to snatch Colonel Vance.

"General," Norton informed Freeman, "that attack in Arizona—apparently there's been a hostage-taking from a hospital in Phoenix. A doctor, a nurse, and two security guards."

"Right!" Freeman said. "For once fate's put me in precisely the right place at the right time."

Well, yes, thought Norton, who'd been with Freeman, but we're a good two hundred miles from Phoenix.

"Activate my ALERTs and get them assembled with choppers. Probable departure zone . . ." Freeman called up the map of the Mojave on his laptop and pointed to a spot not more than five miles from the California-Arizona state line.

The thing that struck Norton immediately was Freeman's satisfied tone. Like Patton, the man lived for action. Even on his holidays in the Southwest, while everyone else was busy playing golf and thinking only about golf, Freeman would be taking in the lay of the land, noting high ground, optimum defense positions, and natural camouflage. Indeed, long before Freeman earned his officer's commission, when he was still a boy and others played with toy cars, young Douglas Freeman spent his paper route money in acquiring a war library. He knew the great battles of the first American Civil War by heart, his hero General Custer—not only the Custer of Little Big Horn, but the Custer of the charge at Gettysburg, who routed Jeb Stuart's "Invincibles" to become, at twenty-three, the youngest general in the Union Army. Custer, like Freeman, had led out front—eleven horses shot from beneath him—and for Freeman the A in Custer's initials stood not for "Armstrong" but for "audacity." The second thing Norton noticed, after Freeman's all but joyous receipt of the news of a militia attack, was Freeman's proprietary use of *my* ALERTs. Admittedly, the general had played an important part in establishing them, and had a ready list on his computer of men he'd fought with, men he trusted to go unhesitatingly into harm's way. But they were hardly his private army.

Norton reminded Freeman that in such situations the Pentagon was under orders from the White House not to send in ALERTs without specific instructions from the President. "We received a reminder about that this morning, General."

Freeman's jaw was clenched. "By God, Norton, is this more political bullshit we're involved with?"

"Afraid so, General. Way the White House sees it, this should be handled by the folks in Tucson. No federals. They say it would be an insult to the Arizona governor—make it look as if it can't be handled by the state government in Tucson."

"Well, *is* Tucson handling it?" Freeman demanded.

"They've dispatched SWAT teams," Norton told him. "Besides, there's another angle from the White House."

"Don't tell me," Freeman interjected angrily. "They're scared shitless again of what might happen to 'investor confidence' overseas if Washington has to take a hand. By God, Norton, I smell Delorme behind this."

"Maybe so, General, but in all fairness, Delorme's duty as National Security Adviser is to advise the President. And he agreed to go along with recalling you out of retirement to keep a rein on the militias."

"He did it *reluctantly*, Norton," Freeman said, looking up, recalling Delorme's comment at the time. "I was told that he thought my mouth could be—and I quote—'as big a threat to the Republic as the militias.'"

"But he did come on our side—eventually," Norton responded.

"All right, but you tell me how in hell I'm supposed to keep *rein* on the militia if I'm not allowed to attack them, goddammit!" Before Norton could offer any defense, the general acknowledged Norton's earlier point about the possible effects on an already skittish Wall Street, should the President precipitously turn federal troops loose. It would indeed elevate what at the moment was a local, state problem into a national one—something bigger than the Randy Weaver and Waco screwups combined. Besides, if the militia types on the run—the likes of Vance, McBride, and the Nazi skinhead, Hearn—got national attention, it would be an enormous shot in the arm for the United States Militia Corps recruiters. The unemployed, and alienated youth, were fertile recruiting ground for the USMC, which now consisted of more than 380 militia groups. Each group had an average of one hundred trained and armed militiamen, for a total of approximately forty thousand. Many had been trained by Vietnam and Gulf War vets who were bitterly antigovernment, believing they had been lied to and betrayed by the government about Agent Orange and the Gulf War syndrome, among other things.

"So," Freeman challenged Norton as they walked back to their Hummer, "what happens if the Arizona police SWAT team fails to free this doctor and nurse and the two security guards, and lets that murderer Hearn get away with Vance and McBride?"

"They're confident they won't, General. Police SWAT teams are heavily armed, well trained, and they've got helos to leapfrog the ambulance convoy. It has to stop somewhere, and they'll be waiting."

"Norton," the general said as the Hummer started and sent up a cough of dry desert dust—in some areas in the Southwest, it hadn't rained in years—"you remember how we routed the militia from Butcher's Ridge up in that Washington wilderness—"

"Sawtooth Wilderness," Norton put in.

"Yes, from there to the Columbia River. We've got to do the same here. Attack before they scatter. Seek and destroy, not wait for them to pull up. Attack 'em when we see 'em. Like Custer did at Powder River."

Norton fell silent. It was difficult to hear in the Hummer, the agile yet solidly built vehicle alternately grinding through sand and bucking loose shale. Besides, while Norton's chief job as Freeman's second in command was to always be truthful, and to restrain the general's volubly violent moments, he thought it would be inappropriate to remind the general that after Powder River there came a place called Little Big Horn and an Indian called Sitting Bull. And the Indians—like the militia—had been notoriously good at hit-and-run—as well as a stand-up fight, if it came to that.

There were now twenty-six squad cars in pursuit as the ambulance convoy sped west along Arizona's Highway 10.

"California bound," Freeman opined when told of the latest police report by Norton.

"How can you be sure?" Norton pressed.

"I can't, but my guess is they want to get to the L.A.–San Diego stretch as soon as possible. Merge with the millions down there. Then it'd be like finding the proverbial needle in a haystack."

Norton nodded his agreement. The general had a point, and as usual, Norton thought, was one step ahead. Freeman asked his driver to bring up Arizona's southwest quadrant on the Hummer's laptop. He turned it on the swivel mount to avoid the hot sun's glare on the computer screen, his finger moving up from the Colorado River's mouth in the Gulf of

California, which lay between the Baja peninsula and northern Mexico, following the course of the river, which formed the border between Arizona and California. "Here," he told Norton, "at Ehrenberg. Once those sons of bitches cross the river—the state line—it's a *federal* offense. The President'll have to turn it over to us. Neither the Phoenix police nor the Arizona Highway Patrol can do anything. He'll have to go federal—national. They're ours, Norton."

Norton hoped not, and James Murphy, the Hummer's driver—known alternately as either Jimmy or Murph—could see the frown of consternation on the colonel's face in the rearview mirror. The last time Freeman had been faced with a militia hostage situation was on the Oregon-Washington border. The militia had taken a bridge, and Freeman, as commander-in-chief of the Northwest Theater, had ordered it retaken. The officer commanding the 82nd Airborne, who'd been parachuted in, told Freeman there were civilian hostages, including women and children. Freeman told him to "take the bridge"—a vital crossing to the port of Astoria on the Columbia's five-mile-wide mouth.

The paratroop general, Trevor, told his men to fire. They'd cleared the bridge. After the battle, General Trevor walked out on the bridge, strewn with the dead. The sight, the smell, was too much for him. He stood by the rail, where a slight breeze dissipated the fog rising above the sea marsh about the bridge, and was shot dead by a militia sniper. The word among the 82nd was that, knowing militiamen were still at large in the marshes and around Astoria, the general had in effect committed suicide. Others said it was murder, and that the real murderer was "George C. Scott" Freeman.

"So," a sergeant from the 82nd had told Jimmy Murphy, "Freeman got his goddamn bridge and got Trevor killed."

"If we hadn't taken that bridge when we did," Freeman had told the press, "we'd have lost a lot more than those civilians killed on the bridge. May I remind you, gentlemen and ladies," he'd said acidly, "the militia weren't taking prisoners. Their leaders, Colonel Vance among them, had told them that, unlike us federals, the militia didn't have the *facilities* for prisoners."

"How does that justify your ordering the killing of women and children, General?" a reporter had asked.

"It doesn't," Freeman snapped. "Nothing justifies the killing of women and children. But we were facing insurrection by a militia that would stop at nothing, and this country was being held hostage by people who advocate the overthrow of this government. Perhaps you're not aware of how this plays overseas—the supposedly strongest nation in the world held to political ransom by rebels. Makes us look like some damned tin-pot Third World Nazi country."

Norton had cautioned him, but as was frequently the case, the general had gone too far with the press. "*Tin-pot* Third World" would have been enough to cause the U.S. embarrassment in the U.N., but "*Nazi*" tacked onto it had caused an uproar. The State Department had been flooded with messages of outrage from Third World countries.

CHAPTER FOUR

Norton knew that Freeman's allusion to a "tin-pot Third World Nazi country" would rebound quickly in the press and come back to haunt him the next time there was any trouble with the militia, as it did now during discussions in the White House as to whether or not Freeman should be allowed to attack the militia when they crossed the Arizona state line. But even Norton wasn't prepared for the cries of outrage from State Department officials who, in their desire to have Freeman permanently retired, were unanimously "shocked and appalled" by what they called the general "habitually riding roughshod over the feelings of valued allies and friends."

"Sack him!" Judy Lamont, the Secretary of State, told the President. "The man's senile!"

The President was toying with a pencil, drumming it on the patent-leather-bound blotter. "He may be a menace, Judy, but he's not senile. Sharp as a tack when it comes to the fighting. He may look like an aging George C. Scott, but he knows his way around a battlefield."

Lamont grimaced impatiently. "With all due respect, Mr. President, we're no longer at war with the militia. We're having this minor skirmish in Arizona—"

"There have been several people killed," put in Walter Shelbourne, the Army's Joint Chief.

"I realize that," retorted Lamont, a no-nonsense, bespectacled woman in her mid-fifties with the harried look of a vice principal on the first day of school. "Of course I'm sorry people have been killed, but across the board we're at peace with the militia in the rest of the country, and I don't think it behooves us to overreact, especially not when we're counseling others abroad—the British government and IRA militias in particular—not to be drawn into any sustained engagement."

"You mean *war*?" queried the President, who by now had learned to quickly decipher State's deliberately obscure language such as "sustained engagement"—they made it sound like someone waiting to get married.

"Yes," Lamont conceded. "War."

"I see your point of view, Madam Secretary, but this Vance and company are making us look like fools abroad. *We* are looking like a Third World outfit."

"And," interjected Treasury Secretary Adrian Nanton, "never mind what it's doing to Wall Street. Overseas investors, just as they do any time we have major domestic problems, get jittery."

"Oh, c'mon, Adrian," Lamont retorted. "Let's keep it in perspective. It's hardly a *major* problem."

The President stopped drumming his pencil. "It is to the families of the dead," he said.

There was a heavy silence in the room before Nanton continued. "Foreign investors think we've got a Quebec—a French Canada—on our hands, a nationwide secessionist movement among the hundreds of militia battalions to break with the rest of the country, especially in the West. And it doesn't help any that French-speaking Cajuns in the South, as far as New Orleans, have bought into it. I think we have to move decisively, Mr. President."

Attorney General Helen Wyeth, like Judy Lamont from State, wanted to calm things down. "We are acting decisively, Adrian. My God, we now have at least thirty police cars—including SWAT teams—in pursuit. This thing could be over in a few hours, by sundown tomorrow at the latest, without any federal intervention."

"Yeah, right!" whispered Walter Shelbourne, who knew just how tough the militia could be.

"All right, Helen," the President said. "And Judy, I agree— what we don't need is overreaction. Another Waco. Let the Arizona state police handle it. And if they need it, they'll ask for federal assistance, and then we can send in the National Guard from . . ."

He paused, put on his reading glasses, and peered at a printout on his desk.

Army's Walter Shelbourne didn't like him. He had one of those silver chains attached to his reading glasses—Christ, all he needed was a pair of long Bermuda shorts and tennis shoes and he could move to Florida with the rest of the Canadians. Shelbourne recalled that Freeman used reading glasses too, but refused to wear the chain—said he looked "damned ridiculous."

"Yes," the President said, his finger following the printout line. "We have a National Guard unit in Phoenix."

Shelbourne didn't know whether to laugh or cry. The guard unit was the 153rd Field Artillery Brigade. Even if

they were called, an artillery brigade couldn't outrun five
ambulances racing west at what the last police report said
was "in excess of a hundred miles per hour." He could only
hope that, despite how tough he knew the militia was, Attorney General Helen Wyeth would be proved right. Outnum-
bering the militia convoy by at least three to one, the
Arizona police should be able to handle it.

The first in the long string of over twenty squad cars from
Phoenix was a Cherokee four-by-four, with a SWAT team
inside. All the vehicles were breaking the speed limit. They
were no more than a quarter mile behind the militia's ambulances, the late yet intense afternoon sun all but blinding the
drivers, including Hearn in the lead vehicle.

"I told those bastards to keep back," Hearn complained to
his driver-cum-guard, a medium-sized, bull-necked man
called Toro, whose complexion was permanently florid.

Toro's quick, darting eyes gave the impression that he was
a heavy drinker, his demeanor one of barely contained
anger. "They figure they'll wear us down," he told Hearn,
whose anger, exacerbated by the sun beating down relentlessly, was as intense as Toro's.

Everyone tried to excuse it away by saying it was a *dry*
heat. Still, it was hot; so hot that back in the third ambulance—
the one holding the doctor and the nurse—there were com-
plaints from the driver about the heat. The sun's light made
the road look like a ribbon of gold stretching into the Sonoran Desert, which spilled over from northern Mexico into
southern Arizona. The air conditioner had broken down, the
driver complained, and the two women hostages were
"whining about it."

"Let 'em whine," Hearn told the driver in a voice that was
breaking up on the cell phone.

Toro, hearing the rush of static, opined, "Must be the cops
tryin' to jam us."

Hearn dropped the cell phone beside him onto the seat
and told Toro to give him the "compact," by which he meant
the palm-sized two-way radio that deliberately scrambled

messages so that only the sender and receiver, their phones unscrambling the message, could understand one another.

"Leader to Five. Come in," Hearn said, holding the radio phone close to his mouth, his posture, which amused the normally unamused Toro, like that of an ostrich sitting up very straight. Like he had a stick up his ass, Toro thought.

"Five to Leader."

"We'll pull up for a rest break soon," Hearn told him. "Time your two guys took a leak."

"Okay."

"They're still cuffed, right?"

"Yessir."

"They want to shit, you uncuff 'em one at a time. Cuff 'em again when they're finished."

"I got it. They're pretty quiet and—"

Hearn cut him off, not wanting to waste any more battery power than absolutely necessary. He put the radio phone down without taking his eyes off the road. "Toro, you know the drill."

"Yeah."

"Christ, I hate those fucking sirens."

"Me too."

"Tryin' to wear us down."

"Psychological bullshit, right."

The SWAT team driver, Hogan, like all the other drivers in the twenty-six-squad-car motorcade, was, as per instructions from his chief of police, ignoring Hearn's order to stop following him. Instead, he was mounting a fifty-yard buffer zone between the SWAT team and the militia's last car, the Cherokee sitting on eighty mph.

"Just a matter of time," one of the four-man team told his buddies. "Keep an eye on their tail from go to whoa. Sooner or later their infrastructure starts shakin'. Lack of sleep, water, food."

"Gas," Hogan said.

"You got it, Hoag. Just wait 'em out. What'd they think?

They're going to get to the river and just be able to skedaddle across the bridge?"

"I don't know what they're thinking," Hogan replied, "but talking about gas, what about our outfit? I mean, all the uniforms behind us? Some of them'll be out of gas pretty soon."

"How do you figure that?"

"Well, most of 'em didn't come from the depot—I mean with full tanks. They responded to the call from all over."

The other SWAT member shrugged. "So some'll have to give up their juice to another car, right?"

Hogan grinned. "You on the ball, Frederico."

"Always on the ball, Hoag."

"How do we know what ambulances the hostages are in?" another team member asked.

"We don't," Hogan said, "but sooner or later they're gonna have to pull up for a piss, gasoline—whatever. Then we'll see."

"Yessir," said Frederico, who was nursing a Remington 870 shotgun; "loaded for bear," as he put it.

"Maybe the militia's carrying extra fuel?" Hogan said. No one knew. "Hey, you heard the one about the militiaman and the federal?"

"Nope," Frederico replied.

"Well, this militia guy and a federal are randy as hell, right, so they're walkin' along this wire fence and see a sheep—got its head all caught up in the wire. So the fed hops the fence, drops his pants, and screws the sheep. When he's finished, out of breath, he says to the militia guy, 'It's your turn now.' The militiaman says, 'No, I couldn't do that.' 'Why not?' the federal says. 'Couldn't get my head through the wire.' "

Amid the laughter came the crackle on the police band. Several cars were pulling off to pool enough gas for one of them.

"Jeez," Hogan said, turning down the volume of background chatter on the police band. "Are those guys gonna be pissed. Sittin' out here—fuck all to do 'cept watch the crows."

"Ah," Frederico said jocularly, "maybe they'll find a sheep."

More laughter, and the militia's last car dead ahead. They had to stop sometime.

CHAPTER FIVE

In the border town of Parker, surrounded by irrigated green fields and desert, twenty-eight miles west of Arizona's Buckskin Mountains, the temperature was still hovering around a hundred degrees as La Paz County sheriff Placido Montoya ordered two patrol cars nose-to-nose to block the two-lane bridge over the Colorado. Here the turquoise rush of water released from Parker Dam to the north passed irrigated fields as it flowed south toward the delta two hundred miles away in the Gulf of Baja. A police chopper out of Phoenix reported that the ambulance convoy had turned north at Quartzsite, heading up Montoya's way on Highway 95.

Place Montoya, a tall, lanky man in his late thirties, didn't say much. His pale blue eyes, now hidden behind shades, usually told the story, along with his ivory-handled Colt .45 six-shooter pistol whose holster was strapped to his right thigh. Three deputies, all older than Montoya, two of them cradling shotguns, the other a .30 rifle, stood behind the two police cars, waiting.

"Don't see," one of them opined nervously, "how we can do much, Place, if they got hostages." The other two deputies looked at Montoya, his back to them as he kept his eyes on 95. The long, ugly white scar across the base of his neck that he'd gotten for breaking up a fight down in Yuma was clearly visible, and in striking contrast to his gray-streaked black hair and the leathery sun-baked brown of his neck.

"You got a plan, Place?" asked the man with the .30.

"Uh-huh," Montoya said.

The deputies exchanged glances. The deputy with the .30 turned to the taciturn sheriff. "Well, hell, Place, ya mind tellin' us, or is it a state secret?"

Montoya looked at the deputy, then across the river toward Earp, on the California side, at an adobe-style house that wasn't there, the red of its tiled roof watery in the mirage. "Stop 'em. Ask 'em to let the hostages go."

The deputy thought about it for a second or two. *Ask* them. Montoya was used to *telling* folks what he wanted—what the law demanded. "And they're gonna release the hostages—just like that?"

"If we're nice to 'em." Montoya paused and with Gary Cooper deliberation took off the shades and slid them by feel rather than sight into his khaki shirt pocket. "Make 'em an offer they can't refuse."

"Jesus Christ," one of the shotgun deputies murmured to his compadre under his breath. "We're in the fuckin' movies again." The quiet, undemonstrative Montoya had a passion for film, and much of his off-duty time—not that he was, practically speaking, ever off duty, given La Paz's shoestring budget—was spent watching videos in his room above Parker's Wrangler Saloon. An only child, born and raised on a small ranch outside Yuma, a hundred miles south of Parker, Montoya had never formed a close relationship other than with Bluey, a lean Australian cattle dog whose abilities— Montoya despised the word "tricks"—had amazed more than one cowboy. In roundup, in response to Montoya's hand signal or whistle, the dog did more work than any two men, Mexican or American. When Montoya was in his mid-twenties, it was said around town—whether the town was Parker, Ehrenberg, or Yuma—that it was time for "young Place" to marry—to settle down.

"He's married to that dog," was the opinion of the Wrangler's owner and bartender, Jimmy Lance, though he didn't say that to Montoya's face, perhaps recalling the time Harry Shead, the local drunk, told Montoya, "I reckon you're a faggot." Montoya felled him with one blow, rearranging Shead's jaw before he hit the floor. "Not that there's anything wrong with it," Montoya had said.

Only one man in the saloon, Jimmy Lance, recognized the line from the old *Seinfeld* episode about homosexuality. A less secure man than Montoya, Jimmy had told one of the deputies later—with Harry Shead present—might have made it his business to go "chasin' pussy" to prove his masculinity, but not Place Montoya. "He don't give a shit. He knows who he is. 'Sides, when the right woman comes along, he'll strike."

"Strike," the deputy had said. "Make 'im sound like a rattler."

Jimmy Lance nodded. "There's a bit of rattler in Place. Unpredictable. Ain't true that all a rattler does is attack. Hell, I reckon that's why they use the rattle—give you fair warning."

Harry Shead could barely talk, his jaw all wired up, but because he'd lost a couple of lower teeth, the sound, albeit muffled and nasal, came out venomously. "Maybe he fucks his horse," he'd said.

Jimmy Lance had looked across the bar at Shead, whose T-shirt and baggy cotton pants were still stiff here and there with bloodstains. At forty, he looked much older. "Haven't you had enough, Harry?" he asked. "Place hears you spoutin' off like that, he's going to fix your *upper* jaw."

"I'll fix *'im*," Shead retorted.

The deputy, Arnie, saw Montoya later outside the only blacksmith shop for two hundred miles and cautioned Place, "Shead's an ornery old bastard, Place. You better keep an eye over your shoulder. He's a bad 'un."

"He was drinking?"

"Yeah, he was drinking, but he's always drinking. Doesn't mean he won't do what he says, Place. He intends to get even."

"How would he do that?" Place asked, lifting his bay's front foot, checking the shoe for stones.

"Hell, I don't know, but he means it."

Place had smiled. Was he taking Shead seriously? If he wasn't, he could end up dead. Shead was the grudge-holding type—like most everybody else—kept it warmer than a hen on an egg. And when the time was right . . .

Trouble was, the deputy thought, if Shead came looking for Place, he'd as likely take out the three deputies as well. No witnesses.

Now, waiting in the hot, dry heat on the bridge, Arnie, who was checking for the sixth time in as many minutes that he'd chambered a round in the .30, was recalling the sheriff's enigmatic smile at the blacksmith's. It had made Arnie nervous then, and it did now, because he linked Shead's threat to what he was sure was an imminent confrontation with the militia— as if Place's laid-back response to Shead's threat intimated too casual an attitude toward the militia. If Place was too damn casual, the four of them could go down in a hail of automatic fire. Phoenix said they were all armed with AK-47s.

"Place?"

The sheriff had picked a dry, straw-colored stalk of passpalem grass and had it between his teeth.

"Place?"

"Uh-huh?" He still hadn't turned around.

"Shead hasn't stopped about you, y'know. Guys in town told me he's sayin'—" Arnie glanced nervously at the other two deputies with the shotguns. "Says you screw Rainboy."

"Not 'less he says please."

Jesus, Arnie thought, the other two deputies sputtering and guffawing. Just like that—without even turning around, still chewing on the passpalem grass. Quick as a rattler.

One of the other shotgun deputies asked the other, "Place cool as that? Or is this all bullshit?"

The other man shrugged. "Beats me."

His buddy's face was creased with anger. "Phoenix boys'll probably get 'em before they ever get here."

The other man said nothing.

                              *   *   *

In the Desert Storm–painted Hummer on California's 95,
moving south parallel to the Arizona border twenty miles to
the east, Colonel Norton's cell phone buzzed. Freeman, in
the back, had been calling up different area maps of the border, moving north to south down the Colorado all the way
from Las Vegas in southern Nevada's Mojave Desert down
through the intermittent splashes of green in and around
Lake Havasu City, halfway down the line, and on through
the Sonoran Desert to the gulf. Though Freeman knew how
to use the laptop—at least its basic functions—and was an
advocate of the best modern equipment the Pentagon's
money could buy, he was not a lover of technology per se.
Like Patton, he adhered to a code of chivalry—the salute of
mutual respect between combatants before the duel, whether
it be in the skies of 1914–18, the time of Von Richthoven, or
back when knights fought each other honorably on horse-
back. The salute had originated then, as combatants raised their
visors courteously and showed their faces to one another before battle, as had the handshake, born as a gesture to show
there were no concealed weapons. For the young Douglas
Freeman at officer school, his discovery that such a code of
chivalry had indeed existed and been obeyed—that it was
not a fantasy of Hollywood but had actually happened—sent
a shiver of excitement through him. The last acts of chivalry
he could remember were those he'd found as a boy in the accounts of Rommel, the Desert Fox, whose behavior toward
the prisoners of war had been documented by British POWs
in Africa's Western Desert before Montgomery's Eighth
Army pushed Rommel's Afrika Korps back from whence it
came. Pictures of both Rommel and Patton, whose forces
had clashed at Qatar, and where the Americans had re-
deemed the lost honor of their ignominious defeat at
Kassarine Pass, adorned the otherwise spartan interior of
Freeman's HQ tent on the California side of the Sonoran
Desert.

Norton, with one hand on the grip above the co-driver's
seat, took the call as Freeman held onto the flip-down laptop

tray, the Hummer swerving to miss a pothole where the desert, like some inexorable glacier, with the help of sudden deluges of unexpected El Niño–generated storms, had slowly but relentlessly eaten away at the edge of the road.

"By God, this is rough," Freeman declared. "Lot of it could've been prevented if the government had listened to Art Bell. But no, they thought Bell's guests were a bunch of kooks. Now we've got more friggin' potholes than Beirut." Norton heard the general's mention of Art Bell, the host of radio's coast-to-coast nightly broadcast, about the only show in America that took unscreened calls from all over. Many of the calls in the past year had been from people who were scared—justifiably, as it turned out—that the effect of El Niño, the Christ Child current, warming up the eastern Pacific over an area larger than the continental U.S., would produce drastic and chaotic weather all over the country— rain and floods in normally dry, drought-ridden deserts, and on the other hand producing such warm water off the relatively cold Northwest that marlin, unknown in those waters, were being caught off Washington State.

When Norton got off the phone, however, the last thing on his mind was the Northwest, which had also been a hotbed of militia activity, and from whence the legendary Lucky McBride had come.

"General," Norton informed him, "Phoenix police say there were six killed in the raid—three police, three civilians, one a little girl visiting on the second floor. Militia apparently. The little girl took one in the shoulder but the wound was fist-sized—lost too much blood before they could help her. Which means the militia must've used dumdum bullets."

"Bastards! Well, they'll reap the whirlwind for this."

Norton knew the general was right. There'd be a public outcry from California to New York. There would be enormous pressure on the President to hand the pursuit over to federal authorities. It would be an unprecedented public relations nightmare for the militia, especially for Vance, McBride, and their rescuers. Norton knew the response from the militia would be instantaneous. Vance, if the high-speed road chase didn't kill him, would express deep regret and sorrow about the death of the little girl—an apology Norton had no trouble believing would be sincere and genuinely heartfelt. But then either Vance, McBride, or someone else in the 380 known militia groups in the U.S. would point out that it had been Freeman who, by his direct order to "take the bridge" at Astoria, had killed—the militia would say "had murdered"—several children. And Norton was sure that they'd also point out—and it was the truth—that unlike the militia raid on Holy Rosary to rescue Vance and McBride, General Freeman must have known the moment he gave the order in Astoria that it would result in the killing of innocents. So Freeman could hardly take the high moral ground now.

By the time Freeman's Hummer, well south of Fort Mojave, had reached a point sixteen miles in the Mojave due west of Lake Havasu City, the temperature was 104 degrees Fahrenheit.

In Arizona, the five ambulances were still heading north toward Parker. Dana Teer and Beverly Malkin, handcuffed, were perspiring heavily in the heat. Their guard told the driver to try the air conditioner again.

"It's still broke," the driver said. "Shit."

The driver had opened the windows, but it made little difference, a hot, hard wind roaring in.

CHAPTER SIX

The imminent confrontation, unless Sheriff Place Montoya let them through, was being hyped by CNN, the three New York networks, and a plethora of affiliates from Nevada to the north, California in the west, and New Mexico eastward. But it was CNN, with its scores of ever-ready freelancers, who was capturing most of the U.S. audience's attention, as well as that of the rest of the world. Among the eager radio listeners was Jeremy Brigham Eleen, a devout Mormon and a battle-hardened militia captain in his late twenties. Eleen had been incarcerated in Camp Fairchild, a federal prison just south of the Fairchild Air Force Base near Spokane in eastern Washington. Despite its innocuous-sounding name, Camp Fairchild was a barbed-wire federal POW camp of over nine hundred militia prisoners—the federals called them "internees"—from which Eleen and other militiamen had made a mass escape. They shot up the Air Force base before many of them had been rounded up and unceremoniously returned to Camp Fairchild and confined to barracks, allowed out only under strict supervision by the "goons," their word for the federal guards. They were forced to fill in "Archie," a tunnel that over fifty POWs, under Eleen's direction, had dug under the wire.

Once a child of Mormon optimism, Eleen had grown up in an increasingly alienated West, and like many other Americans, particularly in the West and South, viewed the federal government's gun laws as a piecemeal attack on the right to bear arms. Further, they believed that the federal government intended to disarm the citizenry of the United States, and thus render it defenseless against the unfettered power of Big Brother. Western militias felt this most acutely in their dealings with the federal government over land and water rights, for while only five percent of all federal land lay in the East, government ownership of land in the West, including Alaska, was over fifty percent. And many saw the restrictions on land use forced on them by Washington, D.C., through such federal agencies as the Bureau of Indian Affairs, the Bureau of Land Management, and the National Parks Service, as stifling free enterprise. Until it was torn down by Camp Fairchild's chief administrator, whom the militia POWs derisively called "Commandant," extracts from a three-quarter-page ad in *USA Today* featuring Charlton Heston had adorned the door of Eleen's thirty-man hut. In the ad, Heston, the president of the National Rifle Association, was exhorting followers to vigorously defend the Second Amendment, claiming that "the doorway to all freedoms is framed with muskets."

It had been and was the rallying cry for all those on the right who, despite differences on other issues, were all united in this war of the Second Amendment, conveniently forgetting or ignoring that part of the ad wherein Heston had mentioned how he'd joined the freedom marches with Martin Luther King, Jr. All that mattered to the thousands of militia and the millions who implicitly supported them in their anger with the excesses of the federal government was what they, like Hollywood's Moses, saw as the "first right among equals": to keep and bear arms.

The militias had used a wide interpretation when it came to what constituted "arms," including anything from a handgun to surface-to-air Stinger missiles bought on the Army surplus black market. Here, due to a simple clerical "error entry" in a defense computer, an "A" weapon that should have been demilitarized—before sale, having its guts pulled out—was often "accidentally" downgraded on the computer to a "C" graded surplus item such as a water canteen. And it had long been suspected by head of the Joint Chiefs, Walter Shelbourne, that the purchase of such items was being funded by secret funds not only from those in the U.S. who supported the militia's agenda, but by those abroad whose interests were served by domestic upheaval in the United States. In this, Secretary of Treasury Nanton was correct. Any disruption of trade flow, as when teamsters had categorically refused to drive trucks on roads staked out by militia snipers, would paralyze interstate trade as well as frighten ordinary civilians off the highways. Until a guarantee of safe passage—almost impossible to get—was obtained from the federal government, all commerce would come to a stop, the flow of goods, including millions of tons of perishables, would be halted, and people would be stymied by just one militia "sniper" phone call and/or land mine scare.

In Camp Fairchild's hut 5A, Jeremy Eleen and most of the thirty men clustered around the smuggled-in, palm-sized transistor radio, four men on either side of the hut on "goon watch." They were listening to the broadcast of the ambulance chase in Arizona, over a thousand miles to the south, and it was providing a badly needed boost in morale. The POWs' hitherto somber mood, most noticeable for its utter lack of optimism and pervasive sense of failure, was a condition Eleen could actually smell—a kind of acidic perspiration secreted by hopelessness and despair. The men who'd been recaptured, instead of feeling part of a cohesive unit, had broken up into cliques marked by hostility, the tolerance of each other's eccentricities so evident in the camaraderie of their tunnel-digging days now gone. Their recapture had given birth to a host of petty disputes that, had it not been for Eleen and other militia officers in the camp, would have ended in violence. Any fight that did break out between the prisoners was now a source of amusement rather than concern for the bored federal guards in the watch towers that stood above the barbed- and razor-wire-topped fence that marked the rectangular perimeter of the camp. POWs who used to flirt with danger, walking near the mined and sensor-planted "No Go" zone that formed a defensive moat around the POW camp, no longer bothered to taunt the guards.

"Shithead!" one of 5A's lookouts shouted. Eleen and the others quickly dispersed amid the triple bunk rows, some to card games in progress, others looking on, a few writing letters for the time when, if ever, the Commandant relented enough in his punishment for escapees to allow letters to be mailed. For a while, once a month, Commandant Moorehead had allowed some letters—those written by "new" POWs; that is, those who weren't recent escapees—to be mailed home. Until he discovered that notes to loved ones written by recent escapees were being slipped inside the new prisoners' envelopes. Since then, Moorehead had banned all letters. The few men who doggedly kept writing were noted by Eleen. Though depressed himself, both over his failure to make good his escape and by a nagging obsession with having left a wounded man, Rubinski, behind while he'd tried to lead his men out of a minefield, Eleen was still officer enough to understand that if he could ever revive a spirit of defiance sufficient to launch another escape attempt, the men he would choose as his cadre of organizers would be the letter writers. It was such men who had at least kept their morale and sanity afloat by writing, though they knew the letters might never get out.

Eleen had flinched when he'd heard the lookout shout his "Shithead" warning. His Mormon sensitivities, despite his combat experience against federal forces, were still offended by any kind of profanity or blasphemy, even used in the most dire circumstances, as when he and his thirty-two men were surrounded under fire near Naches, southwest of Spokane, and he'd left Rubinski, the latter's foot blown off, behind. The nightmare of the battle, the deep snow, the "back out" through the ring of mines that had been dropped by the federal helos, had returned to him every night since his first capture. In the absence of anything else to occupy his mind, the obsession with whether he should have left Rubinski behind had settled upon him amoeba-like. Not even the heavy-booted arrival of Moorehead and four guards in Vietnam-style, tiger-pattern fatigues was enough to evict Rubinski from his mind. He could still see Rubinski's pain-marked face, his bleeding stump reddening the snow, and smell the metallic odor of the warm blood through what had been the bracing odor of falling snow and cordite in the air.

Moorehead was militarily correct but nothing more. "Eleen." He refused to address the militiaman by any rank. "You're the senior rebel in this camp. Correct?"

"I've no idea."

"You should address me as 'sir.' "

Eleen said nothing. He could hear Rubinski crying out for help.

"I'm warning you and every other militiaman in this camp that there'll be no mollycoddling here. This is a federal penal institution. Same rules as any other. All my guards have very clear orders, Eleen. Any of you who try to escape'll be shot on sight." His eyes were now solely fixed on Paterson, a short, stocky man, one of Eleen's NCOs who'd been, in effect, foreman of the tunnel's diggers and instantly recognizable by a white streak of scar tissue beneath his chin in an otherwise tar-black beard. "And that includes you, Paterson. I've heard about you and your friends in this hut having footballs *accidentally* dropping beyond the No Go zone's trip wire to see if you can explode an antipersonnel mine here and there—no doubt trying to figure out the pattern to create a path for a possible run to the main wire. Well, there'll be none of that crap under my administration."

"You're wrong," Paterson said in his characteristic gravelly voice. "I never put a football in the No Go zone."

"Don't lie to me, you little turd. I have it on report that you're a troublemaker. You purposely had footballs drop in the No Go."

"Wasn't footballs. It was a baseball."

There was an outburst of laughter before Moorehead's immaculately shaved face went crimson. "Take him away!" he bellowed at the four guards. "Blockhouse! Now!" As a guard moved to either side of him, Paterson broke out into a wide grin. Moorehead went ballistic. "Right! No baseball for 5A. No football. No sports *period*! I'll teach you bastards what's what around here." His disciplining gaze swept the room. "C'mon, any more smartasses here?"

Eleen felt sick to his stomach, though from his outward calm no one would have guessed it. He didn't know why, and not knowing was more disconcerting to him than the cold-bowel discomfort he was experiencing as Paterson, *the idiot,* was marched off to the six-celled blockhouse near the main gate. Was the icy gut feeling spawned by the déjà vu he was experiencing? Under the previous administrator, Schmidt— before he was run down and killed by a militia-captured Hummer as escaping POWs swarmed across the runways of nearby Fairchild AFB—another of Eleen's subordinates, Browne, had been marched off to the blockhouse.

But there the similarity between Schmidt and Moorehead and all those other militiamen being sent to solitary in jails throughout the country ended. Browne had been a federal plant who was killed during the mass breakout. So what was Paterson up to? Eleen wondered. Surely the federals now under Moorehead's command wouldn't try to repeat the play? Or was it possible in the confusion and inevitable fog of war—in this case the chaos of the breakout and the recapturing of escapees like Eleen and his platoon of POWs in 5A—that Schmidt hadn't passed on to Moorehead the fact that he had been blackmailing Browne? By holding Browne's wife and children in custody, as hostages, in effect, Schmidt had gotten Browne to reveal militia escape plans. After all, it had only been because of one man, Michael Hearn, the Nazi militiaman who'd been in the next cell to Browne and who heard all that Browne and Schmidt had said, that Eleen and his men found out that Browne had been a plant. Or did Moorehead know? Had Schmidt left an incriminating note on the camp's computer file about his stool pigeon Browne before he and Browne were killed?

But it was silly to commit such deals to a file, a computer, or any other recording medium. Such deals were always verbal, so they could be denied should events go wrong. Then again, if Moorehead had learned about it, he might be calculating that the last thing anyone would expect was another plant. It was so obvious, it wouldn't be considered. If Moorehead *was* using "Blackbeard" Paterson, blackmailing him in some way to rat on his comrades, then he was no less audacious than the federal General Freeman, whose credo, *"L'audace, l'audace, toujours l'audace!"* had accounted for the federals' brilliantly outwitting the militias more than once in the field.

Right now, however, it wasn't the art of being audacious that was occupying Eleen's demoralized mood, but rather, the obvious pleasure that Moorehead—roundly booed and called his scatological name by POWs all over the camp as Paterson was led away—was deriving at denying all members of hut 5A any participation in any sports activity. It was easily enforced by placing a guard at either end of the hut— letting no one in or out except for the obligatory lineup for chow delivered by a three-ton truck.

While most of the men in 5A had met Paterson's baseball joke with bravado, and were cheering him on as he was led across the dusty, barren compound toward the blockhouse, Eleen and his NCO, Sergeant Orr, knew that 5A's confinement to barracks would have a devastating effect on morale, negating the optimism aroused by the radio broadcast of Hearn's impending showdown with the federals.

Minutes later a squad of four goons and another federal, his lightning flash shoulder patch identifying him as Signals Corps, came in with a beam direction finder and quickly determined the exact location of the cigarette-packet-sized transistor radio, in the right-hand pocket of Sergeant Orr's militia fatigues. The soldier smashed it under his boot, picking up the two AA batteries and announcing that the "chief administrator" had told him to inform Eleen and all the others in hut 5A that the water, including that piped to the hut's flush toilet, would be cut off as a punishment for the illegal radio. A portable toilet would be placed outside at the eastern entrance of the hut, and only one man allowed out at a time.

"Shitheads!" someone shouted.

"Prick!" another yelled.

"Shut up!" It was Eleen. Punishment was one thing, but Moorehead's actions were beyond that. It was a pettiness, a sadistic intent unbecoming any officer, even a federal, and Eleen knew that Moorehead would impose further punishment in 5A at the slightest excuse. Then it went from bad to worse as half an hour later the PA system crackled to life, Moorehead informing the camp that huts 5B and 5C were also denied any sports activity for two weeks as a "shared punishment for hut 5A's irresponsible conduct." It was an attempt, Eleen could see, to turn huts 5B and 5C against 5A. And with the radio smashed, the spread of any more news about the militia storming of Holy Rosary Hospital, as CNN reporter Marte Price put it, and the upcoming confrontation on the Arizona border, was thwarted.

Eleen, feeling unwell, recalled a line from Shakespeare: "Troubles come not in ones and twos but in battalions."

SWAT driver Hogan heard another rush of static on the police band and saw the red glow of the taillights of the last ambulance in Hearn's motorcade swell in intensity, its driver no doubt pumping the brakes. Because it happened just as he heard the static, he connected the two and turned up the volume on the police band. But a few seconds of idle police chatter told him the two events weren't connected, and he turned his concentration back to the taillights of the ambulance, the distance between his vehicle and the militia's having narrowed to no more than thirty yards.

"You federal bastards!" It was on the police channel. "I told you not to follow me—and that includes your helos, dammit! Remember, we have the two skirts." Abruptly, the ambulances stopped. The line of squad cars led by Hogan did the same, but some, driven by men who were tired and drowsy, didn't stop promptly enough, and for a second or two it sounded to Hogan and Frederico as if a pileup was under way as one squad car bumped into another.

"Keystone Kops!" Frederico joshed offhandedly as he kept

one ear tuned into the police band, waiting for Hearn to say
more. He didn't. Instead, a militiaman—Toro, who'd walked
back to the rear door of the last ambulance—yanked open the
right side of the door and made as if to grab something, but
with some difficulty. Something about the bend of the militiaman's body reminded Hogan of his own reach when he tried to
extract his terrified dog from his four-by-four whenever a visit
to the vet was called for. It was a terrified hostage—one of the
two security men—bracing himself, refusing to come out vol-
untarily. Toro literally hauled him out; the man's cap came off
and fell to the blacktop. The man was bald. Toro punched him
in the midriff and the man doubled over and fell. Toro stood
astride him, bent down, and, in the glare of Hogan's high
beams, cut the man's throat, the body twitching in the black
pool of blood like a stunned fish.

"Jesus!" It was Frederico, out of the four-by-four. Hogan
yelled, "No, they've got the two women!"

Frederico let out a violent kick at the front tire as Toro
ambled away. Hogan noted that—the son of a bitch *ambled*,
as if to say, "Screw you. What can you do?" to the entire
fifty-two-man police contingent.

It would be argued later, as the police column waited, that
the only reason the militiaman used his knife and not a gun
was because of the militia's well-known obsession about
wasting ammunition, much of which was "home-packed" to
avoid leaving a telltale trail of either electronic or paper
records that the FBI, ATF, IRS, or any other federal agency
could follow. But this was, as Hogan said, "bullshit." He
knew well enough why the militiaman used the knife.

"Then tell us," Frederico pressed him.

Hogan was watching the other two SWAT team members
tucking the dead man's hands into his belt, then rolling him
onto the unzipped body bag. "He used the knife," Hogan
said, without taking his eyes off the bag, "because he's like
that bastard Hearn. He *enjoys* it." He paused. "And I thought
the pricks were just stopping to take a leak."

Back in the line of policemen who were taking advantage

of the stop, one of the drivers said he thought the security guard, "guy named Hanson," was married with a couple of kids, but no one seemed to know for sure.

CHAPTER SEVEN

The Mojave Desert

Arms akimbo as he stood gazing up at the darkening sky that hung suspended above the Mojave, Aussie Lewis, a veteran ALERT, proclaimed to the rest of the seven-man team that "tonight there are sixteen million of our fellow Americans who are either doing it, have done it, or will do it before dawn. Screwing 'emselves silly, and here we are—stuck out in the middle of bloody nowhere with fuck all to do except piss in the sand." He paused, shaking his head. "I hate this fucking desert. Reminds me of the fucking outback. Nothing but creepy fucking crawlies and fucking sand."

David Brentwood, team leader from northern New Jersey and a Medal of Honor winner, was lying on his back, hands behind his head, staring skyward. "You're always so eloquent, Aussie."

"Fucking right! Why's the boss got us bivouacked out here anyway?"

"Waiting for Godot," Brentwood answered.

Aussie Lewis turned around. "Who?"

"Godot," Brentwood repeated.

"That's that play, right?" Lewis asked. "By that French fucker."

"Beckett," Brentwood said. "Samuel Beckett. He was Irish but he lived in Paris."

"All right," Lewis responded good-naturedly. "Don't become the know-it-all with me. Why do *you* think we're here?"

"My guess," Brentwood said, "is that he wanted a seven-man team in place for a special op the moment the militia outfit hit that hospital in Phoenix. Wants us to get them the moment they cross the Colorado into California. With two hostages, that'd make it kidnapping across state lines, calling for federal intervention."

"Federal offense wherever it happens," put in Salvini, a native of Brooklyn.

"Yes," Brentwood said. "From what I hear, Washington doesn't want to get involved if Arizona can handle it. But once they cross over into California—"

"And if they don't cross?" Lewis interjected.

"They will," Brentwood replied.

"You sure?"

"No," Brentwood said.

"Hey!" It was Salvini, staring at the heavens. "I just saw a falling star." He paused. "You think there's life out there?"

"Has to be," Lewis said, mildly annoyed that Salvini had changed the subject, and adding, "Bloody arrogant to think we're the only bastards here. Millions of stars and planets."

"You believe in UFOs?" Salvini asked him.

"Dunno," Lewis said. "I figure a lot of sightings are secret military aircraft. Like when they were developing the Stealth."

"I believe in 'em," Salvini said.

"Ah," Lewis quipped, "you'd believe in anything, Sal. Like that blond bird you were banging in Barstow. She told you she didn't have the clap."

Salvini ignored the ribbing, his mind on higher things. "I believe in God."

"Oh, don't get all heavy on us, Sal," Lewis said. "I've got enough to put up with out here without you going all philosophical on me."

"No, seriously," Salvini said. "What do you believe in?"

Aussie Lewis thought for a moment. "A 5.6 millimeter—full metal jacket."

"Seriously?"

"Seriously?"

"Yeah."

"All right," Lewis said with resignation. "A nine-millimeter Browning. Thirteen-round mag."

"Shit!" It was Thomas, a six-foot black ALERT from Fort Walton Beach in the Florida panhandle, as fit and experienced and amiable as the rest of the seven-man team, or rather as amiable as ALERTs allowed themselves to be. He was plugged into his Walkman radio. "Anybody want to listen in?" he asked, pulling out one earphone, offering it. "Militia's closing in on Parker."

CHAPTER EIGHT

Japan

In the teeming streets of Kyoto, two businessmen stepped into a Millennium Electronics Shop, listened intently to the CNN news flash of the raid, then withdrew, saying nothing and making their way to the Tofukuju Temple Garden.

The intent of the garden is to replicate nature's originals, whether these be an untreed plain, a mountain, stream, or sea. But if it's to be a popular garden, it must above all evoke serenity. Jinichi Adachi and Hatazo Fuchida, both men in their forties, dressed smartly in ash-gray suits and

wearing indigo-blue silk ties, sat beneath an azure sky in Tofukuju Temple, looking out at its carefully raked garden of
sand, the darker squares contrasting dramatically with lighter.
Looking at it, it seemed that one were a god high above the
earth gazing down on an ordered universe of immaculately
tilled fields. But for Adachi and Fuchida, any such sense of
order, of balance, in the world was an illusion of harmony,
an illusion of what the Chinese would call the balance between yin and yang. The world was in fact chaotic. And if the
original and sacred harmony between earth and its creators—
the *kami*—was to be reestablished, then those on earth who
pretended to create order while only serving their own chaotic
appetites must be eliminated.

"So the holy one is imprisoned," Adachi, the taller of the
two, said matter-of-factly. He was talking of their leader,
Shoko Asahara, head of Japan's infamous and secretive Aum
Shinri Kyo—Supreme Truth—cult, who had been arrested in
a hideaway near Fuji for acts of terrorism. "But," Adachi
continued, "we know what he wishes—*minzoku joka*—
ethnic cleansing—particularly the materialist barbarians."

Fuchida nodded, his stare still fixed on the squares of
sand, the grains suggesting infinity to him and making him
ponder how, when one dies, one's ashes become the soil of
new growth in the never-ending cycle of death and regenera-
tion. For him the certainty of rebirth after death—in whatever form nature would have it—was the rationalization for
ethnic cleansing, for mass purification, for mass murder.
And if his own people, the Japanese, were so corrupted by
material wealth that they'd had to be punished by Heaven's
avengers, then what of the creators of the gods of material-
ism, the Americans? It was quite clear to both men, as it was
to all members of the Aum Shinri Kyo, what had to be done.
Adachi and Fuchida did not know if the police—Japanese,
American, or Interpol—had them on their list. But at Asahara's warehouse hideaway before his capture, the Tokyo police had found a computer list of over 25,000 sect members
in Russia alone, and the discovery of such foreign lists had
made Adachi and Fuchida nervous.

Other members of the sect, similarly nervous, had refused to carry on the work, but for Fuchida, the thinner and smaller of the two men, this was no surprise. Even the stupid turn-the-other-cheek Christians had their fair-weather members—those who were firm devotees of their saints' gospels and injunctions providing everything was going their way. But the moment things went badly for them, they quickly took leave of their religious beliefs and petulantly refused to obey their religion's calling. Cowards unable to stand their ground, Fuchida thought. It brought to mind the English hymn, "Will Your Anchor Hold?"

The cult's American membership, though small by international standards, was at least twenty thousand. Special messages of encouragement had been sent to all those sects that, like Koresh's Branch Davidians in Waco, Texas, had been or were being hounded by the FBI and Bureau of Alcohol, Tobacco, and Firearms. So many had been slaughtered at Waco, and at Ruby Ridge; Randy Weaver's wife had been shot as she stood in the doorway of the cabin, cradling her baby in her arms, and the FBI had also shot Weaver's ten-year-old son and his dog.

So far, it seemed that the FBI and the ATF saw no link between the militias in the United States and Aum Shinri Kyo in Japan, though the date April 19 was significant to both organizations—the day of the Yokohama chlorine gas attack in '95, and of the Oklahoma City explosion.

"I'm not so sure," Fuchida said now, lighting a cigarette, "that the FBI and ATF haven't made a connection. They don't tell the newspapers everything they think. Only an idiot would fail to see that both groups are committed to direct action in the cleansing. Our ends may be different—maybe not, we both despise the government—but our means are essentially the same. The militias merely have a preference for shooting and bombing."

"You forget Inoue," Adachi put in. He was referring to Yoshiro Inoue. "Like us, he was one of the holy one's faithful followers. But his car, remember, was found loaded with explosives and other bomb-making apparatus along with

Tokyo's subway timetable and maps. He too had a preference for shooting and bombing, so we are not so different
from the militias after all."

Adachi nodded, but then asked Fuchida if he'd heard
about the fuss some in the cult had made about supporting
the American militias who had white supremacist Nazis
such as Hearn in leadership positions. Fuchida drew long
on his Camel cigarette—he loved the Turkish tobacco—
exhaled, and gave Adachi a wry smile, dismissing his concern. "The Nazis made all us Japanese 'honorary whites,'
remember, so that left us to do as we wanted with Asia, and
Germany to do what it wanted with Europe. No, Adachi, the
white supremacists of America do not concern us one way
or another, though the more Nazis we have there as allies,
the better to embroil the United States in unrest. Of course,
those who think the American militias can overthrow their
government are idiots. Not even the Führer Hearn can believe that. Their aim is simply to govern themselves entirely
at the local county level, including immigration, parklands,
and grazing rights. The problem for Washington, D.C., is
that the President cannot permit this. If the U.S. capital is to
enforce its federal law evenly across the board, then it will
first have to disarm the militias, and that is where the militias' threat lies—in tearing the country apart. You see,
Adachi, what the federalists have to understand, something
which they have never understood here in Japan, Ireland,
Spain, Canada, or in the United States, is that different pre-
fectures, different states, are like different children in the
same family. In order to treat them equally, you sometimes
have to treat them differently."

"Just so."

"So," Adachi said, "you will be in New York with the non-
Aryan militias." The tone of Adachi's question begged for
more than a simple yes or no, but Fuchida said nothing, his
silence an answer in itself, namely that the holy one had
trusted him, Fuchida, with a mission in New York, not
Adachi, a mission so grave and important that he was not
permitted to discuss it in any detail.

But if specific operations details could not be discussed, such information being strictly parceled out within the cult on a need-to-know basis, then the overriding aim of the cult's support of the American militias, the massive disruption of American industry, primarily that of the U.S. auto industry, was known by all members of the cult. It was also known by all those representatives of the Japanese auto industry whose interest in sabotaging their U.S. competitors was clearly evident by the millions of dollars they were funneling through the cult for support of the militias. Still, the militias had taken a beating from the federal force under the leadership of the American general, Freeman. In the holy one's view, it was now incumbent upon the U.S. militias, in the light of their recent defeats, to show why they deserved his continuing support in the war against the U.S. government—to do something concrete that would clearly demonstrate an ongoing resolve. To show that while they might have lost the battle for the highly strategic Astoria Bridge between Oregon and Washington, lost the battle of Butcher's Ridge, and taken a whipping in Washington State in the vicinity of Camp Fairchild, they could still take on the federals—and win.

CHAPTER NINE

In Los Angeles, Henry Rice in California Highway Patrol headquarters got the order direct from Governor Fruet himself in the state capital in Sacramento. Fruet had been trying unsuccessfully to reach him for half an hour. "Where in hell were you, Henry?"

Before Rice could explain that he was at a meeting downtown, Fruet was giving him both barrels. "Stop those bastards from entering the state, Henry. I want roadblocks thrown up all along the line. They started this business in Arizona, and goddammit, it's Arizona's problem—not mine. So you make damn sure they don't get across the Colorada."

"I'll sure try, Governor. The Colorado's a long riv—"

"Henry, I'm not interested in anybody *trying*. Voters aren't interested in *trying*. They're interested in *doing*. Cancel all leave. Do what you have to."

"Yes, Governor."

Henry Rice put down the phone. He was more angry with Fruet than intimidated. "Typical," he complained to his second in command, Juanita Gonzales, the first woman in the country to hold the position. "Fruet hasn't a clue how much territory we have to cover. About the nearest they get to the desert in Sacramento is the goddamn beach."

Juanita didn't respond. She had her eye on Henry Rice's job when he retired—top CHIP in the state—and no way was she getting caught up in a squabble between him and Fruet. And so she wasn't about to remind Rice that he knew as little about Sacramento as Fruet knew about the Southwest, namely that Sacramento, being seventy miles inland, *had* no goddamn beach.

Rice's right index finger followed the Colorado. "Fruet calls it the 'Colorad*a*.' He's got no idea."

"Well," Gonzales said, again careful not to take sides, "if this Hearn is heading west along Highway 95, toward Parker, then he must be contemplating crossing over to Earp on our side." She paused, hoping that what she was about to tell him would be well received. "While you were out, I took the liberty of assigning a surveillance chopper to the area."

"Outstanding!" said Rice, an ex-Marine, "outstanding" being his favorite word, which he'd borrowed from the USMC's drill instructors. But in fact there was nothing outstanding about the plan at all. The USMC—United States Militia Corps—saw to that. They had men and women in CHIP who were sympathetic to the militia's opposition to taxes, affirmative action, what they considered the growing power of the liberal left, and the militia corps' fervent support of the right to bear arms, as stated in the Second Amendment.

Within fifteen minutes Governor Fruet's order to Rice, and the assigning of a CHIP surveillance chopper to the Parker area by Juanita Gonzales, was known by the militia in southwestern Arizona and a counterstrike ordered. From four counties, over a hundred militiamen took to their vehicles, mostly four-wheel drives, with desert camouflage nets equally effective in both the Mojave Desert in the north and the Sonoran in the south, to put what had seemed endless weekends of training into practice. One such man was Ernst Schumacher, whose great-great-grandfather Otto had fought in the Southwest's fifteen-year-long Apache Wars (1871–86), and who adamantly denied that he'd had any part in the infamous Camp Grant Massacre. There, over fifty miles north of Tucson, a posse of white Americans, Mexican-Americans, and Papago Indians murdered scores of Apache women and children in vengeance for what the posse suspected were Apache attacks against ranchers. And now Ernst Schumacher believed he was fighting an equally savage enemy, an enemy that would make him and his children criminals for owning a gun, who wouldn't hesitate to shoot them down like they did Randy Weaver's wife and son.

Schumacher set up position on high, prickly-pear-cactus-covered ground west of Earp on the California side of the river, the road below coming directly at him before it entered an S curve. Using the gun's bipod, he set up his ugly, angular-looking Barrett .50 caliber sniper rifle, its anti-matériel rounds capable of piercing armor and knocking out missile launcher control consoles and other *hard* targets. The Surgeon General, reporting to the Joint Chiefs in the late 1990s, had termed the effects of such rounds on the human body as "indescribable."

Schumacher, his four-by-four Blazer hidden in a stony gully five hundred yards behind and below him, now lay

on the high ground, a camouflage net over him casting a
dappled light on his khaki shirt and faded blue jeans. Neither he nor his vehicle could be seen from the air as he
waited, using only one earphone of his Discman to listen to
Marty Robbins belt out "Cool, Clear Water." He adjusted
the scope with all the finesse of a watchmaker, until the target circle was centered on the right-hand lane of the road below him almost a quarter mile away. The sun now finishing
its slide westward cast a dusty light across the cactus-dotted
Sonoran Desert, which contrasted vividly with the luxurious
and cooler-smelling green of the irrigated fields east of his
position.

The California Highway Patrol car appeared no bigger
than a large toy in the distance, and now and then wisps of
dust could be seen, the car magnified in the scope, Schumacher calculating it was speeding in excess of eighty miles
an hour. But no siren.

Beyond the green fields of melon, cotton, wheat, and
other crops around Parker, the township's two-lane steel and
concrete bridge spanned the quarter-mile-wide Colorado in
a gentle arc, the Persian blue of the river turning to gold in
the desert sun's dying rays. Place Montoya, forever casual,
looking relaxed even in times of high tension, only now
pulled out his Colt .45, spun the chamber, and reached over
to the passenger side of his car to pick up a short, stubby
37mm six-round, nonlethal tear gas and rubber slug gun.

"Shit, Place," one of the two shotgun deputies said. "This
ain't gonna be no riot—with rock throwin'. These bastards
are armed with AK-47s, fer Christ's sake."

"Uh-huh," Montoya responded, walking back to open the
trunk. "They got hostages too."

"So?" the deputy said.

Montoya fished about in the messy trunk, pushing aside a
box of clothing, rubber boots, and a bulletproof vest, extracting a shoe box of big, nonlethal 40mm slugs.

"Hell, Place," the deputy pressed. "You ain't gonna use
nonlethals on 'em?"

"They got hostages, Sam. Won't kill anybody 'less I have to."

"What with?" the other shotgun deputy asked.

Montoya smiled, patting his side arm, which was loaded with lethal ammo.

The anxious deputy resented Montoya's cool attitude, which made his three deputies feel "fritzy"—Montoya's word for anyone uncool enough to be nervous or who couldn't hide it.

"You tellin' us to use nonlethal load?" the worried deputy asked.

Montoya closed the trunk. "Relax, Sam. I'm not tellin' you what load to use. Up to you. All I'm saying is they got three hostages—a security guard and two women—and I feel better having nonlethal as well as lethal load. You boys use what you want, but first let me do the talking." It was the longest speech from Place that any of the three deputies could remember. "Be careful, that's all."

The deputy grunted, kicked a stone off the bridge, heard it plop, and told one of the shotguns that Sheriff Gary Cooper didn't realize that not everyone was as calm under pressure as he was.

"Maybe," the .30 rifleman said, "he's as nervous as any of us. Just not showin' it."

"Well, I don't give a shit," the other replied. "Any prick swings a weapon my way, I'm not gonna hold a goddamn meeting about it. I'll blow his head off."

No one spoke, and for a moment all they could hear in the silence about the town—everybody had been ordered off the street—was the sound of the river.

Schumacher was deliberately breathing slowly, knowing that to get excited was to botch a shot. Despite the mottled shade of the camouflage net above his high-ground position, he was sweating profusely, khaki shirt stuck to his back like Saran Wrap. Normally, it was a dry heat in the desert, but he guessed that evaporation moving west of the Colorado River was making it humid. Either that or he was more anxious than he would admit to himself. A scorpion, stingers raised, ready to plunge them into the nearest victim, was trespassing, suddenly scuttling from a stony run of desert onto the square of chamois cloth by the gun, on which Schumacher had carefully placed another three of the armor-piercing rounds. Seeing a fist-sized rock out of the corner of his eye, he kept his other eye fixed on the scorpion, slowly reached for the rock, felt it. The scorpion, sensing danger, froze, as did Schumacher. The scorpion made a run for it, and Schumacher killed it with one stroke.

By now the CHIP car was emerging from a culvert at speed. Yes, it would be a tough shot—to get the driver. But if he did miss the driver, moving directly toward him, he estimated that he'd still have time to get two more shots at the vehicle itself, the explosive armor-piercing bullets hammer blows to a radiator. Without a radiator in the Sonoran, he told himself, the car would be deader than the damn scorpion.

The white dot of the CHIP driver became the size of a balloon in the crosshairs. Schumacher took in a deep breath, began to exhale slowly, then held it, squeezing, not pulling, the trigger. He heard its heavy crack, felt the kick, and saw the tiny dust storm in front of him created by the heat wash from the barrel. There was a squeal of tires, the car swaying violently, then it flipped, rolling off the shoulder into a ten-foot-deep gully, landing upright, one of the wheels blown. Schumacher waited for the mini twister in front of him to settle, alarmed for a moment that he might not see what was happening because of the dust. When he saw, through the scope, the driver's partner extracting himself from the wreck, the car right side up but the hood dented in, Schumacher got the man in the crosshairs, then took his finger off the trigger—the man was bending down low, using the radio. But Schumacher could still see him. What better way to close down the road than to have the sniper attack made public via the police car's radio? he thought. What were they going to do, send another patrol car? "I don't think so," Schumacher said, chuckling. He knew he wasn't the only militiaman on the California side who'd been ordered to "effect stoppage," and that CNN and a host of others, including ham radio operators, would be scanning the police band. It would be international news within minutes. It would stop all traffic, and quickly, allowing Hearn, Vance, Lucky McBride, and their hostages a clear run—providing, that is, that they got across the river at Parker.

Schumacher could see only part of the man's head as the frightened patrolman, side arm drawn, peered about him. Schumacher let him have some rope, as it were, until the man exposed his head, peering up from behind the trunk. He fired then, the man's head exploding like a melon.

The next question was whether Hearn and the boys would make it over the bridge at Parker.

CHAPTER TEN

"Maybe," one of the deputies said, "they're not comin' our way—turned off somewhere—maybe cross the river by boat?"

As if on cue, Montoya heard the faint but angry growl of an outboard motor—probably one of the water-ski boats coming in for the night. He looked northward on the black water to see if he could spot the boat's navigation lights. He was annoyed—he'd told all the marinas, as he'd told the town, not to let anyone go out on the river until this militia business was finished. The boat probably didn't belong to a marina. Maybe a tourist from one of the RV campsites, though he'd made sure the message had been passed on to all marinas along the fifteen-mile Parker strip between the township itself and Parker Dam farther north. "Either a tourist," he said, "or some crazy teenagers out for a thrill."

Montoya's body was a silhouette in the twilight, his voice as dry and as unhurried as the desert that lay beyond the patchwork of irrigated fields.

"Here they come!" announced Sam, one of the two deputies toting the semiautomatic shotguns. He moved closer to one of the two police cars that formed a V-shaped barricade across the bridge, the headlights of the five ambulances coming toward them like some insolent snake.

Montoya, watching the convoy segue, positioned himself behind the southern side of the V, his three deputies off to his left, spaced about six feet apart across the bridge and silhouetted by the light from the snake's eyes, now only a hundred feet away in the right lane of the two-lane bridge.

As the head ambulance's headlights flicked from low to high beams, further illuminating the deputies' silhouettes, Montoya told his men, "Watch 'em! I'm taking out those headlights—hold your fire." With that, he raised his 37mm six-round gun and fired three times—*boomp! boomp! boomp!*—at virtually point-blank range.

There were agonized screams and the clatter of two shotguns and a rifle. Then the three deputies were writhing on the ground like stunned mullet. The three two-inch-square bean bags had struck each of them in the back with the force of a heavyweights' ungloved punch, each man a target well-illuminated by the headlights' glare. Within ten seconds, Montoya had kicked away their weapons, which Toro, the militiaman from the first ambulance, quickly collected. Montoya just as quickly cuffed each deputy and dragged him off the bridge and onto the pedestrian walkway, after which he moved the northside squad car into the south lane. Another militiaman smashed the squad cars' radios, the right-hand lane now open for the militia convoy, with Montoya aboard, to pass through.

Approaching the California side, the first ambulance—

with Hearn driving and Montoya riding shotgun next to him in the passenger seat—slowed.

"No problems?" Hearn asked Montoya.

"None."

"All right," Hearn said. "Now let's hope there aren't any heroes on the west bank. With that old fart Fruet wanting to move from the governor's mansion to the White House, there's always the chance he'll want to try to stop us to earn Brownie points."

"Thought you had that covered?" the normally taciturn Montoya said.

"We do," Hearn answered, "but you know, there's always someone who wants to do a fuckin' John Wayne. Go it alone."

Montoya didn't answer—this was all new to him, and he couldn't help thinking about the deputies. Hearn was known to be prescient—so good at it that Montoya, usually unflappable, was surprised when Hearn asked, "You worried you might've killed a deputy? Hit one guy in the head. That it?"

Montoya felt his gut tighten—something he hadn't experienced since he'd shot a crazy down in Yuma two years ago.

"Is that it?" Hearn repeated.

"More or less."

"Huh!" Hearn said despairingly. "Thought you were a hardass, Montoya. What's it matter? You have to break eggs to make an omelet. Right? These federal bastards have been stickin' it to the West from day one—right?"

"Yes," agreed Montoya, who like so many in the West had grown to detest Washington, D.C., and was as deeply suspicious as anyone else in the Southwest of the East. He remembered a grumpy tourist who made it clear that he hated the desert. "Red dirt," he'd called it, telling Montoya, "New York'd eat you guys alive!" and Montoya believed him, instinctively siding with his fellow southwesterners, who felt their state's way of life constantly threatened by the federal government. Montoya's western bias had made him, like so many others, openly critical of the federals—a potential recruit by a militia that, under Vance, valued an "agent in place" as much as any uniformed militiaman. And now Montoya was talking with a Nazi, a fact about Hearn that he'd brought up to the militia recruiter who'd been sent by Vance to see him.

"What's in a name?" the recruiter had challenged him. "So he's got a few wacky ideas? Who hasn't? He believes in a nigger-free Southwest, more state power, instead of having to kowtow so much to Washington. Let *us* decide what to do with *our* land."

"I guess what bothers me," Montoya now told Hearn, "was firing on them from behind."

"Oh, gimme a break!" Hearn retorted. "When we go up against the federals, there'll be no fuckin' bean bags, I can tell you that. You're damn lucky Vance gave you the okay to use 'em. If it'd been up to me, I would've used live ammo on them."

Then Hearn surprised him again. "You knew 'em, that's what bothers you." Before Montoya could respond, Hearn continued, "Ah, I know what it's like. I've known guys personally, federals I was up against. But that's the way a civil war is, Sheriff. Christ, you think guys didn't know one another in the first civil war—at Gettysburg? Hell, it was brother against brother. That's why it's called a civil war, for Christ's sake." He paused. "You telling me you never put a guy you knew in jail?"

Montoya was nonplussed, unusual for him. He usually knew what was right and what was wrong, but Hearn, this *Nazi*, was, as Sam would have said, "freakin' him out." It was the first time in Place Montoya's adult life that he felt "bamboozled," as his daddy would have said, by another man. Women had bamboozled Montoya all his life, but this Hearn, this Nazi, somehow had the ability to make a grown man, a man who believed it was dishonorable to shoot anyone from behind, feel as naive as a child.

Hearn slowed, saw a man with an AK-47 standing in the middle of the road to Earp, and relaxed. The man was

walking toward the ambulance in the penumbra of the headlights, his right hand giving the thumbs-up "okay" sign.

"Who's this?" Montoya asked.

"Doc Holliday," Hearn said wryly, and wound down the
window, asking the man, "Where's the colonel live?"

"Wherever he is?"

The man, a lookout, had given the correct response. "So
it's clear up ahead," Hearn said.

"All the way. Feds aren't gonna do nothin' so long as you
got them hostages." Suddenly the man's eyes were agog, seeing Montoya's shoulder patch. "Shit, man, that a sheriff?"

"Yeah," Hearn said impatiently, though enjoying the militiaman's shock. Hearn turned to Montoya. "You'd better change
into militia fatigues soon as you can. If you're seen outside
like that, some of the boys'll pop you."

"You have an extra set?" Montoya asked him.

"We've got everything," Hearn said. "But first take off
that star."

"Can I have it?" the lookout asked Hearn.

"No, you fucking can't. It's mine."

"All right. I was just askin'."

"Well, now you know. How far to the next lookout?"

The other's tone turned surly. "Five miles on but you're
clear all the way to L.A. Compliments of Schumacher."

"Schumacher." Hearn was on to it like a shot. "That his
real name?"

"What?"

"Schumacher—is that the guy's real name?"

"Yeah—why?"

"Because, you idiot, you're not supposed to use anyone's
real name."

"Oh, yeah."

"Yeah!"

"Well, everybody knows *your* real name."

Hearn shook his head, more in sorrow than anger. "That's
because I'm famous, you dork."

"What for? Murder?"

"Exactly," Hearn said coolly, taking his foot off the brake and jerking his thumb back in the direction of the two squad cars on the bridge. "Burn 'em!" he ordered the militiaman. "Don't leave anything they can use."

"Hey, smartass!" the California militiaman called after him. "Bet you don't know what my name is."

"I know," Hearn shouted back.

"What is it then?"

"Shit for brains."

If the Nazi hadn't been Vance's designated hitter, the California militiaman would have cheerfully shot Hearn then. The Californian was discovering an uncomfortable truth in a soldier's life: it's possible to hate one of your own side more than you hate the enemy.

Montoya too was learning something—the reason for which Hearn was so dangerous to the federals, and to anyone who crossed his path. The Nazi was totally amoral. And unpredictable—witness his cool, bravely led daylight attack to snatch Vance from federal custody on one hand, yet the willful alienation of a fellow militiaman. It didn't make sense. And the most unsettling thing of all to Montoya, whose name would soon become as infamous as Hearn's for "crossing over," as Marte Price described it on worldwide CNN, was that try as he might as a sheriff, or rather as an ex-sheriff, and as a man, Montoya couldn't dislike Hearn. He sought solace in something he remembered that famous Brit, George Orwell, had said in the thirties. Declaring himself not a violent man, Orwell said that if he had the chance to get close enough to Adolf Hitler, he would surely blow his brains out, but that he had never been able to "dislike the man."

Was it Hearn's daring that he admired? The lightning raid in the middle of rush hour against the odds posed by the entire Phoenix police force? Or was it Hearn's cool repartee with the militiaman they'd just encountered? Montoya didn't know, and it bothered him.

They drove on into the night, Hearn confident in the

knowledge that California comrades, specifically snipers like Schumacher, had cleared Highway 62.

"You know," Hearn said, chuckling to himself in the turquoise glow of the instrument panel as the vehicle's tires hummed westward, "that hayseed back there was right. He never did give us his name, only the greeting. Smarter than I was."

Montoya didn't believe that the militiaman was smarter than Hearn, but in saying so, Hearn seemed likable. Contrary to the stereotype most people had of Aryan supremacists, this Nazi had a sense of humor. It was disturbing.

CHAPTER ELEVEN

No matter that he was traveling first class, Fuchida did not enjoy the bone-wearying flight across the Pacific from Tokyo to Seattle. They had passed through severe turbulence west of Hawaii, and when they stopped over briefly in Honolulu, they weren't allowed out of the first-class waiting area. It was pleasant enough, but he hadn't experienced the beautiful smell of the islands' trade winds, those magical, warm breezes that he remembered as a boy when his grandfather had brought him to see Pearl Harbor and the ghostly shape of the Arizona Memorial where Japan had sunk the great American battleship. The part of his journey that he liked most was the nonstop from Seattle to New York with a half hour stopover in Spokane, where he would make his first call.

Fuchida left on his flight from Seattle to New York after an hour stopover in Seattle. Flying over the darkness of the Cascade Mountains, he saw only one pinpoint of light. He was astounded once again by the vastness of America, particularly the Northwest. It could swallow all of Japan and more. It could swallow an army. The militias' claim that they would first take the entire Northwest—what was called by their commandos the "cleaver," the shape formed by Washington, Oregon, Idaho, and Montana on the chopping block of northern California—was no pipe dream when you saw such vast, uninhabited spaces.

Soon he spotted the sprinkling of lights that was Spokane, typically American in the way it was so spread out, squandering space because they had so much. Everything in America was so big. In Japan his colleagues would not believe him when, after a prior visit to the U.S., he had told them about the size of the American steaks, so big they would cover the plate. And like so many of his countrymen, he was a great fan of American cowboys. He would buy a Texas hat and deduct it from expenses. But the thing Fuchida enjoyed most of all was to see Americans—the citizens of Japan's former enemy—sucking up to him in hopes of benefiting from the holy one's largesse.

Army Chief of Staff Walter Shelburne arrived that evening at the Pentagon in a relatively good mood, but this was soon replaced by a burning anger as he read an urgent report from the Secretary of the Army, who in turn had gone ballistic since he'd received the report from the Secretary of Defense about militias, such as the Scorpions in Arizona, and of wrongdoing in the Army, as well as in the Air Force, Navy, and Marines. The week before, the *New York Times* had run a story on a soldier who was court-martialed for having diverted several M-60 machine guns from a shipment destined for the 116th Cavalry Brigade in Boise, Idaho. On top of this, several news magazines were running more stories on so-called "gangsta"—gang members'—infiltration of the military, building on an investigative story begun back in the

July 24, 1995, issue of *Newsweek*, which had revealed how "gang activity has been reported in all four branches of the armed services and at more than fifty major military bases. The list includes notorious L.A. street gangs like the Crips, the Bloods, and Chicago's Folk Gangsters. The crises include drug trafficking, robbery, assault and—in at least ten cases—homicide." The *Newsweek* story had gone on to describe how at Fort Lewis, near Tacoma, Washington, where drug trafficking was involved, Army gang members had murdered a father and his three children, all hacked to death.

The *Newsweek* story was accompanied by several photos of military training manuals in which it had been discovered that soldiers, as well as demonstrating various weapons, were, unknown to the editors at the time, flashing gang signs. As if this wasn't enough with which to contend, Shelbourne had also received intelligence reports that in the National Guard throughout the country, many of the weekend soldier units had been "infiltrated by members of various militias." Then there was the '97 *New York Times* report about six marines who'd tried "to sell stolen military weapons" to undercover agents, the civilians in North Carolina picked up on "weapons charges which included machine guns, anti-personnel mines, rocket grenades, and plastic explosives," the house in New England where agents found over thirty pounds of C-4 explosives, "sufficient to set off a massive blast," and the Secretary of Defense ordering a review of security procedures at all American bases.

His anger fueled by disgust, General Shelburne issued curt but specific instructions that "as of this hour and regardless—repeat regardless—of time zones, investigations be made by all commands, including the nine unified combatant commands; the National Guard HQ, Arlington, Virginia; and state adjutants general, and marked for immediate and special attention by USACIC–U.S. Army Criminal Investigation Command, Falls Church, Virginia." The general knew of course that, practically speaking, such investigations would be extremely difficult, with one soldier unlikely to inform on another, not simply because of a misplaced sense of loyalty, but because of fear of savage retribution by the gangstas.

CHAPTER TWELVE

CNN's Marte Price, in a tight white sweater and fawn skirt, stopped most channel surfers dead, fingers poised above the remote, but Colonel Norton, on watch at Freeman's mobile HQ in the Mojave, west of Lake Havasu, wasn't so much interested in how Marte Price looked as in what she said about the sniper attacks against the CHIP squad outside of Earp. He dialed Freeman's HQ immediately, the general's response heavy with sleep until he heard Norton announce, "They've done it, General. They've crossed the river. They're in California. They're in our territory now!"

"Right!" It was as if he'd been jolted by a cattle prod.

"A sniper along Highway 62," Norton added. "One CHIP car has been taken out already. The militias've got an open road, General. Just the threat of being fired on has closed it down."

Freeman, getting up from the Army cot on which he had been resting, strapping on his twin 9mm pistols, grunted into the phone. He remembered the I-5 "shutdown" very well in the last clash with militias up in Washington State. Federals had sent troops and Bradley fighting vehicles onto the I-5, only to have them ambushed by snipers of a different

kind—militia firing antitank rounds down on the multilaned
highway and wiping out the federal convoy. Now, as then, it
seemed that the militia could do what it wanted. And almost
before Marte Price stopped speaking, there was another
bulletin from CNN anchorwoman Lynne Russell reporting a
shooting on I-5 in northern California.

"Well," Freeman said, "first thing we've got to do, Norton, is get rid of those damn snipers. Sacramento'll have to
deal with the I-5, but Highway 62 is our baby."

An assistant handed Norton a top secret decipher from
Washington, D.C. "You're not going to send in a federal
convoy, like in Washington State, are you, General?" he
asked over the phone while reading the message—from the
White House.

"Colonel," Freeman said, "I might be just waking up but
I'm not an imbecile. Notify young Brentwood's ALERTs."

"Sir," Norton began, his eyes fixed on the message he
held in one hand, the phone in the other. "I'm afraid that's
out. The President must've anticipated your move. I've got
an *Immediate* and *Secret* from the White House. The President insists on a *measured response* by CHIP and other
California police—but no federal troops as yet. The situation's apparently being monitored worldwide by all the news
services. Markets abroad are—"

"Got a bad line here, Colonel. I didn't get that. Repeat."

Norton couldn't hear any static, not even a crackle on the
line. But he started again. "The White House is telling us
not to—"

"Still can't hear you, Norton," the general shouted, all but
deafening Norton. "Send me what you have by hand." And
with that the line went dead.

By the time a rider was dispatched to Freeman's HQ, the
general had issued a go signal to Brentwood's ALERTs
waiting twenty miles north in the Mojave Desert.

"We have to stop those monkeys before they melt into
L.A. and environs," he told Bentwood and the other six
ALERTs.

"Then, sir, might I suggest a dummy runner, four all-terrain motorbikes, and a FIRST-mounted Hummer?"

Freeman agreed to the dummy runner—a radio-controlled Hummer—the four all-terrain motorbikes, and the fast infrared sniper tracker known as FIRST, but cautioned Brentwood that they would have to be black and rigged, meaning that engine block serial numbers must be rendered untraceable.

"Is Washington that paranoid about having military vehicles on the highway, General?"

"Yes, for now at least. Delorme and the rest of those toadies at the White House would like nothing more than to nail me. And while they're worried about the damn international markets reacting to the sight of our Army being used against fellow Americans, this goddamn hostage taker and the militias are getting away with murder. Imagine what those two gals must be going through."

Brentwood sensed from the general's orders that everything must be "black" and "rigged"—that he might not have "weapons free" status from Washington. And he couldn't help but wonder whether the general—who had once ordered hostages as well as their captors to be fired upon to clear a bridge—wasn't more interested in the glory that would attend the capture of Hearn and the rest than in return of the hostages.

Freeman's voice broke the silence. "Captain Brentwood, if your conscience won't allow you to execute this order, I'll release you, but it might be time for you to remember FDR."

"How's that, sir?"

"President Roosevelt was attacking the Nazis while Congress and the whole damn country were still *debating* the issue. Hadn't been for his 'unofficial' undeclared war on those U-boat bastards—England, our aircraft carrier to Europe, would've gone under."

"Yes, sir."

"All your men FIRST qualified?"

"Salvini and Marsden are, sir."

"I'll send two Chinooks with your equipment. And Brentwood . . ."

"Sir?"

"Good hunting."

When the dispatch rider sent by Norton arrived at Freeman's HQ and delivered the White House's deciphered instructions that all theater of operation commanders were to refrain from intervening "until specifically ordered to do so," the general signed the chit, indicating he had received and understood the President's order, which officially and "unfortunately," he noted in his diary, he had received thirty minutes after he'd ordered Brentwood's team into action.

"All right, listen up," Brentwood told his six ALERTs. "We're going to run a dummy Hummer out front, twenty-five yards ahead of the FIRST Hummer. I'll be driving the FIRST; Salvini, you and Marsden'll be with me operating the FIRST's equipment. Salvini'll joystick the dummy, Marsden will work the step and stare." The step and stare referred to the FIRST-equipped Hummer's rear-mounted gimbal optical method of "ladar," or eye-safe pulsed *laser radar*, which could span at superfast "slew" rates, completing five sweeps a second through the full 360 degrees at an angle of forty degrees.

Next Brentwood turned to Aussie Lewis. "You've won the draw as lead rider immediately behind the FIRST, Aussie. You're Delta One. Keep in radio contact with us. If we get a shooter, we'll give you coordinates immediately and you take off after him. Okay?"

"Sounds like fun," Lewis said dryly.

"Stay about four to five hundred yards back. Don't want to show your hand too early."

"No problem, Your Highness."

"As for you guys," Brentwood told the remaining three ALERTs, "you're on the bikes behind Aussie's diamond pattern and countershooters, should we engage more than one sniper."

"My guess is they won't shoot," Salvini said. "Sniper sees a federal military vehicle, he's not gonna want to take it on."

Phil Marsden, the ALERT who would be working the FIRST and whose moneyed hunt-country New Jersey family had never quite reconciled itself to Philip having joined what Marsden Senior condescendingly referred to as "those people," disagreed with Salvini. He told him that he thought the militias would shoot at anything.

Brentwood cut in. "We don't know where a sniper is until we're on that highway, so pack up your troubles, chaps, in your old kit bags, for our chopper, which should be here—" He glanced at his watch, which, like all ALERTs, he wore under his wrist to reduce the possibility of a giveaway reflection during patrol. "—in six minutes, chaps!"

Aussie Lewis was David Brentwood's best friend—they'd fought together on dangerous "unofficial" missions for the government from the fetid jungles of Southeast Asia to the Iraqi desert—but this "chaps" business got on Lewis's nerves. It was a well-meant British affectation, which Brentwood had picked up at the elite Special Air Service School at Hereford, deep in the English countryside. Lewis had nothing against the SAS. On the contrary, both he and Brentwood knew that they owed their lives on several occasions to having graduated from SAS as part of the U.K.–U.S. Special Forces Agreement to expose the best of the brave to the rigors of both Hereford and Fort Bragg in what was the Army equivalent of SEAL training at Coronado.

Trouble was, Brentwood, through no fault of his own, and because he was American—forthright and open—wasn't wise to the subtle machinations of the British upper-stuffy class. "Chaps" was one of *their* words. "Chaps" promised camaraderie, but a camaraderie underscored by a deeply ingrained belief that they were better than you, a deeply un-American, antidemocratic view, if Brentwood had thought about it. But Lewis knew he hadn't—not because he was unobservant, but because David, in his American way, took people as he saw them, without preconceived ideas. Aussie, on the other hand, wanted to tell the chaps to "bugger off," let them know straightaway that he wasn't going to put up with any upper-class toffee-nosed crap! He'd been schooled by "chaps" in Australia, by the worst of the worst, Australians who'd been such good "chaps" they were more British than the British in their slavish obeisance to all things royal, to preposterous class distinctions, as rigid as they were preposterous, with chapel in the morning and caning in the afternoon; chaps who, despite the scholarship Aussie Lewis had won on merit to attend one of the better schools, had never allowed him to forget his working class origins.

David Brentwood, on the other hand, had come from a well-known eastern family, like Phil Marsden, and when he innocently used the word "chaps," it brought back to Lewis bitter memories of his turbulent youth, where he'd tried to navigate his way in the condescending world of chaps.

Yet he couldn't bring himself, for all his forthrightness, to ask David not to use the word. Indeed, hearing the approaching helo, he announced to his comrades in arms in his usual fashion, "You fuckers ready?"

"Yo," responded Salvini, his blue-collar Brooklyn accent rough music to Lewis's ears.

CHAPTER THIRTEEN

Pursuant to General Shelbourne's explicit order, and regardless of the midnight hour, lights in the headquarters of the U.S. Army's Criminal Investigation Command, in Falls Church, Virginia, came on and the commanding officer summoned the major responsible for the area that included the Tooele—pronounced "Too-ella"—Army Depot in Utah.

When Major Caroline Hart, a pert brunette, arrived, she came armed with the "incident" file.

"Take a seat," the commanding officer said.

"Thank you, sir."

Normally the C.O., old enough to be her father, and who enjoyed having a pretty woman around, would have spent some time on pleasantries, but not now.

"Major, I've just had a call from DOD in Washington, D.C., direct from General Shelbourne's office, to be specific. They're concerned about some apparent error in the Tooele munitions count. The press is on the trail, and Shelbourne wants some answers for the Joint Chiefs meeting on Thursday. Understood?"

Fortunately, Major Hart, tipped off by the switchboard operator, had already made an ACC, or ass-covering call, to the Department of Defense, and so had a general idea of what was up: a discrepancy between the present and the preceding years' count of munitions, including shells that could be used to contain VX, the most poisonous nerve gas ever made, many times stronger than the GB gases tabun and sarin, which were first developed by the Nazis and later used on the Kurds by Saddam Hussein. It was suspected that the fumes from such gases had blown over thousands of U.S. Gulf War soldiers when the Iraqis' chemical depot north of Jahmah was destroyed. "Is that the problem about the number of 155 millimeter shells?" she asked.

The C.O. looked over his reading glasses. "So, you know about this?"

"Yes, sir." She almost added that she didn't know very much, but stopped.

"You know how big a 155mm shell is?"

" 'Bout six inches across and very high," she answered, opening her hands. "Biggest shell that can be handled by one man—which is why it's so ubiquitous."

Sharp, he thought, very sharp. "All right, so what do you make of the discrepancy?"

"It can really be only one of two things, sir," Hart said. "Either someone can't count or there's some shells missing."

The C.O. hunched forward and took off his reading glasses. "What do *you* think it is?"

"I think that somebody, tired at the end of their shift, pressed the wrong button on their calculator."

"Surely the Tooele C.O. would have had the counting re-done if it didn't tally with the previous year's figures? A screwup like this isn't the kind of thing you want on your DD-214." He meant the Tooele C.O.'s service record.

Major Hart agreed but pointed out it was difficult to know just when a counting error had been made. It was quite possible, she said, that, human nature being what it was, a former C.O. might have simply gone with the numbers he was given during an earlier stock-taking account and that the error, unknowingly, had simply been passed up the line to DOD.

"Anyway," she added, "I think he's to be commended for reporting it. The majority of men would simply maintain the old count, afraid to be held responsible for any unexplained loss or theft of CW shells, including 155 VX binaries."

"That's a discriminatory remark against men," he joshed.

"Sorry, sir." She smiled. "A majority of *people* would go along with a cover-up."

"Huh, that's better." He paused, reaching out for her Tooele file. "Do you know," he continued, "how these binaries work?"

"Far as I know, the VX shell is inert. Two chemicals, alcohol and DF, each virtually harmless by itself, are separated in the shell by a membrane. In flight the membrane is ruptured and the two chemicals combine to make the nerve gas. Range of the 155 shell is fifteen miles."

"Hmm," said the C.O.

Did he already know all this? Caroline wondered, or had he just heard it from her? And besides, what C.O. would ever admit he wasn't up to speed on anything in his command? Especially to a skirt.

"You know just how toxic VX is?" he pressed.

"Very," she replied. "But the VX shells with the alcohol sacs in Tooele aren't lethal until they're mixed with the DF, kept someplace else on the base, I assume, till they need the shells. VX is so deadly that at one time the two chemical compounds, by law, had to be kept in different states."

The C.O. pushed himself back from the table. He was in his late fifties, and the strain of criminal investigation command had further creased his already furrow-lined forehead. "I was there," he said, hands clasped together, "when they did the rabbit test. Wasn't pretty." He paused. "A white rabbit. Cute little devil nibbling away on lettuce."

"Uh-huh." She really didn't want to know the details. She liked all animals. "The rabbit died," she said. "Right?" She immediately regretted the "right"; it smacked of impatience and she knew he resented it. He was determined to show he too knew a few things about VX.

"Yeah," he said. "It died. In *seconds*. VX releases a flood of acetylcholine in the body. Uncontrollable convulsions. Your alimentary canal constricts, so do your bladder and pupils, followed by vomiting and diarrhea—a drop or two and it's death on contact. Essentially you die by suffocation." He was about to add that "the penis becomes erect," but stopped short. *Sexual harassment.*

"You know about Dugway?" he asked, and could see her thinking hard. "March 1967?" he added.

"What were the Dugway Proving Grounds?" she asked, sounding like a contestant on *Jeopardy*, but it was clear he wasn't a fan of the game show, missing the allusion entirely.

"That's right," he said, disappointed that she knew.

"Some sheep died," she proffered.

"Huh—*some* sheep. Over *six thousand* were killed by accident. Point is, Major, I'm sorry to have to send you up to Tooele 'round all that other nonbinary nerve gas."

"Going up"—my God, she didn't want to go up to Tooele or any other place in Utah, thank you very much. Nerve gas was now odorless as well as colorless. No way she wanted to do a recount of the chemical warfare shells if there was the remotest chance of an *accidental* leak of chemicals from a nonbinary or any other round. Some of those rounds were pretty old.

"You'll leave tomorrow," the C.O. said. "First thing you should do there is don a nuclear biological chemicals warfare suit, a recently made one, and for God's sake insist on an Abbot. It's a handgun-shaped blister and nerve gas detector. Best there is. If they haven't got one, don't take a step into the CW ammo dump."

"Don't worry, sir. I won't."

"And Caroline?"

It was the first time he'd called her by her first name. "Yes, sir?"

"Don't spend more than an hour in there at a time. You'll dehydrate in those damn suits. It can be hot up there."

"Don't worry, sir. I won't."

"Good gir—good. Call me ASAP." He paused. "I expect you're right, though. It's a run-of-the-mill miscount." He smiled and watched her derriere as she walked out.

CHAPTER FOURTEEN

While Hearn's convoy headed west on California's Highway 62, the ALERTs' two Chinook-delivered Hummers were twenty miles east of them on the same highway, heading east toward the site where the patrol car had been laid waste by Schumacher, the hilly desert all around bathed in moonlight.

The first Hummer, the remote-controlled "runner," moved thirty feet ahead of David Brentwood in the second Hummer, which was equipped with the fast infrared sniper tracker. Salvini and Paul Marsden were in the Hummer with Brentwood. As he drove they worked the FIRST equipment. To avoid possible confusion, because the second Hummer was the "FIRST" vehicle, the runner Hummer out in front was designated "Alpha," and the FIRST-equipped Hummer was "Bravo." As Salvini in Bravo monitored the "remote console" that was programmed to guide Alpha, Marsden was watching the infrared sniper tracker screen, whose laser-radar combination was so fast it would track a bullet in flight, the acoustic wave following the first shock wave in three dimensions. Once a bullet was fired, its muzzle flash and, therefore, its location detected in milliseconds, FIRST's gimbal-mounted countermeasures array, a combination laser dazzler and rifle, would come into play.

That the first Hummer, Alpha, was moving at no more than thirty miles per hour along the flat, desert-surrounded road, struck Schumacher as odd. Never mind that it was dark—a flat, straight road in America, and somebody driving it at *thirty* miles per hour. It was downright un-American. And so, using his "kill flash" infrared binoculars, seeing what looked like a federal soldier driving, wearing the army's standard Gulf War helmet, Schumacher didn't fire. He sensed a trap. And sure enough a second vehicle soon appeared.

Schumacher watched the driver of the first Hummer intently—incredibly stiff, he thought, probably one of those crash dummies the auto makers in Detroit used to test new air bags and seat belts. Schumacher would have shaken his head in mild disgust except he didn't want to have to realign his eye with the infrared scope atop his rifle as he watched the white "shadow," the Hummer's thermal print, moving across a tall saguaro cactus into the scope's circle. He waited till the second Hummer slid into the circle, and as he waited he was, he admitted to himself, spooked. Having his eye fixed to the scope, unable to see anything around or behind him, was akin to that terribly vulnerable moment in the shower, washing his hair, eyes shut, and he couldn't see a thing. It made Schumacher recall Hitchcock's *Psycho*—someone outside the shower curtain coming to murder him. Sometimes his heart just took off in the imagined fright and he frantically opened his eyes too quickly, the soap stinging. But now, despite that rush of anxiety, Schumacher talked himself down, knowing that if he was going to hit his target, his whole body, his breathing, and not just his arms, had to be stilled.

Inside Bravo, Brentwood's Heckler & Koch 5.6mm submachine gun was beside him on the passenger's seat, its barrel pointing away, its safety on but a round chambered, all ready to go. He straightened out his arms against the steering wheel, pressing hard to relieve the tension in his shoulders and noting that driving slowly was a lot more wearing on you than driving fast. Plus he had to keep checking with Salvini at the remote console so as not to get too close to Alpha around a turn, a rocky desert outcrop blocking his view or degrading the remote control's signal. He could hear the soft whir of the tracking mechanism, a squat pyramidlike housing that instead of coming to a peak was blunted at the top, where a transparent upside-down soup-bowl-like basing encased the eye-safe laser radar, Marsden deftly working its controls.

It happened in milliseconds because the moment Brentwood's head moved as he pushed his hands hard against the wheel, Schumacher fired. Salvini saw the muzzle flash on screen, Marsden the coordinates—and the screen went black, a loud pop behind them as the tracking sensor's soup bowl exploded in fragments from the armor-penetrating bullet.

Brentwood recovered fast. "Did you get the coordinates?" he shouted, driving the Hummer off the road.

"No," Phil Marsden replied.

"I did!" Salvini shouted.

"Give 'em to Aussie!" Brentwood yelled, a second bullet slamming into the left rear side panel, red-hot fragments of the door showering the Hummer's interior.

"Goddammit!" It was Marsden, his face bleeding, as was

Salvini beside him, Marsden's left eye blinded, Salvini on the radio.

"Bravo to riders. Latitude—"

The Hummer humped over some fallen rock and crashed down again beneath the protective overhang of an outcrop that looked as if it might break off and fall at any second.

"You guys fit?" It was ALERT shorthand for "Are you able to fight?"

"Yes," Salvini answered, beginning his transmit of coordinates to Lewis, who, a quarter mile behind, was leading the other three bikes behind him in a diamond formation, already punching in the coordinates on his handheld GPS (Global Positioning System), simultaneously giving his Kawasaki 500cc off-road bike full throttle.

Schumacher heard the angry whine of the motorcycles. How many, he couldn't tell. Without getting up, he dragged himself forward until he was beyond the edge of his camouflage net, and fired a flare that appeared for a moment as a red scratch against the moon, then descended, its corona steady under its chute. Schumacher, torso bowed so as to minimize his silhouette, meanwhile made his way down the back slope leading away from the high ground, which he now knew might have been triangulated by the Hummers' radar. He headed for the stony gully where his four-wheel-drive Blazer stood, parked behind a hillock of gravel-studded loam no more than five hundred yards from the highway.

By now the Delta team, Aussie Lewis and the three other ALERTs on the motorcycles, were riding fast through bristly teddy bear cholla plants within a quarter-mile radius of the GPS zone. The moonlight helped, creating an ambient light that made it easier to see through the alien-looking night vision goggles, but it was still dangerous business navigating the cactus-studded terrain at speed. Lewis already felt as if his eyes were being sucked from their sockets, creating a dull, throbbing headache that was the cost of maximum concentration. One of the other three riders, Devane, had already taken a spill, the bike shooting out from under him on a bed of loose gravel, his tank-mounted GPS sheared off, its glass face shattered fragments glinting momentarily in the moonlight like diamonds, his goggles obscured by dust, his left trouser leg ripped and warm with blood. Quickly he regained the bike and slipped it into neutral so he could wipe the lenses of his night vision goggles clean. The few seconds' delay cost him, the first bullet from a militiaman's M-16 hitting him in the mouth, blasting a two-inch-diameter hole in the back of his throat. The other two bullets from the M-16's three-round burst thudded against his flak jacket.

Finn, the last rider, a short, tough, barrel-chested man in his late twenties who'd heard the crack of the enemy rifles and saw Devane fall, hands flailing at his neck, braked hard. He dismounted, his right hand holding his Heckler & Koch, his left pressing his throat mike's bar so he could talk to Aussie Lewis. "Delta leader. Delta leader. Rider down. I say again, rider down."

Lewis had seconds to decide. Was it an ambuscade in force or another sniper? The decision was made for him as hot spots appeared atop a sandy gravel ridge two hundred yards away—a squad of at least eight militiamen had reached the ridgeline. "A fucking trap!" he said as he fired his HK, a fusillade of AK-47s and M-16s opening up in his direction. He braked, momentarily swallowed a cloud of dust. Diving behind a jumble of rocks, he heard a screech owl, bats erupting into flight, and then more enemy rounds, some whistling overhead, others ricocheting from the rocks. The sweet, fruity smell of cactus nectar was turned to aerosol by the shredding impact of enemy fire. Lewis could also hear the engines of his other two bike riders cut out as they took to defensive positions. Then, as low cloud cloaked the white disk of the moon, the firing died down, a fact that told Aussie, as he palmed a new magazine into his HK, that the militia were very short of either infrared or other night vision goggles, the sudden ink-black darkness depriving them of targets backlit by moonlight.

He heard the cough then roar of an engine, sounding like a four-wheel-drive, coming from a rock-obscured depression about a hundred yards behind him, nearer the road. He quickly dismissed any idea of heading for the vehicle and instead turned his attention in the moon-shrouded darkness to getting Devane out. "Delta, this is Delta leader. Zone Lima for Delta, buddy, I say again, Zone Lima!" "Lima" was the ALERTs' phrase for "return to base."

"Roger," acknowledged Finn, one of the remaining two riders of the diamond of four. The other was Thomas, and the two now drew abreast of Devane. Slinging Devane over his gas tank, Finn, then Thomas, started their engines again and, keeping the noise level as low as possible, took off. The militia unleashed a fusillade, aiming wildly, more by sound than sight, as Aussie, who did not leave his position, gunned his downed bike's engine to draw fire, buying time for his buddies to escape. Soon the moon would be unveiled again and cast the twenty-foot-high saguaro cacti in bold relief, the one nearest him looking for all the world like a tall, hatted man, his arms up in a U of surrender.

Devane was bleeding all over Finn's bike, but he was still breathing, his throat making a horrible gurgling sound. He made another rattling sound, then was dead. Realizing as much, and that the extra weight was slowing him down, Finn stopped, slid the body off his bike, then gunned the engine, making up for lost time.

CHAPTER FIFTEEN

Schumacher, his Blazer bucking out to the highway, was heading eastward to where he'd spied the federals' Hummer with the dummy driver or whatever the hell it was. His rifle lay on the floor, covered with a blanket, between the back and front seats. He pushed the glove box button and pulled out a 9mm Glock pistol, slipping it under his left thigh. He slowed as he passed the dummy Hummer that had run off the road when the second Hummer swerved, its tracker-sensing box hit by his fire. He'd pretend he hadn't heard anything about sniper attacks or the police advisory to citizens to keep off the road—play the lone, out-of-touch desert recluse, for which his scraggly beard, khaki shirt, and faded jeans ideally equipped him.

Hands sweaty on the wheel, Schumacher told himself he was either the bravest militiaman in California or the craziest—maybe a bit of both. He laughed despite his fear and could imagine how he'd tell it back in Barstow: "So I just kept my speed real steady like, and I see this Hummer, the feds' decoy vehicle, off to the side, damn motor's still running but it ain't goin' nowhere—flipped on its side, wheels still spinning. So I'm about to drive on. I can hear you guys and the three feds' bikes shootin' up a storm. Anyways, I stop, get out of my Blazer, and go have a peek, because how's just any traveler on the road gonna know about it being a federal decoy vehicle, and if I don't stop and can't tell 'em what I saw, they'll think it was sort of strange—like they might ask why didn't I stop ... you know, could've been someone hurt bad, especially when back a way there's the burned-out CHIP car. So I go over to this flipped Hummer and have a look in. Sure enough it's a crash dummy dressed up like a fucking federal. What? Yeah, sure I walked over with the gun—no, not the rifle, my nine-millimeter with the laser pointer beam. So I get back in the Blazer and drive on, and I'm thinking the control Hummer's just around the corner, but down on the road itself things look a lot different than when I was on the high ground and shot the shit out of that tracker globe. It's further back than I thought. Then I realize they might have shoved it into reverse and hightailed it out of there, pulled off among boulders some-where. But listen up. When I reached the spot where I'd hit 'em—I could tell because of all the splintered glass from the fucking tracker gear—there's no fucking Hummer. Gone! Vanished! I flick the lights on high beams. Nothin'! So I drive on—on the center line—that way I can see the oppo-site road shoulder, right? See if there's any tracks leading off the road. Still nothin'—you guys still banging up a storm—and I hear a couple of their motorcycles fartin' off down the road away from me. I shouldn't've been distracted by those friggin' bikes, 'cause next second I'm comin' out of this dip in the road and there he is—the fuckin' Lone Ranger, 'bout thirty feet ahead, full fed commando gear, flak vest, shoul-der radio and all, pointing this fucking machine gun, an HK, at me, and his hand shading his eyes from the high beams and waving me off to the side—his left, my right. I wind down the passenger's window and ask what's up—all sur-prised like I was a poor local, tourist, or somebody, in the wrong place at the wrong time. Playing dumb!

" 'Pull over!' he tells me, 'and douse your lights.' So I pull over. He's about five feet ahead of me. I cut the lights and the moon's clouded over again. I duck down quicker'n you can say Jack Robinson—pedal to the metal. Fed's quick, though—I give 'im that. Fucking shots crackling above me and a noise like splinterin' timber—windscreen shot to rat shit. I don't even feel it when I hit him, but I hear the thud—next second the fucker's on the hood—no gun, far as I can see, which is fuck all 'cause the windscreen's gone all milky spiderwebs on me. But the fucker's hanging on. And that's what saved me from his buddies. I could hear 'em yellin' as I took off, but no one fired because they might hit this fucker still on my hood—holding on to the fucking wipers.

" 'You turn 'em on?'

" 'Course I did, but they don't move—he's pulling so hard on 'em. Anyway, so now I'm back in the driver's seat—so to speak." Schumacher gave himself a laugh of appreciation for the play on words. Some of the other militia guys wouldn't get it—they were so damn serious.

Schumacher imagined he would tell them how he was back in the driver's seat, and after a mile a Hummer "with these two fed soldiers in it came after me, pedal to the metal, but Jesus, my Blazer just loses 'em in dust. Besides, they still aren't gonna fire because *now* I'm goin' so fast that if they hit me in the back I'm gonna lose control and their buddy's gonna end up squashed 'tween the Blazer and a rock. Then fuck me if I don't see this federal on my hood, reaching for his belt. I would've missed 'im 'cept his buddies in the Hummer have got their lights on high beams—so I can see this guy on the hood through the cracked windshield—like through a shower curtain. Wind's blowing his hair at me like a black mop."

"What's he going for?" one of the militia boys would ask. "Handgun—knife?"

"I wish," Schumacher would say. "No, it wasn't his knife or a gun—one hand, his left, on my friggin' wiper, the other's goin' for a grenade."

"Holy shit!"

"Holy shit's right. Fucker's gonna toss it through the holed windshield, blow the both of us to smithereens. But hey, no way José—so I grab my Glock—"

"Your *cock*?"

"Yeah, very funny. So I give him three—bang bang

bang—right in the fucking head. That did it—lost his grip, slides forward, goes off my Blazer and I hear him bumpin' and screaming underneath me—oh, for about five, ten seconds—then all I can hear is the sound of the radials just hummin' along, sweet as could be."

When he told the story he ended it by licking his finger and stroking the air. "Scratch one more fed." Together with the two CHIP patrolmen he'd wasted, and Devane, it made a total of four federals.

"Good mornin's work, Shoe."

"Fuckin' right."

And Schumacher had been correct. The men from the Hummer had pulled off in a Highway Department culvert. And neither David Brentwood nor Salvini had fired at the militiaman's Blazer because they were afraid of hitting Philip Marsden, whose broken and battered body, unknown to them, now lay on the road like a pile of oil rags soaking in a pool of blood from what had been his intestines. And had it not been cloudy that night in the Mojave, an unusual sight this time of year before El Niño had turned the normal weather patterns upside down and inside out—then Aussie Lewis, even with the help of his night vision goggles, would never have been able to retreat as quietly as he did, the advancing militia having to halt in the sudden blackness of the clouded moon.

"The whole operation," as Lewis conceded to Brentwood, "was not a pretty sight. Tail between our legs."

"How'd we screw up so bad?" Salvini inquired of no one in particular among the four ALERTs—Lewis, Brentwood, Thomas, and Finn—who, along with him, had made it out from what Lewis was calling one hell of a noisy "*clandestine* goatfuck," Marsden's body in the back. They didn't feel like commandos—they felt like dorks. They'd already lost two of their number—these skilled warriors with more than twenty years of hostile ops experience between them.

" 'Course," Salvini said, "we were told to go get a sniper. We didn't know it was a goddamned trap. A friggin' ambush."

No one spoke, and for a while, all that could be heard was the Hummer's engine. Tiny islands of the dashboard lights were the only things that were clearly visible, the moon still in a fibrous shroud. Marsden's corpse bumped with every abrupt turn and jolt as Brentwood, his head, like Lewis's, aching from the strain imposed by the night vision goggles, drove at over thirty miles an hour, very fast for the no-road terrain, until they were three clicks from the road. Then they radioed into Freeman's HQ for a helo extraction. Tomorrow they would have to send in a chopper to pick up Devane's body.

"We should've had more intel on those bastards," Salvini said. "Must've been at least a platoon of 'em."

They hit a deep hole, the Hummer grabbing for a moment before slewing around a scatter of football-sized rocks.

"We fucked up!" Lewis declared. "Plain and simple."

"I don't see how!" Salvini protested. "We didn't know it was a setup—"

"Well, we damned well should have!" Thomas put in.

"That's Freeman's department," Finn said. "Sal's right. If we didn't have the good intel—"

"Knock it off!" It was Brentwood, his voice raised—unusual for him. "We should've been ready for any contingency."

"Too much time off," Thomas suggested.

"Man," Salvini sighed, "is the old man gonna be pissed with us."

"He has every right to be," Brentwood said. "But not as much as Marsden's family, and Devane's."

"Ah, c'mon, fellas," Lewis put in. "So we screwed up. Let's not go jumpin' from any bridges. We'll get another crack at 'em. Pay 'em back. Right?"

"Damn place'll be crawling with reporters come dawn," Thomas said. "Hope there's nothing incriminating there that'll point to the old man."

"Jesus!" Finn said. "What are they gonna do when they find the crash dummy?"

"They won't," Salvini said. "He's in the back—I pulled him out after the hit and run."

"Thank Christ for that."

"Whew!" Finn said. "Thought we were in deep shit there for a moment."

"How 'bout Devane?" Thomas asked.

"Had to leave him," Lewis said.

"Stop!" Finn yelled.

Brentwood braked hard. Finn got out of the Hummer and vomited.

The irony was that although the ALERTs had failed, and failed badly, to neutralize the sniper, the noise of the fierce encounter coupled with the sight of a red flare was enough to give Hearn sufficient pause to make a U-turn and head back east.

"Contingency plan B," he explained to Montoya in an almost flippant tone.

"You have this figured out?" Montoya asked. "Or are you just making it up as you go?"

Hearn didn't answer.

"Playing it close to the chest?" Montoya pressed.

"Uh-huh." It pissed Montoya off, because it was exactly the kind of evasive response he himself might give.

"We're gonna need gas," Hearn said. "When we pull up, I want you to handle it. Explain. Tell 'em we'll pay for all the gas."

"Uh-huh."

"And then rip out the phone."

Shortly after, Hearn's cell phone started beeping. He answered and didn't say anything, which struck Montoya as strange. Hearn just sat there, listening, and when he did speak, he merely said, "Copy that," not as if he was giving an order, but rather as the recipient of an order. Was Vance well enough to overrule his rescuer? Or was it the militant they called Lucky McBride calling the shots?

Hearn flicked his cell phone shut and popped it into its holster on his left side. "We're going back over the river," he told Montoya.

"Back through Earp?"

"No," Hearn said, looking sour, "farther north."

Montoya waited a few seconds before he said, "You don't seem too happy about it."

"What do you care?"

Montoya shrugged.

Hearn looked across at him. Something had changed. Montoya could feel it in the air. "When did our boys contact you?"

"Months ago," Montoya said, certain now that the phone call Hearn received had been about more than a change in the escape plan because of all the shooting they'd heard— that it had something to do with him. Montoya launched a preemptive strike, saying, "Quite a few Yankee lawmen went over to the Confederacy."

Hearn was genuinely impressed. Montoya, in what might seem oblique language to some, had in fact come straight to the point. Hearn liked that. "So?"

"I'm under suspicion. Right?"

Pale moonlight would soon give way to a washed-out dawn over the Mojave on their left and the ribbon of river to the east.

"Right!" Hearn confirmed. "You're under suspicion."

Montoya shrugged again. "Well, you're dead wrong. Haven't other lawmen backed states' rights against the federals?"

"Dunno," Hearn said noncommittally.

"A dozen at least," Montoya said. "Hell, we're locally elected." There was a pause. "Look, I'm not a plant."

A huge whitish ball blew across the road. Hearn braked hard.

"Tumbleweed!" Montoya reassured him.

"You were saying?" Hearn said.

"It'd be too obvious, wouldn't it? Federals using me as a plant?"

Hearn nodded. "That's what I figured."

"So?"

"It's the old man," Hearn said. "He has to be suspicious about everything."

"Don't blame him," Montoya said. "I would be."

They drove along in silence for a few minutes.

"Those deputies you dumped so we could get through . . ."

"Uh-huh."

"Old man had 'em whacked." Hearn waited. "Last ambulance hung back. Toro did the job."

"Uh-huh."

A saguaro cactus, easily twenty feet high, took on a majestic aspect in the fading moonlight, ten-thousand-year-old creosote bushes and the spiky needles of twisted cholla cactus trees looking as if they'd been dipped in silver. West of the river was a bullet-riddled sign:

DANGEROUS DESERT
Lack of water and the high temperatures
in the desert can cause
DEATH
For your own safety
DON'T TRY TO CROSS IT

Montoya walked through the heavy heat of the Arizona night air into the run-down gas station that, standing at the desert's edge, looked like a small, forlorn island, threatened by an ochre-colored sea. The attendant, a tall, fat man in grease-stained blue coveralls, an oil rag drooping from his back pocket, looked as if he was expecting him. It was then that Montoya saw the state trooper standing, like a school principal, behind the attendant in the side door that led inside, the attendant nervously licking his lips between drags on a cigarette, its pungent, un-American odor thick with the heat, as if it had permeated every corner of the run-down garage.

"We need some gas," Montoya told him. "We'll tote it all up when you fill up the last vehicle. Okay?"

"Anything you say, Sheriff. But we're short on gas. Delivery truck's running behind schedule." The man paused. "Trouble on the roads."

It sounded rehearsed, and Montoya, in militia fatigues, wondered how the attendant knew he was a sheriff, then realized that the state trooper must have filled him in. It told Montoya how slow on the uptake, how tired, he was after riding for hours in the federal-thwarted incursion into California.

"*You,*" the state trooper said, "are a disgrace to the uniform. You think you're gonna get away with this?"

"Doing all right so far," Montoya replied wryly. "Matter o' fact, you can man the pump."

The trooper didn't move except for hooking his thumbs defiantly in his belt. "You do it," he told Montoya.

"Hey, hey!" It was the attendant's ash falling onto his belly as he nervously plucked the Gaulois cigarette from his lips. "I'll do it, guys. Let's keep it all nice and friendly, eh?"

"No," Montoya said, looking at the trooper, his voice taking on a more belligerent tone now, as if the trooper's pronouncement had jarred him. "I want *him* to do it."

Montoya figured that if the trooper had been sent ahead to keep up what must be a federally run surveillance, he would have been told not to interfere with Hearn's progress, not so long as Hearn and Montoya were holding hostages. But the trooper hadn't been able to resist telling Montoya what he thought of him.

"I'll do it," the trooper conceded grumpily.

"Thanks," Montoya said, adding by way of a return jibe, "How come you're so cozy with the feds? You rather fight for Washington, D.C., than Arizona? You swore allegiance to the state. Donkey!"

"Hey hey," the attendant said, "let's keep it cool, fellas. What'd you say? No cause for cussin' one another out. Let's just—let's just do it."

"*Just do it,*" Montoya said, asking scornfully, "Your name Nike?"

The big man didn't get it. Montoya wasn't sure the

trooper got it either, but at least he was walking out to put in what gas there was from the single 86-89-91–grade pump.

A door slammed shut. It was Hearn getting out. "What the fuck's going on here?"

Montoya indicated the trooper. "Smokey here doesn't want to fill up our vehicles. He's an ass man from Washington."

"What's wrong with *him*?" Hearn demanded, looking at the attendant. "Gotta finish his smoke, that it?"

"No," Montoya said. "Just thought I'd give Smokey here somethin' to do."

"Let me do the thinking around here," Hearn said, still looking at the attendant. "Let fatso here fill us up."

"Yes, sir," the attendant said with forced bonhomie. "But like I told your buddy, we're short on gas. Mightn't have enough for even one—"

"Shut up!" Hearn said, looking quickly around, spooked by the loneliness of the place. He turned to Montoya. "Get back in the car. We'll fill up somewhere else."

Montoya could see the trooper enjoying Hearn's put-down.

"Hey," Hearn called out to the attendant. "Put out that fucking cigar. He's a cop, right?" he asked Montoya. "Playing at being an attendant?"

"Don't think so," Montoya answered.

"Then how come the fucker waddled out with a fucking cigarette in his mouth?"

"Nervous," Montoya posited. "Either that or he's just stupid. Which is why I wanted to keep him inside and let the trooper man the gas pump."

"Yeah," Hearn said, "that was smart. You were gonna let Dumbo sit on his ass inside while fucking Smokey filled us up, throws some fucking gravel in the tank or some other shit."

Montoya had to agree. "I hadn't thought of that."

"Like I said, let me do the thinking. We'll get gas up in Lake Havasu."

CHAPTER SIXTEEN

The Tooele Army Depot was so isolated and desolate that Caroline Hart thought that this must be the way the first astronauts on the moon had felt.

She'd brought a thick file on binaries with her. One fact in particular stood out, namely that VX, like some other organic phosphates, evaporated very slowly, more than two thousand times more slowly than water. She just hoped that the depot, old-fashioned-looking with its huts and some igloo-shaped storage buildings, was up-to-date with detection drills and a state-of-the-art Abbot detector, as well as the latest NBC protective suit. She didn't doubt that the sacs containing the separate chemicals that would mix to make VX in the 155mm shells were stored separately. But before Congress had passed a bill that required the two chemicals to be stored in different states, there were many land mines, bombs, and rockets, as well as "unitary" 155mm shells, already filled with other nerve gases, and Hart didn't believe that they had all been deactivated. And if they were deactivating them now, the depot would be a doubly dangerous place to be.

A colonel came out to meet her. "Major Hart," he said. "Welcome to TEAD."

"Thank you, sir. I'd be a liar if I said I'm glad to be here."

"Major, I'd be a liar if I said I was happy to have someone from Criminal Investigation Branch. To be quite frank, I didn't think my report of an apparent counting error would get as far as CIB."

"Well, Colonel, someone down the line probably thought it was better to have the situation looked into by us before there's a leak to the press."

"Leak" was not a happy word at Tooele, and Hart regretted it the moment she said it. The colonel didn't comment, except to offer her coffee and a chance to freshen up before she began her "tour."

"No, thank you," she said. "I think I'm alert enough."

The colonel smiled. He liked her honesty. "Most visitors usually are alert. Chemical and biological weapons have a way of focusing the mind."

She smiled in return, but it was a lie. She was feeling far from sanguine about the inspection about to begin, the tiny amounts needed to kill a human being stuck in her mind. "You have an Abbot?"

The colonel was surprised she knew about the detectors. "We have at least a dozen. You want that many?"

Her smile was more relaxed now. "No, one'll be fine."

"First we'll rig you up in one of our protective suits. I guarantee there're no holes in it. I'll don one as well and we can go through together."

"Fine."

As he helped her on with the NBC suit, the colonel had some distinctly unmilitary thoughts about Major Caroline Hart. She sensed it and flashed an encouraging smile. She'd sacrificed a lot of her private life to get ahead in the military, to make it in a man's world, but she hadn't given up her sensuality. And besides, it was time to think about what she'd do when her second stint ended, and good letters of commendation from colonels wouldn't do any harm. As she adjusted the fit of the suit, taking great care that everything was just so, she had an anxious flashback to her college graduation, when academic gown and mortar board had to fit perfectly. They had represented not only the attainment of a bachelor's degree in science, but four years of sacrifice by her parents, her father having to forgo early retirement at sixty and stay on till sixty-five as a sheet-metal worker in the naval yards at Bremerton, outside Seattle.

And she remembered dressing for the graduation ball, vividly recalling the white orchid corsage given to her by one of the handsomest jocks of the class. She'd fretted all day, despite her mother's assurances that in the Ziploc bag in the fridge it would remain fresh. She had worried over the placing of the corsage, her acute anxiety recognized by her mother as a kind of displacement behavior after the sheer unadulterated tension of exam time.

She promised her parents that she wouldn't ride home with anyone who'd been drinking. Her father had promised in return that he or her mother could come collect her, no matter what time it was. "Just call."

She had kissed them both, thanked them again for all their love and sacrifice, and gone to the dance. The jock, he of the white orchid, got tanked, wanted to take her home. She was tempted—he wasn't that far out of it, and besides she wanted to "do stuff " with him. But her father's advice reverberated and she called. Her mother went along with her father. A red Toyota pickup ran a red light and slammed into them at fifty miles an hour. Her father had died instantly. Her mother lasted several days in the intensive care unit at Harrison Memorial before she died.

The colonel handed her an Abbot leak detector. His voice was a hollow, reverberating sound from inside the suit, both of them looking like strange, robotic aliens, despite the flexibility of the NBC suit. "Hold it out in front of you, just as if it were a weapon," he told her, "but keep it about waist high. If you get tired of holding it, change hands or just slip it into the holster and take a break." He adjusted her hood. "Feel a bit claustrophobic in there?"

"A bit." It was a lie. In fact she was terrified—ever since childhood she hated to have anything over her face.

"We can take a break anytime and go outside. Just give me the signal, okay?"

"Okay."

With that, they began their inspection behind the barbed-wire and electronic-alarm fence of the first Quonset storage facility.

"How old are the munitions, Colonel?" Hart asked as they walked slowly down the antiseptic-looking row of 155mm shells.

He shrugged, a gesture that was all but lost in his bulky, protective suit. "At least ten years old, maybe more."

Maybe more. A sloppy answer, she thought, from a base's commanding officer.

Caroline bent low in order to check the details of manufacture stamped on the shell's casing.

In the next hut, nervously walking up and down amid shelves stacked with old ordnance, was Private First Class Robert B. Chas, new to the base and eager to do a first-class job. It was far from a glamorous job, but Chas had figured that if he put in a stint at Tooele, it would be a stepping-stone to higher-profile assignments at other sensitive postings. He was still learning, but one order he already knew by heart was that in an age of unexpected terrorist acts, if anyone enters the facility without the proper identification and/or makes an untoward move, you are to shoot, and you will be exonerated for doing so. He remembered very well the treatment accorded the captain of the Navy's USS *Stark*, who had been too late to fire, though warned of an incoming missile, and the captain of the Aegis cruiser who had mistakenly shot down an Arab airliner as it entered the cruiser's vulnerable area. The captain of the *Stark* lost his command and was humiliated. The captain of the cruiser, though his mistake had killed over a hundred men, women, and children, was completely exonerated for not chancing the safety of his ship, and was subsequently promoted.

Private Chas had read extensively in the Army manuals about the dos and don'ts of guarding chemical and biological weapons, but nowhere was it pointed out that an Abbot detector, like a carpenter's holstered hand drill, looked like a handgun. And in an oversight, the duty officer hadn't mentioned that a visitor would be coming that day. Even so, it wouldn't have happened had the colonel not been called back to his office for an emergency high-level teleconference with the Army's C-in-C, General Shelbourne. But he was called, and while he was driven back in a golf cart, Caroline Hart, having finished the count and anxious to get the whole job over with, moved on to the second storage hut.

Private Chas saw a figure in an NBC suit suddenly appear in a blinding shaft of sunlight, saw what looked like a gun pointing right at him, and fired, twice. The second shot was not a natural reflex, but one drilled into him by the necessity of not taking the slightest risk in any area designated by the skull and crossbones.

The colonel heard the two shots halfway through his teleconference call, but he couldn't hang up on a general, though the remainder of the general's conversation with him was lost.

By the time he reached the storage area, Major Hart was dead, two neat entry holes through her left breast, one of them straight through the heart.

There were two immediate consequences. First, that others who heard about the incident would never shoot to kill until they had ascertained whether a supposed intruder was holding an Abbot detector or a gun. Second, it was not determined whether there had been a miscount at Tooele, or whether the 155mm shells unaccounted for had been stolen. In light of the shooting, operational procedures for a recount would have to be carefully rewritten and rehearsed, and particular attention given to safety procedures regarding the use of the Abbot detector.

There would, of course, be an investigation into the shooting, but PFC Chas was confident that in the end, after all the second-guessing, he would be completely exonerated by any board of inquiry.

And so he was. The answer as to why he fired so quickly— "Because, sir, another step and she would've been close to the stacked munitions, which I didn't want to risk hitting, for the safety of everyone on the base"—impressed the board. To signal all other NCOs and enlisted men on the base that, the tragedy notwithstanding, "PFC Chas performed his duty decisively and well," he was promoted to corporal and a commendation was entered in his service compufile.

CHAPTER SEVENTEEN

By now the arid and normally lonely site of the skirmish between the militia and Brentwood's six—reduced to four—ALERTs was swarming with media. Sixty-two percent of those polled by CNN supported what they believed was an attempt to clear the road of militia snipers. But reports that one federal soldier had apparently been "left to die" of his wounds, as Marte Price described it, while his comrades "fled the scene," was damaging. One of Marte Price's CNN news crew, coming across Devane's body in the morning, filmed the corpse, its eyes gouged out by hawks, staring blackly at the blue expanse of sky, the face set in an expression of horror.

At Douglas Freeman's mobile HQ outside Barstow, the general was, in Norton's words to the staff, "about to go ballistic." Not only had his secret ALERT mission been exposed as a dismal failure, but the federal government in the person of the President was being pilloried by his political opponents not only for "sending too few too late," but for apparently having sent "incompetents to do a man's job."

"By the living Jesus!" Freeman stormed. "Brentwood had better be able to explain this fiasco. Christ, Norton, if those media jackals find they were Special Forces on the fucking road, it'll affect the Special Ops budget from here to Maine. And I'll get fired into the bargain."

"They had no ID on them, General."

"I *told* them not to have any ID, but I also told them to be discreet, and now look at what we've got, the press yelling incompetence and cowardice. *Cowardice,* Norton."

"You don't believe that, do you, General?"

" 'Course not. Young Brentwood, Aussie, and the rest— not a yeller bone in their body, Colonel. But they sure as hell blew it. We'd better pray that there isn't anything on the ALERT who was killed by that goddamn sniper."

"I don't think Brentwood would make that mistake."

"No," Freeman said, but it was as much a question as a hope. The general exhaled, trying to simmer down. A commander couldn't let anger cloud the issue. "Well," he said, without a trace of self-pity, "I'm for the chopper. Any minute that phone's gonna ring, and it'll be Walter Shelbourne. He'll ask me if I had anything to do with it. I'll tell him yes, and next thing you know I'll be CNN's idiot of the week. Play of the day." He sighed heavily. "Well, no use whining. I knew the risk going in."

"It mightn't be so bad, General. Politics make strange bedfellows."

Freeman turned on him, scowling. "Don't give me clichés, Norton."

"All I'm saying is that now it's in the public arena—you never know."

Freeman's scowl grew even more ferocious. "*You never know?* That's a goddamn lottery jingle."

Norton bit his lip in embarrassment. "Yes, sir, I believe it is."

"I don't want goddamn lottery jingles, Norton. I want you on top of this, in the thick of it, wherever you can help protect Special Forces. I'm in deep shit on this one, and I don't want to be held up by my colleagues as the reason a pissed-off Congress'll start cutting the DOD budget, specifically Special Forces. Besides, you know how most brass have it in for Special Forces—think we're a bunch of prima donnas, that we're better than the regular forces."

"Aren't we?" Norton said.

There was silence for a few moments before Freeman answered. "Yes, by God, Norton, we are. We train harder, work harder—I don't know about prima donnas, unless you mean *me*."

"Oh," Norton said, forcing a smile. "You, a prima donna? I don't think so!"

Freeman, not missing the friendly sarcasm, glared at him. "You've got balls to say that, in my present mood."

"General, you hired me to be an aide, not a suck-up. To tell you the truth."

Freeman grunted, turning back to the wall map of the Southwest on his trailer's wall. "Then you think I could come out of this all right?"

"I didn't say that, General. I said we can't be sure. We'll have to wait and—"

"Problem with this fiasco, Norton, is that it'll give those militia bastards an enormous boost in morale."

"You mean all over or just the hostage outfit?"

"Both, and we know there are a lot more militias all over the Southwest, let alone Arizona. They'll be encouraged to take us on."

Norton agreed. Brentwood's team had screwed up royally, and the militia's success on Highway 62 and at the Holy Rosary was already being touted by militia sympathizers all over the not-so-*United* States. Norton didn't envy Brentwood—due back at any moment to report to Freeman.

"They say," Freeman told Norton, "that our ALERT who died looked as if he'd been in agony, that our boys left him, that—"

"I don't believe it, General. Pure press speculation."

"It had better be," Freeman replied. "Goddammit, Norton. It's bad enough they left him."

CHAPTER EIGHTEEN

Wesley Knox, a black thirty-year-old New Yorker, had awesome powers of concentration. He was the kind of man who could think clearly in a storm of construction noise, traffic, and the general din of a city, a man who carried his solitude within and who never depended on external conditions to be conducive to meditation. Now, wearing a dark blue skullcap and a silver coiled-snake earring, he sat in the New York Public Library between stacks of photocopied newspaper reports. Except for the account of what looked like a failed attempt by federal troops earlier that morning to rout militia snipers out near the California-Arizona border, all of the reports that Knox had photocopied were from the *New York Times*, *Los Angeles Times*, *Washington Post*, and *The Christian Science Monitor*, and had to do with the federal siege and attack on the Branch Davidians in Waco, Texas, in 1994. He was marking salient points with a red highlighter, looking for precisely what went wrong with the bungled attack, and, just as important, what went wrong with the Davidian *defense*. The besieged cultists had not expected the tanks that the FBI and ATF agents called in to plow through the compound's walls. At first the federal spokesman said there were no tanks, then that there was only one tank. But aerial photographs showed two M-1 main battle tanks.

It infuriated Knox that Americans had used tanks against other Americans. It showed how big the rift had become between the government and citizens in the United States. He believed it was time for the states to *unite* against big government. Could anyone even imagine the terror of the children in that compound? *Tanks!*

In his notes, Knox asserted that every militia, including his—the Black Brothers of America—would have to train for an armored attack. Russian RPB rifle-propelled grenades and Chinese-type 72-B antitank mines, with a two-year battery life, would be the ticket. He made a note for tractor "spare parts," each weapon in the militias' arsenal having been given an innocuous name should a computer list ever fall into federal hands. Knox thought of the ad for Energizer batteries—"they just keep on going"—and though he was a humorless man, he did allow himself a small smile, picturing the tracks being blown off an advancing M-1 tank. One second an awesome main battle tank, the next an awesome sitting duck.

Normally, even with the relatively low-cost Chinese mine, procuring enough for minimal militia defense would have been "economically unviable," as the militias' HQ Ph.D. economist would put it. But donations were pouring in from all over the country at the moment, which meant that what was normally prohibitive was now very "viable." Knox would report to the meeting of the heads of militias scheduled for later that day. He allowed himself a grunt of satisfaction, remembering how shocked the congressional committee on militias had been in 1996 to have testifying before them not only white militia leaders, but black as well.

"Strange bedfellows, Wes."

"I know, man, but we're united against the federals."

The secret meeting later in the afternoon had initially been referred to as HOM. There'd been strenuous objections, however, that HOM would look a bit like "HOMO"— "homosexual" to some members—and so the acronym was changed to HEM, that is, until someone objected that this would make it sound as if it had something to do with dresses. Commanders of Militia was considered, but COM was too close to communist, and so finally OCM—Officers Commanding Militia—was agreed on. Fax and telephones could be used only for ordinary inter-HQ administration; any "highly sensitive" info was to be relayed by hand, using code. Use of e-mail and/or Internet was strictly forbidden because of the possibility of either an employer snooping or, more likely, a federal intercept by the Pentagon's Automated Systems Security Incident Support Team in Arlington, Virginia, where computers spied on computers.

At the meeting of the OCM, Wes Knox, his skullcap still on, told his comrades that Brother Sammy Davis, Jr., had said it best: "Different strokes for different folks." With the bell about to ring for this next round between the federals and the militia, Knox told them, one militia group, say in Florida, would concentrate on going deep in-country, into the Everglades, while another militia might be waging guerilla warfare in the Rocky Mountains, still others fighting in the Northwest and arid southwestern states. The only unwritten law for *all* militias was never to get into a battle on the Great Plains, where the federals could bring large numbers of their tanks and supporting infantry into play. From all the newspaper reports he'd been studying, the Branch Davidians' defense plan on the plain of Waco never stood a chance. This meant that the militia in the Southwest would have to fight a hit-and-run battle—employing speed in retreat—until they reached the relative safety of high ground. And it meant that those in the militias' four Mobile Emergency Reaction Forces of five thousand each would have to be intimately familiar with Jungle (Florida) Mountain and Plains warfare, in addition to their standard parachute and helo deployment ability.

Here Knox made reference to the number of ex-Army Ranger and superbly trained ex-SEAL warriors in the militias, who numbered no more than a dozen, but whose numbers belied their importance to the militia movement all over the country. The Rangers' and SEALs' experience—three had been in 'Nam, the others in the Gulf War—was pure gold for those in the militia who were already wise in the ways of living off the land, if not fighting in it. The federally trained SEALs, especially, had been subjected to every kind of hazard, from laying submarine demolition charges to high-altitude, low-opening parachute jumps; from escape and evasion techniques to the terrifyingly brutal treatment meted out by instructors acting as guards. The latter's treatment of prisoners had been so rigorous that a score of men from the various federal armed forces had cracked, some having died at the escape and survival training camp in mountainous Bridgeport, California. It was closed after congressional investigations into the psychological and physical torture meted out at the school became known, but not before some of them had joined the militia. And Knox told the OCM that he'd eat his skullcap—which he almost never took off—if there weren't some ex-SEAL types in Hearn's convoy.

The SEALs, he told them, also knew what some, but not all, of the militiawomen knew: how to make demolition charges out of ordinary kitchen ingredients, and how to blow up federal buildings like the Murrah in Oklahoma, with the right mix of ammonium nitrate fertilizer and fuel. Most important, the six ex-Rangers and six ex-SEALs had formed a cadre of instructors for other militias, so that on a "twenty-to-one" multiplier system, every instructor would teach twenty more instructors, and so on until there were thousands of militiamen and -women who knew how to make a bomb for a variety of targets, and just how much material was needed, a vital consideration if supplies had to be rationed under siege.

"Just like making a cake," the instructors had told their eager pupils as they created the potentially explosive mixtures from normal kitchen fare. "Too much, too little, you spoil it."

The Black Brothers of America members, unlike those in the sagebrush states in the West, weren't so much afraid of federal encroachment on land, but like all militias, they were dead set against any attempt by anyone to take away their arms. Because of this threat, Brother Wes Knox told the BOA that if the federals attempted to take their weapons away, all chapters of the BOA militia would need to "liaise" with whitey's militia.

"*Lee* what?"

"Li*aise*—talk to," Wesley had explained.

"I don't wanna become no Oreo cookie," one of his critics charged. "Black on the outside, white inside."

"I don't want you to become no Oreo, brother. All I'm sayin' is we can't let our fight with whitey cloud our strategy. We can settle that later, man, but we have to get our shit together on this federal thing. Bad enough they pushed us into the ghetto, but they ain't gonna take our weapons. Without them, man, we get no respect from nobody."

"Right on, brother!" came a supporting voice. "What you talking 'bout is called a marriage of convenience. Am I right?"

"Hell, no!" another joshed. "One damned marriage is enough, brother."

This got a good laugh and gave Wes Knox a chance to answer. "This ain't no marriage," he said. "It's just that we got to reach agreement with whitey on the issue of the federals tryin' to disarm us, 'specially if the federals drag out the antiterrorist bill, stop and search us like they did after the Oklahoma bombing back in 'ninety-five. Hell, we get the National Rifle Association behind us, man, *we* get clout."

"Amen, but you tell me of jus' one white militia who'll team up with a nigger."

"Yeah, you tell us that, brother!" another challenged.

Wordlessly, Brother Knox opened his concertina file and produced a 1996 *New York Times* photo of Officers Commanding Militia who were present at the congressional hearings on militias following the bombing in Oklahoma. Among the four senior militia commanders facing the congressional committee was a black man smartly attired in pressed militia uniform. "Not all militias are white, brothers," Wes Knox said, holding up the photograph. " 'Sides, you want BOA to be as racist as whitey? Best of my recollection, BOA was founded to fight against racism."

"Yeah, brother, but what happens if *they* don't want *us*?"

"I'm not a fool," Knox answered. "Some o' their militias won't, but a lot will, 'cause when the federal push comes to shove, whitey's militia's gonna need all the shovin' back they can get. And so are we."

CHAPTER NINETEEN

"What in hell do they want?" the President asked his group of advisers gathered in the Oval Office. He was talking about public opinion, how fickle it was. "Now the polls say federal authorities *should* intervene in Arizona, that I *should* deploy the military—because the police aren't equipped to handle it. But you lot advised me no, not to intervene, that the Dow would take a nosedive if foreign investors lost confidence in our ability to move merchandise by road, and therefore by ship or air." The President was shaking his head. "And now you tell me that since some maniac—and General Shelbourne here thinks it might have been Freeman—has loosed federal troops against the militia on some California highway, the White House is looking stupid for not having engaged them in force! Is that correct? Delorme?"

"Essentially yes, Mr. President. Public opinion's like a yo-yo on this."

"Public opinion's always a goddamned yo-yo—and so are yours, come to think of it. Well, first of all I want to know *who* ordered troops against the militia on this damned highway, and second I want to know what we can do about it. Do we accept credit for acting decisively even though it was a balls-up—excuse me, ladies—or do we put someone's ass in a sling for doing it, for going against my express order not to involve federal authorities?"

"We do both," Delorme opined, and before the President could press for explanation, Delorme gave it to him. "We *privately* ream out whoever gave the order for those soldiers to go after the militia sniper or snipers, but publicly we express outrage at the militia for the cold-blooded murder of the two soldiers."

"By God," the President said, shaking his head again, "I thought *I* was a cynical SOB."

"I don't think I'm being overly cynical, Mr. President. Isn't it true that Freeman was way out of line to order—"

"Who said it *was* Freeman?" Shelbourne cut in. "What I told the President was that I wouldn't be *surprised* if it *was* Freeman."

"Who else would it be?" Delorme snapped. "He's in the area—it's a pretty good guess."

"Well," the President said, "I don't want to go before those media vultures out there and not know exactly what the hell I'm talking about." He turned in his swivel chair toward Shelbourne. "General, I want you to get Freeman on the phone right now."

Shelbourne's face was red with anger. "Yes, Mr. President."

"Use the study," the President instructed him, motioning in the direction of the smaller workroom down the hall, which Jimmy Carter and other Presidents had used more than the Oval Office.

When Shelbourne left, the Chief Executive turned back to Delorme. "Go on, explain how we're going to get clear of this thing."

"Mr. President, let the public decide—the public who

elected you. The polls say that the majority of people now favor federal action to get this Hearn and to release the hostages. If Freeman started it—federal intervention, I mean—let him run with it now. And if he screws up, fire him. Either way, the administration'll be clear."

This conclusion met with agreement among those in the Oval Office.

A small orange light lit up on the phone console.

"Yes?"

"Mr. President, General Shelbourne here. I've got Douglas Freeman on the line."

"Put him through."

"Yes, sir."

The President put it on speaker phone so that everyone could hear. "General Freeman?"

"Mr. President?"

"I don't want any hemming or hawing. Did you order federal troops into action against the militia?"

Over two thousand miles away, in the aridity of the Southwest, the starkness of the desert unambiguous in its solitariness and unrelenting heat, General Douglas Freeman forsook the temptation to wriggle out beneath the time-honored "garbled message" excuse. Besides, ALERTs Marsden and Devane were dead, Devane eyeless and Marsden so battered he wasn't recognizable.

"Yes, sir. I did."

The President's indignation collapsed as quickly as Freeman's intent to lie, so taken aback was he by the general's forthrightness. It didn't mean, however, that his anger was gone. "Well, General, you've just put yourself behind the eight ball. You stand to be court-martialed and—"

"I understand—"

"Be quiet, goddammit! For once, be *quiet*." The tension in the room was palpable. "Trouble is, General, in being an insubordinate son of a bitch, you've put this administration and me personally, as your Commander-in-Chief, behind the eight ball with you. And so it behooves you, whether you like it or not, to get us out of the trouble you've gotten us into." There was a heavy pause. "Is that clear?"

"Yes, sir."

"You are now to end this hostage business—and end it quickly, with minimum force and maximum efficiency. You got that?"

"Yes, Mr. President."

"I'm putting you in charge of—" The President snapped his fingers impatiently at Delorme, whispering, "Theater map—quickly! Wait a minute, General. . . ."

Delorme tapped the icon on the President's PC, calling up the theater of operations map. The President peered down at the southwest corner. "I'll inform C-in-C of the Sixth U.S. Army in the Presidio to let you have what you want, but I don't want you interfering or crossing the line into New Mexico. That's Fifth Army sector through Texas and—"

"I know the boundaries, sir."

Delorme also brought up Freeman's DD-214 on split screen.

"Well, General," the President began, looking up at the general's service record, "that's open to question. Your career is studded with misconceptions on where to limit your drives. Norman Schwarzkopf says you wanted to go all the way in the Gulf to Baghdad, fully intending—if I'm quoting you correctly—to 'personally shoot Saddam Insane.' "

"Well, Mr. President, I think we'd be a little further ahead with that—creature—if we'd gone an' dug the son of a bitch up out of that bunker—"

"General! Your job is to obey your orders. Isn't that what you tell your men?"

"Yes, sir."

"Then do as I say. Use *minimum* force with *maximum* efficiency. I don't want anyone dead—if it can be helped. Is that understood?"

"Yes, sir."

There was a long pause. "What went wrong on that highway, General?"

"I underestimated enemy strength, Mr. President. I thought it was so desolate out there, the militia couldn't mount the kind of resistance it did in the short time it had."

"You screwed up?"

"Yes, Mr. President. I won't underestimate them again."

"You'd better not, General, or you're going to be minus a star or two. You started it, now I want you to finish it. And quickly. That is all."

The Secretary of Commerce and Nanton, from Treasury, were nodding in agreement. They, like the President, didn't want to go down in history as the administration that used massive force. It had to be done surgically, but the President had to get a handle on this, get the roads open again with a minimum loss of confidence in domestic as well as foreign markets. And fast. And if not, then he'd give the public Freeman's head on a platter.

At Freeman's mobile HQ in the area where the Mojave Desert meets the Sonoran, Colonel Norton, taking the phone off speaker, was coming to the general's defense, because he knew that beneath Freeman's tough exterior, the general felt responsibility for every man who served under him. "It wasn't right, holding you responsible for *starting it*. Starting what? Damn militia started it the moment Hearn hit that hospital."

Freeman had had a close friend once who was a recovering alcoholic. The man would often repeat something he'd learned at AA, that "regret about the past is spirit wasted." Everything must be directed to the present, the immediate task at hand.

Freeman's forehead was creased with concentration as he walked off into the dawn's early light, hands behind his back, deep in thought. As he'd told the President, he had underestimated the militia's response. He was determined not to do it again, reminding himself of something he'd heard from the myriad newscasts—that militias all over Arizona and in other states were mobilizing once again, spurred on by the victory on the road and Hearn's apparent untouchability. The intelligence report he'd had was faulty. There wasn't one sniper, but a bevy of them.

Freeman knew he needed a plan, something so audacious as to make the media eat their use of the word "failure."

Failure wasn't a word usually heard about ALERT HQ, particularly by the likes of David Brentwood, Aussie Lewis, Salvini, Thomas, and Finn, whose combined battle experience was impressive, and the fact that Freeman didn't ream them out for having lost Marsden and Devane only made their failure—the loss of their two comrades—even more heartfelt.

Walking alone in the desert, head bowed deep in thought, Freeman scoured his prodigious memory for some tactic that could be used against Hearn. But the major problem remained—that along the road, as had happened on Highway 62 on the California side of the border, the militia on the ground could provide deadly sniper fire to keep federals away. And even if the President had wanted to commit all ground forces—tens of thousands of men—in Sixth Army, he couldn't, because it would create the appearance of awesome upheaval, of suppressing a revolution. Besides, Freeman knew that even if he'd been allowed to use a large force, there wouldn't be enough men to string out along every road Hearn might take. No, it had to be done, as his Commander-in-Chief ordered, with minimum force, maximum efficiency. And quickly, before too many other militias followed suit.

CHAPTER TWENTY

When Hearn's convoy pulled up for gas at Lake Havasu, having retreated back across the Colorado into Arizona, Place Montoya got out from the lead ambulance, saw a large man in blue, grease-stained coveralls waiting, and beyond, a police SWAT team placed strategically along London Bridge and a cluster of TV trucks and paraphernalia on the shore of the lake by a replica of an old stern-wheeler bar and restaurant called the Dixie Belle.

Montoya was sure there were other police snipers lurking in and around the fake three-story Tudor buildings, but he kept walking through the heavy heat and told the gas station attendant to "stay cool," that the convoy would be on its way as soon as its gas tanks were filled. On a small black-and-white countertop TV, Montoya could see himself. For a moment he thought it was the gas station's closed-circuit surveillance, but then he realized it wasn't, as the picture changed to CNN's shot of London Bridge across Lake Havasu, Marte Price in a quick aside informing viewers worldwide that, yes, this was the original London Bridge that chain-saw magnate Robert McCulloch had bought, its more than thirty thousand tons of granite torn down, shipped over, and reconstructed over a man-made channel by the edge of Lake Havasu. "Only in America could such a thing happen," announced a condescending German TV commentator on a CNN hookup. Marte Price countered, "Yes," ever so sweetly, and pointed out to the worldwide viewing audience that if they looked closely at the bridge, which had saved the town by becoming the second-largest tourist attraction in Arizona, after the Grand Canyon, they would be able to see the bullet marks made by German Luftwaffe gunners during the terrible Nazi Blitz of London in 1940. For Place Montoya, it seemed for a moment as if he'd wandered onto some bizarre movie set, a surreal feeling finally broken by an uproar he could hear coming from one of the rest rooms. Instinctively, he looked over, and then beyond to the bridge, afraid an overeager SWAT member, the hostages notwithstanding, might try to take him out.

The gas station attendant had also looked up in fright, and when Montoya walked behind the counter, the man backed up like a frightened animal, more relieved than alarmed as Montoya ripped out the phone. Returning to the first ambulance, Montoya glanced back at the other four vehicles, their gas tanks being filled by militiamen, and asked Hearn, "What was all the ruckus about?"

Hearn, who'd been talking on his two-way radio, jerked his head back toward the rear of the convoy. "Oh, I dunno. I think Teer and the nurse wanted to use the gas station's washroom, and one of our guys walked in on them. You rip out the phone?"

"Yes. Couldn't you see?"

Hearn shrugged, and it was then that the truth stole upon Montoya. It didn't come to him in a sudden revelation, but rather incrementally, through Hearn's mood change, from the Nazi's brash confidence at the Parker Bridge to a kind of sullen confusion now as he complained to Montoya, "We should've been in L.A. by now." Montoya realized the federals' skirmish on the California highway with the militia had convinced Vance—or Lucky McBride, if Vance was too ill—that to press on to L.A. was to run a gauntlet of federals, that it wasn't worth the risk. Hearn's decision to turn north then had nothing to do with a plan B because there never had been a plan B. Having hesitated because of Freeman's ALERTs, the militia, at least in the person of Vance,

McBride, and Hearn, hadn't agreed on any one course of action, but were now in effect trying to escape through trial and error, making it up as they went. Montoya turned the air conditioner on full—it was one hundred degrees already outside. Hearn turned it off—"Have to save fuel."

"Listen," Montoya said. "Have we bitten off more than we can chew?"

Hearn squinted grumpily into the sunlight. "Vance isn't well. Gut wound's opened up."

"Huh—thought he was pretty much on the mend."

"So did I. Know what I think?"

"What?"

"That bitch has done something to him."

Place thought about it, looking out toward the Mojave, the heat beating on it in waves shimmering like water. "I don't think so. Doctors take that oath. You know—doesn't matter who you are, they promise they'll help."

Hearn, unshaven, tired, looked across at him. "You serious?"

"Yeah, why?"

"I thought you'd been around."

"I have."

"Oh, where? Big trip to Yuma, was it?"

"You don't need to have traveled," Montoya said, "to have been around."

"It helps."

"So," Montoya said, "what are you going to do to her?"

"Me?" Hearn said, jerking his head up, fighting fatigue. "It's what *you're* gonna do to her."

The sliding door that separated them from the rest of the ambulance opened behind them and a militiaman with a pronounced scar across the bridge of his nose demanded, "Where the fuck are we?"

"Heading north."

"North to what?"

"Alaska," Hearn said, "and close the fucking slot." The man closed it.

Now Montoya's assumption that they had turned north on a whim became a conviction. He told Hearn as much, and

Hearn told him he was dead wrong. "You joined us to be useful, right?" he asked. "Because you state guys are as fed up with federals as the rest of us. You wanted to get their attention? Do something? Demonstrate our power so they know they're going to have to deal with us, give us our autonomy, that there's no other way. Right?"

Montoya nodded.

"Well, that's what we're gonna do. You think we only have one target. Jesus, we've got a fucking book full of 'em." Now Montoya was confused, realizing that what he'd interpreted as simply Hearn's bad mood was in fact the sign of deep concentration. "We would have liked more time—to get to L.A.," Hearn said. "To rest up. But we're gonna have to do it now. We're gonna ask other militia in these parts—maybe Jason Purdy's Four Corners Militiamen—he's reliable—to run interference for us, keep the federals off our backs till we get it done."

Montoya's temper was starting to burn. "Get *what* done? What am I, fried liver? I don't get told—even though I came to help you."

"Need to know," Hearn said, pulling out a pack of Camel cigarettes and lighting one, his other hand doing the driving. "Only Vance, McBride, and I know—better security that way. 'Sides, I told you about the Scorpions, didn't I?"

"Everyone's heard of the Scorpions," Montoya replied grumpily. "You still don't trust me."

"Sheriff," Hearn said, "I don't trust dick. Better for everyone that way. Federals take any of our guys prisoner, they've got nothing to tell them. Better for everyone. That big POW breakout up in Washington—Camp Fairchild, outside Spokane—that almost didn't go down because someone squealed on us. The federals used the safety of his family as leverage. See what I mean?"

"I've got no family," Montoya said.

Hearn shrugged. "Federals recaptured a lot of our guys. They're back behind barbed wire."

"I know *that*," Montoya said irritably.

"You don't want to wind up captured like the rest of those poor bastards up in Fairchild, do you?"

"No."

"Well, then?"

In Camp Fairchild, Captain Jeremy Eleen and his fellow twenty-nine militia POWs in hut 5A were still smarting from what was for them the shame of being recaptured and interned again. He and his men, including Sergeant Orr, who had unwisely begun referring to Commandant Moorehead as "Shithead," and Blackbeard Paterson, who'd been marched off to the six-cell solitary block, were not only being held responsible by huts 5A and 5C for the commandant's canceling all sports activities, as well as being confined to barracks, but were given an extra punishment for their recalcitrance. Moorehead was personally overseeing the water cutoff to 5A's shower, two deep washtubs, and flush toilet. It meant that in addition to not being able to shave—Moorehead wouldn't permit razor blades—the men in 5A were forced to use the portable toilet outside. And since curfew began at lights-out, they couldn't use it during the night, having to defecate in whatever they could till a morning detail could take it out to the portable. Eleen did not excuse himself from the detail. Raised strictly in Utah's Mormon Church, where leadership, service, personal responsibility, and obedience to a higher power than the state were emphasized, Eleen believed, like his federal nemesis, Douglas Freeman, that a leader should lead out front. And this included setting an example, even in 5A's repugnant morning ritual.

Jeremy Eleen had also been taught not to hate, yet while he didn't hate the federals as people, he did hate what they did in the name of centralized government, how they sought to disarm a people—his people, the Mormons—who, if they had experienced anything, had known a life of persecution in the East. There had been so much persecution that under the express orders of John Smith they had made the heroic trek from eastern America to the West, to settle and prosper by the Great Salt Lake. They wanted to be left alone, to carry out their business in freedom, and for a man to have as many wives as consented to marry him. What *business* was it of the state's if a man had six wives through the women's own free will? And try to tell the Mormons to give up their arms! Without such arms they would never have reached the West. And now that they were there, they meant to stay. Big Brother Government had to be resisted, a line drawn in sand.

"Captain?" It was Sergeant Orr, a man who'd been with him in the battle for the Astoria Bridge between Oregon and Washington State, where the Airborne commander had been ordered by Freeman to "take the bridge."

Eleen answered Orr by walking over to the window Orr was peering through intently. Though snow was in the offing over the next forty-eight hours, the weather had been unusually warm for the Spokane area, El Niño depriving the Northwest of rain because of massive high-pressure systems, while the Southwest was experiencing more precipitation in a month than they usually had in a year.

"What is it?" Eleen asked.

"While these goons have got us confined to barracks I've had time to study the situation."

"You can forget any tunneling," Eleen said, recalling the heart-thudding alarm he'd experienced on the day that the previous commandant had found out from his informer, Militiaman Browne, of the existence of "Archie," the name Eleen's escape committee had given the tunnel.

"You sure about that, Captain?" Orr pressed on. "Last thing they'd expect us to try is another one."

"Not now," Eleen said. He motioned out the window. "They're sticking in long needle sensors—putting them in deep."

"We could make cover noise," Orr opined.

"Only way to do that," Eleen pointed out, "is to play sports on the field—make vibrations, overload the sensors. It's one of the reasons Moorehead's confining us to barracks and putting a stop to sports. No, a tunnel's out."

"Sir, isn't it our duty, like every other militia, to run interference for Colonel Vance's escape—tie up as many federals
as possible? To divert them?"

"Yes," Eleen agreed, "it is. But not a tunnel."

"I've got another plan, sir. I think—" He fell silent, a
guard passing beneath their window.

Jason Purdy was a gung-ho thirty-six-year-old captain of
militia in Four Corners, where the boundary lines of Utah,
Colorado, New Mexico, and Arizona intersect at right
angles to one another. Like Orr, he was a former subaltern
of General Freeman, and was also answering the militia's
call to run interference with the federals to draw them away
from pursuit of Hearn, who was now heading north along
the course of the Colorado River toward Arizona's Black
Mountains.

Ahead of Purdy, on Highway 160, lay Monument Valley,
its enormous red stone mesas standing majestically in the
vastness of the Navajo Indian Reservation, whose western-
most region abutted Grand Canyon National Park. Whenever Jason Purdy saw the great mesas and buttes, he thought
of the western movies of his youth, and also how, true to
form, the federal government had caved in to environmentalists and kept vast tracts of the state as federal and not state
inventory.

Purdy, with his "boys," as he called his company of two
hundred militiamen, was intent on "killing two birds with
one stone." He was going to turn the tables for a change—
see how the enviros liked being on the other end of the stick.
He and his Four Corners Militiamen were going to select
and occupy a site under the control of the Federal Bureau
of Indian Affairs as a protest against so much of western
America not belonging to white Americans. Up at Window
Rock, Navajo headquarters, the Navajos, courtesy of the
BIA, had their own laws and system of policing. "So,"
Purdy was asking, "how about a little equality here?" Hell,
yes, it was going to be "peaceful," he told his men with a

wink—just like those Indian rights activists and enviros sitting in the BIA's offices till they got what they wanted. "It's our turn!"

"Go get 'em, Jake!"

"What if they start shooting?" asked Lorne Hays, of 4CM's third platoon.

Jason Purdy looked hard at him. "Well, hell, Lorne, what are *you* gonna do? Sit there like Howdy Doody an' let 'em shoot you like they did Randy Weaver's boy?"

"I'd take 'em out."

"Well, hell, Lorne, that's what we'll do, then. I'll tell you one thing, though. We're not gonna be caught with our pants down by the federals like the Branch Davidians down there in Waco."

"Didn't have their pants down, Jason. Koresh had a lot o' firepower in there."

"Koresh blew it!" Purdy pronounced. "Hell, you can live in a gun shop and not be prepared. We're gonna be prepared!" There was a chorus of approval.

Just after this vocal show of solidarity, Purdy got out to take a leak. The sentinels of Monument Valley looked strong and awesome from any angle, even though the earlier redness at sunrise had subsided, and in the heat bowl of the enormous valley red was now turning to ochre. His back to the assorted Hummers, Cherokee Jeeps, and four-by-four pickups, Purdy took out his canteen, popped two 20mg Prozac pills, and swilled them down as unobtrusively as possible. In the paranoid excitement early that morning, he'd forgotten to take the medication. It amazed him that though he'd been taking the pills for years, he'd forget on some mornings. And every now and then he'd feel that anxiety rushing through him, threatening a panic attack. "Yeah, yeah," he'd told his wife, he should set 'em out the night before on a saucer or something so he could tell at a glance whether he'd taken them or not, but there was enough to do already. He'd been sitting up nights studying the route. Christ, he'd been waiting for years. And federals had been watching him, tapping his phone, for years—even out here where nary a human lived. It was the Internet that had made all the difference. He could contact everyone in 4CM now in a matter of minutes. Near noon Purdy himself had become the recipient of a coded transmit via the Net. It was Hearn's personal request that he put his immediate plans on hold and help take the heat off Hearn's column.

Purdy's 4CM left the 160, swinging south away from Monument Valley onto the 191, heading for Round Rock. After that they'd turn west for twenty-five miles, then south for twenty-five to Chinle at the entrance to one of the most beautiful places on God's earth: the twenty-six-mile-long forked Canyon de Chelly, pronounced "Canyon d'Shay." The canyon spreads east of Chinle in three crooked fingers, as though some enormous arthritic spasm had cleft the earth into three canyons and their offshoot canyons up to a thousand feet deep.

"If we don't make the cover of *Time*," Purdy told third platoon leader Lorne Hays, "you can call me an Indian. I've been working on this plan for years, ever since I realized the federals were closing in. You think that U-2 flights are just over Arabia, and all those lights and stuff sighted over Phoenix weren't UFOs? They were unidentified *federal* objects, like the black holes and Stealth technology experimentation. Government has too much damn power." Lorne Hays was nodding in agreement when Purdy exclaimed, "Ask any small business—all those goddamn forms and red tape. Hell, never mind the small businessmen. Ask anybody. The government has too much power." Sometimes Hays was frightened by Purdy's sudden shifts in conversation.

There were places in the Canyon de Chelly, Purdy told him, where you could stand next to those cool, beautiful cliffs, cool sand beneath your feet, and experience a silence so quiet, " 'cept for the sweet wind through pines," you'd swear God was by your side.

CHAPTER TWENTY-ONE

Fuchida liked America, but he loved Manhattan—always had. He knew what it was about—money and power. He had been specially chosen for the job by the holy one of the Aum Shinri Kyo cult because he got on so well with Americans.

Unlike most of his countrymen who had grown up being taught that good manners dictated that, in business especially, one never looked directly at another person, Fuchida had spent time in America as a child, his father on the staff of the Japanese Trade Association, and had unconsciously learned the American way. When you met someone in America; you didn't bow and avoid eye contact so as not to give offense; you put out your hand and looked the other person straight in the eye. Fuchida preferred doing business in America.

And for Fuchida, the best place to meet someone in New York was, weather permitting, Central Park, midday. Lots of people about, to mingle with and to use as cover if you wanted to shake off anyone who was tailing you. As far as he knew, none of the U.S. agencies were on to him, his membership in Aum Shinri Kyo still secret. Still, this was no reason for him not to be cautious. He loved the park. Here America was on display, the best and the worst, the staid, the wildly eccentric, all in one never-ending parade.

Fuchida entered across from the Plaza, walking toward the rough, U-shaped pond in the park's southeast corner, where he could see a young man, his body wasted away, his eyes holes of despair, begging with a cardboard sign: I'M DYING OF AIDS. NO MONEY. PLEASE HELP.

It was cold but fine, and he enjoyed the brisk walk, foliage here and there glinting and sparkling in the sun that was filtered by the trees into golden shafts of light.

After sitting on one of the benches for a while in a reflective pose, smelling the park as well as seeing it, and confident he was not being followed, Fuchida got up and made his way toward Central Drive and the Heckscher Playground. If there was a chalk mark on the fence post just outside the puppet house, he would proceed north to Heckscher Fields and stop by the baseball diamond nearest the carousel.

He found the chalk mark and, fighting his impatience to get it over with, forced himself to walk leisurely toward the baseball diamonds.

Every one of them was in use, and Fuchida could hear the *thwack* of hard ash on the balls, his eyes surveying all of them but settling on the one nearest the carousel.

A junior team was practicing. A youngster of about eleven, vigorously chewing gum, stepped up to the plate, the bases loaded and a coach bellowing directions to an outfielder. The pitcher, also chewing gum at a ferocious rate, was looking about anxiously at third base, but his eyes didn't convey the impression that he'd look again, and the runner on third was already a pace off the base. Just then Fuchida saw a black man walking toward the diamond from the direction of the carousel.

Fuchida compared him with the description he'd been given in Tokyo: medium build, thickset, skullcap, thirties. Looked like he was wearing an earring. Still, Fuchida thought, that might satisfy the description of any one of a dozen men in the huge park at that very moment. He'd been told that the man was bald, by choice, but it was impossible to verify this as long as the man had the cap on. Fuchida would simply become the bemused Japanese tourist watching the ball game.

They both stood watching the game, along with a dozen

or so other spectators who were intermittently shouting advice at the players. For some reason Fuchida didn't fully understand—perhaps it was the anxiety of the pitcher affecting him, as if by some kind of psychological transference—he suddenly experienced a surge of anxiety. If the FBI, ATF, or some other American intelligence agency had penetrated the BOA and knew of this meeting, they might have substituted one of their black agents for the black man he was supposed to contact.

The black man, hands deep in the pockets of a fawn-colored gabardine coat, his throat wrapped in a red scarf, yelled out his own encouragement to the new batter, the earlier one having struck out, flinging the bat down in disgust.

"How many out?" the black man asked Fuchida without looking at him.

"Two, I think," Fuchida replied, worried now about the gabardine coat. It looked expensive for someone from a supposedly down-and-out radical group.

"Taking in the sights?" the man asked Fuchida.

"Yes."

"Uh-huh. You seen Columbus Circle?"

"Yes."

The batter hit a home run and there was wild cheering. The black man pulled his hands out of the gabardine and joined in the clapping. "So," he said to Fuchida without looking at him, "you like Columbus Circle?"

"Yes. I like the fountains."

"All ten of 'em," the black man joshed, his eyes still on the game.

"I believe," Fuchida said, watching the new hitter, a left hander, step up to the plate, "there are twelve."

"Uh-huh," the black man said, and waited, but the Japanese didn't say anything more. "Is something wrong?" the black man asked him.

"Would you mind," Fuchida began in impeccable English, "removing your cap?"

"What?"

"Would you mind removing your cap?"

The black man took it off. He was bald. "Satisfied?"

Fuchida knew he'd made a tactical error. He knew it was well-known by blacks that most Japanese regarded them as essentially subhuman, that his request about the cap had conveyed the impression of unwarranted suspicion. He half turned toward the black man. "You must forgive me for being so cautious."

"Look, man, I don't go for all this spook shit. Why don' you put your cards on the table. My name's Knox, Wesley Knox, and I know your name's Fuchida."

Fuchida, for all his Japanese self-control, could not hide his surprise. "How do you know this? My name?"

"You think we just a bunch o' niggers you can use to spread Asahara's Aum gospel? Well, fo' your information, we got an agenda all our own. 'S about time we showed Vanilla Ice he can't have it all his way. Now if you can't help us, we'll find someone who can. So don't you come across as Santa Claus to all the li'l black children. Get my drift?"

Fuchida knew what "get my drift" meant, but some of the other references eluded him. The one thing that was clear was that the American was angry—unreasonably so, Fuchida thought. "What we are offering you," he pointed out, "is the means of distribution. This is essential if you desire to target a specific location."

"Is that so?"

"Yes, it is so," Fuchida answered, adding, uncharacteristically, that for the representative of a nascent organization—BOA—in need of assistance, Knox was being very "uncivil."

"Never mind that," Knox retorted. "What I want to know is if the damned thing works."

Fuchida was flabbergasted. Here he was offering the blacks Asahara's blessing, a means of striking a crippling blow—*blows*—to their oppressors, and this man, this black man, was treating him like some sort of *genan*—servant.

"We do this," he told Knox, "as a favor."

"Don't give me that shit, man. You do it because your man Asahara's in prison an' he wants to see everyone else caught in the apocalypse he predicts. Isn't that right?" Before Fuchida could answer, Knox hurried on. "An' when we've done to whitey what the holy one wants to do to his own people, then what's he gonna do with us, man? That's why I ain't no blood brother o' his."

"The holy one has never said such a thing."

"Don't lie to me, Fuchida. Don't you read your sect's own literature? Asahara says the whole world will end except for the members of his Aum Shinri Kyo." Knox paused, his hands still in the pockets of the gabardine. "What's the matter with you, man? You think I can't read?"

Fuchida turned his head and looked straight, unblinkingly, into the black man's eyes. "If the Brothers of America were members of Aum, they would be spared."

After a long silence, and the only time Knox smiled during the whole conversation, the black man nodded at Fuchida. He didn't like a hip Nip at the best of times, but this Nip had thought it through, had anticipated what BOA's concerns might be, and had an answer, or rather, a solution, in mind. Or was he merely a quick thinker—good on his feet? Maybe both. Whatever the reason, Knox was satisfied that Fuchida knew he wasn't fooling around with some half-assed Black Panther movement. "These distributors you're talking about," Knox said, "they're the key to our agenda, man. Are you sure they're easy to put up?"

"Put up?" Fuchida said, like a puzzled schoolteacher to his student.

"Yeah," Knox said, unfazed. "You know—put together. Assemble."

"A child could do it," Fuchida answered, glancing at his watch, starting to worry that they'd been too long talking together in one place. "Perhaps we could stroll a little down to the Literary Walk."

"Okay," Knox said, starting off, impressed by the Jap's use of "stroll." Sophisticated. "So, this distributor," he pressed Fuchida, "is foolproof?"

"Correct."

"Huh," Knox responded. "You know what that old kraut Edward Teller said?"

Fuchida said he didn't know who Teller was.

It was Knox's turn to looked surprised—payback for the way Fuchida had looked at him when the Jap had asked what "put up" meant. "The father of the hydrogen bomb. Thought a Japanese'd know that."

Fuchida said nothing.

"Teller," Knox continued, "said that when you say something's foolproof, you should immediately start looking for the fool. Cool?"

"Very good," Fuchida said, walking with his hands professorlike behind his back. "But I can assure you that the units you will receive are basically of very simple design, though they are difficult to make. Each unit consists of two large, precision-made, two-liter glass containers, welded together like glass fishing floats."

They had now entered the Literary Walk beneath a wide bower of elms still stark and dark against the cold blue sky. "It's very reliable," Fuchida went on. "It was designed by one of Dr. Murai's colleagues."

"The astrophysicist who was murdered?" Knox said. "Someone stabbed him, right? In Tokyo? They said he knew too much—security risk—afraid he might crack if the cops interrogated him. So you wasted him. That right? Did you do it?"

Fuchida pulled his collar up.

All right, Knox thought, don't answer—but just so you know I know: "We have any security problem here *we'll* handle it. Know what I mean?" Before Fuchida could answer, Knox continued, "And we don't want to get no packages that blow your freakin' hand off when you open them—like Tokyo's mayor."

Fuchida looked perplexed. "What is this *freakin'*?"

"Just an expression. We don't want anybody screwin' around with us."

Fuchida glanced to his left at a bronze statue of someone, a poet, it seemed, his name ending in *eck*, the remainder obscured by pigeon droppings and grime. "We have no intention of *screwing* you around, as you put it."

Knox sensed he'd gone too far, but rather than apologize, he asked Fuchida how many units Aum would give to BOA.

"Four," Fuchida said.

"How heavy?" Knox asked.

"Four to five kilos."

"What's that in pounds?"

"About ten. No problem to carry."

"But you can't get it through airport security."

"No, not unless you want to compromise the whole operation. It would show up on the X-ray machines."

"Have the Japanese police ever seen one?"

"No, but any one of their forensic scientists would put one and one together, as you Americans say."

Mention of scientists started Knox wondering how it was that such a prominent astrophysicist as Murai could get caught up in a cult like Aum—believe that the world was going to be destroyed except for members of the cult? He put it to Fuchida.

Fuchida shrugged. "Many people in the West believe a man who was once nailed to a cross and dead and buried will come back to life again. This seems much more improbable to me than believing in Aum. And isn't the prediction of the apocalypse in the Christian's holy book as probable as that foretold by Aum?"

"Shit, man—nowadays people'll believe anything. All I want is the goods. When can we expect delivery?"

"They're coming by container ship to the West Coast," Fuchida said. "There is not nearly as much security as at airports. From there they will be transported by truck to New York." He paused. "We will give you the address when the time comes. I'm sure you understand. Security. The fewer people along the way who know, the better."

But now Knox thought of something else—that the BOA in New York mightn't be the only beneficiary of Aum's self-interested largesse.

They were nearing the end of the Literary Walk, approach-

ing the bandshell off to their right, when Fuchida unexpectedly, passionately, brought his right arm from behind him in
a sweeping gesture that took in most of the park. "Did you
know that at the Plaza they charge at least a hundred and
fifty dollars *extra* for a view of the park? And yet here . . ."

He nodded toward a bundle of old clothes and a shopping
cart, another of the homeless—man or woman, it was difficult to tell. "So many people live here, away in the bushes,
in cardboard boxes, and scrounge the waste bins for food.
An awful disparity."

"What the hell you think the brothers are about? Somethin' to do on a wet Sunday? We're gonna make whitey sit
up an' take notice."

It was as if Fuchida hadn't heard him, the Japanese with
his hands clasped professionally behind his back again. "We
will also be dispersing some money in support of your operations. A lump sum will be given to militia headquarters,
which will distribute it according to need."

"Why didn't you bring it?"

"Someone else has," Fuchida answered. "We like to keep
the left hand from knowing what the other hand is doing, so
that in the event of capture—"

"I understand," Knox cut in. "But you sure as hell don't
think white militias are going to share Aum's pie with us, do
you?"

"No." It was the first unequivocal answer Knox had received from Fuchida. "But the holy one believes you will be
in an unassailable position once you have used the units—ask
for any price you like from your oppressors. Manhattan alone
would pay . . ." Fuchida shrugged. "The amount would be almost incalculable." He smiled. "You would have this Big Apple in the palm of your hand." As soon as he said "Apple,"
Fuchida thought of his colleague Adachi, who, on the opposite side of the country, would soon begin dispensing Aum's
largesse in cash. "I will say so long now," Fuchida said, "and I
will contact you soon. Where should we meet?"

Knox shrugged. Fuchida suggested they meet at the zoo.

"No," Knox said. "I hate cages. How about the Metropolitan—the French Impressionists?"

It suited Fuchida fine. Was the black man trying to impress him? Perhaps Mr. Knox knew a lot about the Impressionists? Perhaps not? Fuchida told him he'd call, pretend he was a dry cleaner, and tell Knox his coat was ready. The time of the call would mean a meeting same time the following day.

"Any problem comes up," Knox cut in, "you tell me that coat ain't ready."

Fuchida nodded. "Precisely. May I ask what targets you have selected?"

"You certainly may," Knox said, and walked away.

CHAPTER TWENTY-TWO

Pearson, the militiaman guarding Dana Teer and Beverly Malkin, told Dana she was the "prettiest damn doctor I've ever seen."

She ignored his remark, taking Vance's pulse and writing it down with the Bic pen attached to Vance's medical chart, which they'd taken from the hospital. Vance was still hooked up to a saline drip, looking worse than he felt, but his stomach was not yet ready for a regular meal. "Your Mr. Hearn," she told Pearson, "shouldn't have had him moved."

"You tell him, then," the militiaman said, handing her a cell phone. She did so.

"Listen," Hearn told her in an even and ostensibly unemotional tone, all the more threatening because of that,

"Vance is your responsibility—your patient. If he takes a turn for the worse, it's your ass."

Nurse Beverly Malkin hadn't been able to hear Hearn's part of the conversation, but from the doctor's reaction, she surmised it was a threat. So had the militia guard. The ambulance driver glanced at them. "Everything okay back there?"

"No," Beverly Malkin said. "Doctor's right. You've messed up, moving Mr. Vance before he's totally recovered. He could have a relapse."

The militia guard, Pearson, said nothing. He sat on the swivel seat, looking up her dress as she sat squashed in the corner at the end of the stretcher bed, unable to keep her starched white uniform pulled down over her knees.

"You guys'll never get away with this," she told him. He grinned at her, his intent as clear as the leer on his lean, chiseled face, his Kalashnikov cradled in the crook of his left arm.

"You better pray we get away with this," he told her. " 'Cause the boys are hornier than a jackrabbit. If they figure they got nothing to lose, well, they're gonna cut up somethin' mean if they don't get what they're after."

"And what's that?" Dana interjected, checking Vance's drip.

The militiaman grinned. "I can't say."

"You mean," Dana cut in, "that you don't know."

The thin-faced man refused to be drawn in. "You ever had a man, Doc?"

Dana ignored him, turning her attention to Vance, who appeared to be sleeping, the hypnotic hum of the tires broken now and then only by the clink of the intravenous bottle as it swung back and forth against its aluminum stand.

The lean-faced militiaman nodded triumphantly to himself. "Didn't think you had. Maybe you and Nurse Malkin here do it to one another. That right? Coupla lesbians?"

"You're disgusting," Beverly Malkin told him.

"Hey, just tryin' to be friendly."

"She's right," Dana said. "You are disgusting."

Pearson's smile vanished. "You be careful, lady. You'll get your tits caught in a wringer. Know what I mean?"

"She's right," came a cracked voice. It was Vance, eyes still unopened, pulling the blanket up to his chin, suffering from a chill. "Should be . . . ashamed to call yourself a militiaman."

Beverly Malkin looked over at the lean face triumphantly, then turned to Vance. "Thank you," she said.

Vance's eyes were closed, the militia guard staring sullenly at Beverly until she looked away.

"Can we stop?" Dana inquired. "We need to relieve ourselves."

The militiaman said nothing, motioning sullenly for them to ask Vance.

"He's fallen asleep," Dana told him. "Well, can we?"

"No."

Dana was sure Pearson was bluffing. She asked him for the cell phone.

"Suck my dick—then you can have it."

Dana didn't blink. "You're not too smart, are you?"

"Yeah," Pearson retorted. "Well, I'm the one with the phone."

"You tell this driver to stop. Right now."

"Suck my cock."

"The doctor's right," Beverly said. "You're not so bright."

"Yeah, well, you and the doc are our hostages."

"Give me the cell phone right now," Dana ordered him, "or you're in deep trouble."

If he didn't, Pearson knew Hearn would chew his ass out. But the two women had now made a permanent enemy. Sullenly, Pearson dialed Hearn, almost shoving the phone in the doctor's face. Hearn ordered the convoy to stop.

Beverly Malkin, humiliated by the spectacle of her and the doctor, two grown women, having to all but beg for a chance to relieve themselves, refused the helping hand Hearn offered her as she stepped down from the ambulance. She stumbled, then fell headfirst on the road's dusty gravel-strewn shoulder.

"Pride cometh before a fall," Hearn said, the five convoy ambulances now disgorging militiamen also taking advantage of the bathroom stop.

Malkin glared at the Nazi and then at Montoya, who was telling her to "hurry it up," pointing out to Hearn that even though the Phoenix police had been stopped by the execution of one of the four hostages, the federals wouldn't be so easily intimidated. Montoya had no sooner finished talking than they could hear the air-slapping beat of a helo in the distance.

The incident of the nurse falling down lasted only seconds, but it diverted militia attention long enough for Dana Teer, waiting to alight behind Malkin, to pick up the Bic ballpoint pen, which she quickly stuck down her front, the pen and Malkin's reading glasses having fallen from the nurse's blouse pocket as she fell. Dana handed the glasses back to her companion.

"Thanks," Malkin said, brushing herself off, then proceeding with Dana toward a clump of sagebrush about fifty feet from the road, the sky above them washed out to a pale blue by the fierce desert sun.

"Watch out for rattlesnakes, honey."

"Who said that?" Hearn demanded.

No one owned up. Hearn's face flushed with anger. At first Montoya thought Hearn's reaction might have arisen from some unexpected well of Nazi gallantry, but this seemed unlikely, given Hearn's ferocious hostage-killing reputation. More likely, he was angry that one of the militiamen had violated his order to neither say nor do anything to the two women hostages without first getting his permission. Montoya had already recognized how unpredictable Hearn could be. One minute you thought you knew him, what he might do in any situation, and then he'd say or do something to trash your assumption.

Eyes narrowed against the desert light, Montoya shook his head in amusement. "They're the same the world over."

"Who?" Hearn asked grumpily, taking off his shades and looking skyward at the black dot that was a helo.

"Women," Montoya answered. "Look at them. Always have to go to the powder room together."

"Those federal bastards," Hearn said, still looking at the sky. "I told them to stay away."

Montoya shrugged. "We don't know who they are— could be civilian aircraft, militia even."

"Huh," Hearn growled. "That's one of the reasons we busted Vance and McBride out. Everybody was going their own way. Never beat the damn federals unless we can coordinate."

"So where are Vance and McBride going to coordinate from?"

"Well, it was going to be from L.A., but now that's been effectively cut off by Freeman's boys."

"But Schumacher and the others beat off the ALERTs."

"That doesn't mean our boys can do it again—not now that it seems Washington has given Freeman the green light."

"Hey!" Montaya shouted at the two women. "Not together. One of you over there—the other by the outcrop."

"Since when are you giving the orders?" Hearn asked with annoyance.

"You let two prisoners get together," Montoya explained, "they start hatching a plot."

It was a surreal scene, a staggered line of militiamen turned away from the women relieving themselves in the desert, the women fifty feet from the opposite side of the road. Nurse Malkin, at once infuriated and embarrassed by the situation, was unable to do anything, convinced, erroneously, that she was being spied upon.

Behind the outcrop of rocks, Dana Teer quickly surveyed the ground for snakes, scorpions, or any reptile that might be baking or moving in the desert heat. She pulled down her white nylon panties, glanced about once more, took them off, and took the Bic pen out. If and when the federals made their move, they'd need to know exactly which of the ambulances, the third and fifth, held her and Beverly Malkin, and the remaining hospital security man.

As she began to write, her hand was trembling, and try as she might, she couldn't rid herself of the fear that some crawly thing would come up behind her. Shortly, Pearson, about fifty feet away from them, gave out a long, piercing whistle like a shepherd to his dog, motioning the two women back to the ambulance.

As Teer walked back, a legion of dire possibilities assailed her, from the fear that she'd been seen to the equally disturbing thought that the federals would never find her message unless she left some kind of trail. This was an unfounded fear, as anyone born and raised in the Southwest, or any other observant traveler for that matter, would see unmistakable signs of tire marks to the road's shoulder, even if they didn't see scavenger birds clumping around patches of soil that had been urinated and/or defecated upon. In her worry, however, Teer didn't take full stock of this and dropped the top of the Bic pen by the shoulder of the road. Suddenly, crashing through her fear, came the realization that if the federals used dogs, they'd find the panties, now held down by a fist-sized rock behind the sage but clearly visible to anyone who bothered to walk over. As if fate had intervened to give her a burst of confidence, she saw Hearn, jaws clenched, still watching the helo dot in the immensity of the azure sky, with only a nascent cumulus cloud hanging rather dejectedly above an ochre-colored mesa that in ages past had been violently thrust hundreds of feet into the desert air.

Montoya was eyeing the helo too. It was easy to feel vulnerable out here, even to a dot in the sky that might well be a federal helo. But Hearn had been in tight spots before, and he told Montoya that they were not so alone after all—radio stations across America were reporting on dozens of other militia incidents, from California to Maine and from Washington State to Florida, breaking out in support of the daring snatch of Vance and McBride.

"The more militia incidents," Hearn informed Montoya, "the more spread out the feds, trying to deal with dozens of brushfires all over the country, instead of just one. Besides, out here we can see for miles whether anything's coming, and if we want, we can stretch their supply lines to the limit."

"There's still that chopper," Montoya insisted.

"So?" Hearn's brief speech to Montoya seemed to infuse the Nazi with new confidence. "The feds can't do a damn thing so long as we have the two bitches. Besides, we're gonna pull the biggest diversion this country has ever seen."

"Which is?" Montoya asked.

"Which is," Hearn said, getting back into the first ambulance, "none of your damn business."

"I disagree," Montoya said coolly. "You're stupid if you're the only one who knows. What happens if something happens to you?"

"Nothing's going to."

"You don't know that. If you're the only one who knows, then—"

"I'm not," Hearn said. "Vance was the one who gave the order. He decides who's to be told—who needs to know."

Montoya shrugged and walked off beyond the road's shoulder, his back to Hearn and Pearson, unzipping his fly while they waited impatiently.

"For two bits," Hearn told Pearson, "I'd leave the bastard here. I don't trust the son of a bitch. Once a lawman, always—"

"Why don't you?" urged Pearson, whose opinion of lawmen coincided with Hearn's.

"Nah," Hearn told him, beeping the horn for Montoya to hurry up, a small whirlwind scurrying across his field of view along the sage-edged road. "Colonel Vance said he'd be *valuable* to us."

"For what?" Pearson pressed.

"For getting us over that fucking bridge," Hearn said, then added, "It's more than that. He's the first lawman—at least the first in the Southwest—that Vance persuaded to come over to our side."

"Before Vance was wounded."

"Of course," Hearn answered impatiently. "Long before he was in the hospital."

"Place," Pearson grumped. "What kind of militia name is that?" He paused. "I don't trust him. Somebody told me he screws his horse. Regular cowboy."

"Don't talk shit!" Hearn said. "He's a guy who's never done it—horse or woman."

In the ambulance, Beverly Malkin and Dana Teer were listening.

"How can you tell?" Pearson asked.

"Dunno," Hearn said, "but you can tell," which meant he was sure but couldn't exactly articulate the reason. "No sex till you're married crap. Last century. Know what I mean? Walks around like he's in *High Noon*. Like he'd never force it on a woman—know what I mean?"

"Yeah," Pearson said, not knowing what Hearn meant at all. They saw Montoya walking back toward their dust-covered ambulances.

"He's a wanker," Hearn concluded. "Plays with himself."

Pearson ducked his head as he entered the ambulance's rear door, and could tell at a glance by the way Beverly Malkin quickly looked away from him that they'd overheard the conversation. "You like that?" he taunted as he pulled the door shut. "Make your pussy all damp?"

"Don't be disgusting!" Dana Teer said.

"You." Pearson gestured with his M-16. "Shut the fuck up or I'll jam this up between your legs. How'd you like that?" Vance's arm suddenly jerked, banging the IV drip against its stand. It gave Pearson pause. Was Vance really coming around or what? Pearson knew he wouldn't like any talk about pussy, and so he fell silent.

Dana Teer looked away through the slide window that separated the driver from the rear and unfortunately could see his eyes staring back at her. She clasped her hands together, trying to thwart his leering stare. For some reason she couldn't understand, perhaps because of Pearson's grossness, she had found a small but much-needed comfort in

Hearn's description of Montoya as, sexually speaking, an unworldly man.

In the second ambulance, Lucky McBride, having rallied since his rescue, was sitting next to the driver, poring over the map of the Mojave Desert in northwestern Arizona where it abuts southeastern Nevada, where the southernmost part of the border between the two states is just seventy miles south of Las Vegas.

Jason Purdy's convoy had been sighted by Arizona state troopers and reported by them to Freeman's HQ, where the general, for lack of any troops nearby in the area of the Four Corners, ordered in a company of National Guard infantry at present on maneuvers northwest of Albuquerque in New Mexico. Freeman's rules of engagement following the cold-blooded murder of the security guard were simple: Stop the militia. No holds barred.

The National Guard company numbered 250 men, and after a year of weekend, part-time soldiering, the company, under the command of Major John D. Eliot, Jr., were spoiling for a fight against what Eliot was referring to as the Four Corners Militia.

"My intention," Major Eliot told his men, his square-jawed features even more emphasized by the stiff spit-and-polish bearing of his short, stocky frame, "that is, *our* intention, gentlemen, will be to box these Four Corner militants into *one* corner, from which they'll have the choice of two options and two options only—to surrender *in toto or die*!" There was a roar of approval from his four platoons.

A jaded cameraman from Albuquerque called from doing his conjugal duty to cover Eliot's foray made a "Yeah, right" face. The cameraman, not yet wired, opined to the reporter, "Thinks he's George Patton."

"So does Purdy, from all accounts," the reporter said. "This should be fun."

"Problem is," the cameraman retorted, checking the camera's gate, "he's playing with real people."

"Who, *Purdy*?"

"Both," the cameraman answered. "And both are prima donnas, egos as big as Freeman's."

The reporter, Brian O'Keefe, felt uneasy. Didn't he want to be famous too—the next Peter Jennings or Dan Rather, with as much "access clout" as Marte Price had, or *more*, to the VIPs of the world? He dreamed of the day when Arthur Brian O'Keefe would become simply "Keefe," known the world over for integrity and courage, a war correspondent par excellence. He certainly wanted as much glory as either Eliot or Purdy. In their own way, he told himself, everyone on earth desired glory.

He had a picture of himself now amid the dust and sounds of battle raging all about him as he coolly reported the clash of arms between Eliot's federal forces and the militia. It did occur to him that he could get shot, but only in that cerebral way in which we acknowledge intellectually the fact that other people do die in car accidents while nevertheless believing it won't be us. Besides, though everyone knew the militias were well armed, the federal Hummer-transported company was equipped with state-of-the-art weaponry, and Eliot's force was rumored to have at least a half-dozen Bradley Fighting Vehicles, equipped with armor-piercing 25mm cannon, machine guns, and TOW antitank missiles. In the view of most professionals, the BFVs alone were capable of wiping out Purdy's entire militia force of over a hundred men. But so far the rumor about the number of Bradley vehicles had not been confirmed, and Brian O'Keefe was determined to find out.

Driving north in the Mojave Desert along the margin between the Black Mountains and the Colorado, Hearn's militiamen had fallen into the silence brought on by the relentless heat of high noon when Montoya reached into the left pocket of his militia fatigues and tossed the panties on top of the dash.

"What the hell—" Hearn began.

"We're going to have to watch her a lot more closely," Montoya explained, spreading the panties out to reveal the black printing, telling whoever might find them that she and Beverly Malkin were in the third ambulance.

"The little bitch," Hearn said, starting to pump the brakes, slowing the convoy.

"No," Montoya cautioned him. "Don't let her know we know. Just make sure we keep an eye on her."

Hearn nodded. Montoya had a point. Why blow the advantage of her thinking her message would get through to the federals, now that Montoya had got the jump on her? "All right," Hearn told him, "*you* keep an eye on her." He smiled. "*If* the feds do get too close, we can always switch her and the other bitch into the lead. Put 'em on the point." His smile now spread into a self-satisfied grin. "See how the bitches like that." Hearn grabbed the panties off the dash and sniffed them.

CHAPTER TWENTY-THREE

Las Vegas

Mario Famano, chairman of the Las Vegas Gaming Association, was on the phone telling Stanley Wright, "We didn't get you elected governor of Nevada so you could sit on your butt and judge beauty contests. We want to know what the hell you're doin' to get these maniacs headed our way locked up. It's bad for business. Already we got cancellations from the charters. People think they'll get shot at. . . . What? Yeah, that's right, shot at while they're in the fucking

plane." He heard Governor Wright making clucking, sooth-
ing noises from his office in Carson City.

"Hey, Stanley!" Famano bellowed. "You don't think these
militia bastards would fire at a plane? They've stopped interstate transport in this country dead in its fucking tracks. The
teamsters are scared of 'em, I can tell you that—after that
California sniping bit. Or they're afraid they'll be shot coming in from the fucking airport."

"Mr. Famano," Stanley Wright assured him, "they're in
Arizona, not—"

"Yes, and heading our way."

"How do you know?"

"CNN. That broad with the big tits has been showing us
satellite pictures of the convoy on the goddamn road. Five
ambulances, for Christ's sake! And they're heading north,
Stanley, so you'd better call out the National Guard."

"Mr. Famano, if I call out the Guard, that will panic
people—tourists especially. Don't you think we should wait—
see if they cross the state line?"

Famano was angry but he wasn't stupid. "So all right, but
what I think *we*—I think *you*—oughta do is have 'em ready.
On standby."

"Mr. Famano, I've already done that."

"You have?"

"Yes."

"Well, why in hell didn't you tell me in the first place?"

"You didn't give me a chance."

There was a pause. "So all right," Famano said. "We can
live with that."

As soon as he hung up, Stanley Wright turned to his aide,
Merle Baker. "Notify the National Guard and ask the White
House whether we can use 'em. Christ, Merle, that's the first
time I ever heard the mob asking for help from the National
Guard."

Merle smiled but thought that Famano did have a point
about a possible threat to Vegas. A lot of militia, especially
those on the religious right, saw gambling as a fundamentally disruptive force in society, especially in the family.

Casinos, in their view, were nothing more than the temples of the money changers, and Christ knew what you did to money changers. In fact everything about big money gambling offended the militias, with their fundamental distrust of an easy life devoid of the kind of self-reliance America's founding fathers had envisioned and encouraged.

In Washington, D.C., presidential approval was given for Governor Wright to mobilize the Nevada National Guard. It leaked to the press, and once Marte Price aired it, cancellations for Las Vegas poured in, when in fact no one from Vance on down through the militia had ever had any intention of crossing over into Nevada. But it gave Hearn an idea, which he wouldn't share with Montoya; an idea, he said, "whose time has come." And now, looking at the map of the Arizona-Nevada border, it hit Montoya as if he'd been roughly jerked aside and punched in the face.

Jason Purdy loved gadgets. He was the first in his Four Corners Militia to own a laser-beam-sighted handgun and the binocular-shaped precision azimuth and elevation module rangefinder. Within its six-mile range, the PALM was accurate judging distances to within fifteen feet, a handy gadget to have anywhere, but particularly in the desert, where distances were notoriously difficult to gauge. With six AA nickel-cadmium cells, it could take a minimum of three hundred range shots.

Perfect for mortar targeting. When Purdy heard on CNN that Eliot's mobile National Guard infantry company from Albuquerque, New Mexico, was on its way to stop him from helping Hearn's column, he did the unexpected, turning around 180 degrees on Highway 160 as soon as it was dark and going on infrared goggles, no headlights, deciding to do battle with them in Monument Valley, putting his earlier destination of the Canyon de Chelly on hold. Simultaneously, he dispatched two of his fastest Hummer mobile recon and rocket-propelled grenade squads to Ship Rock, fifty miles away in the New Mexico quadrant of Four Corners, with orders to relay intelligence reports back to his main force.

Federal authorities would not have been surprised at how well armed Purdy and his followers were. The militias were never to be underestimated. Hearn's raid to free Vance and McBride was an example.

But more than that, it had become common knowledge that military surplus weaponry was in the hands of the militias. In 1996 *U.S. News & World Report* had revealed that hundreds of items marked by the U.S. military for sale as military surplus had been misclassified and so had not been demilitarized. It meant that many items originally graded "secret" and not for sale had been sold. A midwesterner, the subsequent investigation noted, had acquired *eighty* Cobra gunship fuselages through legal bidding; and a private having "mistakenly" graded an item as ready for public purchase could be dishonorably discharged for his "mistake" and retire a wealthy man through "brown envelope" payments paid either directly by the militia or by overseas groups purchasing as much "surplus" weaponry and equipment as could be acquired. Those items that could not be obtained from the cornucopia of American military supplies led Purdy, for example, to obtain the PALM laser rangefinder through Australian suppliers, and led Wesley Knox to approach other foreign sources, in his case, Aum Shinri Kyo.

As Purdy's two four-man militia recon and rocket-propelled grenade squads, led by Lieutenant Ray Fraser, approached Ship Rock—its sharp, towering features so dramatic that it looked like an explosion frozen in time, as desolate a spot as one could find in the North American continent—rain threatened, an all but unheard of phenomenon at this time of year in this part of the Great Basin Desert. Many militiamen were on the religious right, and more likely than most to read religious significance into unusual occurrences. Upon hearing the news of the increasingly strange reversal of weather patterns in South and North America, the worst since 1997–98, when Mexicans, for example, died of snow-induced hypothermia in the Sonoran Desert, Purdy and his followers saw this latest resurgence of El Niño as an unequivocal sign from God, for wasn't the mysterious current El Niño named after the Christ Child?

CHAPTER TWENTY-FOUR

San Diego

"Base security," began the officer commanding the San Diego Sharks Militia, "is more often than not a state of mind, rather than a physical reality." It was, he told them, like those cardboard facades children use as forts and behind which they feel, irrationally, secure. The simple fact was that even during an emergency when federal authorities are on DEFCON 3 alert, the movement sensors around a base can be blanketed by "drown over" sound and movement of a passing truck, so that the relatively lighter footsteps of a break-in don't register.

"How about infrared UGS?" asked a militiaman, referring to infrared, unattended ground sensors.

"You leave that base alone," said the Sharks' C.O. "But remember, a lot of bases don't have UGS of that type. And remember, base guards are like anyone else. Much of their job entails boring, repetitive tasks, all of which is a way of me pointing out that if you want badly enough to get in, you can penetrate most military bases' security. Run your noise suppression, for example, during the changing of the guards. And you can create a false sense of security within the base by arranging for a couple of accidents that cut power to the base in the days preceding the planned penetration. This lulls them, and they start treating power failures as routine, so that on the night of your planned penetration, base personnel won't worry, and you go in during the lull, before the auxiliary generators kick in."

John Delaney, forty-three years old and a longtime member of the Sharks Militia, listened carefully to his commander present clandestine methods of break and enter. He was particularly interested in how he might use this advice to penetrate a federal air base. Delaney knew that the militia at large, including Purdy's force in Monument Valley, had a visceral fear of federal air power. Freeman hadn't hesitated to bomb them at Butcher's Ridge, and Delaney swore that if he could help it, he'd never be bombed with such impunity ever again. He announced that he had a plan, then insulted everyone in the condemned warehouse they were using as an HQ by telling them he'd confide details only to the commander.

"Why?" someone shouted. "Don't you trust us?"

"I don't trust the federals," he said, "and they've got FBI and ATF informers planted all around the country."

"Why should we trust you?" another militiaman asked.

"Because I was with McBride at Butcher's Ridge?"

"So?"

"So I must have been a pretty dumb informer to stay around and get bombed. I've proved my loyalty."

No one challenged him. At Butcher's Ridge, McBride's situation report after the air raid said bluntly that the militia had "had the shit bombed out of them" by Freeman's planes and then were "damn near wiped out" by an ALERT counterattack. Later they learned, from a CNN special report, that the ALERT contingent had included Medal of Honor winners David Brentwood and Aussie Lewis. On Freeman's order, the ALERTs, attacking the dug-in militia position atop the ridge immediately after the bombing by B-52s out of Fairchild, had encountered an unexpectedly stiff resistance from Lucky McBride, John Delaney, and other militiamen who'd survived the earthshaking bombs. At the sound of a whistle—Freeman's radio had been destroyed earlier by militia fire—the entire ALERT force of around fifty men suddenly switched from a spirited attack and reversed direction, fleeing down the hill through heavy brush, the militiamen in triumphant pursuit, like hounds on the scent of a fox. And a fox was what Freeman was, for his ALERTs, all professionals and in much better physical condition than the general run of militia, had suckered the militia into a trap.

Only a minute behind the federals, the militia, their blood up, sensing victory, rushed and rebel-yelled down the hill after the federals who, at a signal, suddenly stopped, wheeled, and fired en masse, catching the militia in the open. The enfillade decimated the militia, which began to retreat back up the hill toward the protection of the bomb craters. The tough physical conditioning of the federals won the day as the ALERTs now pursued the exhausted militia, overrunning most before they could reach the top of the ridge. To this day Delaney, one of the few who, with Hearn and McBride, had escaped into the Sawtooth Mountain wilderness beyond, believed that the bombing could not have been so effective unless there had been an informer among them.

He was wrong—there had been no informer, only the computer-assisted pinpoint accuracy of the bombers. Delaney's paranoid belief, however, now fueled his determination not to reveal his plan to penetrate the enemy base he had in mind: the newly established San Diego Marine Air Base. "To take hostages and swipe one of their planes," he told his commanding officer. "Give Purdy and Hearn some backup."

"With *one* plane?" asked Al Lowry, who had risen over the years from the position of machine gunner in the San Diego Sharks to their commander.

"Well," Delaney retorted, "it's better than nothing. What if Purdy's boys don't have any hostages?"

"Then the federals could send in an air cav unit and shoot 'em up," Lowry said. Before Delaney could counter with the point that one Harrier Jump Jet could do an awful lot of damage to helos, Lowry expanded on what he meant by asking, "But why only one? Why not—"

"Because I've only been able to find one of our guys who can fly a Harrier."

"So why the Harrier? Why not a more common fighter?"

"Because," Delaney snapped, "the Harrier doesn't need a fucking airfield. We get a Harrier, we can land anywhere, take off from anywhere and hit—"

"Not if the feds find out there aren't any hostages with Purdy."

"But *they* don't know."

"Do *you*?" Lowry pressed.

"No, Al, I don't. But that's my point, right? Long as the feds *think* we got hostages, we're safe."

"Until they find out we don't," Lowry countered.

"Who says we don't?" Delaney asked. "We know Hearn does." He paused to let it sink in. "So long as the federals aren't sure, they're going to hold back. Period."

"Yeah," Lowry said sarcastically. "Like Freeman held back at Butcher's Ridge and Astoria Bridge."

"That was under the last administration," Delaney replied. "This is a new crowd in the White House. They do everything by public poll. And no way will the American public put up with that—firing on noncombatants. It'd look like Saddam Hussein strafing the Kurds."

"You sure?" Lowry asked.

"I'm sure," Delaney responded, "that our boys stand a better chance with a Harrier."

"Then do it!" ordered Lowry, who up till then had been playing devil's advocate.

The Sharks were not a large unit, only fifty-three in all, but therein lay their threat to the larger and, of necessity, less mobile units of the federal forces. Single militiamen as snipers on various highways across the country had been able to tie up much larger forces. Indeed, it was militia policy to do just that, a policy that extended not only to all those militiamen in active service against the federal forces, but to those, like Eleen and his men in Fairchild, who had fallen into enemy hands. Whether or not they succeeded, their actions could tie up a disproportionate number of federal forces, particularly in vast and remote areas such as the Southwest and Northwest—federal men and matériel that could otherwise be deployed against other more tactical militia targets. Concerning the men in Fairchild, one escaped prisoner, according to the federal government's own reckoning, required a "disproportionate" ten-to-one federal expenditure of forces.

"Praise the Lord!" said one of the men in Captain Purdy's two four-man recon and RPG squads, thankful for gathering rain clouds in New Mexico's normally bone-dry northwest, enormous ice-cream cumulus bruising above them.

"Praise El Niño!" their leader, Ray Fraser, said, comforted by the thought that *if* the federals sighted two four-man teams and attacked first, their vehicles might be slowed in rain-slicked soil. If it rained. Fraser, like his companions, of course hoped that the federals would not see them at all, for the task of the eight militiamen was not to engage, but to recon and report back to Purdy in Monument Valley as quickly as possible. The two four-by-four modified Dodge Durangos that carried them were hidden behind a section of the miles-long limestone spine that ran out from the base of the massif that was Ship Rock like the spine of a huge prehistoric lizard.

The militia leader of the second four-man squad, Ray Levin, who came from the Utah section of Four Corners, did not have the PALM laser binoculars so coveted by Purdy, but instead relied on older but superbly lensed Zeiss binoculars. Given this, the downside to rain would be the difficulty in estimating distance from, and therefore the speed of, the two-hundred-man federal force being sent up from Albuquerque. The federal force was under the command of Major John D. Eliot, who, from what Levin had seen on CNN, had an ego equaled only by that of Purdy.

As night began to fall across northern New Mexico and on the vastness of the 25,000-square-mile Navajo reservation,

Ray Fraser unloaded his twenty-eight-pound man-portable, extra-high-frequency radio and dish antenna. He was to send details of the federal column to Purdy via the Milstar Satellite Network, using his battery as the external power source.

Major Eliot's mobile infantry column, however, had its own forward scouts in the form of two Bradley Fighting Vehicles, one an M3 cavalry five-man vehicle, the other an infantry fighting vehicle with nine National Guard troops, or "troubleshooters," as Eliot called them. They were ready for instant deployment on the vast, bush-dotted desert that swept up like two long ocean swells on either side of the long, jagged limestone wall running all the way to the fifteen-hundred-foot pinnacle of Ship Rock, known to the Navajo Indians as Tse Bitai—winged rock. Tse Bitai thrust up at the end of the worn, sandy-colored wall, thirty miles south-southeast of the lonely Four Corners junction, where an eerie wind flapped the four state flags and blew across the deserted terrain with a whisper that flowed about any obstacle in its path.

The first Bradley vehicle received a message from Eliot's HQ Hummer far to the south that they had intercepted an uplink radio burst on the forty gigahertz frequency and had, via handheld geosynchronous earth orbit positioner, pinpointed the source of the transmission at 8.1 miles behind the jagged towering rock wall that ran south of the pinnacle.

Accordingly, the two Bradleys, heading north on Route 666 and twenty miles south of Shiprock township, immediately swung westward, each tracked vehicle sending up a rising plume of dust. It was this faint though high twin-tailed wake that Ray Fraser's two four-man squads saw.

At four o'clock, New York time, Wesley Knox's phone rang. "Hello?" he said.

"Mr. Knox?"

"Yeah."

"This is the dry cleaners. Your coat is ready."

"Thanks." Knox hung up, noted the time for the meet the

next day, and made a face. The Metropolitan at noon would be a zoo.

CHAPTER TWENTY-FIVE

Militiaman Alan Orr was determined to escape Fairchild POW camp. It was in the family tradition. His great-grandfather had been one of 500,000 German and other Axis POWs held by Americans in over four hundred camps spread across the United States between 1942 and 1945. Orr even had the same problem facing him, since, having been captured by federal troops in the South, he'd been transported far away, to Washington State. He wanted to escape the vast semi-desert of eastern Washington and get to the coast over the formidable craggy mountains of the Cascade Range, but had little or no information about the local militia who might help him get there. Orr was asking his fellow Washington State POWs so many questions that he'd earned the nickname of "Mr. Jeopardy," after the TV quiz show.

"You should be careful, Orr," his captain, Jeremy Eleen, advised him as they walked outside, to avoid being overheard. "The more questions you ask, the more danger you're in. Remember Browne? He was a plant. Federals threatened his family. So the commandant knew about Archie right from the beginning." Eleen and his escape committee had dug the tunnel they dubbed "Archie" beyond the wire, the committee ordering everyone not to talk about it inside the huts, where it might be picked up by hidden microphones. Nor was "Archie" to be used in any outside conversation as

they ambled or jogged around the No Go zone of antipersonnel mines that lay between them and the wire.

"Well," Orr countered, "if I get out, I want to know where
the hell I am."

Eleen pulled a scarf he'd made by tearing a six-inch-wide
strip off his bunk's blanket tighter around his throat, El Niño
having led to a frigid snap in eastern Washington, when the
temperature around Fairchild would normally have been above
freezing. "Head north," Eleen advised. "To Canada."

"Christ!" Orr retorted, before he remembered how seriously Eleen regarded anyone taking the Lord's name in vain.
"I'd freeze my ass off up there."

Unexpectedly, Eleen smiled. "You people from the South always think that. You head for Vancouver up in British Columbia. Has the same climate as Seattle. Beautiful summers, mild
temperatures in the winter. Wet in winter, but the scenery'll
knock you over. Prettier than San Francisco."

"I'm not looking for scenery, Captain. I just want to get
the hell out. Anyway, wouldn't the Canadians be looking for
escaped POWs?"

Eleen shook his head. "Not nearly as much. Besides, the
border between the U.S. and Canada is over three thousand
miles—longest undefended border in the world. Pick out
some woods near a farmer's road and walk across. Draft
dodgers did it all the time in the Vietnam War."

"Those bastards," Orr said.

"Yes," Eleen agreed, "but Canadian militia groups are
sympathetic to ours."

"All right," Orr conceded, thankful for the advice. "But
what'll happen to me if I get picked up by the Canadians?
They'd ship me right back here, wouldn't they?"

Again Eleen smiled, entertained out of his somber mood
by the younger man's naiveté. They were walking parallel to
the high barbed-wire fence on the eastern side of the camp.
"No," he assured Orr. "You'd apply for refugee status. By
the time the Canadians decide what to do with you, you'll
be an old man, a pillar of the community. They'd hide you

in the basement of the nearest church. You'd be a cause
célèbre. Every liberal in Toronto'd want to put up bail."

"I'd miss the States, though," Orr said.

"I know," Eleen replied. "I would too, but it's worth
considering—give you some breathing time before you're
ready to come back."

Neither spoke until they turned in front of the next guard
tower and began walking adjacent to the southern fence. Eleen
felt ashamed, not because he despised his own government—
Washington, D.C., deserved it—but because he'd just advised Orr, albeit halfheartedly, to leave his own country.

"I'll think about it."

Eleen nodded. "You'll need a compass and—"

"I've got that figured out," Orr said cockily. "What I need
is a list of safe houses. At least I hear there's a list. Can your
escape committee help me there?"

Eleen told him there were a few—farmers who had helped
some men who'd made it earlier in the big break and who,
until they were caught—most of them in the open rather than
in the small townships—had been aided by orchardists and
the like. Eleen also told Orr that he wouldn't give him the
names of any safe houses until Orr made a definite decision,
south or north. No point, Eleen explained, in him giving the
list to a would-be escapee until he was committed one way or
the other. The fewer names people knew, the better.

"I'll think about it," Orr said again.

"Don't take too long. If snow comes early, you'll be in
trouble. And with El Niño, who knows?"

Orr replied that he was ready to try what at least one
member in the escape committee said was a "harebrained"
escape plan. He promised to make his mind up about north
or south by the following morning.

"All right," Eleen said. "I'll pray for you."

Orr started to grin, then squelched it, realizing that Eleen
was in earnest. Eleen *would* pray for him—he prayed for
everyone every night, even for his enemies, that they might
see the light and that the militias—David—would slay the
government's Goliath.

But then, around noon, Orr found out his decision as to whether he should head north to Canada had to be made within eight hours, before nine that evening, because the commandant unexpectedly announced that Eleen's hut, 5A, and several others that had been disciplined for various infractions, were taken off the punishment list and would now be able to resume normal outside activities. Those in 5A could even resume using the washtub and inside toilet.

No one was fooled, however, by the benevolent tone of Moorehead's public address, or by what had at first seemed a conciliatory gesture—at least not for long. The fact was, storms were gathering in bruised battalions above the Cascades, and whereas most of the out-of-season snowfall would be dumped on the Cascades, there promised to be enough to cause unseasonably severe road conditions in the eastern part of the state, including the area around Fairfield Air Force Base and the adjacent POW camp. With this in mind, the commandant knew his transport trucks would be stretched to the limit, and that none could be spared for such daily routines as collecting rubbish and hoisting the portable "johns" outside the "disciplined huts" onto flatbed trucks— trucks that could be used elsewhere, bringing in supplies for the several thousand federal soldiers manning Fairfield AFB and the POW camp.

"The weather forecast," Eleen told Orr, "is for snow over the entire northwestern U.S., and Moorehead will need all the transport he can get to keep us and the Air Force base supplied." He paused. "You have that compass made yet?"

"No, hell, I—"

"Better get moving with it tonight, or don't you need it?" It was his way of asking Orr whether he'd decided which way to go.

"I'll be heading north," Orr told him.

"All right," Eleen said. "I'll authorize your getting a list of safe houses. It's short, I'm afraid. Only three in all. You'll have to memorize how to get to each of them. No paper record must be found on you, in case—"

"I understand."

"All right, then. Get your compass rigged." He paused. He could see Orr's breath in the cold air, and for some reason he could not understand, felt a mixture of admiration and sadness for the man. Despite the assistance he'd get from within the camp, Orr was going it alone. It was a gutsy decision any way you looked at it.

"I hope you've got warm clothes," Eleen said. "It could be hours before—"

"I'll be all right, sir."

"God go with you."

This time Orr didn't grin. "Thank you, sir."

"You get out, Orr," Eleen ordered him. "It's going to be one hell of a black eye for the federals—be in all the papers. They like escapes, the newspapers. One man against the omnipotence of the government."

"Well, sir, I never thought of it that way. I just wanted—I *need* to get out of the joint, sir. It's pressing me down and—"

"Go make your compass," Eleen said. "I'll get you the three safe houses from the escape committee."

Moorehead faced a dilemma which in part was of his own making, and the only comfort he could take from it was that most prison administrators in America and abroad had faced it before him. If you made conditions too harsh, you drove inmates to escape, and security passed from being a pressing concern into an obsession. But if you provided enough activities to relieve the prisoners' boredom and frustration, you only created more opportunities for them, "more avenues," as the Attorney General noted in a memo, for them to escape. Success in being a good administrator—he abhorred the word "commandant," which he knew that the prisoners used—was to discover the right balance, enough opportunities to keep them busy and so push thoughts of escape to a peripheral concern, but not so much opportunity that they could use it either as a means to or as a cover for escape, as Allied prisoners of war did during World War II, building a gym horse out of Red Cross boxes and other assorted timber in order, they told the commandant, to get more exercise. The German commandant had acquiesced, and within days that summer saw the long line of British POWs vaulting over the horse. What the commandant didn't see was the man *inside* the horse, a Trojan horse. Stripped to the waist and wearing only shorts to beat the heat, armed with a trowel and cloth bags and hooks screwed inside on which to hang the bags of dirt he would excavate, he began digging what was to be one of the most famous tunnels of the war, and the means of escape for three British officers.

Jeremy Eleen's hut had already thought of the idea, but the freakish cold weather put paid to the prospect because of the frozen ground, and in any case Moorehead had the "nasty habit," as Orr put it, of making sudden unannounced and nerve-rattling hut inspections, more often than not at night.

"Routine," Moorehead had told his guards, "is the prisoner's best friend. Routine tells a prisoner what we'll be doing at any given hour of the day, and they rely on it to plot and plan. *My* plan is to keep them off balance by checking on them wherever and whenever I like. I'm not silly enough to think we can do away with routines altogether. Of course mealtimes, roll calls, et cetera, will take place as usual. But in addition we'll have these spot inspections." Moorehead had paused, noting how most of his guards were in their late thirties and early forties, men who, unlike the "rebels," as he called the militia, had given their allegiance to federal rather than local "ad hoc" governments. "Most of you," Moorehead told them, "were here before me, and you know how some men, no matter how many amenities you provide, will try to break out. Habitual escapees. Put some razor wire around a compound, they become claustrophobic, just have to try to bust out. Stir crazy."

"How 'bout puttin' 'em in solitary, Major?" one of the guards asked.

"If we had to put every man who tried to escape in the cooler," Moorehead replied, "we'd have to build dozens more isolation cells than we have now. And never mind the paperwork." At this point Moorehead had stopped speaking, waiting for *the* question, because he loved giving the answer. But no one asked, and so he had to tell them himself. "Best way to thwart an escaping prisoner is to shoot 'im! That sends the message—don't fool with federals." He expected a cheer, but didn't get it.

"What if he surrenders, sir, before we can—"

"He won't!" Moorehead said firmly.

"But sir, what if he—"

"He *won't!*" Moorehead snapped. "Besides, it's you or him."

The question of how an escapee could be armed when everything, including their watches, had been taken from them, wasn't raised. And Moorehead locked it up tightly by adding the warning that "if he gets your weapon, you're dead. These fellas we're fighting don't play by the rules. They'll pull every trick in the book and than some. If they didn't, we wouldn't be forced to fight 'em in the first place. They're rebels plain and simple, and sons of bitches have to be taught to heel. *You're* the boss. Not them. Is that clear?"

Now a chorus of yessirs could be heard through the administration hut, which lay barely a hundred yards beyond the main gate.

But Moorehead wasn't finished. "And pay particular attention to hut 5A."

"Eleen," one of the guards said.

"You got it," Moorehead said. "That creeping Jesus might strike you as an innocent Mormon son of a bitch—nothing against their religion, even if they do want more'n one wife. Hell, who wouldn't?"

The boys liked that one—he could hear them guffawing in the back.

"But as I was about to say," Moorehead continued, "appearances can be deceptive. Eleen might strike you as innocent and even religious, but that son of a bitch has already tried to escape once, and give him and his loonies half a chance, they'll run again. Yeah, regular bunch of rabbits over in hut 5A." Moorehead paused. "Now let me give you somethin' you can use on this creeping Jesus if he or his men start giving you any lip. Just mention the name 'Rubinski.' Rubinski was the poor wounded son of a bitch who got left behind at Packwood, west of here, when our boys surrounded 'em."

"I heard—" a guard began, then stopped, sensing the air of disapproval about him.

"What did you hear?" Moorehead growled, then proceeded to answer his own question. "That Eleen had no choice, or that he was plain yellow? Have you asked Rubinski?"

"No, sir, I—"

"No, neither have I, but he was left, and that's a fact." Moorehead paused again. "Anyway, you use what you can on these bastards. Got it?"

"Got it."

CHAPTER TWENTY-SIX

New Mexico

With night having fallen on the cold, high desert, and the intermittent moon visible through sheets of stratus cloud, militiaman Ray Fraser, leading a recon force of eight men, could no longer discern the dust plumes of the two Bradleys from the federal force. South of Dead Man's Wash, Fraser quietly asked for Levin, his second in command, to give him the section's shared night sights, which boosted ambient starlight 35,000 times. The scope picked up the two grayish-colored Bradleys only two miles away. Fraser estimated that the two federal "war wagons," as the militia called them, were traveling in excess of thirty miles an hour through tough rock- and bush-strewn terrain, which told him that the federals must also be using starlight and/or infrared scopes. Purdy's orders to Fraser were clear: to reconnoiter and report back to the remainder of Purdy's column, but not to engage.

The two Bradleys, however, were virtually in the open, albeit moving fast, and Fraser doubted whether such a chance would present itself again. They were well beyond the natural fortification or sawtooth spine of the escarpment that spread out like protective wings from the spectacularly jagged pinnacle of Ship Rock itself. And Purdy was always going on about initiative in the field, about an individual's ability to take any advantage offered, and Fraser was under no illusion about whether the federals in the vehicles, well west of the highway, had picked up his two squads' dust plumes.

Levin, who now looked like a pirate, sporting a bandanna rather than a hat or the World War II surplus steel helmets favored by most militia, noted that the Bradleys were turning at an angle that would bring them toward the lowest part of a dip in the escarpment, or wall, a mile north of the militia's present position. "If they manage to breach the wall," he said, "they'll be able to come around wide an' put 'emselves behind us. Then we'll be between them and the wall."

"All right," Fraser said, his heart beating faster. "Let's move south, away from the wall, and *we'll* get behind *them*."

"We'll have to move and settle before they breach the wall," Levin cautioned.

"Who says they're gonna breach it?" the squad's M-60 machine gunner asked. "The wall looks pretty solid to me."

Fraser, using a red pinpoint flashlight attached to his remote starter, looked at the map but wasn't able to tell for sure whether any part of it was breachable. "Better safe than sorry," he told Levin. "Let's move back from the wall. That way, if they do breach, we'll see them quicker than staying here."

"We'll raise dust," the machine gunner warned.

"Not if we move out fast and settle the plumes by the time they get through."

"*If* they get through," the machine gunner said hopefully.

"They will," Fraser said, "and I don't want to be squeezed in with my back to the wall and nowhere to move."

"If we stay put and stay quiet," a squad man posited, "hopefully they might not see us."

"Murphy says they will," Levin told him.

"Who's Murphy?" the squad man asked, looking around. "Ain't no Mur—"

"Murphy's law, you dork," Levin said.

"Oh. Ah, I dunno, they probably have to go to the end of the wall and around Ship Rock to get behind us."

Levin the pirate looked at Ray Fraser. "Well, do we split and run, or pull back to a better attack position? Your call, Ray."

Fraser's heart was going even faster—he thought it was going to bang right through his chest. Nothing, dammit, ever worked out exactly as you planned it. Did Eliot have air cover? "Shit!" If he did have it, did the White House's rules of engagement allow Eliot to fire on civilian vehicles, without knowing for sure if noncombatants were inside? If he, Fraser, ordered his men to fire on the Bradleys, then his two Durangos *would* be identified as militia. But if he didn't fire, and let Eliot's scouts free range, they could go on and shoot up Purdy's column if, as Fraser suspected, the Bradleys were bristling with TOW missiles. Shit. For some inexplicable reason at this moment of high tension, Fraser was thinking of something that George Orwell, the British author of *1984*, had said about trying to get agreement among the Spanish militias he had fought with and trained—namely, that they'd turn you gray overnight.

Fraser knew he had to decide.

Two miles farther down the sawtoothed wall of rock, Major Eliot's two Bradleys, with all the urgency of a cat after its prey, were racing hard along the base of the wall, looking for a gap.

CHAPTER TWENTY-SEVEN

It began to snow in eastern Washington, and at the POW camp, the militia commander of hut 4B was arguing that Al Orr's escape plan shouldn't be approved by Eleen for that night. The reason, he said, was that the escape committee had already given permission for an escape attempt that same night to a group of eight prisoners from 4B. The fear was that one escape plan would get in the way of the other. Eleen had acknowledged the problem, one that had plagued every one of the five hundred POW camps in the U.S. during the Second World War. But he pointed out that, providing the eight militiamen from 4B and Orr made sure they didn't attempt their escapes at the same time, both parties could go ahead. Accordingly, Orr agreed to let the 4B party precede him by a half hour—since, as Orr conceded, "they've been given permission first."

"Yeah," 4B's commanding officer told Eleen. "But why does Orr have to go tonight? You knew 4B had been given permission."

Jeremy Eleen felt awkward, embarrassed by appearing to break the escape committee's iron law—his iron law—that you didn't allow two breakouts on the same night, neither simultaneously nor staggered. It might have been permissible, provided the escape committee had informed each party about the other's plan, but Eleen, for a very good security reason—to avoid a leak, as had happened with the tunnel—had promised Al Orr he wouldn't divulge his plan, a plan that Orr told him would work only once. In addition, Al Orr, though outwardly confident, was close to what Eleen believed would be a nervous collapse if he didn't get out.

Orr had ceased looking at the worn photo of his wife, Linda, and their two five-year-olds. "Oh, I look so ugly, Al," she had said, her hair tousled, wearing an apron, smiling as she knelt in the kitchen between the twins so that he could get a good close-up. Whenever he looked at the picture of them, he'd experience a smell memory of her making chocolate chip cookies, and he could hear the voices of the two children playing. The photo, a Polaroid, was fading, in part because he hadn't coated it with a protective spray; and it was badly crinkled, because the camp guards had confiscated all personal effects, including wallets. He had hidden the photo in the hem of his pants, and without a protective layer or wallet to protect the photo, he was wearing it out a little more every time he pulled it from his pocket. And he was becoming more obsessive, obeying a crazy impulse, which he seemed to have no control over, to touch the photo a certain number of times every day and the last thing at night, in much the same way he used to feel compelled as a schoolboy to touch his pencil case, as if the photo were a talisman he *had* to touch so many times—seven times at lights-out. It was a small ceremony that, though Orr didn't fully understand it, was somehow a necessary ritual if God, Fortune, whatever, was to reassure him that everything would be all right. That he would see Linda and the boys. Even the most unobservant prisoners had noticed his obsessive-compulsiveness by now, for any prisoner, if he was to deal with the endless sameness of incarceration, noticed such things, grateful for any diversion behind the barbed wire and guard towers.

Eleen assigned two parrots—the POWs' term for lookouts—to aid in Orr's attempt, one at the hut's east end, nearest the main gate a hundred yards off, who would also work the hut's door once the searchlight had swept by; and one who would muss up Orr's footprints in the light snow around the bottom of the hut's steps and the space between the huts and raised portable toilet, which, like most other buildings in the camp, had been deliberately set high off the ground, to prevent tunneling.

In hut 4B the party of six POWs and two other POWs in federal fatigues and coats nervously went over yet again the procedure they were to follow. It had taken weeks for what Eleen, in an unusual display of lightheartedness, dubbed the "covey of warlocks"—ten men in all, drawn from all over the camp, two tailors among them, gofers, scroungers, a thief, and three peacetime handymen—to steal enough blankets, accessories, and make-do dye to fashion two federal uniforms and shape two wooden M-16s. The fake guns wouldn't stand a close inspection from, say, a few inches away, but even by Eleen's exacting standards they were "absolutely real-looking" from a distance of several feet.

"You're gonna get cold, Al," the door parrot told Orr. "It might be a few hours before the feds' trucks arrive."

"I know," Orr said, crouched down by the hut's east door. "But I don't want to leave my move till the last minute. You just tell me the moment you hear the outhouse removal trucks. You'll have to listen carefully—snow'll kill much of the sound, and then there's the noise sometimes from the air base."

"Relax," the parrot told him. "I ain't deaf, and I sure as hell can tell the sound of a truck from a goddamn airplane, snow and all."

"All right," Orr said. "That's good."

"*Hey!*" the parrot said suddenly. "You're supposed to wait till the 4B boys kick up a ruckus and go out. What if the trucks arrive *before* them?"

"Then I'll have to go," Orr asserted with bravado, despite his inner turmoil.

"Man, you do, and they'll be pissed off."

"Who, the guys from 4B or the feds?" Orr said, surprised by his own joke.

"Guys from hut four, that's who."

"Well," Orr said, his outer appearance ultracool, "they have their timetable, I have mine."

"Eleen'd be pissed off."

Orr said nothing. The parrot had a point, but sometimes you just have to take advantage of a situation, Orr told himself. Wasn't Eleen always preaching that federal general's mantra, *"L'audace, l'audace, toujours l'audace!"* Orr silently wished the 4B guys luck, *good* luck, but if the trucks arrived at the gate before they were ready, then he'd have to go. He could feel the photo in his shirt pocket, his heart thumping beneath it.

It was snowing heavily when, amid jeering and shouted protests from the rest of hut 4B, six militia POWs were herded toward the east gate under the bullying of two men who looked like Fairfield guards, carrying the fake but realistic-looking wooden M-16s and yelling orders at their "prisoners." It was chaotic, with men from other huts joining in to vent their spleen, even though most of them didn't understand the escape plan of the men from hut 4B. Many assumed what the east gate guards were assuming—that there'd been a brouhaha in one of the huts, and that two guards were now marching six of the troublemaking POWs through the east gate as the outhouse-removal trucks were entering the camp. Presumably, the POWs were being taken to the newly constructed, special concrete bunker cells beyond the gate, in a compound purposely set aside in a separate containment area a quarter mile outside the main camp.

Now there was more noise coming from the huts as men began to spill out into the snow-covered yard, the guards in the towers stopping their searchlight sweeps and instead bringing the beams to bear on hut 4B and the two huts on either side of it. Meanwhile, the federal drivers in the outhouse-removal trucks that were waiting inside the gate, motors still running, were getting jittery, appealing to the lieutenant in charge of their detail.

"Well," rejoined the lieutenant, a nervous, intense twenty-year-old, "don't worry about it. Just drive slowly through 'em, do the job, and we'll get out of here!" His response filled him with pride because he'd felt the same apprehension as his drivers, but had come back with a laid-back reply. Quickly, one of his men in the truck pulling up by 5A stepped from the back of the three-ton flatbed, one foot on the flatbed, the other on the top of the outhouse. He slipped the U-bolt through the hook, stepped back smartly onto the truck, made a twirling motion with his hand to his co-driver, and heard the half-inch-diameter cable crackle, as the winch, whining as if in protest, took up the strain.

The guards at the gate, fearful of a possible rush toward them by POWs coming up behind the half-dozen troublemakers and their two guards, hurried the two guards and six prisoners through the gate, then locked it, only to have to unlock it again a minute later when the truck, a portable toilet lashed to the flatbed, approached the gate. "Hold it!" the second guard said. "Lock the gate! Boss told us to check all vehicles on the way out."

It was bitingly cold, but not wanting to run afoul of Moorehead, the other guard dutifully held up his hand for the truck to stop and, grunting, his overcoat impeding movement, he bent low and shone his flashlight under the truck's chassis. "Nothin' here!"

"Check the shithouse."

Swearing, the guard hoisted himself over the tailboard and, pulling at the door, couldn't open it because of the ropes holding it down. "Can't open the fuckin' door."

"Well, then," the young lieutenant said, now sitting in the truck's warm cabin, "loosen the ropes, Einstein."

Einstein. The lieutenant liked that. So did the other guard. It was obvious, however, that the guard on the flatbed didn't. Wordlessly, his sullen body language announcing his protest, he loosened the bowline knot and, shouldering his weapon with the sling, jerked the door hard. Then he thought of a get-even reply for the smartass lieutenant and for the other guard. See how the bastards liked this one. "Hey!" he yelled out. "Either of you check those guards' ID?"

"What guards?" the young lieutenant asked, then remembered the two guards he'd seen escorting the delinquent POWs out through the gate.

"Did *you*?" he asked the second guard.

"No, I thought—well, hell, they were—"

"Oh, shit!" the lieutenant said. "Stay here—at the gate." Then he called out to the guard on the flatbed. "Come with me."

The guard liked the lieutenant's panicky tone. *Fuck 'im.* He took his time shining the flashlight into the darkness of the phone booth–sized toilet. "Nothing," he told the lieutenant, who was now on his cell phone, waking up the commandant, and walking, then running, toward the punishment cells and pumping his right arm in the air, giving the guard on the flatbed the "on the double" signal. Stopping, out of breath, he jumped onto the truck's running boards.

Moorehead was awake, barely, and the next minute he was strapping on his .45 with its laser dot aimer and grabbing his coat.

CHAPTER TWENTY-EIGHT

Ray Fraser was right in his evaluation of federal timidity and incompetence at what would be described by CNN as the Battle of Shiprock, despite the relatively few combatants involved. In fact the thrusting rock spires were more than a mile away from the tiny town of the same name. But if the militia had learned something about Major Eliot's National Guard, Eliot, from the two Bradleys' radio reports to him during the skirmish, had learned something about the militia too. He was struck by how accurate the militia's antitank rockets had been. In addition, while the general public had been hypnotized years before by the laser-guided gadgetry and other gee-whiz electronics of the Gulf War, he knew it took guts and training for an infantryman to expose himself to enemy fire in order to aim with such accuracy. "Rebels not only have the hardware," Eliot complained to his officers, "but unlike most ragtag rebel armies, these sons of bitches know how to use it."

Meanwhile the media, its condolences to next of kin notwithstanding, were inferring that Eliot's advance troops were as incompetent as Freeman's ALERTs, who, on orders from Freeman, had tried unsuccessfully with "serious loss of life" to rout militia snipers near the California-Arizona border. The tabloid press had set the accusatory tone, and the mainstream press, while disavowing any impetus from the tabloids, took it from there.

Eliot, in response to the unflattering portrait of him, offered to hold what would be in effect a mobile phone tele-conference as he continued northward, refusing to stop long enough to hold a regular press conference lest he be pilloried for stopping and wasting time instead of keeping up his pursuit of Jason Purdy's militia. In return for his willingness to be interviewed, albeit while on the move, Eliot asked that nothing be reported about his precise whereabouts or his disposition of forces. The reporters, Marte Price among them, were in a feeding frenzy, and smelling Eliot's dismissal by Washington, D.C., they readily agreed to Eliot's terms and closed in for the kill.

Marte Price, however, as well as the dozens of reporters, foreign and domestic, were sorely disappointed. Eliot, an ardent, if somewhat jealous, admirer of General Freeman's forthrightness and élan, adopted a concise, no-nonsense tone. "No," he told the assembled media in Albuquerque, he did not consider the defeat of his men a "stunning blow to federal morale" following what Marte Price called the ALERTs "debacle."

Eliot, a short, blue-eyed man with the stocky appearance of a professional wrestler, never batted an eye and seemed to some to grow taller as he spoke, his tone raspy and unapologetic.

"It's always a blow, Miz Price, for any commander to lose a single one of his soldiers, but the sacrifice those men made up there at Ship Rock wasn't in vain. What they learned about Purdy's militia force is significant."

"And what's that, Colonel?" Marte Price pressed, despite already using up her two-question quota.

Eliot couldn't stand people jumping in, and for a moment he considered not answering, but he knew that would immediately raise suspicions that he was hiding something. He was, but damned if he was going to reveal the content of the Bradleys' last transmit, something he was going to share only with his troops when the time was right. "What we've learned," he told the press via his radio telephone, "is that the militia is clearly led by traitorous Americans—wait till I finish, please. We've learned that U.S. veterans are among the militia leaders. And that, ladies and gentlemen, makes me sick. More than that, it's disgusting that men who daily took the pledge of allegiance to this country have now turned their backs on the greatest country in the world."

"Some of them don't see it that way, Major. Some, like Captain Purdy, feel they've been betrayed by the federal author—"

"I'm not interested in what traitors like Purdy think."

"So anyone who disagrees with the federal government is a traitor."

"I didn't say that."

"You implied it."

"Well, whatever you want to call the militia," Eliot said, flushing angrily, "I call them goddamn traitors." With that, the screen went blank. He had terminated the press conference.

Goddammit, that's not how Freeman would've handled it, Eliot told himself. He shouldn't have shut down the press conference so abruptly. Now he'd be the "rude" commander as well as the "incompetent."

Within ten minutes the White House's Delorme was on the phone to Freeman's HQ.

"General, the President isn't pleased with Major Eliot's teleconference. His demeanor wasn't at all professional. In short, he came across as a rank amateur. That 'goddamn traitors' bit won't go down well in the Bible Belt, or in Salt Lake City. What's the matter with him?"

"He's under pressure," said Freeman, who, looking out from his mobile HQ into the Mojave's early morning light, could see a twenty-foot-high, multilimbed saguaro cactus looking like some giant with its hands up.

"That's not good enough," Delorme said. "We're all under pressure, and it does us no good at all for him to say anyone who disagrees with Washington is a traitor."

"Did he actually say that? That they're traitors?"

"No, he said '*goddamn traitors.*'" There was a pause. Delorme wondered if he'd heard a laugh, or had it been some kind of static?

"Well," Freeman said with transparent gravity, "he shouldn't have said that."

"No, he shouldn't have," Delorme agreed. "You think it's funny?"

"No," Freeman said, "but it's accurate."

"Goddammit, General, you're supposed to be setting an example. He lost it. We're talking about men being killed."

"Listen, Delorme, you're the ones who are losing it. You're more concerned about what public opinion is than—"

"And you're not? Honestly, now? You crave headlines, General. You live for headlines."

"Yes," Freeman conceded. "The right headlines. But now if you're so upset with Eliot, if the public's so put out—which I'm not sure they are—why don't you talk to *him*?" Freeman knew he'd put his foot in it the moment the words left his mouth.

"Because," Delorme said calmly, "you are the force commander for the Southwest, and I didn't think you'd appreciate me blasting one of your subalterns without going through you. It's called protocol." There was a pause.

"You're right," Freeman said. "I appreciate the courtesy. I'll talk to him."

"Thank you, General."

When Freeman got through to Eliot, the latter had calmed down and readily agreed he should have kept his cool. Freeman then asked him exactly what had happened at Ship Rock.

"We got trounced, General," Eliot said. "But . . ." He paused. "And something else happened that I didn't want to talk about in the press conference."

"What's that?"

"The militia surrendered to one of my Bradleys. The Bradley stopped, held its fire, and the bastards hit it with an AT missile."

"Jesus Christ!" Freeman exploded. "Why in hell didn't you tell that to those media pricks?"

"I thought I'd save it—just tell the men."

"Why, for Christ's sake?"

"Because," Eliot said, "that does it for me. From here on in we're not taking prisoners."

There was a long pause. Finally Freeman spoke, his tone as cold as that of his New Mexico commander. "Major, you and I never had this conversation. You understand?"

"I do," Eliot replied.

But Freeman wasn't sure he did, that he was fully cognizant of its horrendous implications.

CHAPTER TWENTY-NINE

Several miles south of Ship Rock the monocular scope that turned night into day was tiring militiaman Levin's eyes. He felt a dull headache radiating into his sinuses, already plugged by the high desert's dust. He saw something move, at a range of about five hundred yards. It moved again. A mule deer. Then he saw the twin dust plumes of the two Bradleys—on *his* side of the escarpment. "Holy shit, they're through!" he said. "They're through the fucking wall!"

"Calm down," Fraser ordered sharply, despite his own fear. "Get the AT." Levin reached inside the four-by-four, grabbing the sling of the carrying case for the 84mm cone-shaped warhead, lifting it high to clear a large sagebrush. He sighted up, the distance between his eight-man recon team and the federals' two Bradleys now about three hundred yards.

"Slow your breathing!" Fraser ordered, but Levin already had, or was trying. He hadn't done this since the Gulf War. Shoulders hunched forward, taking in a half breath and holding it as if stilling himself for a chest X ray, his upper torso and WW II helmet looking as if they were welded to the forty-inch-long rocket, his eye to the sight, he fired. The back-blast kicked up a debris of brush twigs and dust that momentarily obscured him, the fifteen-pound rocket streaking away as the advancing Bradley swiveled its turret in their direction, its 25mm cannon sending out long, lazy-looking arcs of one-in-four red tracer in the militiamen's direction.

The Bradley disappeared.

"What the—" Levin began.

"Where the hell—" Fraser began, equally perplexed, then yelling, "Secondary target. Secondary targ—" But the second Bradley had also disappeared, the AT-4 missile exploding in a brilliant crimson fireball against a rocky protrusion from the wall.

"Right on!" the militia machine gunner shouted, thinking the explosion he'd seen and heard as a loud thump, and the whistling of airborne limestone a half mile away, was the missile detonating against the second Bradley.

"You dork!" Levin shouted in anger. "It missed!"

"Huh? Must've hit some—"

"Shut up!" Fraser told them. "They've obviously found a hole." He meant a depression, no doubt one of the dry creek beds indicated on the topographic map. "Benet!" he called toward the second four-by-four, twenty yards away. "Bring out the other AT." It was their last—only two of the expensive antiarmor weapons being assigned to the eight-man militia squad.

"Should've got in closer," Benet griped.

"Shut your mouth!" Fraser snapped.

But Benet wouldn't be silenced. "Well, we're no fucking closer to 'em now."

"We fucking will be!" Fraser said. "If you move your ass and get over there."

"You coming?"

"Yes. Now get in the back of Levin's vehicle and get ready to fire it. We'll see how *you* do."

"No problem."

"Levin!" Fraser shouted, giving him the GPS coordinates from his handheld unit. "We'll go out first on their right flank and try to draw them out of that damn hole for you. You drive your squad out on the left flank. And Benet . . ."

"Yeah?"

"Once you're close enough, shoot for the tracks. Feds have got packs of appliqué armor front and sides."

Benet said nothing, Levin hopping into the other Durango, driving now by the light of the moon, which was a mottled silver disk in the high desert sky. It backlit the towering beauty of Ship Rock, the fifteen-hundred-foot volcanic plug at that moment resembling a great Gothic cathedral, whose enormous flying buttresses had been pushed inward, so that all that remained now was a magnificent thrust of spires that pierced the moonlit sky.

The two four-wheel-drive vehicles with four militiamen apiece sped over the high desert, jarring their occupants so violently that in the silver light they seemed to be racing each other in some grueling overland trial. Ray Fraser, his head out the front seat's passenger window, braced his starlight scope against the door's frame, navigating as best he could, while the navigator in Levin's vehicle, over two hundred yards away, was "surfing," hanging dangerously out from the vehicle.

Levin, as the commander of the Durango out on the left flank, thought they should be going faster northward, back in the direction of Purdy's 120-man force, but Fraser's rationale was that if the eight militiamen in his mobile infantry force could take out Eliot's two advance Bradleys, it would be such a stunning blow to Eliot and to the morale of the entire federal column that Eliot would hold back, or at least pause long enough for Purdy's force to meet up with Hearn's motorcade farther west. Or long enough—if *both* Bradleys were taken out—to dissuade Eliot from attacking at all. In any event, given the presence of civilian hostages in Hearn's motorcade, it would be a no-win situation for the federals. They weren't keen to walk in the footsteps of General Trevor, who had fired upon the civilians during the battle for Astoria Bridge. Such action would be a career stopper, an impediment to promotion. And never mind the worldwide condemnation that would follow via CNN.

"Jesus!" It was Levin, as he saw what at first looked like a stick protruding from the earth. It got longer. He lost it in the night scope momentarily as the Durango hit gravelly rock, then picked it up again in the scope. The stick was the cannon of the M3, the cavalry Bradley, breaking out of the depression.

Fraser, off to Levin's right, saw it too, the Bradley now about two hundred yards away as the 25mm sticklike cannon began to fire.

"Benet!" Levin shouted over the noise of his vehicle scraping sagebrush and bouncing over the gravel, Levin braking so hard that the silver moon turned yellow then disappeared momentarily in the thick cloud of dust that swept forward over the Durango.

Benet was out, followed by the militiaman with an M-16, who would cover him if necessary.

With radio silence no longer an issue, Fraser notified Purdy, via satellite-bounced signal, that his eight-man, two-vehicle recon squad was attacking. He was confident that Purdy, being the patron saint and proselytizer of initiative in the field, wouldn't try to overrule him. Besides, Fraser didn't see any other realistic response to the Bradleys' breaching the escarpment. Had he run, the Bradleys would have seen the dust trails the moment they breached the wall and spotted the two militia vehicles. This way, attacking the Bradleys head-on, Fraser knew he was doing the most unorthodox, the most unexpected, thing, and sure enough the Bradleys, upon seeing the flash of Levin's AT launch, had run for cover.

The cavalry, or M3, Bradley, its five-man crew having escaped the AT round, and with no way of knowing how many more tank killers the militia had, now burst out of the depression as if catapulted. Its commander obviously keen to hit maximum tactical speed, the M3 raced through the moonlit desert in an evasive quarterback's weaving pattern, to deny any would-be missile a straight-line trajectory.

Benet and his auxiliary rifleman, hidden beneath a clump of purple sage and tumbleweed, could see their two militia

vehicles now ahead of them. Levin's, having made the
U-turn, was to his left, Fraser's on his right. The M3 was
now weaving far right, farther out on Levin's flank, craftily
electing not to get caught between the two militia vehicles.
The Bradley's 500-horsepower diesel was pushing it to forty
miles per hour, its 25mm cannon spitting out armor-piercing
discarding sabot rounds at over 4,400 feet per second. Almost immediately, Levin's four-by-four was hit. It rolled and
ended upright, slamming hard against a boulder and erupting in flame. Levin's body was literally disintegrating as it
took a full burst of the Bradley's armor-piercing rounds. The
navigator raced out of the wreck afire, screaming, the flares
devouring him even as he flung his burning arms up in a
V of surrender. The man stumbled, righted himself, then
stumbled again, falling face first into a bush, setting it aflame.

Its fierce crackling was not heard by Benet. He turned
toward his auxiliary, who, seeing what had happened to Levin,
was in an absolute panic. Throwing down his M-16, he held
up his hands, yelling, imploring the oncoming Bradley,
"Don't shoot! Don't shoot! No, no, we surrender! We—"

There was a loud pop and the high desert turned a shimmering white. A flare.

"Christ!" Now Benet saw that Fraser's vehicle had vanished
from view. Had it been hit or was it playing the Bradley's earlier game, finding its own hideaway? And where was the
second Bradley?

The M3 coming directly toward Benet's auxiliary, carrying five more TOW missiles than the gunport-firing infantry
version, now stopped twenty yards from the unarmed
militiaman. To Benet, the disembodied voice booming from
the Bradley sounded like the voice of God: "Stay where you
are! Don't move." The Bradley's main gun and coaxial 7.62
machine gun were pointing directly at the militiaman who
stood with upraised arms.

Benet, still lying low behind the sagebrush, spotted several figures to his right wearing the wide Gulf War–style
Kevlar helmets that looked like overgrown Nazi helmets. So
where the hell was Fraser hiding? Benet wondered, guess-

ing, correctly, that these eight he could see must be from the
second Bradley, its commander having elected to discharge
his riflemen from the belly of the beast rather than risk total
annihilation from an AT round.

Whatever the case, the point for Benet was the fact that
the cavalry M3 was now still twenty yards away, its gun
trained on his panic-stricken militia comrade, who, like the
Bradley, was stock-still, his hands still up, as he averted his
eyes from the stuttering glare of the descending magne-
sium flare. Benet, bending on one knee, moving his .45 holster out of the way and leaning forward to absorb the shock,
fired his AT at what was virtually point-blank range. The
fiery rocket slammed into the Bradley's left-side track, the
sound of the tread unraveling from its guide train like that of
a ship dropping anchor, the M3 obscured, despite the flare
light, by a pall of dust and debris.

Quickly, Benet scurried off to his right, his auxiliary militiaman knocked over by the shock wave, the M3 Bradley's
coaxial machine gun opening up in concert with the turret's
25mm cannon. But Benet knew they were firing in panic,
firing blind, besides which he was well off to their left now,
amid thick, dry brush—it hadn't rained after all—and so
close to them that even if the turret had swung in his direction, the angle of depression required by the Bradley's gun
would have been too great for them to hit him. The Bradley
suddenly lurched forward a foot or two, then stopped, the
unraveled track bunching up in a tangle, jamming in hard
between the track's guide train and the Bradley's hull. All
right! Benet exulted. It hadn't been the greatest shot, but
buoyed by the M3's inability to move, he knew that the
Bradley was effectively a dead duck.

He saw white smoke seeping out of the hatch, and then
the hatch was flung open. A helmeted gunner appeared,
chemically pungent smoke roiling about him. He was shot
dead by Benet's auxiliary man, who had suddenly decided
he should fight after all. There was a staccato of M-16 fire
from the eight helmeted federals in the penumbra of the dying flare light. The auxiliary man was down, but whether

he'd been hit, Benet couldn't tell. Fighting the impulse to stick his head up and have a look around, he stayed down, his right hand quickly feeling down his right leg for his .45.

Benet heard the *thoomp!* sound of an explosion in a confined space. In the desert? It had to be either Fraser's four-man squad in the four-by-four or the remaining Bradley that had "bought it," as Purdy, borrowing a Limey expression, would have said. Or maybe it had been a federal, or Fraser tossing a grenade into a depression.

But it wasn't Fraser or the other three men in his Durango, which they had sensibly ditched immediately after seeing Levin's vehicle taking a direct hit from the M3 Bradley. The four militiamen, Fraser with his M-16 on point, were now crouching low in a spill of brush on the eroding banks of a dry wash, one of the sun-baked conduits that fed Ship Rock Wash during infrequent rainstorms. Before leaving the four-by-four, however, Fraser and his squad had rigged two claymore mines on trip wires around it.

It was only six minutes later that Fraser's squad lucked out and spotted the second, M2 infantry, Bradley. Fraser's infrared scope had picked up a smear of heat against the background, the result of the temperature differential between the tracks made by the Bradley and the surrounding desert. With his infrared scope, aided by moonlight, he could see the Bradley twenty yards ahead of them, its back ramp down, empty of infantry. Softly, he went to ground, the three militiamen behind him following, Fraser ambivalent about the bright moonlight. On one hand it had no doubt helped him spot the Bradley earlier than he otherwise would have, but it also meant that his squad would have to move with the utmost caution, careful not to present the slightest silhouette in the moonlight.

Carefully, Fraser unclipped a grenade from his belt and waited. He was tempted to seize the moment, crawl ahead on his own, and simply toss it into the Bradley's empty belly, but hearing a metallic noise, he froze. It was followed by a barely audible whine. The ramp was going up. Possibilities crowded in on him. Had the Bradley's infantry been deployed only minutes ago, in which case his squad might be in the middle of them, or had one of the Bradley's three crewmen—the commander, gunner, or driver—simply decided to close it up for safety? If so, had the Bradley's infrared thermal imaging units picked them up during a four-power magnification sweep? But then how would the commander or gunner be sure that the thermal image was militia or federals? The difference between helmet size and shape would be the only giveaway, if anyone was fool or brave enough to stick his head up. Yet Fraser knew that the longer he and his squad waited, the greater the chance that the federal infantry squad would return to the Bradley and maybe stumble across them. The ramp door was closed, Fraser cursing himself now for not having taken the chance.

Then, through the scope, he saw an arc of hot liquid coming from the Bradley. Someone, one of the Bradley's three crewmen, was taking a leak. Even if the hatch was closed, the chances were ninety-nine out of a hundred that it wasn't locked, allowing the man to get back in without having to rap noisily against the hatch. Fraser knew he didn't have much time. Whispering to the militia squad to stay put, he got up and moved quickly toward the Bradley on the opposite side from the man peeing, the Bradley now between them. With five yards to go he could see the hatch was open. All his senses alert, he could smell sweat, urine, and a trace of sage. He came at the turret from its left rear quarter, its guns pointed away from him. Jumping up onto the Bradley's left-hand track, he dropped in the grenade, heard a "What the hell?" and slammed the hatch shut, holding it down. The man relieving himself was now visible to Fraser on the other side and whirled about. Fraser fired the M-16 with his right hand, its stock held tight under his right shoulder. One of the three-round bursts struck the hapless man, his fly undone. It punched him back into a mess of tumbleweed, blood jetting darkly from a gaping abdominal wound as the moon was temporarily hidden by cloud.

By the time Fraser was off the Bradley, its twelve hundred

rounds of 25mm were cooking off, and he knew the whole thing would blow.

The grenade's *thoomp!* saved Benet's life, for upon hearing the muffled explosion, the Bradley's infantrymen, only forty feet away, started back toward their vehicle.

Fraser, meanwhile, knew they would be coming back, but in what direction? He signaled his men to hightail it back, not to the depression where their Durango was parked, but to a point fifty yards beyond. There, sweating profusely despite the cold desert night, they set up a four-man square to cover a 360-degree field of fire. Now that three vehicles— both federal Bradleys and Levin's four-by-four—were finished, gutted, Fraser hoped that the federals would blunder into the two claymores' trip wires.

He had learned a valuable lesson: that while the federals possessed the formidable Bradley fighting vehicles, they had not used them well; all other things being equal, the Bradleys should have won. Then Fraser realized he was getting too far ahead of himself. There were still federal National Guardsmen out there. The question now was whether their squad leader had more savvy than their Bradley crews. Were there any veterans among them, like himself, or were they unblooded weekenders, little more than boys who, when they joined the Guard, never guessed that they would see action?

Fraser, again taking the point, and his three proceeded toward their hidden Durango in the depression a quarter mile off, not far from where Levin and his navigator had let off Benet and his auxiliary. Fraser told his three that it was possible that the federal infantry were spread out between them and Benet, and to be careful not to fire unless they'd ID'd the target as federals.

Benet still hadn't moved from his position near a tangle of brush. He hadn't even moved the expended AT-4 tube by his side, for fear of making a noise that the federals, moving slowly and purposefully through his and the auxiliary man's area, might hear. The stratus cloud passed the moon, and abruptly the desert shapes of cacti and sage nearby stood out in stark relief. Fifteen feet to his right he could see a federal helmet moving cautiously in his direction. Even then, with the enemy almost upon him, Benet wasn't sure he'd use his knife. It was one thing to have fired an antitank missile at point-blank range—he'd done that in the Gulf War—but it was an entirely different matter to plunge cold steel into a fellow human being. The man was coming straight in his direction, and in that moment Benet recalled an old movie he'd seen as a boy, *The Bridge on the River Kwai*, in which a young Canadian, coming face-to-face with a Japanese soldier, had hesitated, rescued only by his officer, who'd stabbed the Japanese. But the federal, bound to be as nervous as he, was almost upon Benet.

Suddenly, there was an M-16 burst from Benet's auxiliary man nearby. The federal was flung back, his rifle clattering on stony ground. In return there was a fusillade of small arms fire, mostly M-16s, and a lot of yelling, as the auxiliary man dropped another federal before he was caught in the apex of a V-shaped field of fire from the four remaining federals, two on either flank.

Then the federal squad leader and Benet heard the sound of an engine coming to life, Fraser's four-by-four, about fifty yards off to Benet's right. The four remaining federals immediately ran toward it, determined to wreak vengeance on the militia by destroying the only means of escape. This was the biggest federal blunder so far in the Shiprock engagement. In their speed, in the anxiety of battle, the four federals assumed that the militiamen, keen to exit the area, were already on board the Durango. Charging down the sides of the depression they fired at the vehicle, and tripped the two claymores on either side. The C4-packed claymores blew, the air filled with the buzz of each mine's fan-shaped saturation charge of over seven hundred ball bearings, which flayed anything within a hundred yards.

When Ray Fraser and his three militiamen came out of their rocky hideaway, three of the four federals lay dead; a fourth, a youth of about twenty with a shock of red hair that took on the color of blood in the moon's reemerging light, begged the militia to finish him, his left leg all but torn off, hanging by a ligament, as he lay writhing and groaning in pain. Morton, Fraser's medic, gave the youth a shot of morphine, but within a minute he too was dead. Soon Benet and his auxiliary man, the latter wounded in the left leg in the federal fusillade of fire and now using his M-16 as a walking stick, came down into the depression.

Now Fraser was faced with the most difficult decision of the night. He'd had no choice but to fight the federals, but it meant he'd failed in his primary mission to assess the enemy column's strength and disposition.

"Feds in those Bradleys," he told his squad, Benet, and the auxiliary man, "no doubt radioed Eliot before they bought it. So four of you had better head back to Purdy. Leave me with the radio, rations for forty-eight hours, and one of you for company, with most of our water canteens."

"What are you gonna do?" Benet challenged. "Walk south and take on Eliot and his outfit all by yourself?"

"No," Fraser said, "but I can check it out, radio their positions and strength back to Purdy."

"Don't be a goddamned hero," Benet told him. "Soon as you make that call, their sigint boys'll have you triangulated. Then what are you gonna do—run?"

"Let me worry about that."

"I will," Benet said with a tone of gruff admiration. "C'mon, who's gonna stay with Fraser?" There was an awkward, embarrassed silence among the other four men; all that could be heard was the faint rustle of wind through the brush, and some tumbleweed that skittered past them like ghosts in the moonlight.

"How 'bout you, Johno?" Fraser asked John Reid, one of the riflemen, a onetime farmer whose father had lost his spread because the Bureau of Land Management had decreed that it belonged to the Navajos, as sacred ground. Reid was fit, in his early twenties, and he knew the land. Still, that didn't mean he enjoyed being slow-fried in the desert.

"I guess so," he told Fraser.

"Hell," Fraser said. "No need to be so enthusiastic."

"Sure." Reid grinned. "I'd love to stay. Get a tan."

"There you go," Fraser said, punching him playfully on the shoulder. "Benet, you four head back to Colonel Purdy. Tell him what happened here, namely that Eliot's National Guard boys panicked—no coordination between the Bradleys and their infantry—but tell him we don't know yet what Eliot's got. If he's bringing up tanks, it could be a different ball game altogether."

One of the militiamen was throwing up and worrying about burying the dead.

"Levin and his navigator only," Fraser said tersely. He didn't approve of any sympathy for the enemy. "Have to leave the federals—not enough time. Eliot's column could be here by daybreak, and I want you guys gone." Then he said something that shocked the other five—except Benet. "We screwed up."

Reid looked askance. "Shit, we killed ten of 'em, counting the guys in the Bradley."

"Can't always tell by the body count, Reid," Fraser answered. "We didn't get past them to Eliot's main force."

"Why don't we all stay?" Benet asked unexpectedly. "Except Mosly here. He'll have to get his leg seen to."

"No," Fraser said, "we've got to get the four-by-four out of here—and we won't break radio silence until absolutely necessary. You take the vehicle, tell Purdy what happened."

The man who had been sick was dry-retching, and no one wanted to sit near him in the Durango. Most of the vehicle's glass was spiderweb white, shot through, and there was a bite taken out of the steering wheel, but the engine responded okay, and as Benet backed it out, he took no care not to run over the dead federal soldiers.

"For Christ's sake, Benet!" Mosly protested.

"Hey!" Benet responded sharply, looking back over his shoulder as the vehicle bucked over one of the bodies. "This isn't some fucking game, puss nuts. It's for keeps. And kick out that fucking glass. I can't see a goddamn thing."

CHAPTER THIRTY

Through the falling snow, a half mile down from Camp Fairchild's east gate, on the two-lane road that ran parallel to Fairchild Air Force Base a quarter mile to the north, the eight escapees were in the throes of that peculiar combination of elation and terror that grips a prisoner who manages to break out. On one hand, they were gaining confidence with every stride, having passed the camp's clump of isolation cells several hundred yards back; the air heavy with snow, clean-smelling and bitterly cold, the snow softening the harsher utilitarian lines of the air base's hangars. On the other hand, there was the ever-present knowledge that if they could so clearly make out the hangars and the perimeter of the base, then perhaps base personnel could see them. Then again, perhaps the glare of the camp's arc lights and the air base's hangar lights bouncing off the falling snow would blind any base personnel, preventing them from seeing beyond the perimeter.

The truck carrying the portable toilet had passed them earlier, the red dots of its taillights now lost in the blizzard. Inside, stiff with the cold and poor blood circulation, Orr pushed out on the two-door standard thirty-by-thirty-inch commode from which the bucket of excrement was periodically extracted. When his two militiamen pals—the two "parrots" from his hut, 5A—took the bucket out during the commotion surrounding the audacious marching away of the six fellow militia "prisoners" by the two militia "guards," Orr had adroitly elbowed himself in and, using the strip of duct tape he'd swiped from under the hut, pulled the commode's door closed from inside the dark space that reeked of spilled excrement and urine.

"Where'd you get that tape?" Eleen had asked him.

"One of our parrots swiped it from one of the drainage pipes in hut four."

"Not very neighborly," Eleen said, allowing himself a faint smile.

"No—ah, they won't miss it."

"Till the next rainstorm."

"Not supposed to rain much up here anyway."

"Tell that to El Niño."

After one of his parrot buddies had helped him to quickly take out the can of excrement, the parrot began to wipe out the inside of the commode, the snow falling so thickly by then that they were hidden from even the closest guard tower. "No," Orr told him, "you clean it up, it won't smell natural like. If a goon opens the door to have a look around, I want him smelling shit." And so it was that after the truck, its ride cushioned by the snow, made its way past the eight militia prisoners, Orr crawled out the back of the portable john from its commode recess. He gulped in the cold, clean air and, with the snow-swirling wind on his face, felt a rush of excitement at having made it, or at least having made it out of the camp.

Though it was hours yet before sunup, the heat was so oppressive that Dana Teer and Beverly Malkin were perspiring heavily, the doctor's nipples sticking to her white cotton blouse, mesmerizing the militia guard, Pearson. As Hearn's motorcade proceeded north on Arizona's 93 through the Mojave Indian Reservation and on to Kingman, Pearson kept finding excuses to switch on the ambulance's interior light. "We're on the 93 now," he informed them, as if neither of them had noticed any of the bullet-riddled highway signs.

The 93, as every schoolchild in this sparsely populated area of Arizona knew, was the way to Las Vegas. The only thing between was the Hoover Dam, which supplied the heavily populated cities of southern California with electric power and irrigation. Behind the dam lay the huge Lake Mead Recreation Area, which straddled the Nevada-Arizona border.

Montoya looked over at Hearn. "I thought all this was about getting Vance and company out?"

"It's about springing *everyone*," Hearn said. "Getting *all* our boys out."

"Whoa!" the normally cool Montoya said. "That's a tall order."

"Hoover's a tall dam," Hearn riposted, grinning now despite his fatigue, the unshaven face emphasizing his tiredness, hiding his youth in the stubble beard of an older man, the smell of sour sweat heavy about him. "What the fuck d'you think we were doing, springing Vance and McBride? So they could take a holiday? We're like the IRA, buddy boy. We *never* give up. Right?" He swerved to miss fallen rock. "Vance has been working on it for a long time—before he was captured. It was gonna happen on the California-Nevada side. That was before we ran into those fucking snipers. So we'll do it from this side. No big deal. And if that old fart Freeman thinks he frightened off Vance, he's got another think coming."

"So how's it going to work?" Montoya asked in unabashed awe at the monumental audacity of what he believed was a plan to deny power to so many at the flick of a switch.

"Don't know exactly," Hearn said, turning sharply to Montoya. "Aren't you listening? I told you it's Vance's baby, and he doesn't say squat unless he has to. It's strictly on the need-to-know." Montoya could tell that Hearn, as well as being exhausted, was embarrassed not to know the plan in full.

"So," Montoya said, as tired and grumpy as Hearn. "You don't really know what's going on?"

"Hey, Jack. Shut the fuck up! I'll tell you what you need

to know when the time's right. I can tell you one thing—it wasn't my idea to bring *you* aboard. Vance said you'd been in place long enough—that it was time." Hearn was so angry, he missed his own pun on Montoya's first name. "Said it was time to activate you. He didn't say squat about you doing anything else."

"Calm down," Montoya said. "I understand. Can't tell every Tom, Dick, and Harry what you're going to do. I understand that."

"I'm tired," Hearn said.

"We're all tired. But can I at least ask what Vance's general plan is? Bottom line? Let our people go or we turn off the tap to California? Is that it?"

In eastern Washington the snow was deep and uneven, blown into high drifts against barns and fences. The wind made the temperature feel like minus twenty as the flatbed transporting the roped-down outhouse continued along at no more than twenty miles an hour. The road's high cane-pole markers on the shoulder were barely visible, the asphalt already buried, the snow muffling the sound of the truck's engine and the incessant whining of its wipers.

Orr heard a bang outside but was unsure, because of the truck's noise, whether it was a shot or a blowout. A second later he heard a bump, then a long, tearing sound like tarpaper being ripped—the sound of an M-60 machine gun—followed by screams.

Unable to see out, Orr couldn't know whether the federal shooters had caught up with all eight of the men from 4B or whether the eight had split up. How many had been hit? He tried to put it out of his mind—he could do nothing to help, and had to focus all his attention on his own escape. Though it was the coldest he'd been in years, cramped in the recess normally occupied by the ordure bucket, Orr was glad it was snowing so hard. The constant white blur beyond the windshield wipers was bound to rivet the driver's attention while he forced the latch on the recess from which the "shit bucket" was daily extracted. Only in this case they wouldn't find any bucket, since it had been taken out by the two parrots to allow him crawl space during the ruckus that covered the march out of the eight escapees from 4B.

The bucket had been put under one of the huts in a snowdrift already in the process of forming. At least there'd be no smell while it was below freezing. Still, Orr realized that sooner or later it would be discovered that a bucket, really more the size of a twenty-two-gallon drum, was missing. But he'd told Captain Eleen he might luck out if the federals didn't connect its disappearance with an escape. After all, when they found nine men missing, they would probably account for all of them by assuming they'd been in the group of POWs marched through the gate.

It was later claimed by Commandant Moorehead on KOMO TV and on a feed into CNN headquarters in Atlanta that the militia prisoners who had escaped—all eight of them—had failed to stop when discovered "by myself and several of my guards," and that two had been "armed with stolen M-16s." The rumor spread by prisoners, he explained to Atlanta anchor Lynne Russell three thousand miles away, that the two M-16s weren't real but "made of wood" was false.

Yes, he said confidently, all the escapees were dead. "These were hard-core militia. They were given the opportunity to be taken alive, but kept running, and I simply couldn't take the risk of them getting out into the countryside and terrorizing the rural population."

"Isn't it odd," Russell asked, "that none of them was wounded, that they were all killed?"

Moorehead nodded, barely able to contain his condescension. "Of course—not all were killed outright. Three men died of their wounds soon after. Unfortunately. The M-16 is a rather unforgiving weapon."

In the camp it was clear what happened. Moorehead had murdered all of them on the spot, telling his guards that it had been "payback time" for what happened to Eliot's federals at Ship Rock. This gave rise to an unofficial militia policy, one that Eleen abhorred but that spread as fast as the blizzard's chill—that if that was the way it was going to be, then so be it. If the federals didn't take prisoners, then dammit, neither would the militia. Tit for tat.

Alan Orr, on the flatbed truck hauling the portable john, was waiting until the vehicle had to slow on a steep hill so he could put the second part of his plan into operation. It was difficult for him to tell just how far the truck was from the camp. At least he knew from the matchbox compass he'd fashioned from a split razor blade that they were heading west.

His anxious frame of mind heightened by the banshee howling of the wind, Orr couldn't decide when to jump off the truck. He had a packet of meager rations with him—a Mars bar traded from one of the guys for cigarettes, some bread now hard as a rock but not mildewed due to the fact it was frozen, and a packet of six fruit strips, also frozen, and brittle in his pocket. His dilemma was that if he jumped off too far from any civilization, he couldn't hope for assistance, the nearest safe house over fifty miles from the camp. But if he stayed with the truck until it reached its depot, he'd most likely be recaptured. And unfortunately, the escape map he'd been given wasn't much help, having only main roads and towns listed, its scale not allowing for much else. He prayed for good fortune, reminded himself of an article of faith among the militia—he who hesitates is lost—and with that in mind, he jumped into soft, deep snow, part of him immediately regretting that he hadn't stayed with the truck, whose ice-covered taillights were quickly swallowed in the snowfall. Then, a few minutes later, in what he attributed to a stroke of luck, divine intervention, or both, he saw a light, then another, winking in the distance, until he realized with the impact of a blow to his stomach that it was the headlights of the truck, which had made a sharp turn south.

In the pale light of dawn, the Camp Fairchild lieutenant who'd caught up with the escaping prisoners from 4B had the dead bodies laid out on the parade square, the khaki ground sheets that covered them almost hidden by the snow by the time six A.M. roll call was made.

"Nine missing, sir," the lieutenant reported to Commander Moorehead.

"Then where are the other two bodies?" Moorehead asked sharply.

"Must have broken away from the main party earlier this morning in the dark," the lieutenant answered.

"Did you look for them?" The commandant's tone was unforgiving.

"Yes, sir, but no luck."

"Huh—snow's probably covered their tracks. Besides, I suppose you didn't search by grid, so if we did find any trace of footprints, they could be yours or your men's."

"Uh, I guess so, sir."

"Do another count," Moorehead ordered. "By name this time."

"Yes, sir."

CHAPTER THIRTY-ONE

Wes Knox was running late, having doubled back on Fifth Avenue outside the Guggenheim to make sure no one was following him. Even so, he was on edge as he walked up the broad stairs of the Metropolitan, pausing halfway up to retie his shoelaces and glance about casually. When he gave the girl a twenty for his admission, he paid scant attention to her giving him his change, after which he passed by one of the gray-uniformed attendants and again assumed a casual air, as if visiting the museum was something he did often, not needing to consult the floor plan pamphlet to find his way up to the second-floor exhibit of European paintings.

It was crowded, groups of people clustered about various guides, their listeners straining, craning their heads to hear every word, some, mostly elderly, giving up any attempt to hear anything over the incessant hum of tourists. Some people were frowning in concentration as they listened intently through the earphones of their do-it-yourself recorded tours.

The drill was always the same. A particular painting, in this case, van Gogh's *Cypresses*, would serve as the point of reference for the meet. If either he or Fuchida were at all suspicious, having sensed they were being followed or that one of the attendants was paying undue attention to them, they would leave after a minute or two; otherwise they would make their separate, unhurried way to the American wing, to the meet's prearranged designated painting.

At first Knox couldn't see Fuchida, obscured as he was by a number of nuns clustered about the *Cypresses*, a painting that Knox normally admired, but today the flamelike contortions of the two deep green trees and the fiery aspect of the sky disturbed him. He wasn't sure whether it was because van Gogh painted it during his stay at the asylum at Saint-Rémy, or if it was the weather—a gray metallic sky over New York, the tallest skyscrapers lost to a swirling onslaught of stratus coming in from the Atlantic; or perhaps, Knox realized as he waited for the nuns to pass on to the next room, it was nothing more than unadulterated fear. He recalled that when he'd met Fuchida for the first time, he hadn't been nearly so nervous. But that was then, and now, with this possibly being his last meeting with the Japanese, the fear of something going wrong gripped his gut. Look man, he told himself, you have to calm down, be cool. He'd taken a milligram pill of sublingual Ativan, but it hadn't done much to steady him, which told him just how keyed up he was.

The last of the nuns had gone and he stood alone, looking

at the *Cypresses* for what seemed a long time, but was only seconds. Fuchida, leaning forward, hands clasped behind his raincoat, read the painting's caption, or pretended to, then stepped back to better study the van Gogh. *What the fuck is he doing?* Then, still looking at the painting, he seemed to sigh before moving off, taking in a few more Impressionists. Knox made up his mind. If the Jap didn't head for the American wing in the next minute, he decided, then he'd go home. But Knox knew he was kidding himself. He'd come too far and waited too long for the goods.

Then, as if he'd read Knox's thoughts, Fuchida, hands still behind his back like a professor, started for the American wing.

Though from a tactical point of view Hearn didn't want to stop, he told Montoya that to keep moving without a rest wasn't smart. Montoya nodded in agreement. "You get too tired, you start making mistakes. Heat gets to you."

"Yeah," Hearn replied tiredly, sardonically. "But it's a dry heat."

Montoya smiled. "Right." It was an old Arizona joke, and inconsequential so far as Hearn's decision to stop the motorcade for a half hour rest, but the exchange between them signaled an ease that allowed for something like camaraderie between them. As the motorcade pulled off onto the shoulder, a red dust cloud sweeping over them, the temperature approaching 103, a sudden quiet enveloped them in the vastness of the Southwest, where a five-hundred-mile travel day wasn't considered unusual, and where the slam of a door a half hour later sounded like a gunshot.

Hearn sat up, the comic, startled expression on his face all the funnier because of the way his hair stuck out at improbable angles. "What the—"

"Changing the guard," Montoya said, not moving from his slumped position, his cowboy hat pulled low over his eyes.

"Noisy bastard," Hearn commented, sliding back into the seat. "Christ, it's hot! Like a—think I'll crawl under the car." He looked across at Montoya. "Hear me?"

"Uh-huh," Montoya replied wearily, face still covered by the Stetson.

"Yeah, well," Hearn said as he grabbed the steering wheel to pull himself up. "Don't drive off without me."

"I won't."

Hearn, despite his fatigue, smiled to himself. It seemed like Montoya was an all-right guy. Still, he reminded himself, appearances were so often deceptive. After having heard the federals describe Hearn in the media, even some of the militia recruits had confessed to imagining a ghoulish face with sharp, devilish features, when in fact he knew that, save for an intensity in his eyes, he had a fairly nondescript look—one that, like the pictures of the Führer in his World War I days, melted into a crowd.

Knox was the first to arrive in the American wing. He was standing in front of Martin Head's *The Coming Storm*, a starkly brooding painting; a great, dark, threatening cloud bank over ink-black water, and a lone sailboat, watched by a lone man sitting with his little dog on a sandy, grass-tufted shore. The sail of the boat was a luminous white fin above the black water, the whole effect one of imminent threat. Lost in it for a moment, Knox suddenly sensed someone behind him. He turned sharply, despite what he believed was his practiced casual air.

"Do you like it?" It was Fuchida.

"Sort of," said Knox, who, for some reason he didn't understand, didn't want to answer with an unequivocal yes, as if that would somehow make him immediately vulnerable.

"It is apt," Fuchida said. "Don't you agree?"

"Has the stuff arrived?"

Fuchida didn't answer straightaway, which meant, Knox thought, that it hadn't.

Fuchida, hands still behind his back, looking at the picture, said, "There was some difficulty."

"Jesus!" Knox said.

"No, no," Fuchida responded, eyes still on the painting, trying to figure out whether the man sitting near the dog was black or white. "You misunderstand," he told Knox. "It's because of the weather. El Niño. No security breach. None at all."

"What am I going to tell the brothers?"

"The truth," Fuchida suggested. "That they must have patience."

"How much patience?"

"Oh, a day or two."

"They're all keyed up."

Fuchida, against character, showed surprise. "But we understood you alone would do it." It was tantamount to a rebuke.

"I will," Knox said. "But the boys are impatient."

"Ah, the American disease," Fuchida said.

"Listen, we've been planning this for a long time."

Fuchida bristled. "So have we."

"Well, then—"

"It will be here in a few days—at most." Fuchida cooled down before he spoke again. "But no more meets will be necessary. I've been instructed because of this delay to deliver some of the material myself. I will book into the Hilton. On the Avenue of the Americas."

"On Sixth," Knox said. He still sounded testy. Only tourists and foreigners called it "Avenue of the Americas."

"Yes," Fuchida agreed. "It is on Sixth Avenue."

"I know."

"I will register in the morning—checkout time. A lot of people will be around. I'll use the name Suzuki. It is a common name in Japan. I will call you and tell you the room number in dollars and cents. I will leave a message and the card key to my room, the envelope for pickup by a Mr. Heade. Leave the key in the room above the bar."

"All right."

"Good hunting."

"Thanks," Knox said. It was said sincerely, now that Knox had cooled down. "The brothers are grateful."

It was appreciated by Fuchida, who smiled for the first time that day.

CHAPTER THIRTY-TWO

It had been a tense rest for Hearn's motorcade, half of them napping, or at least trying to, the other half unhappily on guard, the ear-ringing silence of the cacti-strewn desert broken now and then by the guttural, rasping snoring of those asleep. Before Hearn grabbed some rest, he'd asked Montoya to stand guard by their ambulance. But Toro, Hearn's unofficial bodyguard, who looked like a professional wrestler, and several other militiamen were milling around the vehicle. Montoya knew they were probably still suspicious of him, and the stress of their raid on the hospital and the subsequent chase—until Toro killed the security guard to keep the police cars and other federals back—was etched on their faces.

"Look," he told them, surprising several of the men, most of whom had so far not heard him speak. "What you guys have to remember is I didn't just decide to fight the federals all of a sudden. I'd done that a long time ago. Made the commitment, I mean. You don't believe me, ask Vance."

"Yeah," one of them said. "I think I will."

"He's nodded off again," another militiaman said, referring to Vance.

Two of the men were leaning on the vehicle; the other one, stomping a centipede to death, added, "He's not as good as we thought. He's still sick."

"He'll be all right in a few days," another said. "Give 'im time."

"We haven't got time," came a sleepy voice from the shade beneath the ambulance. It was Hearn. "And leave Montoya alone. He's proved his worth. So drop it." Hearn was yawning, looking down at his watch. It wasn't yet eight o'clock, but the dawn had suffused the sky in a stunning vermilion over the Black Mountains, and you could see for miles. Montoya took Hearn's outstretched hand and hauled him up. He smelled of oil and dust. "I'll see the old boy now," Hearn said, stretching. He walked back to the third ambulance, which, apart from the remaining security man in the last ambulance, was the hostage vehicle. Inside, Vance was not well, as the militiaman had indicated, and Dana Teer didn't mince her words when she told Hearn that in her professional opinion Vance shouldn't be moved anymore. "Not in this heat." It was already over 100 degrees Fahrenheit, the mercury column still rising.

Hearn took no notice of her advice. It was what he would have expected her to say, to try to slow things down.

Vance spoke with difficulty, his tongue bone dry until Beverly Malkin dabbed his lips with water from the squeeze bottle and then cradled his head as he let her pour more water into his mouth. "Thank you," he said simply, his voice croaking. His head turned slowly toward Hearn. "How's McBride?"

"He's fine," Hearn said. "Still a bit groggy but—"

"Don't let me delay you," Vance said quietly, his voice even raspier than before. "You have to be there before they close down for the day."

"I know," Hearn said, realizing the old man didn't mean that the dam closed down, but rather, when the tourist guides finished their day. "We'll be there in plenty of time."

"And the trucks?" Vance pressed weakly. "It's important."

"They'll be on time," Hearn assured him.

"Had to—" Vance signaled Malkin for more water, and took some, fumbling with the plastic bottle. "Had to ask you to do it cold after that ALERT business." He meant the sudden change in the militia's plans after the brouhaha in California, when Hearn's motorcade had turned around on hearing gunfire up ahead between the ALERTs and the California militia's snipers.

"Didn't think I had an option," Hearn said, a mite defensively. "Your orders were to turn back if—"

"I know," Vance cut in croakily. "I'm not being critical. You did the right thing. Couldn't have gone on to L.A. under that threat." He paused. "How about McBride? He clear on everything?"

"He'll stay here with the ambulances when the truck arrives."

There was silence, broken when Pearson shifted his M-16 from one hand to the other. Then Vance spoke again: "You're sure he's up to it?"

"Yes," Hearn assured him. "He's well on the mend. Some bandaging, but Toro says he's been eating like a—horse." Hearn had almost used an expletive, but knew the old man wouldn't approve, not with women present. Vance's sense of propriety saw no contradiction in the fact that under his orders the two women were being held hostage, along with the remaining security guard. For militia business—against the enormous odds presented by the federals—hostages were as necessary as ammunition.

"Remember," Vance said, "don't go right down to the bottom of the dam. It's over six hundred feet thick down there and—"

"So we go for the top half," Hearn interrupted. "I remember." His tone was getting testy. Hell, didn't Vance think he'd gone over it enough in his head? Who pulled off the snatch of him and Lucky McBride from Holy Rosary?

Vance sensed Hearn's irritation, telling him by way of apology, "It's just that you won't get a second chance."

"I know that. We'll do it right, don't worry. McBride's going over the details, coding them for the final fax he'll send."

Dana Teer cut in. "You should have Mr. Vance lifted out by helicopter. Take him to Las Vegas."

"You shut up!" Hearn told her. "That's what *you* should do. *I'm* in charge."

"Then God help us!" she said tartly. Pearson fixated on her bosom, quickly rising and falling in her agitation.

"How's Mon—" Vance began, then swallowed hard and pulled the blanket up near his chin, his whole body shivering despite the heat.

"Montoya?" Hearn said. "He's doing fine." Hearn's face lit up in a self-satisfied smile. "He found a pair of women's undies during the last rest stop. Message scrawled on it by one of the ladies here."

Dana Teer felt rage and embarrassment simultaneously, her face turning as red as the Sedona Rocks at sunset. And she felt utter despair, weakness rushing through her. The bastard had found her message.

"Telling the federals what ambulance she and Beverly here were in," Hearn added.

"So now," Pearson cut in snidely, "you're back where you started."

"Shut up!" Hearn told him.

Vance, taking a big sip of water, beckoned Hearn closer. Hearn listened intently to Vance's whisper, lost to the others because of the air conditioners kicking in. Hearn nodded, brow furrowed, then straightened up and informed Pearson that from now on he would be guarding the security guard in the last ambulance. Somebody else would guard the two women.

Pearson flushed, humiliated that the women had won a victory over him. Vance had no doubt whispered orders to Hearn that he should be moved out.

Dana Teer had strained to hear everything Vance told Hearn. She too thought he'd said something about moving Pearson. But perhaps there had been something else too. She wanted to ask Malkin if she'd overheard what Vance had said, but Hearn waited until the replacement guard arrived before he left.

Through the ambulance's tinted rear windows, Teer could see Hearn walking back, not to the first ambulance, but to the rear. He spoke to Toro, who then disappeared inside the last ambulance for several minutes before reappearing and giving something to Hearn, which Hearn put in his pocket.

Approaching Ship Rock, militiaman John Reid from Purdy's column was not a happy man. His decision to volunteer to keep Ray Fraser company—in reality to cover him while Fraser stayed glued to the binoculars—had not been voluntary, but rather in response to a *suggestion*, which was tantamount to an order. The militia liked to think it was fundamentally a democratic organization, a view that, as in the Spanish Republican militias of 1936–39, sometimes drove its officers to distraction, what with platoons holding meetings before carrying out an order. Reid, on occasion, thought it would be nice to have the autonomy of the Spanish Republicans in their fight against the Nationalists, the kind of freedom to say, "Fuck, no, I'm not going up on a cluster of jumbled and needle-sharp rocks. What happens if Eliot's outfit spots us? Where are we gonna go?"

As he approached the base of Ship Rock, its north and south pinnacles rising like twin spires, the heat was beating down on them. What made it worse was that, courtesy of El Niño, enormous rain clouds were building in what was usually a pure azure sky. Though the humidity wasn't yet high, it was sufficient to override the normally dry heat of the Southwest, so that before he was fifty feet up, Reid's khaki shirt was stuck to him like Saran Wrap. Born and raised in the Southwest, Reid abhorred the sticky sensation as something that properly belonged to a Florida swamp, not a high desert. To add to his misery the jagged lava that formed this enormous "volcanic plug," as it was known in geological circles, was hot to the touch.

Starting at the base of the northwestern aspect, Reid and Fraser climbed slowly. Fraser had advised as much, and after two hours they were only a fifth of the way up. But already Reid could see that Fraser was right, the vista of the desert south of him, three hundred feet below, was breathtaking. After a short rest they began to ascend even higher, both men having gained their second wind, and for a while the climbing, precipitous at first, became easier as they approached an abutment high above the base of the northern pinnacle. The toughest part of the climb lay ahead, but Reid, in a complete reversal of his earlier apprehension about climbing the twin-peaked monolith, was suddenly arrested by a desire to go higher, the spectacular view of the green-dotted, sandy-colored plain exciting him. The rush of adrenaline he felt in such moments, when a misstep would have meant a toe-tingling drop into the abyss, was like nothing he'd ever experienced before. He was conscious of Ray Fraser looking at him, then asserting, "You like this."

"Yeah."

"Well, I don't, but I want to get higher, till we can pick up Eliot's dust trail."

"He's most likely on asphalt," Reid replied, taking sips from his canteen.

"Still be some dust," Fraser explained. "Can't move a lot of vehicles without stirring up eddies."

"Who's Eddie?"

"Yeah, very amusing. Save your wisecracks for the five hundred level. If you've got the spittle for it."

"I have the spittle," Reid said cockily.

"We'll see."

East of them there was a shimmering mirage, a reflection of the bottle-green irrigated fields of the Navajos, which lay eleven miles beyond Route 666, by the Chaco River, and twenty miles from Ship Rock itself. South and west of them stood the long thirty-foot-high radiating arms of lava, the southern arm or "wing," as the Navajos called the three-foot-thick lava, penetrated here and there by wind and erosion. It was through these holes that the two federal Bradleys had breached the wall.

Suddenly—perhaps it was the strong push of wind chilling his sweat-covered back—Reid felt the weird tingling-toe feeling of height fright. He steadied himself and, firmly grasping a spur of volcanic rock, took the next step, watching only the rock face immediately ahead, the pollution-free breeze of the high desert a tonic to his lungs.

"How high is this thing?" he asked, his neck craning heavenward as he gazed upon the two pinnacles that seemed to be moving against the cloud-dotted sky.

"Higher than the Empire State," Fraser said, a fact he usually reserved for tourists, especially New Yorkers.

"You're joking."

"Two hundred feet higher," Fraser said, gazing over the wild expanse of desert.

CHAPTER THIRTY-THREE

Lucky McBride was in good spirits, in defiance of the pain that radiated from a stiff neck down his arms. The duty nurse on his floor at Holy Rosary had given him Tylenol 3s but the effect had worn off hours ago. Unable to sleep, he sat instead at the small fold-down Formica table in the rear of the fourth ambulance, going over Vance's plan, adopting a "keep it simple, stupid" approach that he'd fax to finalize the plan. He knew that of the two vehicles involved—a motor home and a semitrailer—the semi, over ten feet in height, would have to park in either lot 11 or 13 on the Arizona side of the dam. Not superstitious himself, he decided to tell the driver to go for 11, not 13. And what was absolutely crucial, he told the eight militiamen, all of them out of their fatigues and in various civilian clothes, was to keep the cargoes separate until they were only a few miles north of the dam on the Nevada side, the trip from the outskirts of Las Vegas on Highway 93 a distance of about forty-two miles. Only then could he combine the two cargoes. He also made a note of the time of the last public tour of the dam—not the usually favored twenty-five-minute tourist walk-through, but the thirty-five-dollar, hour-long hard hat tour into the guts of the dam. The drill for the semi would be to reach lot 11 at least an hour before the last tour.

"Do you think we'll have to do it?" asked Case, one of the eight militiamen whom McBride had scheduled to help out in the semi before returning to the ambulances.

"Well, Mr. Vance doesn't think so. He figures that the mere threat of closing down L.A. will be enough to get them to release all our POWs."

An astute twenty-year-old who would be staying behind to guard the ambulance asked, "What do *you* think?"

McBride didn't answer right away. The temptation was to lie but he'd be running the mission by radio control and he'd never lied to his men before. The truth might not always set you free, but it at least told you what to expect.

"I don't think the federals'll go for it."

"So we'll have to blow it."

"Yes."

"Shit! I figured the threat would be enough."

"Hey," McBride said in a more upbeat tone, "what do I know? Maybe you're right, Case. But the federals have thousands of us penned up."

"Ah," Case protested, but more in fear than in conviction. "They'll release our boys. The public'd never stand for it. President'll have to release 'em."

"Maybe," McBride repeated.

"How much of a bang will we get?" asked another of the eight, hastily adding for the comfort of his colleagues, "*if* we have to blow."

McBride exhaled heavily. "Four to five times the Murrah Building."

"Jesus Christ!"

"Hey, look," McBride said. "It's like Iraq, right? If we go in, we go in hard. Otherwise, if we can't follow through, what'll our word be worth then?" There was a long silence, pregnant with the full realization of what following through meant. Case, the short, stocky driver, was lighting a cigarette.

"Don't do that after you mix it up," McBride said, attempting a joke, but Case looked insulted.

"You think I'm that stupid?"

"Hey, lighten up," a buddy advised.

"Yeah," Case said. "Well, I'll tell you what I'm worried about. Getting out after."

"No sweat," McBride assured him. "I'm the man on the RCB." He meant the remote control button. "You guys will already be hightailing it toward Purdy's outfit. Once you're with him, he has the firepower to—"

There was an urgent banging on the ambulance door. McBride looked up and saw Dana Teer with her new guard, who looked worried. As McBride opened the door he was struck by what could only be described as the doctor's cool beauty. She was unruffled but quick—to the point. "Mr. Vance is hemorrhaging. We have to get him out of here. Now!"

McBride didn't reply, but hopped down to the roadway's shoulder and strode back to the third ambulance. Hearn and Montoya, already there with Beverly Malkin, stepped aside to let Dana Teer near Vance. His face was pasty and clammy-looking. "He's going into cardiac arrest," she told them.

Vance tried to speak but his lips stuck together. Dana felt his carotid artery while Pearson, watching from outside, saw McBride bend over to hear Vance.

"We can't waste any time," Teer said sharply, anxiety now gripping her voice.

Hearn turned to her. "I thought you brought all the stuff you'd need?"

"I couldn't bring the whole hospital," she countered angrily.

"If he dies," Hearn told her, "you're to blame."

"Don't be absurd! It's you and your crazy militia that's to blame!"

"Knock it off!" It was Montoya, the others surprised, as if noticing him for the first time. "We're only about an hour from Boulder City." It was the township for the dam.

"We need a helo!" Teer said. McBride, Hearn, and Montoya ignored her. A helo was precisely what the militia did *not* want. It would be an opportunity for the federals to get vital intelligence about the motorcade. Besides which, the militia, from past experience and obsession with helos, abhorred the craft.

"Let's go, then," Hearn said.

Dana Teer was utterly exasperated but knew she'd have to settle for the hour's ride, using all her skill to keep Vance alive. "What did he say?" she asked McBride, indicating Vance.

McBride smiled enigmatically, said nothing, and returned to his vehicle. As Hearn and Montoya returned to the lead vehicles, Hearn slapped Montoya on the back. "Sorry I doubted you back there."

Montoya shrugged, wondering when was "back there"— the point at which Hearn had decided to finally trust him.

"I don't blame you," Montoya said. "I would have been the same." He paused. "You think we'll get to Boulder on time?"

Hearn made a face and shook his head.

"What did he tell McBride?" Montoya asked as Hearn turned on the ignition.

"Probably to go on with the plan. He's a tough old bastard."

McBride walked up to the driver's window. "The old man doesn't want to go near a hospital," he told them. "Way he figures it, that'd give them tremendous leverage over us, and he doesn't want that. He makes it or he doesn't."

"You're a hard bunch," Montoya said.

"*We're* a hard bunch," McBride said, pointing at Montoya, who was grateful for being included.

CHAPTER THIRTY-FOUR

"Does Freeman know where they are?" the President asked as he rose from his Oval Office chair. He turned left to his study, situated between the Oval Office and his personal dining room farther down the hall. The study had a more homey, reassuring ambience, with fresh flowers, usually roses, in a vase; his family photos and the famous golf club collection he'd inherited—a place where he could watch TV from the comfortable rocker. But moving from the Oval Office into the study didn't afford him any comfort this afternoon, because as long as the militia had civilian hostages—and the White House believed there were hostages being used as a shield by both Hearn's motorcade and in Purdy's column, which had come down from the Four Corners—federal hands were tied.

CNN's *Headline News* update reported that Hearn's motorcade was heading north on 93 about fifty miles south of Las Vegas, which the White House already knew. "Well," the President asked, "is anyone going to answer me, or am I just the gofer here? What's Freeman doing?"

Delorme lowered the sound on the TV, the President reluctant to admit that he had lost the ability to hear the high tones.

"We haven't heard anything new from him."

"Call him."

"Yes, sir."

* * *

General Freeman was sweating it out—literally. He sat back in the pop-up enclosed umbrella tent that served as a sauna. No hot rocks or steam were necessary, the temperature over 95 and the cumulus clouds moving in making the famous dry air of the Southwest as muggy as the air in the Gulf of California, hundreds of miles south of him. Norton was sweating in the sauna too, but he was not a happy camper. He was well aware of his duty—to accompany and act as a sounding board for his boss—but there were surely more convenient ways of poring over maps than in the tent whose sweaty odor offended his nose and which was known among the general's other sauna sufferers as "Freeman's Inferno." Freeman believed that sweating it out released all the body's accumulated "poisons," which on occasion had led some of his staffers to refer to him as General Jack Ripper, after the mad general in *Dr. Strangelove*, who was so preoccupied with the "Communist conspiracy" against his "vital bodily fluids."

Freeman knew he was called "Ripper" and didn't care. He believed it was an essential component of leadership not to be bothered by such nicknames and comparisons. At least the men, especially his ALERTs, knew he wasn't one of those bland generals who were no more than time servers and place seekers; that his character was strong, and even eccentric enough to devise the unexpected out of the ordinary. He had an extraordinary ability, as Norton well knew, of getting to the kernel of a problem by putting himself in the enemy's skin. Though they had never come face-to-face, Freeman felt he understood the militia's leader. Vance too was unconventional, his tactics, despite the man's urbanity, essentially those of "a thug," Freeman told Norton.

"The day I use civilians as a shield, Norton, you have my permission to shoot me. Matter of fact you won't have to. I'll do it myself."

"So, General, what do you think he's up to?"

"Well, whatever it is, it's in Nevada. Unless he intends to go farther north."

"Maybe he intends to do both," Norton suggested.

Freeman nodded appreciatively for the input. Norton was no lapdog like some other aides—White House aides—he'd seen running around the President. Norton wasn't afraid to speculate, no matter how wild it might seem at the moment. What helped in situations such as this, Freeman knew, was Norton's clear understanding that not only were the militias capable of highly unorthodox tactics, but among the far right militia elements there was a streak of pure, unadulterated madness, a willingness to embrace the extreme, to try anything.

"Maybe they're out to shoot up the MGM Grand," Norton suggested, only half joking, for among the nuts of the militia's far religious right were those who passionately believed that the gambling dens were sinful, that they were a direct and corrupt assault against the work ethic that had once made America great.

"Where were they last reported?" Freeman asked, leaning back in the lightweight aluminum deck chair so as not to let beads of sweat drop on the map.

"Last sitrep," Norton answered, "said they were still headed north on 93. 'Course, they might make a hard right—stay in Arizona."

"Grand Canyon?" Freeman ventured.

"Possibly."

"Well, it's certainly big enough to hide them."

"The problem with the situation reports," Norton reminded the general, "is that even with infrared scopes we can't get too close to the motorcade. Last time we did that they killed a security guard on the spot. Same goes for helos. That Nazi Hearn, remember, said that if he ever hears a chopper, an aircraft, he'll kill another hostage." He paused. "We can't get close enough to find out what they're doing." Norton, perspiring profusely, longed for the cold bucket shower to follow. "I can't take it much more in here," he confessed to Freeman, and, remembering an old *Seinfeld* episode where Kramer was in a sauna with Jerry and George, he commented, "It's like a sauna in here."

"What?"

"Nothing, General. Just a joke." With that, Norton got up and left the tent, the glare of the sun made worse by reflection from a bulbous cumulus cloud towering above.

Whether it was serendipity or not, Norton couldn't say. All he knew was that it happened as he was drying off after the canvas-bucket shower and as Freeman stepped under, soaped himself, and pulled the clothes hanger–shaped plastic handle, the water making his hair look like a gray mop. It was Freeman's habit in the shower to either hum or sing "The Streets of Laredo." If he didn't, it meant he was preoccupied with a problem, and that usually meant everyone at his central HQ back at Camp Pendleton had better be on their toes. Today the general had begun humming the song, but it dribbled off as he stood there.

Freeman had been struck by the apparently idle thought that just as here in the shower there was a finite amount of water, so it was for the earth as a whole. Once you'd fouled it up with soaps and other additives, that would be it. It was a point that environmentalists all over the world were constantly trying to make, the more extreme ones never failing to cause the general's blood pressure to soar. But they did have a point, and as he reached up to pull the plug again to let the water flow, his hand froze on the handle. What had he just been looking at on the map? Staring him in the face. "Well, I'll be—Norton!"

Norton started. "I'm right here, General."

"It's the lake, Norton."

"Sir?"

"Lake Mead. The son of a bitch is going to hold Lake Mead hostage! We play ball or he poisons the goddamn water supply. Cup of liquid VX, he'd wipe out half of California!"

"Where would they get that from?" Norton inquired, feeling his heart pounding as he envisaged the catastrophe Freeman had posited.

"Hell, I don't know. I guess from—"

They both thought of Tooele, Utah. It had been big news,

especially within the military—a major, some skirt, shot while inspecting the base.

"Something about a count error, wasn't it?" Freeman said. Before Norton had a chance to answer him, Freeman told him to contact the White House and ask them to call Tooele immediately.

Norton rang through and handed the field phone to the general. The Tooele C.O. and presidential adviser Delorme were on the line.

"Are we on a scrambler?" Freeman asked, a towel about him making him look like some ancient Roman senator.

"Yes, sir," Norton assured him.

Freeman wasted no time with pleasantries.

No VX shells were missing.

"Goddammit," Freeman said. "Are there *any* kinds of CBW shells missing?"

"None, General."

"Are you sure?"

"I'm positive, sir," the Tooele C.O. replied. "On order from CID Maryland, we've conducted three, I say again, three, counts of individual cradles."

"Cradles?" Freeman asked irritably. "What in hell's that?"

"Each individual shell has its own holder, General—its own cradle. None are missing."

"Satisifed, General?" Delorme asked in a conciliatory tone.

"Guess I'll have to be," Freeman answered. "But I still think they're after the water supply. Militias have been threatening that for years."

"General," Delorme said, "why don't we get the Nevada National Guard down there? Surround the lake."

It would of course be impossible, the general told Norton after, to *guard* the lake. "One bozo with a half-pint jar could slip through the woods around the lake and that would be that." Nevertheless, Delorme's suggestion was better than nothing, and Freeman as C.O. of the Southwest gave the order to the Nevada National Guard's C.O. "Put it out that you're on maneuvers. We've got to keep the reason for the deployment secret."

Fat chance, Norton thought, and he was right. There was a leak from the Guard within an hour, and soon an army of media types, domestic and international, were converging on Las Vegas. Freeman gave it to them straight. Any vehicle passing federal roadblocks set up outside Las Vegas between it and the lake without written authority would be fired on. Deadly force authorized. Ditto for any, repeat, *any* aircraft. He added to the threat by saying the militia had missiles. This applied to Purdy's column, as the New Mexico National Guard—in the form of Eliot's two advance Bradleys— had discovered. Freeman didn't know whether Hearn had them, but omitted to tell this to the media.

Marte Price called in an old IOU on the general. If he would permit her one flyover of Hearn's motorcade, she would be sure "not to overlook your astuteness in all of this, General."

"No dice," he told her. "The militia warned us that if they so much as heard a plane they'd execute another hostage."

In northeastern Arizona, adjacent to New Mexico's northwest corner, Jason Purdy, while waiting for Benet and the other three militiamen to return, heard on the radio that Hearn and his "lads"—as Purdy, affecting a British turn of phrase, called them—were being pursued by overwhelming federal odds. It was a conclusion forced on Purdy by the broadcast of a reporter called "somebody O'Keefe" who was giving a commentary on what he'd heard so far from his rival CNN reporter, Marte Price.

Purdy was no coward. But he was no fool either. Stirred ever since childhood by the Western mythology in which the Seventh Cavalry arrives just in time to scatter ransacking Indians and save the day, Purdy was nevertheless cognizant of the futility of empty gestures. Now that he'd learned from Brian O'Keefe's "update" that the Nevada National Guard was on the march from Reno to protect Lake Mead, he realized that before long the Arizona National Guard, by reason of state pride, would send its Guard against Hearn, and that despite Hearn's effective use of hostages so far, his defense strategy could run only so far on hostages. Once Hitler's admirer used them up—and how many were left, one security guard, a doctor, and a nurse?—Hearn would be out of bargaining chips. With this in mind, Purdy decided the best way to help his fellow militiamen would be to stick to his original plan of occupying land ceded by the federal government to the Indians, and so draw attention away from Hearn. Purdy was under no illusion—he would become the target of federal wrath—but like the harlequin in the rodeo who diverts the charging bull's attention to himself, giving the cowboy time to escape, he would draw off the federals to the perennial cause célèbre in the Southwest: fighting for what many white settlers had believed was the confiscation of land rightly belonging to them. It was a matter of "switching tactics," he told his subalterns, and while most of them had seen action in America's big and little wars abroad and were unquestionably brave, none had quite the courage to point out that it seemed to them that he, Jason Purdy, was merely rationalizing his desire to steal Hearn's thunder—that Jason Purdy was primarily hell-bent for glory.

What Purdy didn't know, however, was that Hearn had no intention of standing his ground, that his modus operandi had been, and always would be, hit and run, the tried and true tactic of guerrillas the world over. Hearn's message to his troops had always been, "Go in hard and get out."

For the first fifteen minutes after he had jumped from the truck, Orr felt frozen to the bone, much of his stiffness caused by having had to stay so cramped in the toilet's recess. But now, walking on the road in the truck's tracks where it had passed but didn't see him—he'd been ready to dive off into the soft powder snow beyond the road should any vehicle approach—Orr started to feel better, the brisk walk warming him. His compass told him he was heading west, and he estimated he was somewhere near Davenport, about twenty miles away from Fairchild, with another twenty miles to go to Wilbur, where a safe farmhouse was located off Highway 2. The mailbox, which Eleen told him was located back from the highway, should read "the Abrems"—the recognition phrase: "I'm a friend of Russell's." But Orr knew that in this weather if the Abrems, a couple in their sixties, couldn't provide him with transportation, there would be no way he could walk farther than Wilbur, his determination notwithstanding. But at least the Abrems' farm could offer him food and shelter until the storm abated.

As he trudged on through the howling snow in this, one of the most sparsely populated parts of America, Orr began to regret his decision not to stay with the truck, wondering whether he'd be better off preferring discovery to starvation. It shocked him, this sudden overwhelming doubt. He was supposed to be the tough one, Eleen's most reliable platoon sergeant. And normally he was. But out here, far away from the camaraderie of fellow militia POWs and the necessity to set an example, he was not the man he usually was, taking more counsel from his fears than he ever had before. "What the hell's the matter with me?" he asked aloud, gathering his courage, abusing the storm, telling it that it wouldn't win, that he'd outlast it.

No sooner had he uttered the words of admonition against his weaker self than Orr saw a light. He stopped and watched it, a patch of white haze reflecting off the snow, and realized it was moving. A few minutes later it seemed to have stopped, and in near-zero visibility it was difficult to judge the distance.

Orr crouched down in a snowdrift, waiting for the light to come closer. When it moved toward him, he felt his gut knotting—it was the headlight of a Washington State Highway Patrol, the cruiser's other light burned out. Orr lay flat in the drift, his face freezing. The last time he'd experienced such a numbness had been at a dentist's.

After it moved on, he wearily resumed his trek westward, the blizzard becoming "thinner," as his fellow prisoners back at Fairchild often described such a weather change in northeastern Washington. But was it only a hole in the storm, or a genuine abatement of the weather? He was only about twenty-five miles west of the camp now, but it might as well have been 225, since he was alone for the first time in the last year, without the mitigating company of fellow POWs. Their conversation, like any friend constantly saying the same things, became boring day after day, but at least it was company, and for a fleeting moment Orr wished himself back into the predictable if suffocating world of the prisoner.

There was more light now, the growing possibility of the storm having truly ended encouraging him to trudge on westward. But there was no pleasing him, for as the sky began to clear, he realized that clear weather was as much an enemy as when visibility was zero, his ability to move off into the snow-covered fields without being seen dramatically curtailed by the threat of open skies. Faced by the contradiction in his wishes, he wondered if prison life, incarceration together with poor nutrition, always did that to you—dulled your senses to the extent that you weren't alert to the most basic paradoxes or capable of making the simplest decisions.

He was lucky, the sun now an alabaster orb veiled by thick gray curtains of nimbostratus cloud, but warming nevertheless, and there was enough mist rising from the earth that it would hide anyone more than a hundred yards away. He saw a mailbox, its ice-covered roof dripping, forming a fringe of icicles. Off the road, thigh-deep in snow backed up to a wire fence, Orr snapped off the ice to reveal the lettering: THE ABREMS.

General Freeman's HQ had become the clearinghouse for any intelligence regarding the anticipated attack on Lake Mead. A high-flying U-2 flight was authorized, its altitude of fifty thousand feet plus making it silent and invisible to anyone on the ground, its digitally enhanced reconnaissance photos transmitted to Freeman's G2 unit at Camp Pendleton.

The cloud cover over northwestern Arizona far below the U-2 had thickened, but two photographs revealed what were

believed to be three ambulances near Lake Mead on Highway 93, the other two presumably under cloud. Five minutes
and twenty-eight seconds into the third transmit of recon
photographs, all five ambulances were identified on the
shoulder of the highway. Norton, always surprised by the
long, stretched look of vehicles in look-down photos, commented to Freeman that the ambulances, the red cross on
their roofs notwithstanding, looked like "five stretch limos."

"More like five hearses," Freeman retorted.

Norton was unsure as to whether the general's remark was
occasioned by what he saw as the fate of the hostages or of
Hearn's militiamen. He was about to ask Freeman when he
heard a whistle from the covey of intelligence officers clustered about the computer, receiving more photos. "Is this
high-tech or what?" one of the officers asked.

"I always thought," another said, "that that business about
our cameras picking up newsprint in Red Square was bullshit."

"What's up?" Freeman asked, turning around from his
map table with a 1:100,000 scale of Lake Mead's 255 square
miles of water; enough, his intelligence people had informed
him, to cover all of New York State in a foot of water.

The lieutenant who had given him this gem was now the
one to respond to Freeman's question. "General," he said, "we
can tell that one ambulance has a flat tire."

"That's why they're stopped." It was more a statement
than a question.

"Yes, sir. Frightened of getting split up, I guess."

"I'll split them wide open if I get the chance," the general
responded.

The lieutenant looked at Norton, the general's comment
not admitting any concern for the hostages, which recalled
for the young intelligence officer the now infamous incident
at Astoria Bridge when Freeman had ordered the bridge
taken at any cost. Norton gave the lieutenant a slight nod,
acknowledging the officer's concern, and said to Freeman,
"Of course we'd have to know which ambulance—I mean
where the hostages are."

"The hostages," Freeman replied without taking his eyes off the U-2 shots, "are in harm's way."

For a man who was famous, or infamous, for plain speaking, it was as ambiguous a statement as a State Department media release, and the lieutenant, Norton saw, was deeply troubled by it. So was Norton.

"Will this cloud cover clear, Major?" Freeman asked his weather officer.

"No, sir. In fact the Southwest is going to be pretty well socked in by tonight."

"Great," Freeman said. "Just what we need. Won't be able to see a damn thing from up there."

"U-2 has infrared, General."

"Yes, all right for clouds, maybe, but not rain."

"Ah, yes, General. I guess so."

"You guess! Goddammit, you're the weatherman!"

"Yes, sir."

The general dropped the photo on the table and returned to hunch over his map. "I'm getting cranky," he told Norton.

"Yes, General, we know. Everyone's under pressure."

Freeman turned to Norton. "Notify the ALERT team I want them on standby." He paused. "Damn, I wish it would clear. El Niño should be called El Pain-in-the-Ass."

"I agree."

"Predictable but unpredictable at the same time," Freeman said, and Norton agreed once more. The general could have been talking about himself.

CHAPTER THIRTY-FIVE

Alice and Melvin Abrem could see him trudging toward the farmhouse, the man following the strip of tractor-graded snow that ran about a hundred yards or so from the main road. The temperature was rising a few degrees, and what had been dry, crisp powder snow was melting. Things that had looked so beautiful, from the big red cattle barn to the grapevines, now appeared in their real, run-down state. Like so many in the region, the Abrems blamed the federal government for the state of their farm, focusing on free trade initiatives and antiherbicide spray legislation, which had hit eastern Washington produce harder than anything since the recession back in the 1970s.

"What d'you think, Alice?" asked Melvin Abrem, a tall, wiry man in his mid-sixties.

"Militia. Why else would he be walking in this weather?"

"Car could've broken down—out of gas."

Alice, a plump woman a few years younger than her husband, sniffed at his suggestion. "If he's run out of gas he's a fool—should know how scarce gas stations are out here."

"Which means he must be militia. Doesn't know the area. 'Sides, where's an escapee gonna get a car?"

"Steal one," Alice said.

"Way out here? In this weather? Why, he'd be picked up in half an hour."

"Guess you're right," Alice conceded. It wasn't that she didn't want to help the militia. All her family were militia sympathizers—had been for years—and her best friend, May Merk, had been killed by an FBI agent down in Yakima. Shot dead—in the hospital. May had gone to visit the Yakima hospital with the intention of killing the FBI agent who'd uncovered the fact that the Merks, who'd had an orchard down near Naches, had harbored a fugitive militiaman and had a cache of weapons. Alice Abrem was as headstrong and antigovernment as May Merk had been, and saw it as her calling to carry on the antigovernment tradition. However, Alice wasn't particularly friendly to any militia who sought her out, at least not at first. She had a curt, bustling manner about her, and a way of making even Melvin's best militia friends feel uneasy, as if she was doing everything under sufferance—a martyr. In fact, she was less promilitia than antigovernment, her support for the militia merely a way of paying back the federals for what she believed had been the government's failure to assist her parents in the face of the bank's Scrooge-like foreclosure of her parents' orchard.

Melvin Abrem walked through the dimly lit hallway toward the front door.

"Don't open it!" Alice commanded sharply.

"Huh?"

"Don't open it. If any federals are watching, that'd look mighty suspicious, wouldn't it? Just openin' the door like that, lettin' him walk right in. Make him knock, like he was a stranger. For all you know, *he* might be a federal."

"Yeah, that's what they do, Alice. They got lawmen who just love walkin' out here through a storm. Part of their basic—"

"Don't you take that tone with me. If it was left up to you, you'd bring in every stray on the road."

"I know what it's like, Alice—on the road by yourself. Can get pretty damn lonely."

"That's no reason to go soft in the head."

"All right, then," Melvin said sulkily. "*You* answer the door—so damn smart. But make sure he uses the right words."

"Yes," she said, "like you were going to do. Just open up an' let everybody in."

They could see him trudging toward the house. Alice, distrustful as usual, slipped the chain on the door. Through the slit she could see another man walking in from the road. "Melvin," she told her husband. "Get your gun."

In the Four Corners, the sun had by now completely burned off the nascent cumulus of morning, and, since high noon, threatened to fry anything that moved, including Ray Fraser and John Reid. The higher they went on Ship Rock, the more exhilarated Reid became. Fraser, ten years older than Reid, suffering from a cramp in his left thigh, had to stop, ostensibly to look for any telltale dust trails of Eliot's National Guard column.

"You okay?" Reid asked.

"Yes. See for miles up here, eh?"

"It's fantastic. Wonder how many people have climbed this."

Fraser shrugged. "Don't know. How are your legs?"

"Fine. Yours?"

"Great."

"Indians thought this was a holy place, right?"

"Uh-huh. Indians think every site's a holy one. They find 'em every time someone wants to drill for oil. You know how big this Navajo reservation is?"

"No idea."

"Twenty-five thousand square miles. Five times the size of Connecticut. And that doesn't include the Chaco National Park, south of us. Got over a thousand holy sites down there. They've got to learn to move over. Purdy's right about that."

The way Fraser said it implied that Purdy wasn't right about everything, and Reid pressed him on it.

"Well," Fraser replied, "I don't necessarily believe that occupying their sites is the best way to make the point, but Purdy says he's killing two birds with one stone, right? Occupies a holy site, he makes it clear to the Indians and the government that they've got to ease up—share the land. 'Specially if there's oil there."

John Reid didn't normally think of oil when he thought of

the militia. He'd seen Purdy's claims to the land as the claim of what was essentially a rural constituency. It had never occurred to him that the militia was as interested in making money as anyone else. He'd made the mistake of many of the younger militia recruits—that the militia was made up entirely of Randy Weaver, cabin-in-the-woods fundamentalist types. It certainly wasn't his, Reid's, type. Indeed, if he thought about it, Reid would have to admit that his own membership in the militia—as that of many of his contemporaries—was largely based on the adventure of it all. The guns. Ironically for some, more than the militia would admit to, hard and fast antigovernment views seemed to follow membership, rather than the other way around.

"We high enough now?" Reid asked Fraser.

"Hell, no."

Way above them they saw an eagle circling lazily against the hard, washed-out blue of the sky.

Orr didn't like the look of the woman through the slit in the chained door. She had a definite mustache and crow's-feet.

"Yes?" Her question was imperious, let alone unfriendly.

"I'm looking for Melvin," Orr said. "I'm a friend of Russell's." He could hear her taking off the chain.

"Come in—quickly."

The gloom of the unlit hallway felt completely at odds with any anticipated relief. It felt unsafe.

"Who's your friend?" It was Melvin, startling Orr, who hadn't seen him.

"What?" Orr said, following the woman over to the living room's window.

She gestured out toward the second man. "Him?"

"Jesus!" said Orr. "I don't know."

"Don't you blaspheme in this house!" she said tartly.

"Sorry, I—" Jesus, she was as strict as Eleen. "I don't know," Orr continued with uneasy suspense. "He didn't come with me."

"Who is he, then?" Melvin Abrem demanded.

"No idea," Orr answered, his fingers hurting as they started to thaw out. "A local?" he suggested.

"Ain't local," Melvin said, and now Orr, whose eyes were growing more accustomed to the house's gloom, saw the gun, an old Colt .45, service issue, Melvin's thumb on the hammer, ready to cock. They could hear the man kicking snow off his boots on the lower step. "You best stand over there," Melvin told Orr softly, motioning to a space near a hat rack behind the door.

It was Alice who opened the door. Melvin, taller, stood behind her, making it evident to Orr who the boss was in this household. "Yes?" she said.

"Are you Mrs. Abrem?" the man asked. He was in his late twenties, possibly early thirties, had a black beard and balding hair, and wore a dark brown woolen scarf about his throat. His breath was visible as he spoke in the frigid air.

"Never mind who *I* am," Alice told him. "Who are *you*?"

"I'm looking for Melvin. I'm Russell's friend."

Looking southeast of Ship Rock, John Reid spotted a high tail of dust as a smudge on the horizon, and he alerted Fraser, who was ten feet below him on a narrow basalt ledge.

"Yeah," Fraser said, standing still, face pressed against the rock, catching his breath. "This is high enough." They were at the thousand-foot level, and Reid was ensconced in a bowl-shaped depression in the rock, about ten feet across and three to four feet deep. It appeared that the thrust of volcanic spew had slackened there for a moment, and Reid thought it was as perfect an observation post as God could have given them. Its only drawback was the fact that, the area being out of the breeze, the temperature in the bowl was about five degrees higher than the already baking surrounding rock. Even so, Fraser, rejecting Reid's proffered hand with "I'm okay," was pleased with the view it gave them of Route 666 as it passed Table Mesa, southeast of them.

"You see the dust plumes?" Reid asked him, reaching for Fraser's binoculars.

Fraser gave them to him and sat down in the bowl, grateful for Reid's preoccupation with the horizon.

"Hard to make out," Reid said, glued to the binoculars, working the focusing sleeve. "Dust is hiding 'em. Wind must be blowing their wakes ahead of 'em."

"Don't worry, we'll pick 'em up soon enough."

"I'm not worried," Reid replied. "This is great."

"Uh-huh," Fraser said. "I'll take the first watch. You can stretch for a while."

"I'm not tired."

"Well, one of us had better rest. It could be a long night."

"They'll pass us 'fore the sun goes down," Reid opined.

"It could still be a long night. Unless you want to scamper down from here in the dark."

"Scamper?" Reid said, grinning, lowering the binoculars. "That's funny."

"Glad you like it."

"Why don't you have forty winks. You look beat."

"I'm all right. But if you want—"

"Sure," Reid said. "Be glad to."

"One thing," Fraser said.

"Yeah?"

"Closer they get, you stay low. Don't move around."

"No problem, but I'll be surprised if they expect us to be up here."

No, Fraser thought sarcastically, we took out two of Eliot's Bradleys and this is the highest lookout in these parts. Why would Eliot think of looking up? "You might be surprised," he told Reid, trying to get comfortable in the aged rock and taking a pull at the canteen.

CHAPTER THIRTY-SIX

"All they have to do," Freeman said, his right hand sweeping across the map of Lake Mead, "is dump a gallon or two of VX from the top of the dam. We've got to prevent the bastards from getting anywhere near that dam."

Norton grimaced. "Problem is, General, Hearn'll shoot another one of his hostages if we get too close."

"And," put in a major normally responsible for coordinating air support, "if we go in with helos, same problem."

"Suggestions?" Freeman asked.

"Road blockade," Norton opined, "raises the same problem. Our best chance is if we could somehow surprise them—not give them enough time to react, to plan anything." He paused. "Like the SAS did with the Iranian terrorists."

None of Freeman's headquarters staff had to be reminded of the Special Air Services' famous commando assault on the Iranian Embassy in London in 1980. If they hadn't seen it as youngsters on worldwide television, they'd seen it umpteen times as a training tape on how to hit hard and fast, so fast that the Iranian terrorists were completely discombobulated, all the hostages but one rescued.

Freeman, jaw clenched, hands on the map table, was nodding his agreement. "You're right, Norton. Hard and fast. Brentwood and his ALERTs."

"Of course," Norton added, "we have to remember SAS had enough cover that they were able to be driven right up close to the embassy. This Hearn could see us for miles."

"And spot any helo," the major said.

Freeman turned, watching the armed services weather channel monitor. He punched in GPS coordinates of the northwestern corner of Arizona, where the great concrete arch-gravity dam stood majestically white between Nevada, left of him as he faced its image, and Arizona to his right. The weather over the dam and the southern half of Lake Mead was socked in by thick cloud cover from three to seven thousand feet, with only a thirty percent chance of clearing in the next twenty-four hours.

"All right," Freeman declared, his combative tone directed at the inclement weather. "We've got to get men atop the dam wall, and if that's the way it's going to be—" He paused and looked across at Norton. "—we'll go in HAHO." There was a somber silence in the room. He was talking about the ALERTs parachuting in, but because they couldn't go in high altitude, low opening—because of the cloud bank, they wouldn't be able to see the dam until they were practically on it, its curving top only forty feet across—it would have to be a high altitude, high opening insertion. Then they could go high enough that the plane wouldn't be heard by Hearn or anyone else, and opening, their chutes high enough, they could avoid a dangerous low opening in the thick cloud directly above the dam. In HAHO they could jump well north of the dam, allowing them time to glide in under the cloud cover, to better time their approach and surprise. It would all be a matter of exquisite timing, like skydivers who at times can land within a ten-foot circle when it's clear weather. Of course, they didn't have to carry an eighty-pound war load.

"Risky," Norton counseled.

"Crossing the street's risky," Freeman retorted.

"Not the same order of magnitude, General."

"ALERTs are trained to take risks. Goddammit, that's how they earn their pay."

"If there's a screwup, General," Norton said bluntly, "Hearn'll shoot hostages."

"I *know* that. But what would you have us do? Stand by,

let them toss that shit in the lake? Poison everyone, for Christ's sake?"

The air support major and other HQ staff said nothing, but Norton stood his ground. This was how he earned his pay, as devil's advocate to Freeman's gut-born hunches. Norton glanced at his watch and then delivered what Freeman called his "whammy." "General, it'll mean them jumping at night."

"Jesus!" the major said before he could stop himself.

"What in hell's the matter with you?" Freeman declared. "I'm surrounded by a bunch of goddamn ninnies."

"That's unfair, General." It was Norton. Everyone else thought the general would be infuriated. Instead he surprised them, as he sometimes did. He stared hard at Norton for a moment, then relented. "You're right, Norton. I'm well rebuked. Sorry, gentlemen. I appreciate your concern. It's just that we have to do *something*." He paused. "Anyone got a better idea?"

"Approach by boat?" the signals captain proffered.

"No," the air major replied. "Hearn's outfit'd hear them coming a mile away."

"Then it's insertion by HAHO."

No one objected, but no one looked happy.

"All right, Major," Freeman said. "Organize it with Nellis Air Base. We'll jump soon as it's dark."

"By *we*," Norton said, "I take it you're speaking figuratively. You're not going to jump."

"Why not?"

"You're too old."

Everybody busied themselves looking elsewhere in the HQ—at anything but the general.

"You're a cheeky bastard!" he told Norton. "I'm as fit as any man here. Besides, can't ask my men to do something I wouldn't."

"Is this White House approved?" Norton asked, knowing very well it wasn't.

"I don't need the permission of a bunch of politicians to tell me what I can do."

"Well, perhaps not, General, but last time I checked, the President was your Commander-in-Chief."

"He's given me wide latitude."

"Ah . . ." Norton said, seeing that this was an argument he wasn't going to win, at least not in front of the other officers present. Freeman told signals he wanted scrambled phone contact with David Brentwood's team.

"Brentwood?"

"Sir?"

"I want you and your team to get your ass to Nellis—I'll send a chopper—and prepare for a HAHO drop over Hoover Dam. Thing isn't too wide at the top, and it's socked in, so you'll have to glide approach."

"Yes, sir."

"David, I want you to listen to me—carefully." Freeman walked out of his HQ into the blazing sun. "Go in hard and fast. I'll fax you via scrambler with the layout of the dam. We're going to have to stop these Nazi bastards in their tracks. Take them out."

"Shoot first, questions later?"

"Yes."

"How about the hostages, General?" There was a long silence. Brentwood could hear Freeman breathing.

"David, earlier today I spoke with Major Eliot, C-in-C of the Albuquerque National Guard. He tells me that one of his Bradleys—before it was taken out by the militia—had held its fire when a militiaman surrendered. It was a ruse. The moment our Bradley stopped, it was taken out by an AT."

Brentwood was still waiting. The general had given him the rules of engagement for the militia combatants, but not the hostages. He asked the question again. "How about the hostages, General?"

"David, I'm convinced that the militia's directly responsible for the theft of nerve gas, no matter what the depot count says. Could've substituted a dummy shell for a stolen one."

Brentwood remembered hearing about the incident, the

shooting of a woman, a captain called Caroline Hardwick, Harcourt, something like that.

"The fact is, I'm convinced they're going to dump this poison in Mead. If hostages get in the way of preventing you from saving millions of people from this act of terrorism, then you'll have to take them out—I'll back you."

Brentwood didn't reply, but Aussie Lewis and Salvini noticed his fist idly thumping his thigh, a sure sign that he was feeling distinctly uncomfortable.

"You there, David?" It was Freeman.

"Yes, sir."

"I'll back you. I don't let my people dangle in the wind. Another thing—there'll be no nosy media types there."

What he's telling me, Brentwood thought, is that probably no one would see it happen. "Can I be frank, General?"

"Shoot." It was an unfortunate choice of words.

"I'm not comfortable with this, General."

"Captain," Freeman began more formally, "no one's *comfortable* with it, but the numbers are staring us right in the face. Millions of civilians at risk versus three hostages. Hell, it might not arise. You might neutralize these pricks with minimum casualties."

"Yes."

"All right then, let's do it."

It occurred to ALERT Thomas, as the big black man picked up his load, that the general might have it all wrong. "Maybe," he told Brentwood, "Hearn and his bunch are just gonna drive right across the dam after all."

"Yeah, right," Brentwood said.

Salvini asked how high they were going.

"Thirty thousand," Brentwood answered.

"Gonna be a bit nippy up there."

"Yeah," Finn agreed. "Well, don't forget your oxygen."

CHAPTER THIRTY-SEVEN

"You know one another?" Melvin Abrem asked, regarding both Orr and the black-bearded newcomer with suspicion.

"I know *him*," the newcomer said, indicating Orr.

Alice Abrem was looking sternly at both of them, trying to deduce which one was lying, or whether both were. "You know him?" she asked Orr.

Orr looked closely at the man. "No. Doesn't mean much, though." He saw Melvin Abrem's finger moving back and forth nervously around the .45's trigger guard and didn't like it. "Look," he told Alice, then shifted his gaze to Melvin, "Fairchild's one hell of a—"

"We won't have bad language," Alice cut in. "Not in this house."

Orr was flabbergasted, vetting what he'd just said for any trace of profanity.

"He's right," the other man said. "It's a big prison camp— a thousand or so of us."

"Can I ask him a question?" Orr said, hardly able to believe he was actually asking this woman for permission, but conscious of the necessity to suck up. "Ah, I apologize for the language, ma'am," he added.

"Go on!" she commanded him. "Ask away."

Thank you, you old bitch, Orr thought, and turned to the man. "What hut?"

"Four B—right next to yours." He put out his hand. "Brody—Neil Brody."

"No last names," Alice put in. "Security."

Brody shook hands, but Orr was obviously uncomfortable. "You're one of Eleen's guys. Right?" Brody asked Orr.

"Right."

"There you are," Brody told the Abrems. "Neighbors."

"Then how come he doesn't know you?" Alice pressed Brody.

Orr figured it was time to return Brody's favor of having recognized him, Orr reiterating how big the POW camp was and how a lot of men were growing beards, many unwillingly, in the face of the commandant's "no razors" rule. "Brody here is one of about two hundred POWs in the camp growing beards. It's warmer too. There are about forty men to a hut—you can't know all of them." Orr turned to Brody. "So you were one of the eight 4B guys?"

"Yeah, that's right."

Orr wondered, was Brody—if that was his real name—telling the truth or merely latching on to what was offered? "Were there any guards with you?"

"Yeah, two of us were dressed up as guards—pretended to be marching the rest of us to the punishment cells outside the main gate."

"Which gate?"

"East gate. Why?"

Alice knew why, and so did Melvin. They were watching Brody's every move. And Orr's.

"Where are the other seven?" Alice asked.

Brody was breathing hard, like an asthmatic, as if he couldn't get enough air. "Shot—all of 'em. Son of a—" He stopped, waylaid by Alice's reproachful scowl. "Federal gate lieutenant and two guards woke up to our caper not long after we were through the gate. Everything went haywire. I dunno—I mean they just started shooting. It was snowing like, really heavily. I ran—fast as I could." Eyes bright, teary, he looked over at Orr. "I managed to get up on the flatbed of your truck. Didn't know you were in the sh—in the john—until I heard you push the recess door open and saw you go off the truck. I didn't know what to do, stay with the truck or follow you. I dropped off 'bout a quarter mile after you."

"You followed him?" It was Melvin, and when he heard Brody say yes, he lowered the .45, though he still had one more question for Orr. "Sound right to you?"

While Brody was telling his story, Orr had been recalling the truck ride, the muffled sound of the truck's engine, the bump he'd heard as it passed the isolation cells, and the awful tearing sound of an M-60 and men screaming. "Yes," he told the Abrems; Brody's account pretty much fit his own.

"Well," Alice said, her voice softening, "you both had better sit down, warm up, have a meal. Then we'll see what's what."

"Thank you, ma'am," Brody said. "I could eat a horse."

"No horse, son," she replied, "only beef."

Melvin chuckled. She was some card, wasn't she?

Orr was luxuriating in the hot wash of furnace air that came rushing from a grate grid by the kitchen table, telling himself to relax. Hadn't Brody known the pass phrase for the safe house as well as he himself did? Besides, there was the thump he'd heard on the flatbed, one of several in fact, as the portable john had risen an inch or so, despite the guy ropes, as the truck trundled over deep potholes that hadn't been filled with snow. Of course he could ask Brody about the light—the lone headlight—or rather, *not* ask about it, just ask if he'd seen a *pair* of headlights. See what Brody said.

"We don't have any liquor," Alice told them. "Coffee?"

"Sounds great," Brody said, rubbing his hands, flexing them over the heat outlet.

"And you," she said, turning to Orr.

"I'd love a coffee."

Melvin gave them a wink. A promise of something stronger? Orr reminded himself that a lot of guys with beards, particularly medium, stocky types like Brody, were hard to tell apart in fatigues unless you were right up close, which he hadn't been with anyone in 4B.

"Chicken gumbo!" Alice announced, her voice reverting for a moment to her earlier unapologetic tone, as if to say, "Like it or lump it."

Orr didn't mind. He was getting used to the old tartar. Besides, fair was fair. These people were taking a hell of a risk. If the federals were on the trail and found the Abrems harboring fugitives, they'd face mandatory fines and imprisonment, as well as lose their property. Those odds would make anyone think twice. These folks were sticking their necks out. No need to feel offended by their caution. And chicken gumbo was way ahead of the crap Moorehead's goons dished out.

Orr almost burned his tongue, he was so hungry, Brody blowing circumspectly on his soup.

Now it was clear to John Reid that the distant spirals of dust were Eliot's National Guard column proceeding at some speed, at least for the Bradleys and ancillary infantry and other vehicles. Through the binoculars he could see packs that looked like huge slabs of milk chocolate affixed to the Bradleys, especially on the glacis or sloping front around the lower section of the turret, and on the track skirting. They were appliqué armor packs, sandwiched layers of ceramics and other protective material making the Bradleys less vulnerable to antivehicular missiles. It was a protection that the two reconnaissance Bradleys taken out near Ship Rock lacked, probably a trade-off, less armor for more speed, the appliqué packs more common after severe criticism had been leveled at the Bradleys during some nasty Pentagon infighting and criticism of the vehicle in the late 1990s.

Reid was excited and frightened, wondering if he should wait until the federals came closer along the 666 or wake Ray Fraser now. Fraser, in a deep, openmouthed sleep, was snoring so loudly in the rock bowl, which magnified the sound, that Reid had a fleeting irrational concern that if any of Eliot's men came near, they would hear him despite the fact that the column was still miles off. He woke Fraser, who gulped and burst awake as if he'd been hit with a cattle prod. "Wha—What's wrong?"

"Nothing, but those federals are coming faster than we realized."

Fraser, shielding his eyes from the sun with his hands, yawned, moved to Reid's end of the rock bowl, and took up the binoculars. He made a mental note of the vehicles: twelve Bradleys, three of them taking up the rear of the column of ten troop- and supply-laden trucks. Either he could radio Purdy now, he thought, or he could wait to send a more detailed report when Eliot's column drew adjacent to the rock seven miles off to his left on the 666 and he could identify more precisely what the column consisted of apart from the highly lethal wire-guided TOW antitank missile arrays that lay ready in the launcher modules on the Bradleys' turrets.

"We'll wait," he told Reid. "You see those appliqué packs?"

"Yeah. Bad news. Need CAS for those fuckers." He meant close air support, which the militia craved but did not have. Fraser, in an uncharacteristic moment of wishful thinking, told Reid that he wished they had just one Cobra right now, but he knew he had to be content with the fact that the nonintervention of federal air power had been carefully gained by the militia's holding civilian hostages. God help Hearn's column, he told Reid, if the federals ever discovered the vehicles in which the hostages were being held. A federal gunship could take out the other ambulances in a matter of minutes, or even less in the open desert. Fraser handed Reid the binoculars and grabbed his radio's headset. Then, without looking directly at it, he figured out roughly where the sun was, and glancing at his watch, had a flash of brilliance: he and Reid would observe Eliot's column as it drew closer, but wouldn't radio it in until well after dark, by which time the federals would be well past them en route to intercept Purdy's column. It was still dangerous, Fraser told Reid, if the federals were carrying a direction-finding radio beam detector. They could quickly pin down the coordinates to Ship Rock, but he was banking on the fact that once well past Ship Rock, Eliot would probably not bother to send any of his force back.

In the lead Hummer, Major Eliot and his driver, Peter Lowe, were at odds. In civilian life, Eliot worked for the IRS, something that his driver, a small businessman, could not abide, convinced as he was that the IRS was dedicated to driving small business out of its cotton-picking mind. Every President promised to decrease the amount of red tape involved, but every year it seemed to get worse, and Major Eliot was no help. Lowe having complained once about too many damn taxes—"Ends up I'm workin' six months of the year for the government"—Eliot had replied, unhelpfully, that "rules are rules."

Though Lowe didn't like the militias in general, he did sympathize with their attitude toward the IRS. Whereas Eliot had grown up with the belief that the IRS was a moral institution—taxes necessary to provide health care, roads, dams, etc.—Lowe had been taught that the purpose in life of the IRS was to dream up ways of taxing you into the grave. "Why do they bury dead IRS agents ten feet deep?" his father had asked him, and answered his own question, "Because *deep down* they're nice people." It was this tension between Eliot and his driver that had set the stage for the argument they were having, Lowe insisting he'd seen the flash halfway up Ship Rock's northeastern side, Eliot just as certain that the reflection of the sun on whatever it was had been higher. Such disagreement between a commander and a private was more likely to be sustained in the National Guard than in the regular army, in which, if the commander of a column had said the sun rose in the west, the driver would let it go. But Lowe thought that as a successful small businessman, his opinion about anything was at least as good as that of Major "Rules Are Rules." Hell, he knew exactly where he'd seen the flash, like that off binoculars, with his own eyes.

"Well," Eliot retorted censoriously, "whatever it was, it

came from Ship Rock. And it's one doozy of an observation post."

"Yeah," Lowe had to agree. "But don't the militia use smoked lenses like we do? You know, antireflection?"

"Maybe it was off a weapon. Something flashed, I agree, and I want everyone on it. After last night I don't want any damn sniper picking off any more of my men."

Lowe had to agree with that. After all, he was in Hummer One, and as such he would be a prime target, along with Eliot.

Following Eliot's order that he wanted "everyone on it," it seemed the entire column suddenly sprouted binoculars. Every man, including those relatively safe within the rifle ports of the Bradleys, was looking at Ship Rock. The threat of being fired upon by militia snipers who, in the understatement of the year, Eliot had described as having the "high ground," focused everyone's attention.

"Are we sure it's militia?" the commander of the four platoons of Bradleys asked over the radio. "It could just be a regular climber."

"Who's dumb enough to climb that?" It was the driver of the lead Bradley.

"Militia's dumb enough," the Bradley's gunner opined.

"Yeah," the commander caustically replied. "Like those dumb bastards last night who took out our two Bradleys and infantry guys. Or had you boys forgotten?"

The Bradley commander asked whether he shouldn't take part of the column over to the rock, now several miles away to the column's left, looking deceptively small because of the lack of anything else near enough with which to compare it.

"I'm not sending any force over there," Major Eliot replied, "unless we start taking fire from it."

"A burial detail surely," the Bradley's commander proffered.

"Ah, of course," Eliot replied, embarrassed by appearing callous to the memory of those National Guardsmen whose bodies now lay rotting in the sun. The actual site of the battle was hidden from view to anyone on 666 by the high southern wall of one of the two lava "wings" that ran out from the thrust of spires that formed the impressive-looking ship of rock.

But the major warned, "Keep your eyes open over there. We don't know whether any of them are still around. I don't want any more of my men bushwhacked. If it's one thing those people know how to do, it's to dig in and—"

"There it is again," Lowe interrupted.

A Bradley sergeant commander doing an Israeli—standing up, head out of the turret—also saw it through his binoculars. It was about two-thirds of the way up, he said, and several other men without binoculars also claimed that they'd seen the flash.

"Major?" It was the column's Bradley commander. "You want us to check it out while we're over there?"

"Might as well," Eliot answered, "but don't linger unnecessarily."

" 'Linger unnecessarily,' " the Bradley commander parroted once off the line. He spoke to his second in command, a captain. "What the hell does he think we'll do—break out and party?"

The captain grinned. "Rules are rules."

"Okay," the captain told the two Bradleys he'd selected. "Let's get it over with—bury our guys and rejoin the column. On the off chance we do see any rebs, remember what the old man told us—they suckered one of our Brads into thinking the militia was going to surrender. Guy apparently had his hands up, white T-shirt, the whole bit, and when our boys stopped instead of shooting him, some other militia prick hit us with an AT-4. A setup. You know what that means?"

"No prisoners."

"I didn't say that," the commander said. "Did I?"

"No, sir."

"All right, let's move out."

"You think they've seen us?" Reid asked Fraser.

"No, probably just intent on burying their dead."

It was Reid's turn with the binoculars. "I dunno, Ray. Looks like they're heading straight for us."

"So? They'll swing south behind the lava wall once they reach the rock—using it as a point of reference. They're looking for their dead, trust me."

"You're the boss," and by way of reassuring himself, Reid added, "and anyway, I suppose there's not much they could do even if they think there's anyone up here."

Fraser said nothing, pulling out a stick of lip balm.

"Is there?" Reid asked.

"What?"

"I said I suppose there's not much the federals can do even if they saw us. I mean, we could be anybody. Right?"

"Right," Fraser said, applying the balm, but his tone carried little conviction.

"I mean," Reid said, worrying it like a terrier, "we could just be a couple of climbers."

"Right."

Reid watched Fraser recap the balm and slip it into his pocket, and asked, "Why you so worried about your lips getting burned? Sun'll be down in a while."

"Not for an hour or so. I hate getting dried out."

Neither spoke for several minutes, Fraser checking the radio and his M-16 while Reid stayed glued to the binoculars.

"Shit—Ray?"

"Uh-huh?"

"Those bastards are on to us! They're looking at us."

"Let me see," Fraser said, and Reid handed him the binoculars. Fraser got the strap out of the way and looped it over his head. Despite the dust the federals were kicking up, he could see half a dozen or so individuals in Hummers and Bradleys whose binoculars were pointing in his direction. But they could be studying the rock's north-side wall, or lava wing, searching for a hole through which they could pass, rather than having to negotiate the stony ground around the rock itself to get to their fallen comrades.

But Fraser was asking himself whether the nonchalance with which he'd answered Reid's question was in part an act of self-deception, the art of double-think, of holding two contradictory beliefs simultaneously. The climb had been hard on his nerves. "Look," he finally confessed to Reid, "I don't know what they'll do—whether they've seen us or not—but just in case, let's be ready. I mean, load and lock, check your canteen—know where everything is. Come dark, we don't want to be fumbling around."

"Well, if some of this cloud is burned off we should have moonlight, enough for us to be able to—"

"Yes, but you can't count on it," Fraser replied irritably. "Might get more cloud moving in. You need to know where everything is."

"Right." Quite suddenly, Reid was afraid, bowel-clutching afraid. His youthful exuberance had fueled his ascent, but now, with night approaching, his earlier excitement had been replaced by a gnawing anxiety fueled, albeit unconsciously and somewhat ironically, by his older comrade's experience of such predicaments and by his attempt to prepare him.

CHAPTER THIRTY-EIGHT

Driving south of Las Vegas, the twenty-four-foot-long "Road Clipper" recreational vehicle, plastered with every decal imaginable, from Lake Mead RV Parks to SAVE THE WHALES from Oregon, was humming along down the highway, its driver an overweight man in his mid-forties, his window down not just because it saved energy by giving the air conditioner a rest, but because Jimmy Sarna liked the wind on his face—gave him that sense of freedom, open road, open sky, the road like a long black ribbon stretching, undulating, to infinity. Jimmy Sarna was in such a buoyant mood that he could ignore his two kids—Darlene, twelve, and Danny, ten—fighting over some fool puzzle book, his wife Karen, having her period, aching and telling the kids to shut up. The fight subsided for a few minutes then flared up again. Karen snapped, turned toward the kids and smacked Danny awkwardly on the thigh. "Now just stop it! Give me the book!"

"She started it."

"Give me the book! Right now, Daniel!"

"She started it," he said again, reluctantly handing over the puzzle book.

"I don't care who started it. Knock it off!"

"Why'd ya hit *me*, then?" Danny complained.

"Because you're the nearest. And if I hear any more ruckus from you, Darlene, you're gonna get it too."

"You take some Midol?" Jimmy asked her.

"Yeah, but it's not helpin'. Why those idiots went and changed the ingredients years ago I'll never know. Doesn't work as good as the old one."

"They *are* the old ones," he said, gesturing to the blue and white box between them on the seat. "See, it says 'traditional' on the box."

"D'you ever listen to me?" she asked him.

"Yeah, why?"

"Because if I've told you once, Jimmy, I've told you a thousand times. They put 'traditional' on the box because they want you to think it's the original formula. Traditional means old, see?"

"Hell, I know that, but I thought—"

"No," she said sharply, her voice rising over the hum of the V-8. "They've stopped using that cinnamedrine. Besides, the new ones have acetaminophen in them 'stead of aspirin. Does nothin' for me."

"Ah," he said, adopting her annoyed tone. "Same all over. They're changing everything. Can't leave well enough alone, can they?"

Karen didn't answer, looking out the window at what for her was just another dreary desert.

"You want to stop for a while?" Jimmy asked.

"Yeah," Danny said.

"I was talkin' to your mother. Karen, want to stop, hon?"

"No," she said. "Sooner we get this done, the better." She turned away from the desert to look at him. "We go to Lake Mead first, right?"

"You betcha!"

"How long will it take?"

"To the lake? Not long. I'd say we'll be there in an hour."

"Not the lake. I mean the other. How long will it take?"

"Oh—hell, ten, twenty minutes at most."

"What's 'the other'?" Darlene piped up.

Jimmy was watching his speed. Last thing he wanted was to be pulled over for speeding.

"What's *the other*, Mom?" Darlene repeated.

"Oh, Daddy has to see an old friend. He's dropping us off at the RV park first. We'll stay with the Haleys until he gets back."

"Why'd you call it 'the other'?" Danny persisted.

"Because I can't remember his name, Mr. Big Ears."

"Name's John," Jimmy put in. "John Smith. I want him to fix something in the RV—water pipes."

"Daddy," Darlene said, "I think I'm gonna throw up. Can we stop?"

Jimmy pulled off onto the gravelly shoulder. "Darlene?"

"Yes," came a quavery voice.

"Get out and do it on the other side of the road," Jimmy told her. "Don't go back and use the toilet. There's too much stuff back there."

"Okay . . ." She opened the door and was sick. Karen got out to help her.

"Poor little mite," Jimmy said to no one in particular. Glancing in the rearview mirror, he asked Danny, "How you doin', son?"

Danny gave a sulky shrug, still smarting from the slap. "I'm okay."

"Feel better, sweetie?" Jimmy asked Darlene as she got back into the car.

"A bit," she answered.

"All right. How you doing, Mom?"

"I'm all right. You're very jolly."

"I'm gonna catch the biggest fish in the lake."

That was what Karen couldn't understand, Jimmy being so—so cheery, because if they caught him, they'd put him away for life or give him the lethal injection. But then Karen had never understood Jimmy's total commitment to the militia. Didn't they usually use loners for this kind of stuff? But she knew she was being naive. Vance was said to be married. Most militiamen were. In fact it was when they got married that their commitment usually increased, because they saw the future not in terms of themselves but in terms of their children. It was strange, though, how Jimmy was such a worrier about everything, seeing federal conspiracy everywhere, from the government's refusal to admit there were UFOs way back to the shooting of JFK, but when the time came, he was so relaxed. It was as if now that the die had been cast, the green light given by whomever—they said Vance, but she suspected it was Hearn—Jimmy, faced with doing something concrete, as opposed to the free-floating anxiety induced by just waiting, had jettisoned all the worries he'd had during the more nebulous planning stage. Now everything was in place, and in any case it was Hearn who had the major responsibility.

"Kids," he said as they started off again. "You know what Hoover Dam used to be called?"

"No," Danny said, uninterested.

"Darlene?" Jimmy asked. He glanced again in the rearview mirror. She didn't answer. She looked pale. "You okay, little one?"

She nodded unconvincingly.

"Well?" Karen said.

"What?"

"Are you going to tell us or do we have to beg?"

"You really want to know?" he asked enthusiastically.

"No," Karen said.

"Boulder. It used to be called Boulder Dam. Some fool civil servant changed it to Hoover."

"It'll be dark soon," she said. "Will you be back before then?"

"No problem. We're practically at the RV park."

Hearn, driving the lead ambulance, was frowning, concentrating on what the militiaman was telling him by cell phone from the Nevada side of Lake Mead. "You're breaking up," Hearn told him. "Say again."

There was a garbled word then a rush of static that sounded like stir-fry.

"Dammit!" Hearn complained to Montoya. "Now we don't know whether it's go or whoa!"

"Can we reach anyone on a land line?" Montoya asked. "As a backup?"

"Yeah," Hearn answered, "but that means one of our guys'd be in a fixed position—by the phone—and if the federals are listening, they could pounce on him."

"We may have no choice," Montoya said.

"Sure we do. We can go for it—just do it. We've got hostages, remember."

"So you're saying even if the federals are waiting for us at the dam, we'd go in anyway?"

"That's right. No reason to think anything's wrong with our security. Besides, we've already got men in there, so we're halfway committed right now."

"So you're still not going to tell me how we're going to do it?"

"Hey, Montoya, don't take it so personal, man. There are only five guys who know exactly how it's going down. Vance, McBride, me, and two on the Nevada side. That way it's safer for everyone."

"So not even the guy on the cell phone knows."

"No, he only knows whether it's a go or whoa. He gets a call, that's all. Just a messenger in the loop. That way if the feds do penetrate our security, he can't tell them dick. Same as you. It's for your own protection."

There was a sudden thump and a rolling noise from under the chassis. "What's that?"

"Fuckin' squirrel. You think I'm nuts, playing it so close to the chest?"

"No. I can see how—"

"But you're pissed I'm not telling you chapter and verse. Still think I don't trust you. Right?"

Montoya thought about it for a minute. "Yeah, that's right. Besides, how will you know unless you give me something to do?"

"Who said I wasn't gonna give you somethin' to do?"

"Oh," Montoya riposted, "I get to park our ambulance."

Hearn, despite his fatigue, was smiling. "No way, José. You get to do a lot more than park the car. Yessiree, Bob! I'll tell you one thing," he continued. "When we get there, it'll be after dark. The breeze off the lake'll be pretty nippy. You'd better wear your vest."

They drove on for a while, Hearn looking at his watch, then at the sun in its western arc, sagebrush rushing by.

"You said we have guys in there?" Montoya asked.

"What—yeah."

"I suppose it'd be too much to ask how many?"

"It would. We've got enough, though. Going through on the last hard hat tour." He paused, then explained, "They run tours of the dam all day. A quickie takes you twenty-five minutes. Hard hat lasts an hour. Costs more."

"Then you've been on one."

"No," Hearn said sarcastically. "Vance gives me federal targets I know nothing about." Before Montoya could respond, Hearn added, "I know every inch of that mother from intake towers to control and back. You know how much concrete they used building that fucker?"

"A lot."

"Over three million cubic yards, bud."

Montoya shrugged. "That a fact?"

"You've got no idea how much that is, right?"

"A lot."

"Enough," Hearn said, ignoring Montoya's deadpan delivery, "to build a highway from San Francisco to New York."

How come, Montoya asked himself, Hearn was telling him everything he didn't want to know and not a whit about what precisely they were going to do?

CHAPTER THIRTY-NINE

Freeman was furious. He'd had a direct call from Washington, D.C., from the President, his Commander-in-Chief, that the general was not, repeat *not*, to participate in any combat, that he was to remain cognizant of both the Hearn problem and the increasing danger of Purdy's column, which looked as if it was positioning itself to aid and assist Hearn.

"Norton?"

"General?"

"Did you contact the White House about me going in with Brentwood and company?"

"No, sir, I did not."

"Well, goddammit, find out who did. I'll skin him alive. It's a serious breach of security. My God, the White House is like a sieve. Next thing we know we'll have the press camping out near Lake Mead, and if Hearn hears that our ALERTs are on the way, the whole element of surprise is gone. He'll cut them to pieces the moment they set foot on the dam."

Norton understood. He had weighed this possibility of jeopardizing the five remaining ALERTs of the seven who had run afoul of the militia on the California side, and decided that the general's active participation in such a raid could jeopardize the overall coordinating strategy needed to deal with *both* Hearn's and Purdy's militia. The President was right—they needed a general to orchestrate overall policy.

When Norton assured the general that he had not contacted the White House, he was telling the truth up to a point—namely that he hadn't literally called Washington himself. But he had told one of his subalterns to report the general's intended participation in the raid to the White House, and told him to stress that he, Norton, didn't object to the general's participation because of any concern that the general, though in his sixties, was physically unfit. Indeed, in Norton's view, Freeman's daily workout regimen would give many a fit forty-year-old pause.

Norton, however, *did* call the White House shortly after the general's tantrum. Freeman, despite his legendary status, was as bad tempered as any fighter pilot who, already in the cockpit, was told he had to stand down. Norton told the White House that, given that federal authorities knew the militia had infiltrated every major organization in the United States, including the armed services and police forces, if there was such a leak about Brentwood's clandestine ALERT raid—Brentwood and the other four commandos in the Hercules, already in the air out of Nellis—then the aim of the mission would be jeopardized. To underscore his point, Norton explained to Delorme that in a clandestine high altitude, high opening mission—unlike high altitude, low opening, when the ALERTs jumped out at thirty thousand feet and opened their chutes falling at around twenty feet a second—it would be anywhere from twenty-five minutes to half an hour before they touched down, depending on the winds.

"A half hour?" Delorme was incredulous.

"You've been watching too many movies," Norton told him. "Skydivers are dropped over target, but HAHO is indirect. The jumpers are dropped some distance from the target, whether for security reasons or weather problems. They steer their chutes in. It's quite an art."

"A *half hour*?"

"Yes."

"We'll try to prevent a leak," Delorme assured him.

"Thank you."

The police, who'd been following Hearn's motorcade but, under the threat of having more hostages shot, had kept miles back, out of infrared scope range as well as out of line of sight, now arrived at the rest stop where Hearn's ambulances had obviously pulled over to the shoulder, their tire marks still plainly visible in the desert dust. It was fair to say that they were the grumpiest police in Arizona, probably in the entire Southwest, having been thwarted these past two days and nights by a known Nazi and felon, and now having to line up again like so many schoolboys, twenty on either side of the road, on a walk search through the desert of sagebrush and tumbleweed. Despite El Niño's temperamental predilection to send storm clouds over the arid Southwest, it was perceived as being hotter than usual, the clouds locking the heat in and turning the humidity way up.

"If I get near that bastard Nazi," a veteran of ten years on the force said, "I'm gonna blow his fucking head off."

"Get in line," a younger cop said. They saw a gum wrapper, colors bleached white by the hard desert sun; the remains of a blown tire scattered about; the grayish white of a cow's skeleton; and footprints made by militia boots, more of them east of the road than on the west side, most too lazy to cross the road for more privacy amid dusty green sagebrush.

"All right!" called out the search master, an overweight roly-poly sergeant who was not enjoying the heat at all and was holding the samples of Dana Teer's and Beverly Malkin's clothing that had been sent on from Phoenix. "Send the dog over here."

The dog, a bloodhound on a leash, was brought over by his handler, and after having his nose in one of Nurse Beverly Malkin's blouses, proceeded to sniff, chaotically at first, the dog's nose skimming the desert so close to the ground that he seemed somehow attached to it like a rapidly moving magnet. Then he began a more purposeful trace, not backing up or going off on wild tangents, but more or less on a straight line to the spot where, as the veteran of ten years commented, the nurse "must have taken a piss." Then his younger partner, the "get in line" cop, saw the rectangle of paper, about six by four inches, in the middle of a sagebrush about twenty feet to the right. The young cop reached into the bush, extracted it, and could tell immediately that it was graph paper, like that used for a patient's chart. It had *Charles Vance* typed on top and a hastily scribbled note: *We are in third ambulance. Security man in fifth.*

"Over here, Sarge!"

Roly-Poly looked at it, breathing hard, sweat pouring down his neck. "Third ambulance. Third from which end, for Christ's sake?"

"Ah," the young cop ventured, winking at his partner, the veteran with the dog, "there are five ambulances, Sarge."

"So?"

"Well," the dog handler explained, "third in is third in— doesn't matter when there are five ambulances."

The sergeant still didn't get it, mopping his forehead with a Kleenex that was rapidly coming apart. The veteran, rolling his eyes at his young partner, bent down and poked five holes in the dust. "Doesn't matter what end you start with, Sarge. Third in is the same from either end."

"Oh, yeah."

Walking back to their cruisers, the veteran complained to his younger partner, "And he was promoted ahead of *me*?"

The young cop made a sympathetic face. "It's not what you know, Greg, it's who you are."

"Ain't that the truth."

Roly-Poly was already on the radio to Phoenix. "I've found a note here. . . ."

Phoenix told him they'd relay it to Freeman's HQ.

"Ya hear that?" the young cop asked Greg. " '*I've* found a note.' Says *he* found it."

"He's an asshole," Greg said. "Pity they didn't take *him* hostage."

"There you go."

For Aussie Lewis, jumping from the stupendous roar of a four-engine Herky Combat Talon—a Hercules M-130—was like making love. It was always the same and different every time. As he, Brentwood, Salvini, Thomas, and Finn moved awkwardly, shuffling rather than walking, toward the door ramp, they were feeling hot from the special ops Gore-Tex insulation suits, Spectra shields over eight times stronger than steel, their parachuters' helmets, infrared goggles and gloves, and from hauling eighty-pound packs of extra ammo and canteens. If, God forbid, Freeman was correct about the militia's intentions concerning Lake Mead, they would find themselves in the ironic position of the Ancient Mariner, with water everywhere but not a drop to drink.

Normally, on such a mission, Lewis favored the seven-round quiet shotgun specially designed for silent clandestine ops, but a shotgun's pattern was too wide where hostages were concerned. Instead, each of the five ALERTs carried the new short, bullpup-sized laser-sighting individual combat weapon, or I-COW, with its revolutionary under/over barrel configuration weighing in at just over eleven pounds and sporting a top 20mm barrel mounted over a 5.56mm NATO-round barrel, with an eight-round box magazine for the high-explosive rounds situated behind the pistol grip. The top section of this magazine fit into what would normally be the stock, and the 5.56mm-round magazine went under the barrel, like the banana-shaped mag of an AK-47.

Each man checked his wrist altimeter. The loadmaster, satisfied that each man was ready, gave the A-OK signal, and seconds later the huge rear door ramp of the Hercules yawned open. The sustained roar of the 4,300-horsepower turboprops was even louder as they shuffled down the ramp and fell into darkness five miles above the earth, and miles away from the cloud bank that lay like a huge blanket over the southern reaches of Lake Mead and the dam wall itself. The ALERTs were supposed to land not near the curved forty-foot-wide two-lane road that formed the top of the dam, but right on it. But all this was ahead of them, and falling initially for ten seconds at two hundred feet a second until well clear of the Hercules, they were preoccupied with staying in pattern, not colliding, popping their rectangular arching chutes at 28,000 feet as they began working the toggles, making sure of free flow between the lower and upper panels of the canopy. They glided toward the dam site over fourteen miles away at an acute angle, going in "by the side door," as they called it, hoping to slip under the cloud bank that lay only two to three thousand feet above the lake and dam wall.

Lewis, pulling hard, keeping the toggles hard up to maintain the glide, ruminated on the fact that if the cloud cover over the southern part of Lake Mead lifted, there was a danger they might be seen in the moonlight.

For Brentwood, the fear was coming in at too acute an angle without having time to spiral, crashing into the road instead of on it, or, just as humiliating and dangerous, with his heavy pack hitting the water instead of landing nicely on the road atop the dam wall.

Salvini was just happy to be out of the Hercules, for no matter how many times he heard the statistics citing air travel as the safest mode of transport, he distrusted planes and knew of instances where, though publicly unknown, Herk pilots had made an error over the drop zone and men had died.

Thomas, the ALERT squad's medic, or "Doc," was watching his wrist altimeter, feeling his body losing its heat, worrying about whether he'd packed everything in his medic's bag, and hoping he wouldn't have to use it on anyone.

Finn was having trouble. Despite his having carefully gone through his checklist, his toggles were acting up, sluggish and unresponsive, the sound of his breathing loud through the oxygen mask. He worked the toggles hard again but couldn't feel any noticeable change in the air flow through his canopy. Murphy's law.

CHAPTER FORTY

Eliot's men weren't eager to bury their dead, killed by the militia the night before in the running battle behind the lava wall. Already putrefaction had set in, the carrionlike stench in the desert heat as offensive to the burial details as the sight of dismembered corpses after nocturnal animals had had their fill, half-eaten entrails spilled out and lying broiling and dirty under the sun's dying light.

"C'mon," the commander of the two Bradleys said. "Let's get to it before the sun goes down."

The most distressing sign of all—especially for those who, unlike the older members who had been in the Gulf, had never seen dead bodies before, at least not in this state—was the horror they experienced when they came across the remains of their fellow soldiers who'd run afoul of the claymore antipersonnel, antivehicular mines. The ground was stained with what was now hard, cracked brown blood fired under the relentless sun, with pieces of unidentifiable body parts strewn about, most of which had been gnawed to the bone by nocturnal scavengers or pecked clean by hawks, one of whom perched defiantly on a burned-out Bradley's cupola as if it had taken sole possession of the fighting vehicle. Appearances were deceptive, however, and externally the Bradley looked in fairly good condition, if one made allowances for the dust. The fire started by the militiamen when they'd charged the vehicle, and which had set some ammo off, had died. Still, the commander of the burial team warned his men that it was bound to be a pretty ugly sight inside if any of the concussed crew had been unable to get out. In the twilight, the long, serrated tops of sandstone-colored rock forming the lava-flow walls took on a golden hue, and for a brief but dazzling five minutes or so, Ship Rock looked like clusters of golden spires towering over a thousand feet into the blue that would soon be night.

Whether it was the ironic sense of deep serenity that enveloped the burial detail at this transcendent moment, or whether they were merely tired, the Bradley commander couldn't say, but as the first man up on the Bradley, taking advantage of what twilight remained, opened the hatch, there was an explosion so ferocious that it decapitated him. The air vibrated with shrapnel, his grotesque headless torso, spurting blood, actually standing up on the Bradley, fully erect, as if an invisible head was somehow still there, only to tumble a second later off the vehicle into a clump of sage. It was a turning point for both the veterans and the younger soldiers in Eliot's column: their realization that Americans could booby-trap their dead, to kill other Americans—something that hadn't happened since the first Civil War—driving home the fact of just how bloody and unforgiving the war had become.

Fraser and Reid heard the explosion, muffled somewhat by the lava wall and the western side of Ship Rock.

"What the hell was that?" Reid inquired.

Fraser shook his head. "Don't know."

"Maybe one of the Bradleys went up—fire in its belly not out yet."

Fraser shook his head again.

"Booby trap?" Reid suggested, though he didn't remember Fraser giving Benet, or anyone else for that matter, orders to booby-trap anything.

"No," Fraser answered, declaring, "I never told anyone to do that."

"That's just what I was thinking," said a relieved Reid, who'd been brought up to believe Americans didn't do such things. Japs, sure, Chinese in Korea, gooks in Vietnam, and towelheads in the Gulf, but not Americans. But Ray Fraser had seen it done before—on Butcher's Ridge, by the militia.

What might have been a relatively short delay for the men Eliot had sent to bury the dead near Ship Rock now turned into a longer mission for the burial party, namely to seek vengeance for their booby-trapped comrade who'd opened the hatch of the Bradley whose crew had been killed in the skirmish with the militiamen.

The C.O. of the federals' burial party didn't want to hang around Ship Rock, taking the view, as Eliot did, that a delay here could only give Jason Purdy's militia column west of them a better chance of eventually linking up with Hearn's motorcade. But sometimes short-term vengeance couldn't be denied if a C.O., like Eliot, was to maintain morale in the long term. And again the fact that Eliot's column was made up of volunteers, weekend soldiers who, much like Purdy's militiamen, knew one another in both civilian and military life, meant that close bonds had been formed between men from the same township, often the same street. Major Eliot well knew that this counted for so much in creating unit cohesion. Men who were from the same town, same block, would not break as quickly as men who were thrown together from all over the place. Because of this, Eliot realized that to ignore the profound shock his men had experienced upon discovering the bodies of their comrades shot down by the militia, further defiled by nocturnal predators from the desert, would be deleterious to his command. Yet he didn't want to waste valuable time on the burial with what was essentially a side issue to his main mission.

Eliot's answer to this dilemma was to leave one of the two Bradley Fighting Vehicles that made up the burial party with a squad of eight infantry to deal with what the Bradley com-

mander, Sergeant Norris, described as "those scumbags up
on the rock." The sole Bradley was nothing less than a
highly mobile heavy machine-gun post and TOW missile
launcher which, once the position of the men on the rock
was pinpointed, could be fired to blow them to smithereens.
There was no shortage of volunteers to make up the eight-
man infantry squad for the Bradley, their only beef being
that killing the "scumbags" with either a TOW blast or
25mm cannon would be too quick. Eliot seized upon this
complaint, pointing out that if the militiamen could be
rooted out alive, they might be useful for extracting intelligence about Purdy's column.

However, the eight men, who would be under Norris's
command so long as they were at Ship Rock, while agreeing
with Eliot about the usefulness of gaining intelligence from
the militiamen, had decided among themselves that they
weren't bringing in any militia prisoners to be questioned
politely and then sent to some POW camp where they might
spend the duration of the war.

It had by now been determined that there were in fact
only two militiamen on the rock. One of the federals suggested taking them both alive. "We shoot one," he said, "and
the other guy'll tell us what we want to know."

"That would make us as bad as they are," Sergeant Norris
pointed out.

"Oh, fuck it," said another outraged recruit, who'd had to
scoop up the innards of what had been a federal infantryman
and bury them. "I say no prisoners. Look what happened
here last night—that militia bastard surrendering, hands up,
the whole lot, and what happens? Our Bradley stopped, held
its fire, scumbags opened up on 'em. I'm sure as heck not
gonna believe any militia scumbag who puts up his hands.
Fuck him—he goes down, man."

"Ditto here," said another.

Sergeant Norris knew as they made their way to the base
of Ship Rock, using his infrared scope, that it didn't take a
Navajo tracker to follow the footprints of the two militia because the more compact sand depressed by the militiamen's

boots gave off a discernible heat signature on the green background. Within ten minutes Norris announced to his eight infantrymen inside the Bradley that he'd found the spot where they'd come up against the base of the fifteen-hundred-foot-high rock and begun their climb. He figured they wouldn't try a descent at night, even if they were equipped like him with infrared scopes or goggles. It would certainly be crazy to try to climb at night, even given the moonlight. Infrared wasn't *that* good. Norris told his men that he'd move the Bradley around to the eastern side of the rock and they'd wait till first light and "canonize," a bon mot that Norris thought was very clever, the "bastards." But if he could, he wanted to put the wind up the scumbags—break up their sleep. Get 'em on edge and wear them down.

For a second or two John Reid, taking the first watch, had glimpsed the Bradley coming from the southwest where he, Benet, Fraser, Levin, and the rest had clashed with the federals. After that it disappeared behind the massive rock. To the east of him, Reid could see Eliot's column reaching the hump of the long dip before the town of Shiprock, its relatively few lights twinkling like a clutch of stars. Fifteen minutes later Reid experienced a shock as he saw two batteries of 155mm towed artillery, six guns in all, preceded by two command Hummers, another six Hummers and ammo supply trucks coming up from the rear. His first impulse was to wake Fraser, but he hesitated. The federal column still had hours to go before it would meet up with Jason Purdy's. No sense in waking up Fraser until it was Fraser's watch, and, in accordance with Fraser's wish, he would let the federal column get well north of the rock before he transmitted their strength to Purdy himself.

Suddenly night became day, a flare and an arc of tracer tattooing the rock face a hundred feet above him, splintered debris showering down into his and Fraser's rock tub.

"Wha—" Fraser began, waking up at once, startled and confused.

"Federals!" Reid said.

Fraser pulled him down below the rim of the tub. "Keep your head down."

"They can see us!"

"No, they can't," Fraser said. "They're just peppering the general area. Want us to panic, make a move."

"What are we gonna do?"

"Right now, nothing."

Soon the firing died down. Cautiously, Fraser moved his infrared scope above their natural foxhole's ruin of ancient lava and looked down at the general area from where the tracer had come.

He could see nothing. "Bastards must've pulled back. That was twenty-five-millimeter tracer. They're using a Bradley. Trying to scare us."

"Well, they sure as hell scared me," Reid said.

"Point is," Fraser said, speaking softly, "not to show it. I mean not to do something stupid."

"Like what?"

"Like firing back tit for tat. They'll go quiet now, otherwise they'll be kept awake by their own noise."

"You sure?"

"No." He paused. "You grab some shut-eye. I'll stand watch."

Reid lay down on the hard, pockmarked lava, wide-awake. This wasn't how it was meant to go, he thought.

CHAPTER FORTY-ONE

Driving alone south from Las Vegas, Jimmy Sarna had no doubt he was doing what he told Karen was the right thing.

"So no one'll get hurt?" she'd asked.

"I didn't say that. You know what they say. 'You can't make an omelet without breaking eggs.' " She'd heard this before from the militia.

"So who are the eggs?" she'd pressed.

"Federals, of course."

"How about ordinary Joes like you?"

"Isn't complicated, Karen. Those who are against us are against us."

"Like anyone who disagrees with you?"

"Nope. Like I told you, anyone who is against us. Anyone who stands in our way."

"What's it going to prove?" she asked. Even though she didn't know exactly what *it* was, she told him that she knew it was going to involve a clash.

"Maybe not," Jimmy had told her. "Everybody does what they're told, won't even be a punch thrown."

"I don't want you getting hurt."

"I won't."

"*If* they don't do anything."

"They won't. Nobody wants to get hurt. You ask people, when other people aren't around, and you'll find a lot of 'em don't like the federals. Besides, we've talked ourselves silly

trying to get Washington to listen to us—give us more control over our own resources. Look at—"

Jimmy had stopped himself because he'd almost said,
"Look at Hoover Dam," instead of "Boulder Dam."

Now Jimmy saw the lake and the turnoff coming up to the
isolated log cabin by the shore where he was to meet his
other half in the project. He was glad Karen didn't know the
details, because then if, God forbid, something went wrong
and the federals came around, she could say with all honesty
that she didn't know. Or was he only kidding himself? What
else would the militia be doing, meeting at the southern end
of Lake Mead? Going fishing? But there were some things
between man and wife that each sensed were off limits,
bound to open up old wounds, things you knew but by an
unspoken agreement and in the little word games you played
to cover real intent you simply didn't talk about—like Karen
believed aliens had definitely come to earth and were among
us. For her, watching *The X-Files* was like going to church.
You messed with that and you'd find yourself on the maca-
roni and cheese dinner for a week.

They could agree on UFOs—no problem there. Militia all
over, especially in the southwestern states, knew about the
Phoenix Lights, for example, and that in New Mexico,
Colorado, Arizona, and Nevada black projects were going
on. Even commercial pilots, trained observers, professionals
who, though they wouldn't identify themselves because of
fear of being fired by the airlines they worked for, had seen
any number of UFOs, disks moving with incredible speed.
For Karen and a lot of other folk, these were alien UFOs.
For Jimmy and his ilk in the militia, the UFOs were experi-
mental federal projects—antigravity machines? Whatever
they were, the federal government was lying through its bu-
reaucratic teeth, and on that, he and Karen, like many others, had found common ground—a deep distrust of and
hostility to *all* federal enterprise.

A tall man in blue coveralls emerged from the log cabin,
and Jimmy could hear the mesh door slam shut.

"How ya doin'?" Jimmy shouted, turning his motor off. "Can you tell me how far it is to Boulder Dam?"

"You mean Hoover Dam?" said the other man, whose blue coveralls, Jimmy thought, were not a good idea.

"I like to call it Boulder," Jimmy said. He could see the man relax, his walk toward the RV more casual than when he'd come stiff-assed out of the cabin. Jimmy still didn't like the coveralls—made the guy look like he was ready for heavy work, which it was going to be, but he should've put on a pair of shorts or pants, like he'd come to Lake Mead, like most people, for the recreation. Jimmy was sure that Mike Hearn would sure as hell disapprove of blue coveralls. A small point, maybe, but the federals were alert to such things. Jimmy felt his chest tightening. It always did when he felt obliged to say something that might offend, but this was the biggest militia op ever in the Southwest, so he told the guy what he thought about the coveralls.

"I mean," Jimmy went on, "I'm no genius, but for a guy to turn up for a tour tomorrow in coveralls might look kinda strange."

"Where is it?" the man mumbled.

Jimmy, a little flushed, indicated the back of the RV. "It's in there."

"I know it's in there," the man replied. "Where exactly?"

"In a tank under the bed," Jimmy said.

The man mumbled something else.

"Say again?" Jimmy said politely.

"You have tubing?"

"Yeah, in the kitchen."

"There's been a hitch."

All right, Jimmy thought, now it's my turn not to answer. But his sense of urgency wouldn't allow it. "Hitch?"

"A guy from the Scorpions was supposed to help me get it ready but he's gone sick on us. 'Least that's what he told me."

"Chickened out?"

Coveralls shrugged, and it teed Jimmy off. Here he was

trying to be polite, get along, and all Coveralls could do was mumble and shrug at him.

"Well," Jimmy said, "my job was to deliver the stuff, and here it is. I'm expected back at the RV camp."

"Don't matter to me, but Hearn wants it there—" He glanced at his watch. "—in an hour."

"Well, I'm expected back at the RV camp."

"You're not listenin' to me," Coveralls said with surprising clarity. "I told you there's been a hitch. You and I are gonna be stirrers. Everything's been moved up for tonight." He was angry.

"Why not tomorrow?"

"Because Hearn's moved it up, that's why. I thought you'd been told."

"Tonight? No one told me. What am I, the friggin' gofer?"

"You gonna help me or not?"

"Oh, shit!" Jimmy said, suddenly more afraid than at any time in his life. Delivery of material was one thing, but hands-on was irrevocable. With delivery you could always say you were just delivering. Like a gun shop clerk, right? He sold the guns, but he didn't load the chamber. What was done with the gun was up to the shooter, not him.

"If you don't help me, Sarna, it's in the toilet."

Shit. The guy wasn't supposed to know his name, just the greeting about Boulder and Hoover. It seemed to Jimmy like everything was coming apart.

"So," Coveralls pressed. "I tell Mr. Hearn you won't help."

"I'll help, goddammit!"

"Drive the RV down by the lake, then back it right up to the semi. I'll get you a pair of coveralls."

Oh shit, Jimmy thought. You're in it up to your eyeballs.

Coveralls could see how upset Jimmy was, and in what was for him a generous moment, he sought to quiet Jimmy Sarna's fears. Besides, he didn't want Jimmy to freak out on him. Not now.

"Don't sweat it," he told Jimmy. "The six guys out of Las

Vegas designated to take the hard hat tour are already there. Went in earlier. There are a thousand places to hide in that place. It's huge. They're all set to help us the moment Hearn arrives."

"Help us? But we'll be in the car park."

"In the bus park," Coveralls corrected him.

"We'll still be in a parking lot. They're inside. What can they do to help us?"

"Hey, calm down. The guys inside are gonna help us unload. 'Less you want to do it all yourself."

Shit.

CHAPTER FORTY-TWO

In eastern Washington State it was not yet dark, and having let Orr and Brody rest up in the afternoon, Melvin and Alice Abrem were discussing what they should do with the two POWs. If the Abrems hadn't seen eye-to-eye on it much earlier in the day, they were now agreed on one thing: that the two POWs shouldn't be encouraged to stay any longer than necessary. The rule was to keep escapees moving along until, with a hundred dollars and whatever papers were needed, they were delivered back into the mainstream, where their anonymity stood a better chance than in isolated farmhouses. Melvin and Alice thought it was best if Melvin took both men on to the next safe house, up around Omak, around forty miles to the northwest.

Orr asked for their opinion about heading for the Canadian border.

"Not as strange as it seems," Melvin had said. "Anyone escapes from Camp Fairchild, all the authorities are notified, especially now with this Hearn fella causing trouble down south. You get across into Canada, you stay out of circulation for a while, the Canadian militia'll look after you. Then, when it's time, you cross back over. Our cops aren't lookin' for Americans coming back to the States. Lot o' guys during Prohibition used to go across into Canada when things got too hot for 'em in the States."

"I'm not a bootlegger," Orr told him.

"But you're tired, right? Need a place to build up your strength, give you time to think."

"I don't need time to think," Brody said. "I want to get back to my unit."

"Where's that?"

"North Dakota."

"Then don't try to do it on your lonesome from here. Not a direct line, I mean. Not from here in this weather. You'd be smart too if you made the loop through Canada." Melvin looked around at Alice, who told him it was time to get going.

"I don't want you out all hours of the night," she said.

Orr was surprised when Melvin told him he was going to take both of them to the next safe house. Eleen hadn't said anything about the safe houses looking after two escapees at a time. "Isn't that a bit risky?" Orr asked. "I mean, shouldn't we be separated? You know, one at a time?"

Alice was shaking her head. "I don't want Mel doing two runs a night in this weather. B'sides, people are nosy 'round here, just like they are everywhere. If they were to see Mel making two trips the same night, they'd start to wondering."

"It's okay with me," Brody said.

"Yeah," Orr said. "I was just making a—yeah, it's fine."

"Anything to get us farther away from Fairchild," Brody said. "Not that I don't like your chicken gumbo, Mrs. Abrem."

Orr could see she was pleased, and he felt awkward about bringing up the prohibition against moving two men at a time. It made him feel odd man out, as if he was a whiner, ungrateful for the help the Abrems were giving him and the risk they were taking, harboring fugitives. Maybe it was because he resented Brody showing up, as if the man from hut 4B had taken away, or at least split the attention of, the Abrems. Then again, Alan Orr was conscious of the jealous streak that had made life miserable for him since he was a child, a trait that as an adult he had tried hard to suppress. Or maybe, he thought, he was being too hard on himself. It was natural to feel on edge, with fears of being recaptured always on your mind.

Or was he resentful of the relative calm with which this Brody seemed to be accepting everything, telling Melvin during the gumbo feast that he, Brody, was relaxed about how and when he was taken to the next safe house? "I just go with the flow," Brody had said. One of the things that still bothered Al Orr was that he couldn't place Neil Brody in hut 4B. Every time he tried, Brody's bearded face would meld into all the other beards he'd seen in Camp Fairchild. And also eating away at Al Orr was another face, that of Browne, a federalist plant who, in return for the promise that his family would be looked after rather than pursued by federal officials, had told the previous commandant about "Archie," the tunnel. Of course, Orr knew that Brody might well be suspicious of *him* being a plant, set loose by Moorehead under some equally invidious kind of blackmail, to be passed from one militia-sympathetic household to another in order to blow the network of safe houses throughout the state.

Alice, less anxious seeing them leave than when they had arrived, one literally on the heels of the other, actually smiled and wished them well, passing them a large thermos of chicken gumbo, for which Alan Orr thanked her and over which Neil Brody gushed like a schoolboy on his first date. What bothered Orr most was that Brody had such a bonhomie attitude not more than twenty-four hours after his comrades had been machine-gunned to death—at least that was Brody's story—outside the camp. Or maybe Brody was the type who possessed the envious ability of being able to put the bad behind him immediately and get on with his life.

Melvin Abrem had left his station wagon running for a while, but even so, it was bitingly cold for the first half hour of the journey to Omak, Abrem trying to reach a compromise with the heater: too low and the windshield would fog up, too high and it was too stuffy. The last thing anyone on this trip wanted was to fall asleep. Miles to go.

Colonel Jason Purdy's column was about to undergo a radical change in strategy, one that Purdy himself had not contemplated until he heard the media reports, mainly those of CNN's Brian O'Keefe, warning—in spite of Freeman's request to the media not to go public—that Hearn's column had been sighted heading in the direction of Hoover Dam and Lake Mead, Nevada, and that the Nevada National Guard had been called out by the "decisive action" of the governor.

Purdy was no coward, as his record in the Gulf War showed. Neither was he a fool, and as anyone who could read a map would see, the situation had dramatically changed, what with the Nevada National Guard stepping into the ring. Only an idiot would willfully continue along the path of his original plan, and thus sandwich himself between hostile and larger forces. Along with the media bulletin about the Nevada National Guard, Purdy's receipt of Ray Fraser's recent radio message from Ship Rock, informing him that Eliot's force had been bolstered by the presence of two batteries of 155mm artillery—the big killer in wars—convinced him that a radical change in strategy was called for. He ordered his column to turn about, heading back east along Highway 64, or what he said the "damn defiant Indians" called the Navajo Trail.

Purdy's soldiers were at once stunned and relieved that Purdy for once was following the old and much admired military tactic of retreat being "the better part of valor." In this way, his men believed, Washington, D.C., wouldn't be pressed to unleash an air attack on the militia, a tactic that had so far been ruled out by the administration because of the humiliation that would follow with CNN footage of Americans bombing their own. In fact, the administration's reluctance to bomb or strafe large numbers of fellow Americans from the air had as much if not more to do with the belief that, like Hearn, Purdy had civilian hostages, the latter's existence something the militia would neither confirm nor deny, despite the media's best efforts to find out.

O'Keefe's report of the retreat of Purdy's column, aired every fifteen minutes on CNN's *Headline News*, had been met with audible sighs of relief in the White House. It was only at Freeman's HQ in California that the news was met with less than enthusiasm. Watching the broadcast, the volume up so as to override the concomitant noise of air conditioners, computers clacking, and the purr of laser printers, Freeman shook his head.

"That Purdy bastard is up to something," he said. "He's one of those shit stirrers from Four Corners. That's hard country and hard men. This is a tactical withdrawal if ever I've seen one."

"Possibly," Norton answered. "If he'd kept going westward, he would have been wedged between a rock and a hard place. Nevada National Guard to his front, Eliot coming up his rear. And that O'Keefe seemed pretty sure of—"

"He's sure of nothing," the general cut in. "Strikes me as a kid who's flying by the seat of his pants. Grab anything he can and run with it. You'll notice Marte Price didn't file a report about any goddamn retreat, and she's the leading pro in Vegas. O'Keefe's just a stringer. Marte would've unearthed anything important."

"Maybe the kid outgunned her?"

"Marte? With that pair of jugs on her? I doubt it. She's on a first-name basis with every man wherever she touches down."

"Yes, but stringers sometimes get a break, General."

"That's true. And sometimes they get bullshit fed to them. BS that a pro like Marte Price can smell at a hundred yards."

The general looked up at the TV screen and a photo of Jason Purdy, who had an unremarkable face, even blander since he'd shaved off a mustache.

"That Purdy son of a bitch," Freeman declared, "is up to something."

"An attack," Norton ventured, "on Eliot's flank."

"Hmm ... alert Eliot to the possibility. Last thing we need is more bad publicity."

We might spare a thought for the men, Norton thought, never mind the PR.

"And more casualties," Freeman added, as if reading Norton's mind. "Like those ALERTs we've lost and ..." He paused, looking up at the map of the Southwest. "Norton—Brentwood and company are in transit as we speak. Correct?"

"Yes, sir."

"What's touchdown time for Brentwood's boys?"

Norton glanced at his watch. "Twenty minutes, possibly thirty, depending on local air currents."

"Cloud still over the southern part of Lake Mead?"

"Still there, sir."

"What's its ceiling?"

"Three to four thousand feet."

"But it is clear between the top of the dam and the underside of the cloud cover?"

"As of ten minutes ago, yes, sir. We'll be getting an update anytime now."

CHAPTER FORTY-THREE

Jimmy Sarna had helped Coveralls unload the bags of airtight-sealed three-by-two-foot bags into the semi trailer, in the dim Coleman light, and by the time he'd finished, his brow was covered in beads of sweat. He could feel the itch of perspiration running down his neck. He didn't mind unloading his RV—that was part of the job he'd agreed to—but the idea of actually going in the semi took him that much closer to the final act of having everything ready for Hearn, whose motorcade, he knew, was now pulled off the highway somewhere on the Arizona side, waiting for the final dash to the dam.

The six militiamen posing as tourists, who had taken the hour-long hard hat tour, were mingling in a crowd of other sightseers. While passing through the enormous rooms, or "galleries," as they were called—man-made caverns that housed everything from the massive hydroelectric generators fed by the water rushing down through huge thirty-foot-diameter steel pipes to the brutal aspect of the gigantic shaft gallery and the more sedate pastels of the control room—the six militiamen, now wearing blue coveralls, had easily secreted themselves in several of the myriad nooks and crannies available in the maze of steel and concrete that made up the more than seven-hundred-foot-high dam.

Once Hearn knew that the semi had arrived on the two-lane road atop the crest of the dam, he would move in with one ambulance—two militiamen, Toro and Montoya, accompanying him—and use hostages Dana Teer and Beverly Malkin as a shield. While he was waiting for the signal from Toro, who was now using an infrared scope to signal the moment the semi was approaching the crest, Hearn spoke to him over the walkie-talkie. He told Toro that when he saw the semi, he was to go get the doc and the nurse and to tape a shotgun's muzzle to each of their necks, using the surgical tape from the kit they'd brought for Vance.

Toro saw the semi, signaled Hearn, and walked off to get Teer and Malkin. Montoya thanked Hearn.

"What for?"

"For letting me come along—for finally trusting me."

Hearn never shifted his gaze from the crest of the dam, a long, gentle curve between Arizona on his right and Nevada, across the canyon, on his left. His tone was dismissive. "Yeah, well, it's come time, I guess, to put you to work." As he was speaking, two militiamen from one of the other ambulances, dressed in coveralls and wearing security badges in the manner of the dam's night-shift personnel, squashed into the back of Hearn's ambulance.

"What do you want me to do?" Montoya asked.

"You're a big, strapping boy," Hearn said. "We need you and some of the guys to help roll some barrels in."

"Barrels?" Montoya said.

"Yeah. What's the matter? You deaf?"

Montoya heard Toro coming up behind, the jackboots he habitually wore shucking gravel on the highway's shoulder. When he turned, he could vaguely make out a clump of three people, including Teer and Malkin, a yoke of plaster tape about their necks, a double-barreled twelve-gauge at the junction of the Y-shaped yoke so that if the gun went off, it'd kill both of them.

"How about the security guard?" Toro inquired.

"Leave him here with the motorcade. He's our guys' insurance while we're at the dam."

Through the night vision scope, against its luminous green background, Hearn could see the whitish block of heat formed by the semi truck's cabin and engine, and a white rectangle of the semi's trailer sliding into view behind it, less distinct in the scope because it was not as hot as the engine and cabin. In the cabin he could make out two men, one of whom he knew must be Coveralls, the other another militiaman. Hearn and Coveralls were in what the militia called "Sanyo range," referring to the remarkably secure Sanyo 917 cordless phone, its digitally coded spreading spectrum impervious to anyone trying to listen in. But the perennially suspicious Hearn, always aware of the rate of technological breakthroughs, would not talk in plain language, using allusions instead. When he asked, "Ready to roll?" he wasn't asking Coveralls if he was ready to drive, but whether he was ready to roll in the barrels.

"Yes."

With that, Hearn, Montoya, and Toro moved off in the lead ambulance toward the dam. Montoya was still unarmed, so he guessed that the ever-cautious Hearn wasn't yet ready to trust him unconditionally, which, in all fairness, Montoya understood. He was still wondering what he was supposed to do if, contrary to Hearn's explicit instructions, the Nevada National Guard had sent sharpshooters to the lake's edge behind the dam, or even atop the four intake towers, two on the Nevada side, two in Arizona's water, the boundary between the states running straight through the middle of the dam and the lake. Unknown to Montoya, however, Hearn had already searched the lake's near shores with the infrared scope; a coyote and some kind of waterborne rodent were the only heat signatures he saw.

Halfway down to the crest, Montoya driving, Hearn, still looking through the night scope, uttered a curse and switched the Sanyo to the most frequently used military channel. But before he spoke, he told Montoya to brake. His speech was articulate, brooking no misinterpretation, his tone hard as flint. "Listen, you federal assholes. I see boats, three of them, two hundred yards from the dam's crest. You tell those fuckers to get lost, and fast."

There was a surge of static, a confused mélange of voices

beyond the phone's five-mile range, or were they trying to patch him through?

"Nevada National Guard here. Major Innes. To whom am I speaking?"

"Hearn. Get those fucking boats away, *now*—or you're gonna have one dead lady on your hands." Now there was no static, the National Guard commander coming in loud and clear.

"Ah, Mr. Hearn, those boats are empty, I believe. Just moored to the lake's edge by some tour—"

"Move the boats, asshole! You've got five minutes."

"We can't possibly move them in—"

"Four minutes, fifty seconds!"

"There's no one in them. I—"

"Prove it! Toss a grenade in each one. Four minutes and thirty seconds."

"Jesus Christ!" Innes said. "We don't have time to go out and— Stay on the channel."

Brentwood, Lewis, Salvini, Thomas, and wrestler-chested Finn, all at plus or minus ten thousand feet, still had a little over eight minutes to go until, providing they could slip under the blanket of cloud that hung over the southern end of the lake, they would reach the curving, two-lane highway that formed the dam's crest. So when Brentwood, through his night vision goggles, saw white-hot streaks flickering momentarily like a weak neon tube hidden within the cloud cover below, and heard the faint yet distinct rattle that experience told him and the other ALERTs was machine-gun fire, he felt his heart start to race and his gut constrict. How in hell did they know he and the others were descending north of the dam? And once he and the other four broke through the cloud to slip into the dam, would they suffer a combat parachutists' nightmare, to be descending under fire? But they were going in, and Brentwood, like the others, knew better than to break radio silence. They were committed and that was all there was to—

There was a blossom of light in the cloud below them,

followed by a shock wave of sound several seconds later as one of the boats, its gasoline tank punctured by the white streaks of incendiary tracer fire, exploded. Major Innes, not having had the time to send men out to move the anchored boats, had ordered them shot up to allay Hearn's suspicions. A little over a minute later there were more white streaks in the low cloud, but this time not so much noise as the second and third boats erupted, burning to the waterline, casting frantic dancing patterns of orange flames across the black water.

Brentwood's five-man team was now six minutes from what they hoped would be touchdown, and fearful that their parafoils would be picked up in the reflected firelight.

"That's more like it!" Hearn told the federal major. "Now pull your men back from the lakeshore and away from the dam!"

"Roger that," said an obedient Innes, or at least an ostensibly obedient Innes, who less than fifteen minutes before had dispatched six swimmers across the lake to the Arizona side only two hundred yards from the remaining four militia ambulances. And when Innes saw Hearn, Montoya, and Toro with both women, he made a fatal mistake, for in the confusion that invariably attaches itself to such hostage situations, Innes had been told that there had initially been three hostages in the ambulance motorcade instead of four, and knowing that a security guard had been shot in cold blood two days before, he concluded that there were now no hostages remaining in the motorcade. His swimmers, equipped with M-16s and grenades, which they had floated across via black buoys that couldn't be seen against the dark water, were preparing to attack the four remaining ambulances in the motorcade, which, with Hearn and the others at the dam with the two women, Innes believed were hostage free.

Touchdown for Brentwood and his ALERTs was now four minutes away. Unfortunately, the shooting following Innes's order to his troops to open up on the three now sinking boats had been heard up and down the lake, Jimmy Sarna's wife panic-stricken that Jimmy might have been caught up in it. Residents' telephoned reports of gunfire at the lake were interpreted by the assembled press in Las Vegas and Nellis Air Force Base, seven miles north of Las Vegas, as proof that hostilities had begun in earnest, that the earlier need for security was now negated. Freeman, also believing his ALERTs were now in combat, ordered a CH-7 Chinook helo in toward the lake with instructions to stay out of range of small arms fire but to hover behind the protective barrier of the hills on the Nevada side, ready for a quick extraction of the ALERTs if necessary.

Jimmy Sarna and Coveralls were now in the semi's trailer, and Jimmy was perspiring again, this time from fear, as he helped to roll out a half dozen of the sealed forty-four-gallon drums down the semi's ramp. The two militiamen from Hearn's ambulance, and Montoya, began transferring the barrels toward the dam's entrance, where one of four militiamen emerged to help Jimmy Sarna and the semi's driver to unload large black rectangular plastic bags from the semi, marked as MOSS. Another militiaman was holding one of the control room shift hostage, a sawed-off shotgun taped to his neck in the same way as Dana Teer and Beverly Malkin were being held by Toro to guarantee safe passage of the drums and bags to the control room.

In the control room, two members of the dam's eight-to-four watch, occupying two of the high-backed blue upholstered chairs, were gagged and bound, sitting in obvious discomfort, their wrists tied behind them with duct tape, forcing them to lean uncomfortably forward. A militiaman dropped two tire levers on the floor. Hearn pointed to the trussed-up controllers. "Get them outa here!" he barked.

The first of the black drums was rolled in, Toro standing in front of the huge control panel, which dwarfed him. He jerked Dana Teer and Beverly Malkin to a stop, the nurse pale with fear, thinking the sudden pull on the shotgun meant it was going to go off. Toro, his right hand on the

twelve-gauge, his finger hard on the trigger guard, was looking up like an airport traveler, watching the new state-of-the-
art TV security monitors. He grinned and gave a little wave
with his left hand. Ha, ha! The drums kept rolling in until
they lined the control-faced wall like so many black sentries.
By the time he was finished, Jimmy Sarna and Coveralls
were dripping with perspiration, the two of them ordered out
by Hearn, who told them to go join the motorcade.

"Will there be room for all of us?" one of the drum rollers
inquired, meaning Jimmy Sarna and Coveralls.

"Yeah," Hearn answered sharply. "Now get a move on.
Toro, you stay here with the two women. Montoya, hand me
one of those two tire levers; you use the other one. All
twelve barrels have to be opened."

"Right!" Montoya said, levering open the end drum on his
side of the control room. As the lid was pried off, its teeth
clasps giving way, Montoya instinctively jerked his head
away from the foul-smelling mixture, then made what up to
that point must have been the dumbest remark he could remember. "You need this much stuff to poison the lake?"

"What in hell are you talking about?" Hearn said. "This
isn't poison, you dork. It's slurry—fertilizer and diesel fuel,
ammonium nitrate plus." Levering open another drum,
Hearn added, "We got three times the amount Tim used."

"Tim?" Montoya said, prying off another lid.

"Yeah," Hearn growled, working hard, having gotten the
lid off the seventh drum. "Timothy McVeigh."

"My God!" Dana Teer said before she could stop herself.
"You mean—"

"Shut your mouth!" Toro said, jerking the shotgun stock
back like a choke chain.

"Yeah," Hearn continued, ignoring the doctor's outburst.
"Three times what he used on the Murrah Building. Gonna
be quite the little bang!"

CHAPTER FORTY-FOUR

Brentwood's five were a minute from touchdown, each man coming out of the gradual angle of his glide approach, pulling down hard on either left- or right-hand toggle to effect a tight rotation, or "screw" descent, beneath the crescent-shaped canopy chute. Each of the five lowered his twenty-foot-long, rope-tethered, eighty-pound pack, containing their weapons, ammo, and emergency medical and rations supply. With the dam's crest sliding up at them through their night vision goggles, they braked, pulling both toggles at once, a maneuver that would allow them to virtually step down onto the crest with no more jarring than hopping off a slowly moving train, if done correctly.

With thirty feet to go they heard a series of explosions that sounded like fireworks. They were under the cloud, and saw gun flashes a hundred yards or so up the road on the Arizona side of the dam's crescent, where the National Guard swimmers were attacking the four ambulances. There was a lot of yelling and screaming, the militiamen quickly returning fire.

Finn was the only one of the ALERT team who didn't see the firefight, his four comrades touching down after their packs with a balletlike deftness worthy of Baryshnikov. As Finn braked, a sudden gust coming from the lake behind the dam swept him hard into the Nevada-side intake tower and concussed him, despite his helmet. He went limp beneath his canopy like a stricken bird, his pack, having preceded him, dragging him under the black water.

Beverly Malkin had seen many of the worst of the trauma cases brought into Phoenix's Holy Rosary Hospital, but now, with the crackle of the firefight going on outside, and her realization that the remaining security guard in the ambulances must be dead, she began sobbing uncontrollably.

"Shut up!" shouted Toro, who, like his two hostages, was listening to the crackle and rattle of machine gun and other small arms fire.

Norton, meanwhile, as duty officer at Freeman's HQ, was listening in on the Nevada National Guard frequency and cursing the commander for having jumped the gun, not getting it straight that the militia still had one Holy Rosary security guard in the ambulances. Now that the fight was joined and the element of surprise lost, Norton thought, he had to advise Freeman to send in the Chinook from Nellis for an emergency ALERT extraction.

"I concur," Freeman said rather formally, a sure sign that he was not amused by the National Guard's intercession. "That stupid son of a bitch Innes. Oughta be drawn and quartered. He'll be lucky if he ends up Corporal Innes after this."

Norton wasn't listening, having ordered the communications operator to signal Brentwood that the CH-47 helo would be standing by on the Nevada side in the next eleven minutes, for evacuation.

"Copy that," Brentwood said tersely, having just unlaced himself from the canopy. Grabbing his weapon, he flicked off the safety and did a quick head count. One of his men was missing. Salvini was by his side, his Vibram soles noiseless on the crest's cement road.

"It's Finn," Salvini told Brentwood. "Looks like he went into the drink."

"You see him hit?"

"No."

"All right. Do a quick check. Have a look over the side."

By then Lewis and Thomas were running toward Brentwood from the Nevada side of the dam's crest. "No Japs on the crest!" Lewis reported. "They've got to be inside."

"None in the semi either," Thomas said.

"Let's go," Brentwood said. Salvini, now coming up the rear, had failed to see the pinpoint of light that would have been visible if Finn had pulled the inflatable tab on his Mae West.

The four ALERTs, in the stop-rush-stop of commandos covering one another, passed through the main door and lucked out, or so they thought as they saw one of the trussed-up employees rolling frantically about like a beached whale. Aussie Lewis had sense enough not to rip the duct tape off the man's mouth, and went as slowly as urgency would allow. Nevertheless the man winced in pain.

"Sorry, bud."

"It's—" He gasped for more air. "They're in the control room, I think. It's not poisoning the water they're up to. They're gonna blow the dam."

Brentwood looked questioningly across at Lewis, the explosives expert on the team. "Aussie?"

"You know what he's using?" Lewis asked the man.

The man shook his head. "A lot o' barrels being rolled in. 'Bout ten of 'em. Stank pretty bad."

"Like what?"

"Diesel. I hate—"

"Probably ammonium nitrate and fuel slurry," Lewis told Brentwood. "But this sucker is over 650 million tons of cement. That Murrah Building in Oklahoma City was a grocery stand compared to this. This is like a whole city compressed into—"

"Shush!" It was Brentwood. Someone was coming from the direction of the control room. Brentwood gave the hand signal to disperse and hide.

Seeing Dana Teer and the nurse whose name he couldn't recall coming through the doorway from the interior of the dam, the shotgun forming the stem of the sticky plaster Y behind their heads, Brentwood knew that any precipitous move would mean their death. Suddenly, Toro jerked them back, the militiaman either hearing or sensing that something was amiss.

"What's the matter?" It was Hearn's voice in the rear. He carried the radio remote control switch, Montoya behind him, the tire iron he'd used to open the drums still in his hand. Toro's eyes moved momentarily away from the hostages immediately in front of him as he turned to warn Hearn. Montoya's police training and experience as a sheriff kicked in then. Abreast of Hearn, Montoya struck with the tire iron, taking Hearn down. With his other hand he got his right thumb behind the shotgun's trigger as he shoved the shotgun's barrel ahead, forward of the two women's heads, and meanwhile brought the tire iron around, smashing it into Toro's hand. The shotgun went off inches from the two hostages' heads, its heat wash searing Nurse Malkin, who was now hysterical as well as deaf. Toro, having let go of the gun, screamed in pain, the tire iron having broken three fingers of his right hand.

By now, Hearn had somewhat recovered. He managed to tackle Montoya from behind. Grabbing the shotgun, Hearn pulled the two women back, screaming, "Stop or I'll fire—stop!" forcing the four ALERTs to freeze, a kill shot impossible in the melee. The two hostages were so close to Hearn that the slightest movement would convulse the Nazi's trigger finger, even if they hit him. "Put your weapons down or I'll do 'em," he yelled. "Honest to Christ I'll do 'em!"

"Easy," Brentwood cautioned him. "Easy."

"Easy—fuck you! Put your weapons down and take off your goggles. You!" He was yelling at Salvini. "Call in a chopper. Parking lot thirteen, Arizona side. Now!"

"We don't have—" Salvini began.

"I can fucking *hear* one, you moron! And I want it down here *now* or I'll do one of these two. Get on to it!"

Salvini shot a glance at Brentwood, who gave him a nod. "Go ahead! Call 'em in."

"Toro!" Hearn shouted.

"Yeah?"

"Get their weapons and their goggles. No, no, walk around me. Watch 'em! Don't get between us." On the marble floor, Montoya was groaning.

"Shut the fuck up!" Hearn said, giving the sheriff a vicious side kick to the head.

"Helo's coming in!" Salvini told Hearn.

"Fuckin' better be."

There was a mad gleam in Hearn's eyes. It had been touch and go there for a second, but he'd won. He was still in charge. Toro had an armful of I-COW guns. "What'll I do with these?" he asked stupidly, his right hand bleeding from Montoya's blow. Outside they could hear the National Guard's attack on the motorcade coming to a climax. "Hearn, what'll I—"

"What d'you think?" Hearn shouted at him. "Throw 'em over the fucking side on our way out." Suddenly the lights flickered and went out, the result of a cable brought down during the National Guard–militia shootout.

Swapping one of the four ALERTs' night vision goggles for his monocular night vision scope, which he pocketed, Hearn now had the clear advantage. Toro also grabbed NVGs, then dumped the I-COWs over the dam's downstream wall. Their clatter down the seven-hundred-foot face seemed to last minutes as Hearn, with the two women and Toro, made his way toward the parking lot.

Toro ran forward and climbed into the Chinook's cargo bay, the helo manned by only the pilot, copilot, and crew chief. Toro was watching Hearn approach with the two women when he saw a heat blur in his night vision goggles, the shape of a fat man moving awkwardly but determinedly toward the helo.

It was Finn, who, having come to as he sank into the lake, had managed to pull the CO_2 cartridge tag after all, inflating his Mae West. It now made him look obese in Toro's NVGs, but failed to activate the light, its bulb smashed to pieces by his impact with the water intake tower. Despite his confusion, Finn had run toward the helo, thinking it had been called in by Brentwood for extraction of the hostages.

"Get inside!" Toro said, waving a gun at him.

"What?" Finn began, only dimly realizing now that the man with the two women was no ALERT or other federal, but merely someone who didn't like him and who had a 9mm Beretta to his throat. Finn began to climb into the Chinook, water still streaming from him, the crew chief moving forward to help him.

"Stay away!" Toro told the chief.

"I was only trying to—"

"Sit down and be quiet!" Toro said, then took over shotgun duty from Hearn, forcing the two women farther into the rear of the Chinook as Hearn dragged himself aboard.

"Take her up!" Hearn shouted, and the chopper began to rise. Hearn allowed himself a grin of satisfaction as he saw the four ALERTs standing impotently down on the crest's curving roadway, looking up at the fleeing Chinook.

Hearn was shouting something at Toro above the *wokka-wokka* of the CH-47, the Nazi obviously untroubled by those he'd left behind, including Vance, who would have understood the harsh no-holds-barred necessity.

"What'd you say?" Toro bellowed.

"I said, now for the frosting on the cake!" And with that, Hearn pressed the remote.

The very air seemed to shift as the shock wave of the blast that utterly demolished the control room and caused adjacent galleries to cave in was felt high above the dam, punching the chopper hard to the left. Hearn, who through the NVGs was able to see the effluent of cement dust and smoke pouring out of the ventilator shafts, knew he'd pulled off the perfect militia sabotage—no broken dam as such, no godawful flood from here to the Gulf of Mexico killing thousands, destroying millions of hectares of crops, but a dam with its guts ripped out, its control center, its brain, atomized by what Hearn gleefully referred to as a "Timothy McVeigh special." Hearn gestured for Finn to move to the helo doorway. Suspecting the worst, Finn refused.

"Do it!" Hearn shouted. "Or I'll shoot you!" Hearn held

up his 9mm Glock, motioning Finn to the doorway. "Do it or I'll have some fun with the ladies."

Finn looked into the dimly lit rear section of the Chinook. The women were traumatized, Beverly Malkin's face frozen in shock, Dana Teer's expression evidencing more life, but she was trying desperately to swallow.

"You're such a bastard," Finn told Hearn.

Hearn shot him point-blank in the face. The commando was thrown back against the doorjamb, hands cupped to his face as he fell out, his agonizing cry quickly lost, whipped away by the slipstream. The crew chief's eyes bulged as if they were about to come out of his skull. "Jesus Christ!"

"Now you know," Hearn bellowed at him, pointing the Glock at him. "Don't fuck around with Mikey Hearn. You sky jockeys do exactly what I say. Understand?"

The chief could only nod. He'd been in the Gulf War and Haiti, but hadn't seen anything as brutal as this.

"Now," Hearn shouted. "You tell one of your drivers to come here."

The crew chief stared at him, terrified.

"Nah," Hearn said. "I'm not gonna shoot him. Need to tell him where we're going, right?"

The chief nodded.

"And I don't want any shit about you people running out of gas. If we need gas, we'll get it. Got it?"

"Yeah—yes, sir."

"Good, now bring me a chart of northern Arizona. And quick!"

The Nevada National Guardsmen had overrun the ambulances parked on the Arizona side of the dam. There was only one militia prisoner—the remainder, including Vance, were dead—and the sole prisoner, a man who, the press were told, was the rebel captain Lucky McBride, would have been dead too—something not divulged to the media—except for the fact that he'd been wounded, which was noted, and by then there were too many witnesses to condone shooting him again.

Brentwood and his men looked like they'd been rolled in gray flour, their flak jackets and faces covered in concrete dust blown up out of the wrecked control center that had fallen like volcanic ash.

Major Innes told Brentwood that several of his men had seen what looked like a body dumped from the Chinook above the eastern shore of the lake and he'd sent a squad to investigate.

Everything remained in darkness, the entire southwestern grid out of Hoover Dam knocked out. The militia had unmistakably flexed their muscle. The warning was clear: Do as we say or suffer more of the same.

The White House's response was just as unequivocal. In the President's words, "We will not succumb to terrorism!"

CHAPTER FORTY-FIVE

West of Danville, passing through the Colville Indian Reservation in north-central Washington, the windshield wipers fighting in the snowstorm, Melvin Abrem spotted the eyes of a coyote loping across the snow-buried road. "Sign of good luck," Brody said, riding in the passenger seat of Abrem's station wagon.

"Never heard that one before," Abrem said.

"I made it up," Brody confessed good-naturedly. Abrem was leaning well forward, almost against the steering wheel, anxious about not letting the car wander off to the high snowbanked shoulder, his station wagon having a definite pull to the right.

Alan Orr was sitting quietly in the backseat, watching the road, shifting his focus every now and then before the falling snow coming at them like tracer mesmerized him into a headache. And every few minutes he checked the rearview mirror. Though he didn't expect many cars up in the rolling northern reaches of the state, he would have almost welcomed another pair of headlights as evidence that there was someone else in the world. On the other hand, the snow would slow down any patrols the federals might have launched out of Spokane, now far to the east of them. And though it was letting up some, Abrem said it would be another hour before they reached the safe house, the exact location of which he wouldn't reveal lest they were unlucky, Brody's coyote sighting notwithstanding. What Brody and Orr didn't know, they couldn't tell, should they be captured and interrogated.

Brody asked Abrem if he could turn on the radio. Abrem nodded, concentrating on a small bridge ahead that looked particularly narrow, leaving, as he put it, "nary spitting distance" either way. Brody was unsuccessful with the radio, picking up only crackling static and occasional surges of a talk show out of Canada, the Seattle broadcasts shut down by the Cascade Range.

"Anyone for chicken gumbo?" Brody asked enthusiastically.

"No, thanks," Abrem said, intent on crossing the bridge.

"How 'bout you, Al?"

"Not for me," Orr said, knowing he should have thanked Brody for the offer; but he couldn't—or wouldn't.

He found Brody's optimism off-putting. Here he'd planned a gutsy escape, *mano a mano,* as it were, while Brody had had the comfort of a group, if he'd really been in the group, as he'd said. Besides, there was in Orr's mind something disproportionate about Brody's cheeriness—the coyote quip, his munching of the saltine crackers and noisy slurping of soup. He had no right to be so damned relaxed. Hadn't he heard what the federals did when they caught you? They asked you questions about who helped you in and out of the camp, and if you didn't answer, or if they didn't like your answer, the bastards shot you on the spot, especially after the news reports, infuriatingly vague though they were, of some skirmish between federal National Guard troops and militia around some place called Shiprock, which, Orr wasn't certain, was somewhere in either New Mexico or Arizona—somewhere it was damn hot anyway.

Colonel Jason Purdy's column, having retreated beneath a fibrous white moonlit sky from the possibility of a fight on two fronts—any military commander's nightmare—was approaching Chinle Wash, which, on the rare occasion it received rain, flowed into the Colorado. For the first time in years, because of El Niño, Purdy was seeing massive storm clouds gathering over the wash, extending from the Navajo Trail fifty miles south over Canyon de Chelly National Monument, the massive three-pronged canyon area immediately east of the small Navajo town of Chinle. Purdy's thoughts were not about Canyon de Chelly, however, but on how best to attack and, if possible, annihilate Eliot's federal column, now two hours away to the east in the desert foothills of the Chuska Mountains. The sitrep from Fraser and Reid at Ship Rock, fifty miles northeast of him, revealed that Eliot's column contained two towed artillery batteries, each consisting of six big guns. Purdy knew that if he and his men were to make a name for themselves and for the militia in general—badly needed now that Hearn's motorcade, according to ABC radio reports from Las Vegas, had been wiped out except for Hearn, Toro, and his hostages—then their first order of business was to deal with the federals' artillery. Artillery was and always had been the great killer. It wrought more damage in most armed clashes than any other weapon, including bombing, a fact that Purdy believed Washington, D.C., well knew, and was prepared to use, even while avoiding aerial bombardment, in deference to American public opinion.

In the predawn light, Purdy called his platoon commanders together. Everything, he told them, would depend on the speed of their four-by-fours and the militiamen's ability

to "shoot straight while in the saddle." This was his unambiguous reference to the seemingly endless hours that his
"pickup army," as he called his two-hundred-man company,
practiced fighting on the move, employing techniques such
as "ahead aiming" to enable men to shoot down moving as
well as stationary targets. And of course there was room for
deception. To this end, Purdy ordered his intelligence officer,
Lieutenant Cooper, to undertake deception measures within a
half hour of his column's estimated visual sighting of Eliot's
column, on the understanding that visual sighting in poor
visibility due to dust storms might not occur until the two
forces were almost upon one another—a matter of minutes.
Cooper, a Gulf War veteran, was a religious man, and he
prayed fervently that what had been strong gusts of wind
would subside into nothing more than gentle zephyrs blowing across the enormity of the red butte- and mesa-domi-
nated desert with only an occasional tumbleweed rolling
across the pickup army's front. On the other hand, a clear
desert would allow both the militia and Eliot's federals a
longer visible window of opportunity in which to act.

"Half a dozen of one," Cooper's sergeant opined, "and six
of the other."

Cooper, recalling his own intel reports to Purdy about
Eliot, pondered the fact that Eliot was a civil bureaucrat by
profession. Could he, Cooper, advise Purdy that Eliot's most
probable tactic would be a frontal attack with possible flank-
ing movements? Cooper decided not to say anything because, on the basis of evidence he couldn't explain, he had a
sixth sense that a "rules are rules" man during the workaday
week might well become a freewheeling commander in
combat, the very opposite of his normal self, as some people
are in their extracurricular activities—such as making war.
Perhaps combat was Eliot's outlet, and the militia could expect unorthodox tactics befitting Douglas Freeman, who in
any case was probably overseeing Eliot's strategy as his column crossed from the desert sage of New Mexico to the
desert brush of Arizona. But no matter what Eliot might do,
Cooper knew the militia would have to be quicker in their

reaction time. Even with computers to quickly figure out elevation, wind direction, humidity, propellent charge, and gun barrel wear and tear, it would take a highly trained federal gun crew from twenty to twenty-four minutes to set up their towed 155mm howitzers. But once set up, each of the federal gunners, twelve in all, backed up by their loaders and gun bunnies, would be able to deliver three ninety-pound high-explosive shells a minute—one every five seconds if the batteries fired in sequence. Cooper gave orders to "prepare for tails," and every man instantly became a scrounger. Dried animal bones, sagebrush weighted down with stones, and cacti were cut down or lassooed by a few would-be cowboys, piled in the back of the trucks, and stuffed into every available space next to TOW missile mounts and heavy machine guns.

"We use 'em now?" one overanxious militiaman asked Cooper.

"No," Cooper said. "Don't worry. I'll tell you when."

"I'm not worried," the man lied.

Cooper looked out on the desert. The wind seemed to be picking up a bit, or was it his imagination? Before combat, you were naturally stressed, worried about everything from your wife or girlfriend to the children, your nerves, the weather, and just how dedicated the enemy might be. The National Guard units were entirely voluntary, so they must be willing. Hell, the militia was voluntary too. Control your breathing, that's what Purdy always emphasized: "It's amazing what proper breathing can do for you. Gives you a sense of control that you never thought possible. Relax." Relax? Cooper thought. Fucking artillery would chop you to pieces. Drive like hell, that was the only way. Attacking or defending, drive like hell. Either that or dig a hole so deep it'd reach China.

When Cooper drew abreast in his truck—Purdy didn't want to use radio unless absolutely necessary—he saw that Purdy had put on his Rommel gear, a high, peaked cap, which he'd achieved by bending a piece of a wire coat hanger inside the peak, and desert goggles. The wind *was* picking up.

"How we doin' with tails?" Purdy asked.

"We've got enough stuff now," Cooper yelled.

"Very well," Purdy replied without turning his head, his gaze fixed eastward. He was tempted to break radio silence to Fraser and Reid at Ship Rock, because it might prove crucial to his tactics if the federals' guns were short-barreled 155mms; the M-198 having a range of eighteen miles, the M-109A eleven miles. For a moment Purdy glanced skyward, estimating the speed of the clouds, dark battalions of them moving in from the west. The one thing he was relying on was that the federals were, for the moment, ironically, handicapped by their most destructive weapon—the guns. The federal column's speed was regulated by how fast the guns, each weighing up to seven tons, and the trucks towing them could move. Certainly they couldn't move at anywhere near the speed of his own pickups.

What Purdy feared most was that Eliot's ammo-laden trucks were carrying beehive rounds packed with thousands of steel darts, which, if the guns ambushed his militia, would be fired at point-blank range.

CHAPTER FORTY-SIX

In Manhattan, Wesley Knox looked up appreciatively at the morning sky. It was clear and cold, wind cups on the anemometers at LaGuardia and Kennedy hardly moving, the weatherman said, so slight was the breeze.

Perfect. The city that never sleeps was picking up its tempo, the crowds surging, reading the moving neon lights:

MASSIVE DAM EXPLOSION IN SOUTHWEST THREATENS SOUTH-
ERN CALIFORNIA . . . MILITIA CLAIMS RESPONSIBILITY . . .
BOMB THREATS CLOSE LAS VEGAS AIRPORT, LAGUARDIA, JFK,
AND PHOENIX . . . MILITIA BELIEVED RESPONSIBLE.

And it struck Knox how much information people take
from the media unquestioningly, and how important it
would be for the militias to grab the TV and radio stations
immediately—and the newspapers. Sure, people pretended
they didn't believe anything they read in the newspapers or
saw on TV, then turned around and told you something or
other happened, and if you doubted it, they started quoting
the media: "I just saw it on TV," "I read it in the papers," or
"It's on the radio." Wesley Knox was on the toilet when JFK
was killed. And when his twin teenage brother yelled out,
"Hey, man, they shot Kennedy, they shot the President,"
Knox said, "Good," tearing off another piece of toilet paper
so violently it set the whole roll unraveling. "One less
honky." Everybody weepin' and wailin' in the streets, black
folks too, bawlin' their eyes out 'cause the honky President
was dead. And white supremacy—man, it just kept rollin'
along. And never mind Colin Powell. Man, he didn't even
look black—from Jamaica. As Knox told his black militia
brothers, Powell looked like "a honky with a nice tan. He
ain't gonna make a difference—just make the whiteys feel
good pretendin' they support a black man. Way to make a
change, brother, is the big move—somethin' spectacular."

As Knox left Grand Central, the black transit cop at the
turnstile asked, "What you got in the bag, brother?"

Knox looked up. America's transit authorities were paranoid about bombs, he thought, so naturally this mother
wanted to check out the bag. "Glassware, man," he answered and unzipped the bag. "An analyzer. Medical stuff."

"Uh-huh. You deliverin'?"

"Uptown. Manhattan Medicinal."

"Uh-huh. What's that liquid in it?"

"Don't know. Some kind o' liquid used for the analysis, I
guess. Huh, looks like piss, don't it?"

"How come you're deliverin' uptown? Shouldn't you have a truck or somethin'?"

"Truck!" Knox looked incredulous. "Man, this is expensive glassware. I mean we're talkin' big bucks here. They don't put this baby on a fuckin' truck. They give me a twenty, man, just to hold it. Know what I mean? This is *glass*. Could break real easy."

"You got an invoice, somethin' like that?"

"Sure do." He fished for it in his back pocket, and a couple of idiots, late teens, moved up on a white dish, big tits, coming out of the tunnels, trains rumbling down below.

"Hey!" the transit cop yelled. One of the teenagers, a long, lanky brother, cap backward, wearing baggy gray overalls and a blue T-shirt, gave her the kissy-kiss look, smacking his lips at her. She was walking fast, looking straight ahead, as if she didn't see them. Scared and pissed off at the same time. The other brother, of medium build, was giving the transit cop the finger, "Come an' get me, motherfucker" all over their faces. The tall one leaped the turnstile, looking back, all Dentyne teeth. Come on, mother. The shorter one leaped the turnstile. "Hey!" the cop yelled.

Knox was watching the woman gripping her handbag under her left arm and telling himself to relax, to be cool. The woman slowed down to let the two brothers move past. They slowed down too. "Miss!" the transit cop yelled, signaling her to stop, to back up, so he could help her. But either she didn't hear him or, if she did, she thought it was another brother dissing her. In panic, she kept walking. The two brothers slowed down. Now she didn't know what to do. More people were coming behind her. She waited.

"This way, miss!" the transit cop yelled, moving away from Knox toward the turnstiles—holding his bag. Shit. Then, still walking, he shot a glance back at Knox a few yards away. "You wait there!" Then he used his walkie-talkie as he walked toward the woman, telling every cop within hearing distance of Grand Central what was goin' on. But was he talking about the white dish or the bag?

Knox, seeing his chance, moved quickly into the flood of

people exiting the station. Foxy Knoxy's already in the out crowd, he thought, parallel with the transit cop but twenty feet away in a fast-moving stream of passengers spilling out onto the street.

The woman waited with the cop until another transit cop arrived to escort her out, to make sure the two black youths had beat it.

When the transit cop who'd been with Knox radioed in that he had a bag with some kind of glass jars in it and what looked like a fan, one of the bomb squad detectives asked if there was anything inside the glass. The transit cop said there was a liquid, the color of apple juice.

"Apple juice?"

"Yes, sir. Guy said it was some kind of analysis machine. Actually it's the color of pee."

"Pea soup color?"

"No. Piss."

The detective, just recently promoted to that rank, had to think hard about this one. If it was a bomb, he sure hadn't heard of anything like it, and to close the entrance of Grand Central was to cause major disruption all through the subway system for thousands of morning commuters on their way to work. He thought of the Atlanta bombs—pipes stuffed with glass, ball bearings, nails, whatever. But nothing like this. He checked with his chief, who was just winding up a stoppage at LaGuardia over an unattended satchel. It was nothing, full of papers, but the chief had given the businessman who'd forgotten it by the bar what the detectives called "quiet shit." The chief knew he was out of line, dressing down the civilian, but the drain on the department's time and public money for these false alarms was enormous.

"What does the transit cop say is in it?" the chief asked the detective.

"Liquid—color of urine or apple juice. Take your pick. And a fan."

"What line's he on?"

"Line two."

"Put him through."

"You got it."

The bomb squad chief asked the transit cop if there was any smell or noise being emitted from the bag.

"No, sir. There's something that looks like small fan blades, a couple of wires and batteries."

"Batteries?"

"Yes, sir. Looks like they're nine volts."

"What do *you* think it is?"

The transit cop felt honored that his opinion was being sought, but he didn't have a clue what it could be if it wasn't an analyzer. "I don't know, sir. Could be stolen property. He said it was expensive."

"How'd he strike you?"

"Full of it—jive-talkin' me."

"All right. I'll put you through to the sketch artist. Give him a description."

When the transit cop turned away from the phone, he couldn't believe it—the bag was gone.

CHAPTER FORTY-SEVEN

The dam's crest looked like the wreck of the Hesperus. Though the structural integrity of the high arch gravity dam had not been breached, debris from the explosion was everywhere, and a dispirited ALERT team, now down to four—Brentwood, Lewis, Salvini, and Thomas—waited to have their request for transport approved. They might have been down at the moment, but a seething, collective rage at the way Hearn had murdered and dumped their comrade was replacing their disappointment, and they had requested transport from Freeman not for evac, but to take them east in Hearn's wake to get him. The problem was that while the Chinook with the Nazi, Toro, and two women hostages aboard could easily be tracked by radar, communication had been severely disrupted between Hoover Dam and Freeman's HQ. It had not been the blast so much as static caused by what the meteorologists were calling "significant electrical disturbance in the advancing front of El Niño–generated cumulonimbus." Lightning.

Eventually, a half hour later, when Freeman did get through, he told them that they should go, but that should they end up anywhere near Purdy's militia column, they would be under the nominal authority of Major Eliot. "Nominal" was Freeman's code, which the ALERTs understood, an ass-covering order to satisfy Washington, D.C.'s inherent distaste for "cowboys," by which they meant special forces who tended to be a law unto themselves, or rather a law unto Freeman.

Montoya, though suffering from a king-sized headache, insisted on accompanying them. After investing in so much caution for so long to disarm Hearn's suspicion of him, he'd failed to capitalize on the one clear moment he'd had to stop Hearn and his brutal sidekick. He wasn't about to give up now.

"Sign this," Aussie Lewis said, producing a torn piece of paper that had come out of a ventilator.

"What is it?" Montoya asked.

"A release form." Montoya signed and Lewis immediately crumpled it up and threw it over the side into the lake. "Cleared for mission." He smiled.

Salvini looked at Thomas, whose black face, still covered in dust, looked like an old vaudevillian's, and shook his head. Even in the most down moments, the Australian had an irrepressible spirit—something they'd all need if ever they saw Hearn and his thug again.

* * *

"You sure Vance is dead?" Freeman asked.

"Yes, sir," Brentwood reported.

"Well, that's good news. I'll tell the President."

"Yes, sir."

"David, I'm concerned with you boys not having any wheels. Makes you dependent on Eliot, and you may have occasion to break away from the main column—with Major Eliot's permission, of course."

"Of course," Brentwood said, tongue in cheek despite his somber mood. He was remembering the look of sheer terror on the faces of the nurse and the doctor.

"It's rough country over there, and hauling fuel's a problem, a real problem, so I'm going to have a Herky paraglide you two Mark Three JO-TEVs. Have 'em on standby just in case."

"Thank you, General. Here or on site?"

"On site, and David . . . ?"

"Sir."

"I'm sorry about Finn."

Within minutes the Chinook arrived, landing in parking lot 11 on the Arizona side, where Jimmy Sarna and Coveralls lay dead. They were the first two gunned down by the National Guardsmen, who had then gone on to virtually wipe out the militias' five ambulances. Lucky McBride was the only one fortunate enough to escape, and was now in custody, en route north to Camp Fairchild.

Crouching low, the four ALERTs and Place Montoya ran to the waiting chopper, and within minutes were airborne in increasing cloud cover moving in from the Grand Canyon. They were heading for the area north of Canyon de Chelly and west of the Arizona–New Mexico border, approximately halfway between Shiprock to the northeast and Canyon de Chelly to the southwest. The chopper pilot informed Brentwood that the distance from the dam to Eliot's last reported position might well exceed the Chinook's range of 345 miles, but that it was with this in mind that General Freeman had arranged for two JO-TEVs to be paraglided in.

"What's a JO-TEV?" Montoya asked, the roaring of the twin engines all but drowning his voice and making his headache worse.

"Joint tactical electric vehicle," Brentwood answered. "Bit of a misnomer, really. It's also switchable to diesel. Goes over bumpier ground than a Hummer, smaller and quiet as a mouse when you select electric drive only. Prototypes."

"Uh-huh," Montoya answered, not much wiser for the explanation but grateful that Freeman was in the picture.

"Mounted with a fifty-caliber," Salvini added.

"Machine gun," Lewis added.

Montoya knew very well what a fifty-caliber was, but the idea of a jarring ride over and through boulder-strewn terrain didn't appeal to him, especially with his headache, which was now spreading up around his forehead and down deep into his neck muscles. Thomas offered him a Tylenol 3, not part of the standard unit-one medic's bag but an addition that he had found effective.

"No, thanks," Montoya said.

Thomas knew the type well—wouldn't take a pill unless his leg was cut off, and then only when pressed.

The Chinook had reached its maximum speed of around 180 mph, but was now being met by a steadily increasing headwind from the southeast, which was putting the needle back to 150 mph, which meant a later ETA and more fuel sucked up.

"We should lose this blow halfway into the Navajo Reservation and pick up a tailwind," the pilot told Brentwood.

"Well," Lewis shouted over the noise, "it means Hearn is up against it too."

"True," the pilot replied, "but he's still 'bout thirty minutes ahead of you. Other thing is that we don't know exactly where Purdy's militia column is under this cloud cover, but last time we heard from Eliot his forward scouts had put him well west of Eliot, which means Hearn and his hostages'll be with the militia column before you get to Eliot."

"You're a cheerful bastard!" Lewis told the pilot.

"Just giving you the facts."

"Fact is," Lewis retorted, "if Hearn gets away on us, we're gonna have egg all over our face. Again."

Montoya looked up, wondering whether Lewis meant him as well—his failure to down Hearn at the dam. But it didn't really matter whether Lewis meant to include him, because Montoya knew well enough that he'd fumbled the ball at the dam. Now he wanted to get Hearn even more, not only because of the fear he'd seen in the two women, but to redeem himself in his own eyes.

CHAPTER FORTY-EIGHT

The pounding sound of the two transit cops echoed along the platform at Grand Central as they ran, yelling, after a youth who, seeing the turnstile cop on the phone, had snatched the bag. And then thirty feet in front of him by the tracks, another cop stepped out from behind a pillar, gun raised in both hands, legs apart in the crouch. The bag snatcher, a black youth, saw he had two ways to go: the electrified tracks on his left or the pillar to his right. But by now the other two transit cops were behind him. He stopped, dropped the bag, and put up his hands. "Hey, man, don't shoot!"

They asked him what was in the bag. He said he didn't know, he hadn't looked. They believed him—there hadn't been time. They arrested him and one of them took him away.

The bomb squad detective, Ron Wallace, advanced slowly, like a pregnant green alien, his head made enormous by the suit's armored and gas-proof hood. He stood over the bag, holding a gas sniffer similar to the one used by the now-deceased Major Caroline Hart at Tooele, recording through his transmitter everything he was doing so that should he make a mistake and die, the next man or woman to approach any similar object would not be going in cold. "Gas sniffer registers zero. Am now unzipping the bag . . . Bag unzipped . . . The contents are two glass containers . . . joined . . . a spiderweb crack running through both of them. Must have happened when the snatcher dropped it." The man's voice rebounded off the inside of the hood, sounding as if he were in one of the subway's tunnels. Trains had been stopped, waiting for the okay to proceed, some of the more claustrophobic passengers already becoming panicky as they waited for an all clear.

Now Wallace reported, "There's a small fan fixed to the inside of the bag to my right with wires . . . batteries attached. Nine volts. Fan is not operating. No timer indicated." He was now drenched in sweat. "I suggest we containerize in the vehicle and remove to Rodman's Neck." It was the police firing range in the Bronx.

"Roger," came his commander's voice. "You need a hand with it, Ron?"

"Negative. It's relatively light, but better play safe and back the vehicle in as close as possible."

"Roger."

Despite the possibility of danger, a crowd had gathered at the entrance to Grand Central. It was moved back beyond police barricades and yellow tape as the green-suited Wallace carefully, slowly, carried the bag to the bomb disposal containment vehicle, a truck hauling a cement mixer–shaped, very thick steel container into which the bag was placed.

Within seconds people in the crowd were screaming, falling, clutching their throats, others already going into anaphylactic shock, urinating and defecating, dying, enough of the odorless, colorless sarin nerve gas having escaped from the bag, through the spiderweb-thin crack, wafting into the onlookers. Within minutes six people were dead. Dozens of others were violently ill, the stench of vomit thick in the air.

"Christ, what happened?" the police commissioner demanded. He was talking to the bomb disposal unit's Captain Dick Blaney, a tall, lean black man, impeccably dressed in dark gray suit and tie. "I've got the media all over me here. The mayor's office is on the phone. I thought your man had checked for gas. Isn't that standard?"

"Yes, sir," Blaney answered. "He did test it. Either the detector was on the fritz or the liquids didn't mix until a minute or so later as the bag was being carried to the drum."

"The drum?"

"The steel container."

"Listen, Captain," the commissioner said, "the shit's coming down fast and heavy on this one and we have to move quickly. I've seen your initial fax on this, and from what I've read, this is no do-it-yourself project."

"I concur," Blaney said. "We've had a closer look at the glass containers and fan, and this is a pretty sophisticated, albeit simply designed, apparatus. You don't get blown-customized-glass tubing like that in the basement. Has to be specially made."

"You have any leads on that?" the commissioner pressed.

"No," answered Blaney, who now patched in Ron Wallace for a three-way phone conference call with the commissioner. "It wasn't that intricate, was it, Ron?"

"No, but it was precise."

"How 'bout the fan?" Blaney asked.

"Beautifully made," Wallace told him. "Hardly a sound. Very quiet purring. Steady. West German–made is the guess downtown. Pressed carbon fibers—space station stuff."

"How about batteries?"

"Energizers, Captain," Wallace said. "Just keep on goin'."

"Never mind the comedy," the commissioner cut in. "We've got to find that son of a bitch who first had the bag, and find out if there are any more. You get a good description of him from that transit cop who called it in?"

"Reasonable," Wallace said. "Black, medium build, thickset, skullcap, late thirties."

The commissioner sighed. "That's about a quarter of New York City."

"We'll have an identikit Xeroxed in twenty minutes," Blaney assured him.

"Good. Get it to all media, onto the Net, patrol cars, and all our men on the street."

"Yes, sir."

"Another thing," the commissioner said. "Now we know that it's sarin—nerve gas like those Japanese religious nuts used on the Tokyo subway—you'd better contact Tokyo police and get whatever you can. See if there's any terrorist group connection."

"We're doing that now, sir," Wallace replied. "Our labs're running a spectrometer analysis to see if we can get a chemical match with the stuff that cult outfit used in Japan."

"Good. Another thing we should—" The commissioner was interrupted by his assistant, who told him, somewhat awestruck, "It's the President. He's on Air Force One."

"Mr. President."

"Commissioner. I believe we have a problem in New York. Poison gas?"

"Yes, sir. Eleven dead. Sixteen in critical condition. Several on life support. Some nut carried it into Grand Central. We didn't get it in time but it could've been a lot worse if we'd had it leak into the subway's lower levels."

As he was listening to the commissioner the President cupped the mouthpiece, asking Delorme, "What's his name again, Ryan?"

"Yes," Delorme told him. "Terrence—Terry Ryan."

"Well," said the President, "I know you're doing what you have to, Terry. FBI's working on this with you. I don't want any jurisdictional disputes. Our collective responsibility is to get to whoever's doing this and get to them quickly. I want you to feel free to call my office if you need any over-ride authority."

"Thank you, Mr. President. I appreciate that."

"Thank God we've got our antiterrorist bill in place after Oklahoma."

"Yes, sir."

"I'll leave you to it, Terry. We'll talk again."

"Yes, sir."

When he got off the phone, Terry Ryan rang home. "Marlene—"

"Terr, are you okay? I've been watching CNN about—"

"Yes, I'm fine. Listen, you won't believe it, I just got a call from Air Force One."

"From the *President*?"

"The one and only. Calls me Terry."

On CNN, news anchor Linden Soles reminded listeners that an hour-long special, "Terror at Grand Central," would be aired that evening. And among Larry King's guests would be the transit policeman who found the "gas bomb," the mayor of New York, the commissioner of police, and a political scientist—an expert on terrorist gas attacks through-out the world. The second half of the show would be about the dangers posed to the public by escaped militia POWs in the Pacific Northwest.

Meanwhile, the managing editor of the *New York Times* received a call, a male's voice, claiming that more people would be killed unless the *Times* published the manifesto of the Black Brothers of America militia. The manifesto, said the man, was addressed to the managing editor and was al-ready in the mail, and if post office officials weren't busy shooting one another today, it should arrive that afternoon "special delivery." The managing editor did not dismiss it as a prank call, though it could have been, and notified the mail room to hold any "special delivery" packages and to make certain that they went through the mail room's combination sniffer and X-ray machine.

At police headquarters it was rumored that someone was

in "deep shit." The six-volt batteries in the gas sniffer that
Ron Wallace used were dead, a no-brand generic kind that
"some idiot in Purchasing," or so said the rumor, had
bought, trying to save the department the cost of a more expensive brand name. The two liquids in the glass containers
had apparently already mixed when the bomb squad arrived
on the scene, and because of the dead batteries, the sniffer
hadn't been working.

"You mean to tell me," Blaney thundered, "that we have
eleven people dead and I don't know how many near death
or dying because some asshole in Purchasing bought two
fucking dead batteries?"

"That's it, sir!"

"Send me the chief purchasing officer right now. This
minute!"

The head purchasing officer was a woman by the name of
Ellen Rose, and when she walked into Blaney's office, she
looked him straight in the eye.

"You wanted to see me, Captain?"

"Rose, did *you* sign a purchasing order for—"

"I don't sign purchasing orders. My clerks do that."

"Are you abnegating responsibility?"

"I'm not *abnegating* anything, sir. I'm just telling you I
don't sign purchasing orders."

"All right, you want to play pickass, we'll play pickass.
Did you authorize in any way, shape, or manner the purchase of substandard six-volt batteries?"

"They're not substandard. I made sure of that."

"They *are* substandard and *you* authorized them verbally
to save a few lousy cents."

"A penny saved is a penny earned."

"Hey!" He jabbed his finger at her face. "Don't you screw
around with me."

"I would *never* screw around with you."

Ellen Rose thought he was going to jump over the table.
"*You* authorized them!" he shouted.

"I did, but I understand *you* have a problem."

"*I* have a problem? We have people *dead* because of *you*!"

Ellen Rose suddenly leaned forward, both hands on the police captain's desk. "You have fatalities because someone in your bomb squad skipped procedure and didn't test the *fucking* batteries before they got near the *fucking* bag. And if you don't get off my back and instead track down the mad-*men* who did this, I'll call every fucking paper in New York and tell them that *your* squad screwed up. Now go intimidate somebody else!"

CHAPTER FORTY-NINE

The sun, locked out by the cloud, could manage only pale dawn over Ship Rock but it was light enough for the Bradley's gunner to fire a burst in the general direction of where they thought the two militiamen were holed up. There was no return fire. This posed a problem for federal Sergeant Norris, in command of the Bradley Fighting Vehicle and the burial squad of eight infantrymen it carried. He had already stretched out the time allocated for his burial detail, and knew that Major Eliot had passed Ship Rock and was heading west. The burial detail, having performed its grizzly task last night, should now move on to rejoin Eliot's column.

The fact that Eliot, in the main National Guard column of 240, had not contacted him from the HQ Bradley didn't mean that Eliot's patience wasn't being tried, but that the major wanted to keep radio silence as long as possible. Norris wanted revenge for the slaughter of his buddies, wiped out two nights before by Purdy's men, but he knew he could wait only so much longer now that dawn had passed and the

desert cool had been evicted by the fierce sun, whose rays
were reflected by increasing cloud cover over the Southwest.
So Norris decided on a compromise, ordering the infantry
squad back into the Bradley, after which he told his driver to
head west-northwest on a heading that would take them
back to Eliot's column.

Once behind the western face of Ship Rock, he stopped
the Bradley, and four infantrymen—the top four marksmen
in the squad—disembarked. On the two militiamen's blind
side now, two of the marksmen moved in closer, deep in the
shadow of the west face, hugging the rock. The other two
marksmen meanwhile edged around the warmer northern
side, the four men hoping to get the two militiamen whom
they'd spotted near dusk the evening before in a cross fire,
should the militiamen decide to come down now that it was
light and they could see the Bradley moving eastward, returning to Route 666. Norris figured that driving the Bradley at no more than thirty mph would allow his four shooters
about half an hour at the rock, during which time he hoped
that the two militiamen, probably getting short on water, if
not rations, would descend. All that his four marksmen
needed was a brief look at the two men.

Norris stared back at the basaltic monolith but could see
no movement on it. "If they stay up there," he told his driver,
"they'll fry."

"Good," the driver said. "Either way, we'll get 'em."

Norris was trying to decide what he would do if he were
in the militiamen's shoes.

Just south of the small township of Omak, in Washington
State, it was still dark, the snow flurries roiling about in the
car's headlights as Melvin Abrem pulled off into a snow-
choked driveway. Shifting into low gear, his body even
closer to the wheel now, wipers humming, heater on full
blast, and the smell of chicken gumbo farts filling the car—
no one claiming responsibility—Abrem felt the snow tires
gripping, but the vehicle was only crawling ahead, the snow
piling up to his headlights.

"Thought he would've graded the driveway," Abrem complained.

"Probably hasn't got one," Brody said easily. "Normally don't get that much snow up here, do you?"

"He's got a snowblower," Abrem replied.

"We can walk in from here," Orr offered.

"Hang on," Abrem said. "We'll make it. Besides, I have to take you up personally to vouch for you. You could be a coupla federal dicks."

"Right," Brody said, again in the easy, relaxed tone that bothered Orr, since he himself didn't feel relaxed.

"How far are we from the border?" Orr asked.

" 'Bout forty miles," Abrem answered.

"Do we have one more stop after this?" Brody inquired.

"Don't know," Abrem told him. "I'm only one cog in the wheel. Security, right?"

"Right," Brody said. The driving snow was giving way easily now, perhaps because of warmth from the house. It was an old house, built in the 1930s—a wide veranda almost at ground level forming a moat of snow.

The door opened and a man in his mid-thirties, wearing a royal-blue down vest and sporting a goatee beard, came out waving in the penumbra of headlights. Abrem wound down his window. "Got a delivery for you."

"Bring 'im in."

"Two of 'em."

The man smiled. "Okay, bring in both of 'em."

When Orr got out, he felt cramped and stiff, his body having been unable to relax during the trip.

"Name's Ken," the man said. "And you are?"

"Al—" Orr told him, almost using his last name.

"Neil," Brody said, and shook the other man's hand, smiling.

"Lots of room," Ken said. "Wife's down in Seattle."

"Oh," Abrem said, and Orr guessed from his reaction that the wife's absence wasn't the normal state of affairs.

"Yeah," Ken said. "Been separated two months now. Can't say I don't miss her."

Mel Abrem looked like he was about to say something, but it just trailed off into a mumble.

"But by hell," Ken went on, "I can make coffee!"

"Sounds good," Brody said, "but not before I try to go to sleep. We're moving on today, or later on."

Ken pursed his lips as if thinking about it for the first time, which struck Orr as disorganized for an escape route. "Well, how 'bout we move off around ten? That way you fellas can grab a bit of shut-eye."

"Sounds good to me," Brody said. And it suddenly hit Orr that Brody might simply be one of those habitual optimists, and that perhaps because of his own perennial suspicion, he was making too much of the other man's hearty hail-fellow-well-met attitude. Orr recalled, then, that when he'd gone to Captain Eleen with his escape idea, he too had been optimistic, excitement boosting his morale along with his adrenaline. Maybe what irked him about Brody was the man's simple ability to take things as they came, whereas he couldn't accept his good luck, as if God wouldn't allow him such a relatively easy ride to freedom.

Another thing that bothered Orr, now that he ruminated on his own pervasive pessimism, was the necessity of having to go to Canada first before he could reenter the States. The only thing he knew about Canada was the little Eleen had told him, and that years ago the Canadians had helped get some American hostages back from Iran. Still, Eleen had said that once he was near the border, he wouldn't know the difference between the U.S. and Canadian side. He'd just walk over the border between friends—the longest undefended border in the world.

Ken offered to "rustle up" some pancakes. Brody, big gumbo eater that he was, said he could down "a couple—of dozen."

It got a good laugh from Ken, and Orr told himself to lighten up, not to be such a grumpy son of a bitch.

The first of Norris's two marksmen at the base of Ship Rock's western face had worked his way around to the

southeast far enough to view the area where the two militiamen had been sighted the evening before. He saw movement, but not enough to risk a quick shot that might take out
one of the militiamen, leaving the other to wait until the federals either left or began to climb up after them. There was
movement again, and the second federal marksman at the
base of the western face saw the two of them about six hundred feet above, a third of the M-16's effective range. "They
starting down?" the first marksman asked.

"Don't know. Looks like it. Have to wait a bit."

By now the other two marksmen, working their way around
the northern face, were approaching the farthest point on the
eastern side they could reach without being seen by the militia. They were awaiting a signal from the other two, now
about 150 yards away, as to whether they could see the militiamen. And then, out of the corner of his eye, the first of the
two at the base of the eastern cliff glimpsed the two militiamen. One of them was moving cautiously down the rock
face along a rocky, sawtoothlike parapet; the other, his head
barely visible in what seemed to be a depression in the rock,
was covering him. The marksman on the eastern side signaled the other two marksmen that he too could see one of
the enemy coming down, the other positioned to provide
covering fire.

It was a dilemma. What would Norris want them to do?
Go for a shot at the man moving cautiously down the
acutely angled parapet, and by doing so, warn the other militiaman? Or wait until the two of them were closer together—if the two militiamen allowed that to happen? Norris
would soon be on 666, and he couldn't wait all day if he was
to rejoin Eliot's force in time for any impending action
against Purdy's militia. The marksman who'd glimpsed the
militiaman on the parapet told his companion and signaled
his other two comrades, 150 yards away, that they should all
swing out simultaneously and fire at the man on the parapet.
The marksman raised his M-16 high above his right shoulder, switched the safety to the off position, and, teeth

clenched in anticipation, raised his left hand, ready to drop it, as a signal to shoot.

He saw that the other two marksmen were primed to step out from the base and start shooting, and his comrade behind him also ready to go wide. He dropped his left hand and stepped out, taking a second to aim and fire, the sound of the four M-16s' three-round bursts, twelve bullets in all streaking toward the militiamen, echoing off the rock. There were puffs of rock dust about the militiaman and he fell back, away from the parapet into a two-hundred-foot fall to the abutment of rocks below.

The impact of Ray Fraser's body was so violent as he hit that the two marksmen on the south column base heard his back break like a twig snapping, his skull bursting like a melon.

Return fire had come almost immediately, as John Reid, heart racing in fright, opened up on the marksmen. But all they had to do was step back in against the protective walls of rock that formed Ship Rock's base.

One of the two marksmen at the eastern face fired an orange flare, and as it burst beneath the bunching cumulus, Sergeant Norris turned the Bradley about to pick them up. It was a pity, he said, that his men got only one of the bastards, but one was better than none. Let the other guy rot, too scared to come down lest there be one or two men waiting for another turkey shoot.

As a thoroughly demoralized Reid watched the Bradley returning to Ship Rock, losing sight of the vehicle for a minute while it presumably stopped to pick up the federal shooters, then seeing it draw away from the rock mountain, westward, its desert camouflage paint making it increasingly difficult to make out, he felt indescribably alone and afraid. A short time ago Ray Fraser, in so many ways his mentor, had been a sentient human being. Typically courageous, Fraser had insisted on going down first, exposing himself in the event that something might go wrong. Reid's throat was as dry as the red desert dust, and though he took a gulp from

the canteen, a minute or so later the parched, leathery feel
returned and he had to force himself not to guzzle away his
shock. The plan had been to report via radio telephone to
Purdy and arrange for pickup. But then everything had gone
bananas.

Reid began to swear violently up at the cathedrallike
spires of the majestic rock, seeing it no longer as an inani-
mate upthrust of basalt, but as a malevolent force that had
failed to protect his friend and comrade in arms, and had allowed the enemy to kill him. A part of him knew he was being irrational, but the other part, the outraged militiaman in
him, swore anyway—anything to vent his sorrow and his
anger.

In fact, Sergeant Norris's assumption that the second militiaman, Reid, would stay holed up on the rock for fear of
snipers, proved inaccurate. With the Bradley no more than a
khaki dot east of the rock, Reid started down the narrow
ledge toward the sawtooth parapet, which then dropped
away to shadow.

He was halfway down the sharply inclined ledge when he
saw Fraser's blood splattered on the rock face, and chips in
the basalt where the M-16 rounds had struck, some of them
after passing right through exposed flesh. What made it
worse was that in the heat, antlike insects were swarming
out of crevices in the rock face, making haste toward the
streaks of blood. By the time Reid descended another two
hundred feet to Fraser's broken body, he was soaking in
perspiration. He took another gulp of water, only to throw
up when he saw that Fraser's face was a seething mass of
red ants, every orifice alive with the frenzied flesh-eating
insects.

Michael Hearn had fled the dam site but he was under no
illusion as to what Freeman would do. The general had egg
on his face. Hoover Dam had been shut down, certainly for a
matter of months, leaving entire regions of the American
Southwest, including California's Imperial Valley, the salad
basket of the nation, high and dry. And while the death toll

did not begin to match that of the Oklahoma bombing, the economic implications of failed electric power and water supply to farms, hospitals, homes, industry, and cities in populous southern California alone was enormous.

Hearn's half hour lead on the ALERTs was increased now by the southeastern tailwind that came down through Utah and Arizona's Monument Valley, the famed setting for so many classic Western movies and commercials with cars perched precariously atop the stunning, towering, vibrant red rock buttes and mesas. Whereas the headwind blowing east from the New Mexico desert had reduced the Chinook's speed to no more than 150 miles per hour, the tailwind coming down from Four Corners' Monument Valley on through the Great Basin Desert and as far south as Fort Defiance now bolstered the helo to two hundred mph, making up for lost time and delivering Hearn, Toro, and the two women hostages to the general area of Purdy's militia column. Purdy's burst-coded radio message was received by Toro. It placed Purdy southwest of towering Roof Butte and about twelve miles north of Canyon de Chelly, where Purdy estimated his militia column would be well-placed to hit Eliot's federal column on its southern flank.

Accordingly, looking at the eastern horizon, Purdy gave orders to ready the "stand-ins," an expression he'd picked up from TV's Hollywood reporters when describing the use of look-alike actors and actresses to block, that is, to set up, all the camera positions, lighting, and so on, prior to filming the real stars. The stand-ins in this case weighed fifty-four pounds apiece, each packed in its own large hard plastic suitcase, which the militia had either stolen from Armored Division bases or bought for two thousand dollars each from highly questionable civilian dealers of military surplus.

What Purdy was most afraid of were the guns Fraser and Reid had reported that the federals were hauling. Would Eliot separate his guns from his main force, that is, position them no more than five miles behind in the case of the 155mm howitzers, or fifteen miles for the longer eighteen-mile-range 155mm guns? They could then provide an offensive barrage of covering fire for the federals' Bradley-mobile infantry. Both columns had about the same number of infantry, two hundred men each, but Purdy knew that the guns would settle the matter in the federals' favor if he could not neutralize the guns. But first he had to know where they were.

In addition to the pickup-borne scouts he'd already sent out, he called Ship Rock again, but, as in the case of Reid, who'd tried to call him, atmospherics were bad and all he could get was static. "Keep trying," he told Benet, a celebrity in Purdy's column since he'd taken out the Bradley during the night skirmish at Ship Rock.

"They could be dead," Benet said.

"I know that, dammit, but keep trying."

Benet reached Reid on the third try, and Reid told Purdy that Ray Fraser was dead.

"Sorry, Johno," said Purdy, who knew most of the militia under his command by their first names. "But you've got work to do. We have to know where those twelve guns are." A rush of static invaded.

"We're losing him," Benet said.

"Can you hear me?" Purdy hurriedly asked Reid.

"Barely . . . you're fading."

"Where are you?"

"Say again?"

"Where are you?

"Shiprock town. Got myself a motorcycle and—" There was more static.

"Listen," Purdy shouted, as if volume could somehow overcome the static. "You see any frogs, you call in. Fire a green and red and—" The static surged and drowned out Reid's response; and on his end, all Reid heard was "see any—" and then there had been a word that sounded like *frogs*.

As Purdy was leaving Benet's pickup to turn his attention to the myriad details a commander worries about, he ordered Benet, "Get ready for coat-tailing."

"Yes, sir."

A militiaman manning the M-60 machine gun swivel-mounted on Benet's pickup's roof waited until Purdy was gone, then asked Benet, "Did he say *frogs*?"

"Yeah."

"What the fuck have frogs got to do with anything?"

"How the fuck should I know?" Benet retorted. "Ask Freeman."

"Federal Freeman?"

"Yeah."

"What about him?"

"Don't you know?" Benet asked grumpily, then proceeded to answer his own question. "Purdy used to work under Freeman. Desert warfare school before they went to the Gulf."

"Shit," the militiaman said, not willing to take any crap from Benet, Bradley killer or not. "I know that. Lot of our militia guys were in the Gulf. What's that got to do with fucking frogs?"

"I told you, how the fuck should I know? But it's the kind of thing Freeman would come up with. He'd study an area for weeks before he went into action, find out all kinds of strange stuff. Like Patton, who knew the Germans were finished because of carts. He had a dream about all the hand carts he'd seen—Germans using the handcarts to carry away their dead. It meant they'd run out of gasoline and were ripe for finishing off."

"Well, I'll be fucked."

"Not so loud," Benet said, lightening up a bit. "We got some randy guys in this outfit. They might jump you."

CHAPTER FIFTY

By the time Brentwood, Salvini, Thomas, Lewis, and Montoya had deplaned from their Chinook, the Hercules MC-130, with a speed of 350-plus miles per hour, twice that of the Chinook, was already overhead, circling, ready to send down the two JO-TEVs by paraglider. The Hercules flew in and out of the bunching cumulonimbus clouds, waiting for Brentwood's radio call. When it came, it was chopped up by the atmospheric disturbance and had to be repeated several times. Finally the loadmaster got the go signal from the pilot, and the two big, wide, 5,100-pound, six-foot-six-inch paraglider crates rolled noisily down the ramp out into the gaping void. The paraglider wings folded back neatly atop each box, until each of the boxes was well clear of the plane's ramp. Within seconds large chutes blossomed, the boxes' fabric wings unfolding, becoming inflated with air, each flying winged box guided by Global Positioning System receivers. High above the protective gully into which the ALERTs and Montoya had deplaned, each descending box in effect became a glider, their awkward appearance notwithstanding, reaching over seventy miles per hour, the seventy-eight-foot wing span and another large drogue chute deploying to break impact. One box glider slammed into a man-sized boulder, bits of flying cacti and crate wood from the box flying high, the pieces of wood sounding like boomerangs chopping the desert air.

"Fuck a duck!" Lewis said. "Scratch one JO-TEV!"

"Not necessarily," Brentwood responded, more out of hope than from conviction as the five of them split up, Lewis and Salvini heading for the box glider that had come in beautifully, Brentwood, Thomas, and Montoya going over to inspect the other.

Brentwood's optimism turned out to be well-founded. The JO-TEV had been so well packed that, though broken Styrofoam buffers and other packing littered the area about the boulder like rectangular bits of snow, the vehicle was intact. Neither its "midships"-mounted electric motor, tucked away behind the driver's seat, nor its diesel, forward of the driver, nor the eight-hundred-pound battery pack beneath the driver's seat, seemed damaged. The JO-TEV vehicle, as Aussie Lewis had already told Montoya, didn't look at all sexy, but like an open, cut-down four-by-four, with room for only driver, co-driver, and machine gunner in the back; the .50 caliber gun on a swivel mount was well above the two front riders, the gun mount's steel post protruding above the crisscross roll-bar assembly.

Since the box around the JO-TEV had literally come apart at the seams, the extraction of the vehicle was almost immediate. Within a few minutes Brentwood had engaged the 2.1 Peugeot turbodiesel and, in effect, driven out of the crate.

"You tinny bastard!" Lewis said, *tinny* being his word for someone who was extraordinarily lucky, a lottery winner. "Here poor Sal has to unload this fucker, and you tootle out like Little Lord Fauntleroy."

"Tough tit," Thomas joked. "Time you did some work."

"Oh, I don't work," Lewis said, affecting a condescending British upper-crust tone. "My man Sal will unpack."

"And fuck you too," Salvini said.

It was the only light moment that morning for the ALERTs as they buckled up—Brentwood and Montoya in JO-TEV Alpha, with Thomas manning the machine gun; Lewis and Salvini in JO-TEV Bravo, Lewis claiming driving privileges till noon, Salvini on the fifty-caliber. They donned goggles and disposable surgical masks against the dust, preferring the discomfort of traveling one behind the other, thus confining the dust trail they'd kick up to one wake rather than two when they headed for Eliot's column, which, if the GPS was correct, should be in sight as soon as they were out of the gully. But before they began, Thomas held up his hand for silence, the sound of a vehicle approaching beyond the rise.

Three of the men, including Montoya, scattered, taking cover behind the nearby boulders. Thomas and Salvini remained, cocking the machine guns. Suddenly there was no sound, just the ear-ringing silence of the desert. Thomas and Salvini intuitively, and from force of habit, had divided the field of fire, Thomas's gun pointing east, Salvini's west, though he could not swing the gun to cover the full 180-degree arc because of the JO-TEV's crisscrossing roll bars. As insurance, Salvini cocked his I-COW, selecting the 25mm "air-burst" mag. Then, just as unexpectedly, the noise of a bullhorn filled the air.

"This is FEDFOR National Guard, Albuquerque. Identify yourselves."

Eliot's men?

None of the ALERTs or Montoya responded. If it was militia aboard the unseen vehicle, that's exactly what they would say to trap you—tell you they were federals.

"Identify yourselves," the voice repeated.

Thomas had his heavy machine gun pointed in the direction of the voice, but out of the corner of his eye he spotted Brentwood working his way forward from boulder to boulder on the northern flank. Thomas assumed that Lewis, perhaps with Montoya, was doing the same on the southern flank.

The ALERTs and Montoya positioned themselves as best they could against attack and waited. The hailer sounded again. "What is your recognition word?"

Brentwood could see Lewis across from him on the southern side of Thomas's machine gun, and he raised his arms in a questioning gesture.

Lewis gave him the same signal back. Brentwood, with

one more glance to see that every ALERT was ready to go, answered, "We are FEDFOR but we have no recognition code. Send one of your men forward unarmed."

"Negative. Put down your arms."

"Fuck you!" It was Lewis's voice bouncing off the boulders. Finally the hailer agreed: "One man from us. One from you."

"All right, send your man forward."

"Send yours!"

Brentwood, the other three ALERTs and Montoya, with his Colt, covering him, put down his weapon and walked out from the boulders, arms fully extended, palms open to the front. After a few uneasy seconds, another figure in desert fatigues appeared at the top of the rise fifty yards away, arms also extended, palms open, looking down at Brentwood.

"You should have a recognition code if you're FEDFOR," the other said.

"Well, I don't," Brentwood replied, his manner sharp, impatient, un-Brentwood-like.

It would be argued later that Salvini had taken an enormous risk, the risk of a "blue on blue," a so-called "friendly fire" incident, which was never "friendly" to those being shot at. But Salvini would tell them that it was his knowing about the "Israeli fighters' side mirror" that had made him recognize the incongruity of a federal force having a mechanical cherry picker arm—the kind used by electric companies to hoist men high up to power poles—peeking, rising above the crest of the hill, an M-60 barrel extending from it. As he put it to Lewis afterward, it was the extended arm of the cherry picker that had "alerted this ALERT."

"Oh, very droll," Lewis would answer laconically, but he nevertheless admitted to Thomas that Salvini's instant assumption had been "one hell of a smart move."

"How'd you know about the Israeli stuff?" he asked Salvini.

"One of Freeman's lectures. He told us about how the Israeli fighter pilots discovered they had a blind spot—you know, like when you check your rearview mirror to change lanes and miss seeing anyone who's at about seven o'clock."

"Yeah," Lewis said. "So?"

"So you need a side mirror. Israeli pilots told their ground crews, who went out immediately and bought a bunch of auto side mirrors and stuck 'em outside the cockpit. Problem solved. It wasn't part of standard equipment. It was innovative, something that would take our Pentagon bureaucracy about a year if not longer to investigate and approve. When did you ever hear of a goddamned cherry picker as standard FEDFOR for the National Guard or the Army?"

"Never heard of it," Thomas had to admit.

"So you guessed it was militia trying to con us," Lewis told Salvini. "You clever little bastard."

Salvini had been watching the man in the FEDFOR uniform when he spotted the edge of a beige fiberglass bucket at the end of the cherry picker arm. He fired a long burst from his .50 caliber machine gun, and saucer-sized pieces of fiberglass flew into the air like errant Frisbees, one of the pieces making a distinctive, wobbly *whoop! whoop!* noise, like someone flexing a thin piece of particle board. The militiaman from Purdy's column in the cherry-picker bucket took Salvini's full burst in the chest, literally disintegrating inside the disintegrating bucket.

Brentwood was down, hugging the dry red desert dirt as a fusillade of small and medium-sized arms opened up, the gully reverberating with the crack and crackle of gunfire as Salvini, Thomas, and Lewis let fly. Brentwood, Montoya closest to him and covering him, performed what Montoya would describe as the best crab scuttle he'd ever seen, quickly finding refuge, his militia counterpart on the ground also, arms out imploringly, shouting, "Don't shoot! Don't shoot! I'm unarmed."

Salvini shot him anyway—the bastard might have his battle smock pockets full of grenades, he thought, and the story of how the militia had suckered the Bradley at Ship Rock was by then well known to all the federal soldiers.

Their bluff having failed, the militia pickup, on whose flatbed the cherry picker was attached, started up with a roar, followed by a screech of brakes as it went into reverse before making a dust-churning U-turn, not heading back east, from where it had come, but north on a stone-strewn stretch of sagebrush desert. However, before it traveled more than a hundred yards, Lewis and Salvini's JO-TEV had gained the rise, and Thomas, in the other JO-TEV, was laying down heavy machine-gun fire at the pickup's rear tires. One of them blew, the vehicle's driver losing control. Three militiamen fell off the flatbed like rag dolls, two of them already dead, raked by fire from Thomas's fifty-caliber. The remaining militiaman, who'd been momentarily airborne during the pickup's slide, rolled over, still stubbornly grasping his M-16 and getting off a three-round burst before he too was felled by Brentwood, who delivered a fatal shot from his I-COW's 25mm.

As the dust cleared, the pickup's driver could be seen hung upside down by his seat harness. The four ALERTs and Montoya approached in the two JO-TEVs. Surprisingly, the militiaman, having shaken his head like a boxer intent on regaining full consciousness after a hard hit, released himself, fell into the passenger seat, drew the handgun from his shoulder holster, and started shooting. Brentwood squeezed off three 5.6mm rounds, the man's body flexing into a spastic arch before it crumpled.

Montoya had never seen anything like the ferocity of the short militia/ALERT engagement, and recollected the words of Thomas Hobbes, whom he'd studied in college and who had talked about the life of man in the natural state as being "nasty, brutish, and short." No quarter had been asked or given by either side. Most impressive, he thought—or shocking, depending on how you looked at it—was the all-but-palpable hatred of the militia for the federals, the militia driver's refusal to surrender in what was clearly a no-win situation for him. It was an augury, Montoya feared, of what might happen should the two columns, each eagerly looking for the other, clash.

"Better bury them," Montoya said, his tone conveying respect for the dead, even if they were the enemy.

"No," Brentwood said calmly; almost regretfully, Montoya thought. "We haven't got time," he explained. "Keep an eye open for any more militia while we right the truck."

"What for?" Lewis challenged. "Leave the fucking thing where it is. We've got the transport we need."

But Salvini was on to it right away, answering, "Because, you dork, we can use the cherry picker. When you put that arm up vertical, you'll be able to see another couple of miles."

"Oh," Lewis said, embarrassed and at an unusual loss for words.

"What you think they were using it for, Aussie?" Thomas joked. "Pickin' cherries?"

"Fuck the lot of you," Lewis said. "So what are we gonna use for a basket, now that the other one's shot to rat shit?"

"Aw," Salvini said, "we're gonna stick it up your ass, Aussie, 'fore we hoist you up."

"Yeah, yeah," intoned Aussie. "Very funny, you wop!"

Montoya had thought he was a hard man, but these guys had just killed six men, and were now joking with each other.

"All right, you know-it-alls," Lewis said, walking over to the cherry picker. "Get the friggin' thing up. I'll stand on the frame. Dollars to doughnuts we see fuck all."

"I dunno, Aussie," Brentwood said, topping up his 5.6mm round mag. "How do you think they saw us and sent out a reception committee?"

"Because," Lewis began, pausing to sling his I-COW and Brentwood's binoculars over his right shoulder as he stood on the bottom rung of what had been the basket, and grabbing the top of the frame with his right hand, "they saw the JO-TEVs' drogue chutes coming down. Those things are big enough!"

"Maybe they spotted the chutes from the picker," Brentwood said.

Lewis shrugged and worked the cherry picker's control

toggle with his left hand. He was about eleven feet off the flat, stony desert, gazing north to south, when he saw a faint scratch of dust against the southwest horizon. It might be nothing more than a wind swirl whipping up loose soil into a spiral, he thought. Adjusting the focus on the binoculars, he leaned forward against the frame of what had been the cherry picker's fiberglass bucket. Now he could see at least three other plumes adjacent to the first one. "Son of a bitch!"

"What's up?" Brentwood asked.

"Something's on the move," Lewis said.

"What?"

"Can't tell, but whatever it is, it's churning up the dirt."

"How far?"

"Four, maybe five miles."

Brentwood was a decisive leader, but he was also a team player, as all the ALERTs had to be, in addition to being highly self-reliant, and he was never afraid to seek the others' counsel. "What do you think, guys? We take a ride out there for a closer look before we make for Eliot's column, which should be east of us?"

"Eliot's probably got scouts out already," Thomas said.

"Can't see anything eastward yet," Lewis said. "Enemy or FEDFOR."

"Let's take a run out for a couple of miles," Thomas pressed.

"Well, if it is Purdy's outfit," Salvini opined, "we can't take the whole two hundred of 'em on. We'll need Eliot's boys for that."

"Agreed," Brentwood said, "but if we can pick out where Purdy's guns are, that's going to help Eliot's column."

"Let's go," Lewis said, shifting the toggle into the down position. "Pity we can't take this cherry picker with us."

"Why can't we?" Montoya asked.

"Because," Lewis explained, pointing to Thomas, "that fucker shot the shit out of its tires, and we're not gonna get far driving over this rocky ground on fucking rims."

"Well, smartass," Thomas replied, "somebody had to stop the mother while you were there pickin' your nose!"

"All right," Brentwood said. "Saddle up. Let's go!" Then, as an afterthought, he told Montoya, "You don't have to come along, Sheriff. If you want you can stay here and—"

"I'm in," Montoya said.

Brentwood nodded at one of the dead militiamen. "Guy over there has a three-ought rifle. Maybe you'd rather pack that, along with your Colt—just in case."

"Good idea," Montoya said. He walked over and pried the rifle from the militiaman's hand, sincerely hoping he'd have no call to use it. Maybe, he told himself, the militia, confronted by the sight of Eliot's big field guns, would throw in the towel.

CHAPTER FIFTY-ONE

"Hey, my man, you lookin' to make some cash?" Wesley Knox's face was the picture of beneficence, ready to help the two brothers hanging out by the steps of a Harlem tenement.

"Who we gotta kill?" the shorter of the two asked.

"Don't have to kill nobody. Just make a delivery. I got twenty bucks for each o' you if you deliver right now. A hundred each when I know you delivered it."

"How you gonna know that?"

"Man is waitin' for it. Certain place. He tells me it's there, it's there. You just made yourselves a hundred. *Each.*"

"Uh . . ." It was the shorter man again. "What's in the fuckin' bag, man? Head shit?"

"No drugs, man. Absolutely."

"Fuckin' bomb!" the taller one piped up.

"No bomb," Knox said. "You have a look."

He unzipped the bag. Both of the men craned their necks to see without actually getting closer to the bag. The taller one lost interest when he saw it wasn't a bomb. The other one was still looking at it, his pride doing battle with curiosity. He saw what looked like two glass bowls, some kind of small fan attached, and a small claw hammer. "This ain't no fuckin' bomb," he said.

"I told you," Knox replied. "Hey, you guys ain't interested, that's cool." He zipped up the bag and started walking off.

"Hey, man, I didn't say no."

"You didn't say yes. Other brothers can use the cash."

"Hey, hold on, man. You goin' too fast."

"Fuck I am. I got business."

"Where you wan' us to take it?"

"Underground parking lot. World Trade Center."

"Uh-huh, so we take it in just like that, huh? Just carry the fuckin' bag past the eyes, man. Right through the front door. That right?"

"Hell, no. You park the car. Get out, go up to the lobby, walk out. Nobody gonna ask you what you doin' comin' out."

"Where's this fuckin' car comin' from?"

"That's not your business."

The short one laughed derisively. "Fo' a hundred an' change? You jerkin' us off, man."

Fuck it, Knox thought. 'T ain't no help these days without crossin' the palms with silver. You think they were all Jewboys 'stead of the Brothers of Farrakhan. Shit, he'd do it himself. Besides, the newspapers were jerkin' him around. They published the Unabomber's shit but not his. So you had to show 'em you were serious, that you meant business. He kept walking down the sidewalk, careful not to step on any cracks and counting his footsteps between the pavement blocks, because if you stepped on too many cracks, it was a sign.

"Wes, my man!" It was a brother coming down onto the sidewalk, where he stood unsteadily, smiling at Knox.

Knox acknowledged him with a wave of his hand, then went to the nearest drugstore, where he bought a tear-off pair of transparent plastic gloves.

Purdy, as Brentwood surmised, had seen the big drogue chutes and decided it was time to start coat-tailing, an old trick of Douglas Freeman's. His militiamen had deployed ropes attached to fishing nets containing the rocks, cacti, and sagebrush he'd ordered collected earlier. The thick dust trails raised by dragging the weighted nets behind thirty militia-equipped pickups now proceeding abreast rather than in column were enormous, convincing the ALERTs that there were at least four times as many militia as they'd assumed now moving fast, eastward, to attack Eliot.

The four ALERT commandos came to a conclusion that struck Montoya as singularly impressive, though it wasn't the stuff of Hollywood movies: five of them could make little or no difference against what seemed a broad and large conventional force whose dust trails they could see over a front a mile wide; particularly since they'd lost their most valuable weapon—the element of surprise. Besides, Brentwood reminded his comrades, their mission was to rescue the hostages, not to fight a full mobile infantry column head-on.

"Best we can do," Brentwood said as the two JO-TEVs paused, "is find Eliot and offer our services to him."

"Problem is," Lewis said, "that fucking Nazi and the two women will be in that column."

"I know that, Aussie," Brentwood retorted. "And if you've got any ideas about how to go get them right now, I'd welcome them."

Lewis thought for a moment. "Nah," he said finally. "I can't think of anything. Just pisses me off to think of that bastard out there somewhere—banging those two women."

"And here I thought it was your humanitarian concern," Brentwood said.

"Yeah, well, that too," Lewis mumbled. It amused Thomas to see Lewis embarrassed by his genuine concern for the two women Hearn had used as a shield.

It was another hour before Montoya and the ALERTs contacted the most forward elements of Eliot's column. They were the surveyors for the two batteries—twelve guns in all—looking for high ground from which they could lay down heavy barrage fire should the militia force, in the words of Sergeant Norris, who accompanied the surveyors, "refuse to surrender."

"I beg your pardon, Sergeant?" Lewis said with exaggerated politeness. "Did I hear you say *surrender*?"

"Yes," Norris said, despite Lewis's incredulous tone.

Lewis jerked his thumb over his right shoulder in the direction, miles away now, of the disabled cherry picker. "Sarge, let me tell you about the militia and surrendering."

Norris listened to Lewis's account of the short, fierce fight atop the gully, and it confirmed for him what he already knew, despite Major Eliot's hope of a surrender: the militia wouldn't so easily capitulate.

"We'll pulverize them with the howitzers," Norris told Lewis and his mates. "It'll sort things out quick smart."

And what about the women? Brentwood wondered, a sinking feeling in his stomach. Purdy could use them, as Hearn had, as a shield.

But Hearn had already offered them to Colonel Purdy, who forcefully, indeed indignantly, declined.

"It dishonors the militia," he'd told the Nazi bluntly. "I won't deny that I've let the federals think I might already have hostages as protection against possible air attack, but I was wrong in doing so. I won't do it again."

"No," Hearn said contemptuously, "because you don't have to. They know you do have hostages now. Mine!"

"We're not using them," Purdy said. "It's—it's ignoble."

"Oh, yeah, well, wait until they start with the artillery. See what your boys say then."

Purdy turned on him. "They're under my command, not yours. You'll do as I say."

"Hey, Jake, I do what I do. I came here thinking you were someone who'd go to the edge."

"I won't use the women!" Purdy said. "And, you insolent bastard, address me as—"

"Shove it!" Hearn told him. "If you won't use 'em, I will. I didn't come this far to end up as fucking artillery fodder. Big Tits and the other one stay with me and Toro. I want someone with me who knows the area."

"And what if I refuse?"

"Hey, Jake, you're not listening to me. I did my bit at Hoover. I've earned the right. I told you, if you don't intend to use the women, I will. And if you're so damned concerned about their safety, you'd better get me a good guide and half a dozen good shooters to get me outa here. Because they go where I go."

Reluctantly, Purdy told him, "The best chance to hide would be in the Canyon de Chelly National Monument. It's really three big canyons twenty miles south of here. I'll give you one of our guides. That's the best I can do."

"I'll want two pickups," Hearn demanded. "One for me, Toro, Big Tits, and the nurse. One for the shooters."

Hearing Hearn's demands, Purdy was forced to concede that for once the media, which he thoroughly distrusted, had been right in calling Hearn a "ruthless Nazi sympathizer" whose reason for joining the militia was to overthrow the government in order to establish a white supremacist regime across the United States, as well as in the Pacific Northwest, where the Aryan Nation already had numerous sympathizers. Watching Hearn's arrogant stride, and his equally arrogant dismissal of one of the militiamen whose truck he commandeered without a thank-you, Purdy pondered the fact that only a day or so ago he'd been prepared to take his column to rescue Hearn's.

The other thing that struck Purdy was Hearn's apparent lack of interest in what had happened to the militiamen, including Vance, in the four ambulances the Nevada

National Guard had overrun and, with the exception of Lucky McBride, wiped out. For Hearn, it seemed, other people were mere pawns, objects to be moved in the service of his will. The only regret, if it could be called that, that Purdy had about Hearn's impending desertion of the column was that Hearn's departure would mean the loss of the Nazi's undeniable fighting skills. His cowardly use of hostages notwithstanding, he was a fearless fighter, as evidenced at the Battle of Butcher's Ridge against Douglas Freeman's federal forces.

"Colonel?" It was one of the forward scouts in the column returning to report to Purdy that two vehicles with what looked like five federals had been spotted and were now heading northeastward.

"All right," Purdy said. "Those stand-ins ready?"

"All set to go, Colonel," militiaman Benet replied. "Just give us the word."

"Shortly," Purdy said. "You and your scouts go out front as far as you can, Benet. The moment you see their artillery, fire a red flare." He added by way of explanation, "They may have radio jammers on."

"Yes, sir."

Next, Purdy turned to his second in command. "Make sure all our drivers know to split up as soon as we bring the stand-ins into play. Tell them I don't want any pickup closer than fifty yards to another. Whatever we do, we mustn't bunch up and present the federals a concentrated target."

"The drivers have already been told, Colonel."

"Tell them again."

"Yes, sir." But Purdy's second in command doubted they'd see any artillery for a while. Except for the five federals Benet had seen, there had been no sign of the forward elements of Eliot's column, let alone artillery.

Wesley Knox took the bag past a beggar sitting on the pavement, his dog and cup next to him as he read, to the corner of Fifth Avenue and Forty-seventh Street. The street was known as Diamond Alley, and it was crowded with tourists and Hasidic Jews in beards and stovepipe hats. Everyone gawking at so much wealth in the shops, Knox thought—all of it so near yet so far. That's why he'd come here. Screw the World Trade Center—bad vibes from the brothers. Besides, this was his best bet. Everyone in a hurry, so that no one, including the cops in their booths along the street, would notice the plastic glove on his right hand carrying the bag. And if they did, they wouldn't give a shit.

He noted the breeze was coming from Sixth Avenue, put the bag down in front of one of the barred-window jewelry stores, and unzipped it. He reached in with the plastic glove, took the claw hammer and smashed the glass ampoules, then let the hammer drop into the bag and kept walking down Forty-seventh Street *against* the wind. Before he got to Sixth Avenue, where he turned the corner past Rockefeller Center, heading toward Central Park, there was a commotion about fifty yards behind him. People started screaming.

On Sixth and Fifty-second he saw a one-act play going on between two cops and two men with an old flatbed truck loaded with oranges, one guy at the wheel of the truck, the second guy alternately yelling at him and telling him the cops wanted to see a permit to sell oranges, the second guy assuring the cops he'd move the truck. Then the cops heard the screaming and took off.

A policeman called in the location of the disturbance, his partner pulling violently at his collar, saying he couldn't breathe. By the time the other policeman realized what it was, he too was gasping for air, dying.

As ambulances screamed in from Bellevue, their drivers overcome with the sarin, cars crashed, piling up both at Forty-seventh and Sixth and Forty-seventh and Fifth, bodies strewn everywhere.

CHAPTER FIFTY-TWO

The four ALERTs and Montoya—none of them easy men to impress—were nothing less than astonished by the two JO-TEVs, and indeed the vehicles were to play a vital part in what would become known as the Battle for Chinle Wash, the latter the clear, shallow creek, a scratch on the map, north of Canyon de Chelly.

It was in this canyon, where the wash flowed amid the vivid polished greens of cottonwood trees, beneath towering, awesomely beautiful six-hundred-foot layered sandstone cliffs, that Purdy had once wanted to make his stand, before Hearn's raid in Phoenix caused him to change strategy. The "White House" ruins were located there—the stone remains of ancient pre-Navajo Anasazi cliff dwellers.

The wash north of Canyon de Chelly, though a clear, sandy-bottomed creek, was surrounded by rough desert country that challenged the toughest of four-wheel-drives. It was here that the JO-TEVs impressed the ALERTs, the highly extolled and versatile Hummer a distant second when it came to negotiating the rough ground, impassable by any other four-by-four. As the five men hurried toward the coordinates of Eliot's column's last position, with neither surprise nor silence a consideration, both Brentwood and Lewis hit the yellow button selecting the 2.1-liter Peugeot diesel capability of the hybrid diesel/electric vehicles. Speeding eastward, looking for the column, they thus saved their electric power, the JO-TEVs' big sixty-kilowatt alternators pro-

ducing over fifty times the electric power produced in a
normal four-by-four.

"I feel ill," Beverly Malkin said.

"Then open the door," Toro said gruffly. "Don't be sick in
here."

"Leave her alone," said Dana Teer, in handcuffs in the
front passenger's seat, Hearn driving, Toro and Malkin in
the back.

"You," Toro retorted, smacking her hard on the side of her
head, "be quiet and do as you're fuckin' told."

Hearn slid the automatic into low gear, the pickup negotiating a sharp incline north of Chinle, where tourists
often stopped to hire Navajo guides, as required by law, to
see one of the three canyons in the national monument:
Canyon del Muerto, the northernmost depression; Black
Rock Canyon, the middle; and Canyon de Chelly itself, the
farthest south.

Hearn hadn't said a word for miles since leaving Purdy's
militia column, paying close attention to the map of the area
and in particular to the location of a little-known slot canyon
that Purdy had mentioned, more out of consideration for the
safety of the two women than for him or Toro. Even with
the rising wind, Hearn knew he would be visible for miles
in the high desert terrain. But he also assumed that whoever
saw him and the six militiamen accompanying him would
probably think he was trying for a run south of Purdy's main
force, in order to make hit-and-run attacks against Eliot's left
flank. Indeed, Hearn had a similar misconception when he
saw the spiral of dust left behind by the ALERTs as they
made their way toward Eliot's column. It never occurred to
him that it was the ALERTs. He assumed that the men
they'd defeated so soundly back at the dam were still there.

Meanwhile, Purdy continued advancing eastward. But
until he was sure where the federals' towed artillery was, he
knew he could not hope to attack with confidence, and as
yet he hadn't heard from John Reid, who should be somewhere behind Eliot's main force. Perhaps Eliot's federal

column had simply stopped, Purdy thought, and was digging in. Or had Eliot withdrawn after hearing news of the Nevada National Guard overrunning Hearn's ambulances near Hoover Dam?

In fact, neither was the case. Eliot's column had split in two, his mobile infantry moving fast in an outflanking movement to the north, the slower artillery turning to the southwest to try to catch Purdy's militia in a pincer movement. The artillery, Eliot hoped, would panic the militia, which would flee in disarray eastward where the federals' concentrated mobile infantry could exact a heavy price, turning disarray into a rout.

The wind had risen in the high desert, visibility declining, and John Reid, on the old Harley-Davidson motorcycle he'd rented in Shiprock township, was finding it increasingly difficult to follow the tracks of the federal column, signs of the tire marks obscured by the wind. Riding nervously on the motorbike, which had seen better days, recalling Ray Fraser's violent death on the rock and worrying that at any moment he would be confronted by the federals' rear guard, Reid was about to witness the strangest sight of his life.

He sensed movement somewhere in front. Or was it, he wondered, a sudden gust, a change in the predominant direction of the wind? But then he saw movement again. This time it was more definite, a brown arc in the reddish brown dust—something, he guessed, about the size of a tennis ball, maybe even smaller. Despite the rising wind, he'd been able to distinguish between the traces of the Bradleys, other vehicles, and those of the towed guns. But now the wind was winning the battle, erasing tire and Bradley tracks altogether. Reid stopped the motorbike and sat there shaking. He felt suddenly weak, perspiring, and a heart-stopping panic attack had him in its grip. He was afraid of going back, terrified of going forward. He was sure he was dying.

The panic attack left Reid feeling utterly exhausted, his palms and neck sweaty, clammy to the touch, a stickiness he knew was due more to his mental state than the humidity of the cumulus-invaded sky. He could smell impending rain. It calmed him, not completely, but enough that he knew he wasn't going to die in the next few minutes. After he'd seen the first frog—the quick, brown arc in the dust—it was only a matter of seconds until he saw another half dozen or so, then even more. It was an astonishing sight, something he'd never seen in the desert before: a proliferation of life that he expected in swampy lowland, not in the high desert.

Praying that the static wouldn't be as bad as it had been earlier, he called Purdy's force. There was static dancing in the background, but Purdy told Reid he could hear him, barely, and Reid told him about the frogs—they were in fact toads, not frogs—which Purdy knew were spadefoots or *Scaphiopus couchii*. The toads spent most of their life in these arid climes dug in several feet below the surface, but today, mistaking the sound of engines immediately above them for thunder, they had dug their way quickly up to the surface, excited by the prospect of rain puddles in which to mate.

"It means," Purdy explained to Reid, "that heavy machinery of a certain tone has passed over them."

"The trucks pulling the big guns!" Reid said.

"Give . . . man . . . Kewpie doll," Reid heard before static drowned Purdy's voice.

But Reid didn't need any more. He knew what to do. Wherever the rumbling of trucks pulling guns had passed, toads in the hundreds would be present. It was ironic, Reid thought, that what with the El Niño–driven weather going as crazy as it was, there was a very great possibility of thunder and rain anyway. Till then, however, the artificial thunder of the trucks pulling the six-ton 155mm howitzers would suffice.

CHAPTER FIFTY-THREE

Alan Orr and Neil Brody were informed by the man they knew only as Ken that they had to leave Omak and surrounding environs.

"When?" asked a sleepy Brody, who had dozed off while waiting for his mug of coffee to cool, his beard having soaked up some of the pancake syrup.

"Right away!" Ken told him. "Just got a call from the militia down in Bridgeport. That commandant at Fairchild—"

"Moorehead," Orr said.

"Yeah. Apparently he's going ape and knows it's you two who are missing."

"Huh," Orr said disparagingly. "Wouldn't take a genius to figure that out."

"Yeah, well, apparently the boys said your POW buddies managed to cover it up for a while, one guy crouching, moving down the lines as they counted heads. Counted him twice and another guy who was covering for you. Point is, fellas, the feds've now got your names and faces from their Polaroid collection, and every sheriff from here to Walla Walla is gunning for you. They've put it out that you're armed and dangerous."

"Who?" Brody demanded, his question devoid of his normal good cheer.

"Both of you," Ken told him. "Nothing for it but to make a daylight run to Nighthawk. A farm up there right near the border. They'll send you across tonight."

Abrem, Orr noticed, had already left for home, forgetting the gumbo thermos.

"Oh, shit," Brody enjoined, manifesting signs of panic at odds with his earlier nonchalance. "Have to use the bathroom," he said.

"Yeah, all right," Ken answered. "But hurry."

The blizzard in eastern Washington had abated, the snowfall now light and melting the moment it struck Ken's windshield. Orr, gazing out at the virgin snow, missed the hard blow of small-grained powder snow. While it had reduced visibility to zero, it had also given him a reassuring, almost cozy feeling of invulnerability, being in a safe cocoon from the hostile world outside. Now, visibility was a quarter mile or so, just enough that if you suddenly saw a vehicle coming at you, you had time to worry but not enough time to do much about it. Brody, however, appeared unfazed by the change in the weather; if anything, the increased visibility seemed to make him more optimistic.

"How far's this farm?" Brody asked Ken.

"Not too far," Ken replied edgily, obviously still spooked by the urgency of the phone call that had catapulted him into action, belying his earlier calm. "When you go across tonight," he told the two of them, "don't bunch up."

Brody laughed. "Bunch up? Heck, there's only two of us."

"Coupla guys got caught like that," Ken said, as if Brody hadn't heard him. "Sticking together like Mutt and Jeff."

"Mutt and Jeff?" Brody said.

"Comic characters," Orr explained.

"Gotta keep well apart," Ken reiterated.

"Yes," Orr said, "but it'll be dark. Have to be able to see one another." Jesus, Ken was spooking him.

"Yeah, I know that," Ken said, "but not too close. They shone a light on those two and both of 'em stood out like sore thumbs. Get what I mean?" Then, conversely, Ken reassured them, "You'll be fine. It'll be moonlight. On the snow you'll see one another real easy, just keep about ten feet or so apart. If that second guy hadn't been so close, he'd've never gotten caught. All he had to do was stand real still and the feds might never have seen him."

"What did they do to him?" Brody asked.

"Shot him. Said he was trying to escape."

"Well, he was, wasn't he?" Brody said.

"Yeah, but I mean when they were taking him back to Camp Fairchild." Brody for once didn't try to joke it away. Instead he made a face at Orr. "Not nice."

"No," Orr said, "it isn't. We'll—"

"Car coming!" Ken shouted and both of them slid down out of view.

The oncoming car passed, but Ken told Orr and Brody to stay down. "Farm's coming up," he added. "Another few miles."

" 'Bout time," Brody said, and it was the only time that Orr sensed that he and Brody were on the same wavelength, both of them tiring of Ken's nervousness, which had by now spilled over to them.

A few minutes later they were passing through a stand of firs, Christmaslike, with the branches laden with snow. Now and then they saw clumps of it falling off the trees like lumps of icing sugar. Orr, in his anxiety, pushed the image of collapse out of his mind, for he knew how vulnerable he was at such times to "signs" and "omens." He told himself it was simply snow melting because, though still cold, the temperature had obviously risen a couple of degrees. If he had taken the melting as a sign, he told himself, he could look on it as the end of danger, the thaw after a tense, icy journey, a melting away of adverse conditions, a sign that once he was in the farm, the tough part was over. The trouble was, he knew deep inside that the tension he'd felt was far from a spent force, that the toughest part, psychologically, would be the "walk" to the border. In the Abrem house and at Ken's, they had referred to it as a "walk," as if it were no more than a Sunday picnic in the woods. "No problem," Ken had said, or had it been Mrs. Abrem? It bothered Orr that he couldn't remember exactly, because he thought it might be a sign of Alzheimer's. But he wasn't old enough for that, or maybe age wasn't a factor? He remembered something about vitamin E slowing down the process. Jesus Christ, where was the damn farm? Of course, he reminded himself, snow melting was always depressing, the once beautiful forms covered in deep blankets of snow now revealed for what they really were.

Reid tried to contact Purdy a quarter hour after his first call, but without luck. When he did manage to reach him, Purdy's militia column was twelve miles north of Chinle, following the line of the wash, and there was no static.

"Colonel, I've got more damn frogs than I know what to do with. The big guns are maintaining the same heading toward the Hard Spring area 'bout ten, twelve miles north of Chinle. Looks like they're gonna hit you in the wash."

"That's a good bet," Purdy told Benet wryly, his voice muffled by the surgical mask he was wearing against his column's coat-tailing dust. "The wash is over seventy miles long."

In fairness to Reid, however, Benet pointed out to Purdy that if the guns were on a vector toward Hard Spring and Eliot's mobile infantry farther north, that was enough information for Purdy to act on.

Purdy agreed. "Good job, Reid. Keep following them. Call in if it's important."

"Yes, sir."

Purdy studied the sandy bed of Chinle Wash immediately to his south, its banks fringed by a verdant green that spread out to a lesser green as sage took over where cottonwoods trailed off. He took a bearing to Hard Spring, but all he could see was a dusty horizon.

"They should be in sight soon," Benet told Purdy, who knew that this was Benet's way of telling him he'd better hurry now that they knew what Eliot was up to.

The federal commander, probably under Freeman's overall command, was sending in his artillery to pound and panic the two-hundred-strong militia company, causing them to withdraw in haste. Then Eliot's mobile infantry, Purdy conjectured, would hit them hard on their right flank, when they were at the maximum point of disarray, relying on the age-old terror infantry experienced in the face of the big guns.

Benet, who had been the coolest of the cool at the skirmish of Ship Rock, now seemed agitated. "Sir," he said. "Sir, we've got to—"

"Yes, yes," Purdy snapped. "We've got to keep their guns down here to give our infantry time to engage their infantry without having to worry about their guns *reaching* up north." By "reaching" he meant that the federal artillery's 155mms, their dust cloud now rising on the eastern horizon, had a reach of eleven miles. It would take them at least fifteen minutes, even half an hour, to set up with their surveyors' poles. During that time, the armed pickups of the militia column could race to engage Eliot's mobile infantry—not in panic, not in disarray, but *before* Eliot expected it. As with so many things, it was all a matter of timing.

"Sir—"

"Yes. Break out the stand-ins."

The stand-ins in this case were twelve new inflatable Army surplus M-1A1 tank decoys, impossible to differentiate from the real thing beyond three hundred yards. They were inflatable by portable Yamaha air compressors, or, in an emergency, by their CO_2 gas cylinders. So convincing were they that they came with an inbuilt "break-a-bag" chemical heat source to duplicate an M-1's heat signature, should they be viewed by enemy infrared scopes. In minutes, behind the thick rising dust curtain, an ochre-red in overcast filtered light, twelve M-1 tanks were born, each complete with fake 120mm main gun, auxiliary 7.62mm machine gun, and thermal sight.

In the twenty minutes it took for Eliot's artillery and Purdy's fake tanks to come within good binocular range of one another, militiaman Norris was enormously impressed by the courage of his fellow tank handlers. Staying behind, they'd had to marshal the phony tanks in convincing loose deuce formation, where each lead tank was flanked by two other tanks, or "wingmen," just enough men visible to Eliot's artillery that it would convince the federal gunners, now racing to set up their guns, that a standard tank-led infantry advance was under way.

"Holy Mother!" an ammo carrier, or gun bunny, said, taking a quick binocular look at the tanks.

"Don't worry," the gun chief told him, "those tanks' 120 mil have only got a range of five thousand yards."

"Yeah, well, it's too fucking long for me, Jack," the gun's second bunny said.

"Ah, quit your moaning," the gun chief told them. "We got three times their range."

"Yeah," the first bunny mumbled, lending a hand with the transom, "but those mothers are *movin'*, Chief. 'Sides, it only takes them a couple of minutes to cover a thousand yards. That could put 'em at our throats before we set up."

"Then shut up and *work*!" the chief shouted, anxious to get the gun rotated, elevated, and aligned with the surveyors' poles. What the chief of this gun and the chiefs of Eliot's other eleven guns in the four batteries were counting on was that the tanks, delayed by what the chiefs believed were the militia infantry coming behind, would be able to advance only at walking pace, unable to dash ahead any earlier and do battle with the federal artillery.

On the opposing side, Purdy's eastbound infantry was relying on the hope that by the time the federals' artillery had engaged the fake tanks and discovered the militia's ruse, it would be too late for the federal artillerymen, no matter how efficient each of Eliot's federal gun crew was, to engage them. By the time Eliot's artillery had packed up, hooked up their guns to the trucks, and headed northeastward to try to support their mobile infantry against the militia's high-speed attack, the battle would be joined, the mobile militia and mobile federal infantry so intermingled, at close quarters, that it would be impossible to use the artillery.

CHAPTER FIFTY-FOUR

It looked like aliens had landed on Forty-seventh Street between Fifth and Sixth Avenue, the nuclear-biological-and-chemical suits similar to the one Caroline Hart had worn when she was killed in Tooele. Several of the NBC-suited emergency response team members were also holding gunlike pistol-grip gas detectors.

Despite a cool breeze coming in off the Atlantic, it was a sauna inside the suits, some of the visors misting up. Soon the detectors' needles were dropping to zero, but police and ambulance personnel, quite a few of them women, were too terrified to take off the suits despite the intense discomfort. By now all the bodies had been removed. Thousands of panicky people were evacuated from buildings in the surrounding blocks, scores of people ill and still sitting curbside awaiting attention, many of them robbed as they lay incapacitated on the sidewalks. Traffic was snarled to a stop on Fifth Avenue, mounted police moving in as the all-clear was finally given.

Police investigative teams also moved in, a two-detective team, a man and a woman in their early thirties from Midtown North, starting at the shop window where the bag containing the sarin had been placed.

The shop reeked with the smell of vomit. The owner, a

gaunt, elderly Jewish American, and his son, a stocky man in his forties, lay dead on the floor, one of the glass cases opened, the owner's key chain still out of his pocket, lying next to him. A chalk outline near the door marked the spot where a customer on her way out had unwittingly moved closer to the source of the sarin gas just outside.

There were chalked outlines all over the street, the irony being, as the *New York Times* noted, that the elderly owner of the shop, an indelible Auschwitz number on his wrist, had survived the death camps of Nazi Germany as a young boy, only to be murdered by Nazi-derived gas, sarin, in America. The *Times* was reporting that several neo-Nazi skinhead militia hate groups of the kind the fugitive Hearn belonged to had phoned in claiming responsibility, several warning that "niggers and faggots are next."

On closer examination, the two detectives from Midtown North found several diamonds that had spilled out from the black velvet cushion pad in the now open display case and onto the floor, rolling under the edging of the case. While the female detective used the pair of tweezers from behind the counter to put the diamonds back, the male detective moved toward the curtain separating the front of the shop from the rear, noting a video surveillance camera above him on the left.

Behind the curtain, he looked at the monitor and saw a hand behind the countertop, his partner's as she retrieved the diamonds from the floor. The rest of her body was a blur, being too close to the camera, only the remainder of the small storefront properly in focus. He could see the chalk outline of the dead customer, and was wondering why the ambulance attendants hadn't taken the old man and his son away with the customer; possibly because all the ambulances were full, he thought. When he saw that the video camera's red light was on, he felt a rush of excitement. Some of them did that, record for six hours at a time and then record over. He was about to tell his partner, but decided to wait. If anything, there'd probably be only a glimpse on the video of anyone outside at the time of the sarin attack. And a number of things might obscure any such image; the sun, or rain. Had it rained earlier? he wondered. He'd been in his cubby-hole doing paperwork.

He stopped the tape, removed it, put it in the monitor, and pressed Rewind gently, as if any rough treatment of the machine might screw up the tape. That'd be it, wouldn't it? A prime suspect and you screw up the tape. It was different equipment from his own, and he had a second of panic when he thought he might have pressed the wrong button. After several seconds of whiny rewinding, he stopped it and pressed Play.

"Found anything, Ralph?" his partner asked.

"Not yet," he said casually. Mama mia, this could be his ticket to stardom. He saw the tape start and pushed Fast Forward, but everything was going too fast, like Keystone Kops. It seemed as if someone was coming in or going out of the store every couple of seconds. All right, he realized, unless he took it back to the lab, he'd have to watch all of it here. No telling when the old guy had started the tape.

"What are you doing?" his partner asked, pulling aside the black curtain. She could see he was exited. "You're not telling me it was on Record?" she said.

"Yes, it was."

"Jesus, Ralph!"

"Don't get excited, Beth. Whoever dumped the bag would have been recorded through the glass. Maybe there were too many reflections for a clear image."

"Well, have you seen anything yet?"

"Not on Fast Forward. Have to watch the whole friggin' thing."

"Yeah, but you'd pick up a guy with a bag."

"Yeah, but you blink for a fraction of a second and it's gone."

"It's not *that* fast! Here, let me have a go."

"All yours."

Ralph was excited but anxious. Wasn't there a point of professional etiquette here? That is, if they got an image of whoever dumped the bag, who would the credit belong to? He was the one who'd seen the red recording light on.

"You can have it," she said, without taking her eyes off the screen.

"What d'you mean? Have what?"

"You know. The glory." She was reading his mind.

"Hey," he said. "We might have squat."

"In that case," she said, her eyes still on the screen, "we'll share it."

"Fair enough."

CHAPTER FIFTY-FIVE

Approaching Chinle, Hearn looked up and didn't like what he saw—a sky grown lumpy and sullen from the invasion of cumulonimbus clouds that had been turning darker by the hour. The last thing he needed was rain, which could turn the desert into a quagmire, inhibiting his run into Canyon del Muerto—the Canyon of Death—so-called because of the massacre in 1805 by Spanish soldiers of over eighty Navajos. The Indians took refuge in a cave located over five hundred feet above the northernmost of the three canyons that formed Canyon de Chelly National Monument. But Hearn's luck held as he and the second pickup, carrying six of Purdy's militia "shooters," passed quickly through Chinle township, past the campground a mile or so west of the Navajo township, past Blade Rock and Antelope Point, then turned left, heading east-northeast into Canyon del Muerto itself, where a sign warned that the trail was only for four-wheel-drive vehicles and that by law a Navajo guide must accompany all who entered. They continued for another three miles beneath cliff dwellings, the Navajo Fortress, Battle Cove Ruins, and still farther into the thousand-foot-deep Canyon del Muerto, and past another sign indicating that the trail ahead was only for four-wheel-drive vehicles. And a relatively new sign warning of fallen rock as far in as Massacre Cave, eleven miles into the eroded but at times relatively wide V-shaped canyon. Some offshoot "slot" canyons narrowed to a matter of feet, the main canyon going on for at least another twelve miles, the sheer walls as enclosing as they were awesome.

Hearn was past the slot canyon entrance before Morgan, the scout Purdy had assigned to him, realized it. Hearn, however, though tense, showed no irritation with Morgan because, as he told Toro, if one of Purdy's best guides could miss it, then so would anyone stupid enough to try to follow him.

"Oh, shit!" It was the first time since they'd left Purdy's column that Toro had spoken, apart from when he'd smacked Dana Teer and told her to shut up.

"What's with you?" Hearn demanded.

"These vehicles. What are we gonna do with 'em? Federals'd see them and—"

"No problem," Hearn assured him. "Christ, you think I'd come all this way without thinking of that?"

Toro shrugged, his way of apology. "So what do we do?"

Hearn indicated the group of six militiamen, all of them out of the vehicle, stretching their legs. "Two of these guys'll drive the vehicles farther into the Canyon del Muerto a couple of miles, pick out a nice wide part of the canyon and hide 'em, then walk back."

One of the two militiamen Hearn pointed to was frowning, complaining, "That'll take a while."

"Oh, gee," Hearn said, oozing sarcasm. "I'm sorry, boys. I didn't mean to drag you away from a chance of getting killed by federals. You just take it easy here. Sit down a while, have a cup of coffee. Wait till the federals come along

and see the two fucking pickups here that'll take them right
to the slot. Now, my guess is they'll shoot you on the spot
after that little incident at Ship Rock I heard about. On the
other hand, they might take pity on you and ship you off to
Camp Fairchild. It's nice up there—'bout ten below fucking
zero. All right?"

None of Purdy's six volunteers said a word, though if
looks could kill, Hearn and Toro would have both been
dead. The two men Hearn had chosen walked sulkily to their
respective pickups.

"Wait till we unload," Hearn said, looking over at Toro
and shaking his head.

"Can we please get out?" It was Dana Teer. "And go to
the bathroom?"

"Shut up!" said Toro, who turned to Hearn. "That's all
they ever do—piss."

"Let 'em out," Hearn instructed him. "Uncuff 'em, but
have 'em go do it inside the slot canyon. Not here outside. If
the feds are stupid enough to follow us and bring dogs, I
don't want them picking up—"

There was the sound of thunder, or what sounded like
thunder. "It's the guns," one of the four remaining militiamen said.

As Dana Teer and Beverly Malkin went through the entrance to the slot canyon, so called because of its narrowness
and depth, over six hundred feet deep at this point, they
stared upward at the sheer sandstone cliffs thrusting into the
sky. Strange, eerie, and at times changing patterns of light
flickered now and then, as if reflected from hidden subter-
ranean pools, striking shades of pink and ochre throughout
the exquisitely layered sandstone rock. It was at once awe-
inspiring and frightening, the kind of fearful excitement that
embraces scuba divers when, passing through an opening
just wide enough to squeeze through, they discover caverns
of stunning and lonely grandeur.

Suddenly the light disappeared, the bruised clouds moving so fast above the slot canyon that it seemed to the two
women that they were the ones moving. And then all they

could see passing high above the slot was solid gray. Rain clouds.

Teer understood why Hearn hadn't worried about them trying to run off. She'd peeked at the map on the drive down, and the main Canyon del Muerto went on for over two miles, its wash shrinking to a narrow waist in places where the cliffs were only a few feet apart, as opposed to the football-field-width floor of the canyon farther in, where cottonwood trees and pine apparently flourished beneath the site of ancient, little-known cliff dwellings.

"You can't run forever," Teer told Hearn after she and Beverly reemerged.

Hearn smiled. "None of us can run forever, sweetheart, but I intend to stick around a lot longer than you."

A chill passed through her.

"I have a bad feeling about this place," Malkin whispered in what was the understatement of her life. "I feel so closed in. Claustrophobic."

"Hang on," Teer implored her, talking as much to herself as to the nurse.

CHAPTER FIFTY-SIX

"Load!" Eliot's gun chief ordered. "Fire!" They were using high-explosive, ninety-pound rounds plus propellant, "adjusting" rounds, readying the howitzers for what Eliot advised his gunners would be a "fire assault"—a concentrated artillery attack upon the tanks, with intermittent smoke rounds to confuse those tanks not yet destroyed and to produce an obscuring screen of smoke and dust through which the militia couldn't see. After that, if the tanks attacked, it would be "target of opportunity" firing.

One of the gun chiefs used a palm-sized microtape recorder rather than a notebook for his gun log, to keep tabs on how many shots and what type were being fired, information that would be utilized and gone over later to ensure correct servicing and aiming of the guns. Between shouting his orders and talking into the mike, which was practically in his mouth to override the collective boom of the guns, the gun chief noted that a star parachute flare round had been loaded instead of an H.E. What he said to the two gun bunnies wasn't nice, his right thumb on his recorder's Off button as he castigated the hapless Guardsmen for fouling up the intended five-rounds-per-minute delivery.

The truth was, some of the gun crews were tiring prematurely, the extraordinary amount of nervous energy required in this, the first battle for some, draining them. The relatively new Guardsmen were easy to identify because of their nervous haste, as opposed to the equally fast but more rhythmic delivery of shells into the breech by veterans. The heat of the barrels, the unusual humidity of the high desert, the ear-dunning sound of the twelve 155s, the yelling of the gun chiefs, the pungent stink of cordite, and the dust from the barrels' heat wash, all combined to almost overwhelm their senses.

It was a full ten minutes—a long time in any battle, an eternity for some—before several of the gun chiefs, amid the cacophony of battle, noticed that something was awry. Before smoke had been laid, so densely as to obscure the militia's view of the artillery, two of Eliot's gun chiefs were puzzled by the lack of what they believed should have been direct hits on the militia's armor. Perhaps the enemy tanks were pulling back? A sensible move for Purdy if, as was the case, the federal howitzers were beyond the maximum five-thousand-yard range of the tanks. Now more smoke had been laid, this time between the tanks and howitzers by the militia's 81mm mortars. The initial confusion was made worse when the officer commanding Eliot's artillery sensibly ordered his gunners to switch from "contact" to "proximity fuses." Given the literal fog of war created by smoke rounds from both sides, it was a smart and responsible move, because the smoke and dust had thwarted the guns' laser and thermal sights, whereas the proximity fuses were set to explode if in the near vicinity of solid objects, such as a tank. However, except for one of the proximity shells, which blew one of the militia's 81mm mortar–mounted militia pickups to pieces, along with its four occupants, nearly all of the proximity rounds exploded on the ground—as if there were no tanks there, sending up spumes of red earth and rock. Eliot then ordered the commencement of a rolling barrage, which, beginning at four thousand yards, would move through the "tank" area northward. This would hopefully achieve two things simultaneously: dissuade any of the militia's tanks from attacking through the smoke, and destroy any other mobile militia infantry in its path.

Also fearing that some of the mobile militia infantry might break through to the guns—when in fact at most Purdy had no more than fourteen men with his fake tanks—the federal gun chiefs ordered beehive rounds brought up from the ammunition trucks. If the militia infantry did break through, then the federal gunners, providing the howitzers could be loaded fast enough, would fire these shells, packed with thousands of metal darts, at point-blank range. Now, however, because of the danger of overheating the guns, the rate of fire had to be held at no more than three a minute with over three hundred rounds.

More smoke appeared from both sides, curling within the blankets of smoke already laid, and no one knew what to expect.

It was in this confusion of smoke, much of it blowing over one another's lines, that John Reid fell. The gun chief from the federals' second howitzer spotted the militiaman as he emerged ghostlike from the man-made fog of war and shot him dead, the young militiaman obviously, bravely, coming up behind the guns to take out as many of the gun crew as he could.

Six miles away to the northeast, a furious running infantry battle was in full swing. Here too, smoke from both militia pickups and Eliot's mortars had been laid. But where Eliot's infantry were dug in, the militia were attacking under cover of 81mm mortar and heavy machine-gun fire. Their heavily armed pickups had not stopped since racing there from the smoke-obscured artillery battle south-southwest of them, where gun chiefs, gunners, loaders, and gun bunnies kept up the rolling barrage, with murderous intent.

The ALERTs weren't used to being in, or in this case confined to, a defensive mode. Eliot refused their request outright. He didn't want any "hotshots" doing a "Rambo," with the possibility of his Bradleys mistaking the ALERTs' unorthodox JO-TEVs as militia "dune buggies." But they told him their whole reason for being was to attack.

"As you did," Eliot coldly reminded them, "at the dam. With humiliating results."

Along with Montoya, the ALERTs wanted Hearn badly, but soon found themselves fighting for their lives as the mobile militia, over 150 of them, hit Eliot's dug-in position front and side. The major had ordered his Bradleys into action and was confident he'd win, though with the militia pickups afforded the cover of dense smoke and dust, which would affect the guidance of their TOW missiles, Eliot knew it would be a close-run thing.

Despite the Bradleys' 25mm cannon, the faster pickups time and again burst through with their lethal shoulder-fired antitank missile, the pickups' souped-up acceleration and tight turns more than once overcoming the Bradleys' maximum turbo-driven speed of thirty-eight miles an hour.

Faster speeds, of course, meant more danger for the pickup drivers, as Lewis and Brentwood witnessed while firing their I-COWs. They saw a dark khaki pickup turning hard right into the path of an oncoming Bradley, the pickup literally bouncing off the Bradley, then rolling, spilling out its

complement of four militiamen in the back. The Bradley's
7.62 machine gun raked and killed two of them before they
could get up, the 25mm cannon chopping two others to
pieces. But the driver in the badly dented cabin had managed to crawl free, and grabbing the truck's AT-4, he fired it
at point-blank range, shrapnel from the hit killing him and
setting the Bradley afire. The crew was shot up by another
pickup, which emerged briefly from the choking haze of
mixed black and white smoke, then disappeared.

Salvini, on Lewis's left, let fly with a burst of his I-COW's
armor-piercing and incendiary 25mm, which they could
hear rattling about in the pickup before the vehicle blossomed with orange flame, swayed violently, and stopped,
now a faint shape in the smoke-riven dust. One man, covered in flame, leaped from the burning truck, screaming, another militiaman throwing earth on him, yelling for him to
lie down. But the man fell, a shriveled black form curling
into the fetal position, dying as they watched. Brentwood
fired, and the militiaman, Benet of Ship Rock fame, who
now looked like a picture Brentwood had seen of a monk who
had immolated himself during the Vietnam War, toppled
sideways, dead. Montoya felt sick but forced himself to keep
his eyes to the front, and saw a pickup bearing down on him
out of the smoke. He didn't panic, but simply went flat in his
slit trench, the pickup hitting the hard-piled earth in front of
the trench, its rear wheels, a foot above the earth, missing
Montoya by inches. Montoya fired his 3.06 at the vehicle's
extra gas tanks and, to his disgust, missed by a wide margin.

The desert wind was picking up, blowing away the smoke
cover, the militia, having exhausted their supply of smoke
grenades and mortar rounds, becoming more visible. Purdy
had a simple, stark choice: throw everything into a final concentrated attack before all the smoke was gone, or pull back.
The truth, however, was that neither he nor Eliot nor anyone else really knew which way the battle was going. It was
a confusion of noise, tires squealing, the relatively quiet
rush of the Bradleys' turbos, mortars exploding, and geysers

of earth erupting, taking on a chocolatey hue in the fading smoke.

Purdy knew that in ten minutes or so he'd have a much better idea of what was happening, but right now, in the almost indescribably cloying humidity and chaos, ten minutes was an eternity, the air, now that the smoke was clearing, pierced by dozens of TOW missiles streaming out from Eliot's Bradleys. It left Purdy wondering what Freeman, his old boss and now his enemy, would do in such a situation. Meanwhile, a crazy incident was unfolding on the federals' right flank, as Salvini and Thomas moved to occupy a forward position where two of Eliot's men had been killed. A militia mortar squad, as Purdy now gave the order for one final, and hopefully overwhelming, attack on the federal position, fired an 81mm mortar smoke round. Lewis heard the pop and, sensing in that mysterious way some soldiers have of knowing that a particular mortar was heading for him, he took cover, not knowing it wouldn't be an H.E. round. As the smoke began to dissipate, a federal soldier, an M-60 machine gunner only twenty yards from Thomas on the right flank, "lost it," as Thomas described it, screaming, "Gas! It's gas!" At which point he ripped his Atropine shot from its plastic bag, plunging the needle into his right thigh muscle, bringing on violent illness before the Diazepam in the antitoxic mix took effect. Then he lay down, no longer "giving a shit" about what was going on.

What had gone on was an aborted militia attack, aborted because of the cries of "gas" that spread through the battlefield on both sides, the federals equipped with masks, the militia not. It turned out that the federal soldier, or "Screamer," as he was called afterward, had been spooked by the radio reports of the gas attack in New York.

When the smoke cleared, Purdy saw for the first time the extent of the carnage, caused mostly by his TOW missiles in the relatively smoke-free interval. The battlefield by Chinle Wash was littered with weapons and over 120 dead—a catastrophic kill rate for any commander—Purdy realizing that the federals' Bradleys, for all the past criticism, especially about their armor, had won the day. Against the militiamen's war wagons, no matter how brave the militia had been, the Bradleys were simply too much. As with all battles, those who weren't there could fault both sides for this and that error, but the end result was unequivocal: Purdy's militia had been thrashed, and he knew that unless he wanted to see them all dead, there was only one honorable, indeed responsible, thing to do. He ordered the remainder of his spent force to surrender.

Eliot, unseen by most of his federals during the battle, preferring to stay back and command his men from higher ground, now appeared. He didn't make any apology to his men, many of whom he knew would consider him at best a backseat driver, at worst a coward. He knew he was no coward, but unlike Purdy, and Purdy's onetime mentor Freeman, Eliot found being right at the front confusing, leaving him unable to see the woods for the trees. Neither was he a fool, and in a cold, unemotional command—which only some of his survivors heard, those still with or near radios—he instructed his Guardsmen to shoot first should there be any possibility of the militia pulling a "Ship Rock" ruse.

To say it began to rain would be an understatement. There was lightning, which some men on both sides thought was the artillery still firing to the south, and then the sky opened up. It was as if El Niño, having turned the weather upside down—with the temperature reaching freezing in L.A. and in the eighties in New York, when it should have been the other way around—was determined to finish the job, the rainfall in the high Arizona desert breaking all records. This, like the smoke, cut down on visibility and added to the confusion of the militia's surrender. The federals, nerves strained, exhausted, running on nothing but adrenaline and the sugar shot of Hershey bars, were not about to take a chance with men who'd cut down their buddies at Ship Rock. A federal, seeing the quick arm movement of an advancing rain-curtained militiaman, fired his M-60, cutting the militiaman down. Suddenly everyone was firing at the militiamen, many of whom were now unarmed.

"Cease fire!" yelled Brentwood and the other ALERTs, but by then those militiamen who still had weapons were going down in what was fast becoming a field of red mud.

Eventually, probably because ammunition was running low on both sides, some even running out of ammo completely, the firing ceased, albeit with a few last defiant shots.

Eliot's federals had lost eighteen men dead and had twenty-seven wounded; the militia thirty-one wounded, one hundred fifty-two dead, one missing, and six with Hearn in Canyon del Muerto. One of the last militiamen to die was Jason Purdy, who, bending down, trying to help another wounded militiaman, was shot by a federal who in the downpour mistook his action, thinking he was reaching for a weapon.

To the south, where Captain Andrew Arnold was commanding Eliot's artillery, the carnage was proportionally even worse than at the site of the infantry battle. None of the militia had been left alive, the battlefield littered not so much with bodies as with body parts, primarily limbs, intestines, and unidentifiable lumps of flesh. Torsos had been decapitated and ID tags were gone, making it virtually impossible to identify which limb or head went with which body. The rain quickly cleansed the scattered remains, washing off the dust and creating a more macabre sight as body parts began to float in the torrential downpour, the reddish water looking like a river of blood.

Captain Arnold, unlike many of his men, wasn't fazed by the cannon-butchered militia. His view was that the militia had started "this business"—he'd merely finished it, in this area at least. But what angered him, what would stay with him till the day he died, was the discovery that the militia's tanks weren't tanks after all, but were what he called "fucking blow-up things, goddammit! *Balloons!*" Inwardly, he cringed at the thought of the embarrassment that "these militia bastards" had caused him and the Albuquerque National Guard, which, under his direct command, had expended in excess of $1.5 million in shells at a bunch of decoys. And what did he have to show for it in terms of damaged enemy matériel after the smoke had cleared? Nothing but the vinyl remains of the twelve dummy tanks, the compressed-air-filled dummies having deflated after they'd been hit several times by rounds passing straight through them before exploding. The tote bag–sized Yamaha generators, unless hit themselves, had been capable of keeping the "hot-air balloon" upright while also giving off a convincing heat signature to any of the federal guns' thermal sights that managed to penetrate the thick, roiling smoke and dust. In any event, among the line of bedraggled and utterly defeated militia prisoners of war being attended to by Eliot's medics before being marched off to the trucks that would start them on their long journey up north to Camp Fairchild, Captain Arnold would be known as "Hot Air Arnie," or "H.A." for short.

This was not, however, how he was presented on CNN and affiliates around the globe, his triumph against the "rebels" complete, the media army ordered to keep away from the battlefield itself, happy enough to settle for photo ops with Eliot. The major, in a willfully dramatic understatement intended to impress, said, "Rules are rules. The militia broke society's rules and they've paid the price."

CHAPTER FIFTY-SEVEN

When the ALERTs and Montoya, looking for Hearn, Toro, and the two women, walked in the rain through the remnant smoke of gutted, burning pickups and failed to find any sign of them, the conclusion was clear: Hearn had fled the scene either before or during the battle.

"But where?" Thomas asked.

Lewis, Brentwood, Montoya, and Salvini questioned the militia POWs now being strip-searched under a hastily erected canvas lean-to. None was in the mood to tell them anything.

"Listen!" Lewis said. "I can understand where you guys are coming from, but your mate Hearn's a first-class bastard. He's holding two women hostage. Now do we have any *gentlemen* among you?"

"Fuck you!" one militiaman said, which was followed by a murmured agreement down the line. Lewis remembered the chilling report he'd read in *Time* in the aftermath of the Oklahoma bombing, how so many antigovernment people showed no sympathy toward the victims of that blast. Such antigovernment types were certainly not going to care about two hostages.

Then the ALERTs got the first break they'd had in days. "There's some Indian from down in Chinle on the blower," Eliot's RO (radio operator) said to the major, "doing a war dance about some of our guys tearing through town without registering or something."

"Who is he?" inquired Eliot, who was then told by his R.O. that the Indian claimed he was a Navajo sheriff. "He's pretty pissed off, Major."

Eliot got on the line, having difficulty hearing the Navajo lawman because of the rain drumming on the roof, but with bits and pieces he managed to put together the fact that access to Canyon de Chelly was restricted, and the Navajo police didn't take kindly to tourists or, in this case, soldiers violating sacred ground and going in without Navajo guides.

"How do you know they were soldiers?" the humorless Eliot asked.

"They were in soldiers' uniforms," the Navajo told him, "roaring through in four-wheel-drives."

"Hummers?" Eliot asked.

"No, other kinds, but painted army khaki."

"Militia," Eliot told him. "Stop anyone from going into the canyon without my permission. I'll send some men down to investigate. How many were there?"

The Navajo sheriff paused. "I think about eight, maybe ten."

"Any women?"

"I don't know. I just glimpsed these guys in the distance. There was a lot of dust. I think there were eight."

"Armed?"

"Yes, a bunch of guns. I saw them." The Indian added, as if it were Eliot's fault, "There are press people coming in too."

"Coming in where? To Chinle?"

"Yes, there's a landing strip outside the town."

"How far is it from the three canyons?"

"The town's about—"

"No, the landing strip," Eliot said, snapping his fingers impatiently for his R.O. to get the topographic map.

"Not far," the Navajo said. "Maybe a mile."

"You need any help down there, I mean policing the place? I don't want anybody else wandering into the canyon."

"No, I got a lot of deputies I can call," the Navajo said. "And guides if I need 'em. You need guides?"

"One'll be fine," Eliot told him. "The leader of my team will be Captain Brentwood. They're heading off now." Eliot turned to the ALERTs and Place Montoya. "How far is it?"

"As the crow flies," Lewis said, measuring the distance on the map, "about eleven miles . . . a half, maybe an hour, given this deluge we're under."

"An hour," Eliot told the Najavo. "Maybe less."

"There'll be a lot of mud," the Navajo said.

"He says there'll be a lot of mud," Eliot told the ALERTs and Montoya.

"Tell me somethin' I don't know," Lewis replied.

"Anyway," Brentwood put in, "tell him we've got four-wheel drive. We should be okay."

Aussie Lewis held up his hand to get Eliot's eye. "Major,

ask if we can have two guides." Brentwood, Salvini, Thomas, and Montoya looked at him.

Eliot, nonplussed, nevertheless passed on Lewis's request.

"Why two?" Brentwood asked Lewis.

"In case one gets shot," Lewis answered.

A line of strip-searched militia POWs, about thirty in all, were now shuffling past Eliot's lean-to, the rain drumming so hard on the canvas that Brentwood knew he would have to shout to be heard by Eliot. "Major, can you have your arty towed a few miles south within range of the canyons?"

"I could, but since when are we allowed to bombard national monuments?"

"When there's a civil war, Colonel," Brentwood answered. "Besides, we might need ammo resupply. If you want, get permission from General Freeman."

"Very well," Eliot agreed.

"Just don't shell the White House," Lewis added jokingly.

He was referring to the White House Ruins in Canyon de Chelly itself, the only ruins tourists were allowed to visit without a guide. But Eliot didn't get the joke.

"You know," Lewis said as he and the others walked briskly toward the JO-TEVs, keen to get under way, "it's been proven that only about three guys out of ten in the Army can read a map properly?"

"Is that a fact?" Thomas asked dryly. "I suppose that makes us the elite, right?"

"Right," Lewis responded, "all of us except Sal. He can't read any fucking map."

"Up yours too, Aussie."

The A-frame cedar farmhouse near Nighthawk was secluded between a small apple orchard and a hillside of pine. The thaw in northern Washington State had been hit by another front moving in fast from the Pacific, and everything began refreezing, making for treacherous ice conditions leading up to the farm. The house had a cozy look, the rich red paint of its A-frame and matching window boxes in pleasant contrast to the snow. A high spiral of wood smoke was rising above the pines where it flattened out, sinking back into the trees, making the tops near the house appear as if they were wreathed by fog.

The owners, a couple in their late fifties, gave Ken, Orr, and Brody a warm reception, but Orr, given his paranoia of the last few days, told himself not to let his guard down; as if, perversely, a good beginning would somehow become a bad ending. Brody, however, was as friendly as always, shaking the man's hand vigorously, as if he was a long-lost uncle bearing gifts. The man introduced himself as Norm and his wife as Helen. They were rather dumpy and short and on a quick pass looked like brother and sister, which the effervescent Neil Brody happily pointed out.

"Folks are always saying that," Norm said, smiling. "But I can promise you we're not." Even Ken laughed, much relieved now that he'd delivered his charges safely. Still, he was keen to return to his own place, and still unnerved by the phone call about Camp Fairchild's commandant and federal authorities launching what had been described as the biggest manhunt in Washington State history. Before he left, Ken asked Norm and Helen whether they'd heard the news.

"Yes," Norm told him. "It's all over the news, that and what was done to our fellas down in Arizona. Those federal bastards. With that many dead, you have to figure it was in cold blood, right? I mean—"

"Norman!" Helen chided him good-naturedly, "don't frighten the boys."

"Oh—uh, yes, of course. Sorry, fellas, didn't mean to be the voice of doom. You hungry?"

"You could say that," Brody responded. "At least I am. How 'bout you, Al?"

"I could handle a sandwich," Orr said, excusing himself to get nearer to the wood-burning Fisher, holding his hands above the boot-black stove.

"Feels good, eh?" Norman said.

"Sure does," Brody replied.

Orr thought, He's not even near the damn stove. The

sooner they were across the border and he could go his own way, the better.

"Heats the whole house, I bet," Brody added.

Helen brought in a tray of sandwiches and told the "boys," as she called them, that if there was something they didn't like, to just holler.

Norm let them eat in silence in the kitchen while he went into the living room and turned on the TV, looking for a weather report or bulletin. Orr could see it flickering, and wondered why a TV always appeared blue from outside a house. Norm came back looking dejected. "More snow tonight."

"We're not going?" Brody said.

"Don't know. Have to hear from the Canadian side. Don't want to run into any patrols."

"They patrol a lot?" Brody inquired, helping himself to the Dijon mustard and ham.

"Nope," Norm said. "Hardly at all way out here. But we like an all clear just in case. 'Course, we don't say that on the phone. We've got a dialogue about the weather in case the feds've got the lines tapped."

"Well, whenever you do go over," Helen said, "you'd better wrap up. Any of your clothes damp? You can dry them by the stove."

"Or *in* the stove," Brody joked. "Like Kramer in *Seinfeld*."

Norman and Helen looked blank. "We don't watch much TV up here. Mostly rubbish. We get the Canadian news channel. Comes in clear."

"So you're not on cable?"

"No," Norm said. "Mostly rubbish."

"It's not all bad, Norman," Helen cut in. "I'd like to see some more channels, but Mr. Tightwad here won't pay for it."

"Get a dish," Brody suggested.

"I guess," Norm said. "Trouble is, I—" The phone rang. Norm stopped talking and listened. It rang four times, then stopped.

Brody wanted to say something, though his mouth was stuffed with Black Forest ham. Norm held up his finger for

silence. After about ten seconds, the phone rang again, and
this time Norm answered it, his tone no longer serious, but
lighthearted. "How you doing, Charlie? Yep, pretty well
snowed in here too. Roads are passable, though slippery as
all get out. So how's Brenda? On the mend? . . . Oh, good.
Well, you say hello from us, all right?"

When he put the phone down he wrote on a Post-it
notepad, walked through to the kitchen, and put it down on
the table: *Nine P.M. Tonight.* What in hell? Orr thought.
What's with all the drama? Why couldn't he have simply
said it instead of using a note, which Norm now crumpled
and tossed into the fiery interior of the Fisher. The kitchen
clock said ten after two.

When they were left alone to finish their sandwiches and
coffee, Brody nodded to the stove. "What was all that about?"

Orr shrugged. "Makes it more interesting, I guess. All
hush-hush. Thinks he's in the Maquis."

Brody was into the Dijon again. "What's that?"

"Maquis was the name for the French resistance. World
War Two."

"Huh," Brody said, but Orr could tell he wasn't interested—
either that or he was faking it.

In New York it was five P.M. Two detectives in their navy-
blue jackets, NYPD emblazoned in white on the back, stood
on either side of the door of the dingy, poorly lit tenement
apartment, breathing heavily in their alienlike gas masks.
The air was heavy with the cloying odor of rodents. The
other two uniformed policemen, also wearing gas masks,
crouched down on the stairs below the line of fire from the
apartment of suspect Wesley Knox, the man with the bag
whom they'd seen on the jeweler's video surveillance tape.
They had a rammer. One of the detectives nodded, and the
other knocked once. Then, his gun held high in both hands
like his partner's, he announced, "Mr. Knox—police. Open
up!" His voice, coming from behind the mask, was thick
and nasal.

No answer.

"Open up!"

"You got a warrant?"

"Fucking lawyer," the other detective said. "Yeah, we got a warrant. Open up!"

Nothing. The cop nodded to the ram crew. "Let's go!" The two rammers came up the steps, stood about six inches from the door. Their voices low in unison, they said, "One, two . . ." then hit the door, knocking it right off the bolt and chain, the rammer hung up momentarily halfway through the door, delaying entry. The first detective inside saw a dirty translucent curtain ballooning into the room from the fire escape. Then Knox fired twice, from the rear right corner of the room—the sawed-off shotgun blasts blowing the detective out the doorway, the second detective firing as he was slammed hard against the splintered door frame. He and Knox were both hit, Knox in the chest, the detective in the neck and sliding down, dropping the gun. With both his hands he tried to cover the wound, the sound of ambulance men running up the stairs swallowing all other noises.

After the ambulance attendants came the bomb squad, and in the bathroom, in the badly chipped old-fashioned bathtub, they found two other tote bags, each with one-liter connected glass flasks containing the chemical components for sarin. Enough, the police lab said, to kill well in excess of a million people; enough to wipe out Manhattan, they added, seeing ten poorly drawn but eminently workable plans for pouring the stuff into the ventilation systems of major buildings, one building clearly targeted in the amateurish drawings—a shaded area on Sixth Avenue between Fifty-third and Fifty-fourth Streets.

"The Hilton," one of the cops said.

The neck-wounded detective died en route to Bellevue; the other was in critical condition. They worked hard on Wesley Knox.

"Knox!" one of the cops said. "Where'd you get the glass dispensers?"

"He can't hear you," his partner said. "He's in shock."

"Shock! Hope the fucker dies, but not before I talk to him."

CHAPTER FIFTY-EIGHT

The two JO-TEVs had never faced a test like it. Initially, the run down south, adjacent to the Chinle Wash, didn't present any problems. Despite the fact the wash was already swollen, a thousand smaller, local streams draining the high country in the downpour, there were a lot of sandy side washes that posed no problems for the massive hydraulic-damping, valve-equipped shock absorbers, which were capable of taking the kind of punishment that would have drastically slowed a Hummer and stopped any other four-wheel-drive. But Lewis knew the real challenge would be in Canyon del Muerto, where there could be rock slides and erosion caused by the sudden rush of unseasonable rain through the sandstone, shale, and limestone. He told the other ALERTs, yelling above the sound of his JO-TEV's diesel, that the water would carve out a significantly different route in the canyon than that indicated on the map. There, the water would rush through the green of Russian olive, tamarack, cottonwood, and sage, wreaking havoc with the Navajos' carefully tilled vegetable gardens of beans, squash, and corn nestled in the canyon's floor, where they were normally irrigated by the natural springs that formed small oases at the base of the towering rocky cliffs.

Normally, it was the vast silence of the canyons that affected everyone who entered them and took the time to stand, look, and feel, but for the ALERTs and Montoya, there was no time to pause and reflect on the insignificance of man in the awesome silence of the high desert. Now the desert was roaring with cataracts, and ahead, after they had picked up the two Navajo guides in Chinle, lay Canyon del Muerto, darkened by the storm, illuminated now and then by lightning. There was a hideout somewhere in the canyon, including two innocents, the doctor and the nurse. The ALERTs, with the world media monitoring the situation, knew they had to rescue the women if the militia in the Southwest were to be seen as having been decisively beaten and federal authority reasserted.

Salvini, rain streaming from his face, yelled out to Montoya and the guide to hang on as he saw Lewis and Brentwood's JO-TEV in back, Thomas bringing up the rear, climbing a pile of debris at an angle that would have been impossible for almost any other vehicle, the guides hanging on to the roll bars. Then the two JO-TEVs hit a deep muddy patch just beyond the entrance to the Canyon del Muerto, which necessitated low gear and stop-go acceleration to inch out of, like driving in snow, both drivers elevating the JO-TEVs' clearance from ten to fifteen inches with the hydraulic adjuster. A bolt of lightning struck the cliffs high above them, its bluish white light filling the canyon like a spluttering flare, the swirls of different pinks and rust-red slabs of rock momentarily illuminated, the thunder that followed rolling through the canyon like a creepy artillery barrage. There was another crooked, spastic arc of lightning, a sharp crack high above, heard through the noise of the reverberating thunder, and a tree atop a seven-hundred-foot precipice towering above them split asunder. It burned fiercely, a warning, Montoya thought, to stay the hell out of Canyon del Muerto, to leave it with its holy places, its ancient cliff dwellings and ruins. The guides said they should go no farther—that surely the gods were speaking.

"When we find out which way Hearn went!" Lewis assured them, though he now knew that any tracks left by Hearn's vehicle must have been obliterated by the rain. The Indians of course knew this too, and they were looking for some other sign of the white man having invaded their place. Montoya also looked. It was highly unlikely, he thought, that Dana Teer, who had left a sign before, wouldn't leave one now, when Hearn and Toro were no doubt more desperate than before. But then, with all the water around and—

Suddenly, through the rain, Montoya, higher up than the others, saw two men in fatigues. Thomas swung his JO-TEV toward them, yelling a warning. There was a burst of fire, the sound of glass splintering. Thomas's head snapped back and he was dead, the JO-TEV turning sharply. Salvini got off a side burst as the JO-TEV hit a rock and flipped, throwing out Montoya and one of the guides. Lewis had stopped his JO-TEV, and Brentwood was returning fire with his I-COW. One of the two militiamen screamed and went down in a chocolate-brown, ankle-deep torrent, the water making a rapids out of his head, streaming over it. The other man threw up his hands. "No, no! Don't shoot!"

Lewis, his .45 in one hand, had pulled the hand brake so hard with the other that Brentwood thought he'd stripped it. The Australian was now out of the car, splashing his way to the remaining hapless militiaman, who'd been one of those charged by Hearn to take the two four-wheel-drives farther down the canyon, then walk back.

Lewis racked the slide on his .45 and jammed it under the militiaman's chin. "How's Thomas?" he yelled.

"He's gone," Salvini said, closing the black man's eyes.

"All right, puss nuts," Lewis told the remaining militiaman. "Where *are* they? Right now! Or I blow your fucking head off!"

The militiaman nervously jerked his thumb back toward the beginning of Canyon del Muerto—now about five miles away. "A slot canyon," he said, gasping for air, Lewis having forced the man's head up and back, the barrel hard under the militiaman's chin.

Lewis pressed harder, the man almost on tiptoe. "You take us there now, dickhead!"

"Yeah, sure," the militiaman said. "But there's only room for one person at a time through the entrance."

"Then you're first through!"

"Yessir."

In the interim, while they'd been coming up the canyon, deadwood, sagebrush, and other debris had come floating down along what a half hour earlier had been dry creek beds. The JO-TEV that had been driven by Thomas was righted with the winch of the first JO-TEV, Salvini bruised from the roll but nothing more. Worst off was Montoya, who felt he'd cracked a rib, the pintle gun mount punching him hard in the chest as the JO-TEV went over and threw him clear.

Though unable to see the contours of the ground beneath the swirling chocolate-colored water, except where a rapids was obviously foaming, Lewis pushed hard on the accelerator. Salvini in the second JO-TEV, with Montoya now in the passenger seat, Thomas's body strapped to the base of one of the roll bars, did likewise. The noise of rushing water in the canyon was growing, and Brentwood, on the machine gun, the militiaman's hands tied to the roll bar, realized why Lewis was intent on driving so damn fast. If this rain kept up, they would soon be in the middle of a river up to half a mile wide, bringing down more debris, and the light was starting to go.

"You bloody beauty!" Lewis yelled, his voice barely audible above the sound of a dozen creeks that had materialized on both sides of the canyon. He was talking to the vehicle. It was performing magnificently, shocks continuing to take brutal punishment, and with the high clearance, each wheel capable of being lowered and raised individually at the flick of a switch, it was like playing a fast-moving video game. It was a skill that his generation of warriors had learned in the arcades of the land, to their parents' displeasure, skills that had been useful in the Gulf War, when every combatant, from infantryman to fighter pilot, had the manual dexterity of the robotics and cyberspace age, as the generation before them had had with a standard shift. It became part of them, and Lewis now had his JO-TEV at forty miles per hour—breakneck speed, given the conditions—enjoying every second of it. He was in control and on a high, marveling at the vehicle's rugged flexibility in hitting rocks that would have dewheeled and/or stopped everything from a jeep to the most rugged Hummer. The wheels rose with fluidity, overriding obstacles with an ease that would have been the envy of every automotive engineer since Henry Ford. "It's a beauty!" Lewis had once told a fellow commando in the Mojave. "And the fucker just keeps on going. Tell me anything else that'll climb a forty-eight-degree grade like that."

Meanwhile, Salvini, who had known some rough driving of his own over Brooklyn's potholes, was straining to keep up in what was literally Lewis's wake, the wipers of Salvini's JO-TEV on full power.

The captured militiaman directed Lewis to the southern wall of the canyon, to where the slot canyon, its entrance all but hidden by cottonwood saplings, cut into the high mesa between Black Canyon and Canyon del Muerto.

"It's through there," the militiaman told him, pointing at the saplings. "You'll have to go around them."

"Bugger that," said Lewis, who, like any good driver, had been thinking ahead, knowing that any delay would raise the risk of not being able to get into the slot canyon at all if the rain kept up. He slipped the JO-TEV into its lowest gear and hit the saplings, busting through them, the cracking of the wood and the shower of leaves adding to Salvini's momentary sense of chaos in the second JO-TEV. Then suddenly, as if a curtain had been ripped aside, they were through a six-foot-wide gap into the slot canyon.

"You know this canyon?" Lewis shouted at the Navajo guide.

"Yes," the guide said. "It narrows here, widens a half mile up, then closes again. There are old Pueblo dwellings high in the cliff. If I was on the run, that's where I'd go."

"How far up?"

"About a mile, maybe less."

"No," Lewis shouted. "I mean, how far up the cliffs are the ruins?"

"Eighty feet, maybe more. Been a long time since I've been there. Very few people know about it."

"Hearn knew."

"Who's Hearn?"

"Jesus! Don't you read the papers? Watch TV?"

"No."

"He's a Nazi son of—" The JO-TEV hit a rock the size of a forty-four-gallon drum, the right wheel starting to slew before Lewis held on firmly and rode over it. "He's a Nazi son of a bitch with two women hostages, and he's on the run. He's got a gaggle of militia with him."

The Navajo guide said nothing, gripping the roll bar.

"Is there a path up to them? The ruins?"

"A ladder," the guide said.

At first Lewis was pessimistic about the chance of Hearn leaving a ladder against the canyon wall, figuring the Nazi would haul it up, as did the ancient Indians to secure themselves from attack. But then, as Lewis took the next mud-filled pothole, the wheel going down a foot before recovering, he realized there was a good chance Hearn had left the ladder intact. If he thought he was safe, why go to all the trouble of hauling the long, rough wooden ladder—the guide had said eighty feet or more—up the side of the cliff? And there were the two militiamen Hearn was expecting back sometime during what would be nightfall.

They came to a narrowing of the slot canyon, Lewis braking hard, his wake of six-inch-deep muddy water rushing back and hitting Salvini's JO-TEV, sending a muddy sheet of water over the windshield. "Thanks a lot, you Aussie prick!" Salvini yelled.

But Lewis didn't hear the curse through the sound of the rain pelting down on the JO-TEV's hood.

The slot canyon's pinched waist drew in to a width of less than six feet, which would have been fourteen inches too narrow for a Hummer, but the JO-TEV's sixty-five-inch width sneaked through with no more than three inches to spare on either side.

"How far are we from the ruins now?" Lewis asked.

"A mile at most."

"Right!" Lewis said, and turned his head to look behind him. Salvini hated rain, and it showed. "Sal, we're about a mile away," Lewis shouted.

"Then we'd better go on quiet. Can't risk the noise of the diesel getting through."

Lewis gave him the thumbs-up sign and they both switched from the diesel engine to the silent electric-drive motor, bringing the nickel-cadmium battery into play.

Waterfalls were cascading down the sheer canyon's wall, flashes of lightning momentarily illuminating the dazzling beauty of the walls. Layers of red sediment from eons ago were distinguishable, the wavering reflections of red rock and water merging, separating, and merging again, like the mottled patterns cast by hidden pools. The JO-TEVs were moving quickly, the sound of the water swirling about the two vehicles drowned by the sound of the rain and myriad cascades.

The lights of Nighthawk glittered like cut diamonds against the snow, and in the farmhouse, Neil Brody and Alan Orr were getting ready for what their host, Norm, referred to as the "crossing." His wife, Helen, gave them each a large plastic Ziploc bag containing sandwiches, fruit, two Hershey bars, and bottled water.

"Don't think you can just eat the snow for your thirst," she told them. "That'll satisfy you for a while but it'll chill your gut."

Orr nodded. He'd known that since he was a boy, but he noticed that Brody took the information as if she'd just split the atom. "Huh—never thought of that. That's smart."

"And," she said, "don't go opening the bag and eating anything till you're sure you're across. Dogs'll pick up the smell of food a lot quicker if you open the Ziploc."

"Dogs?" Brody said, and for the first time since they'd met, Orr saw Brody's friendly demeanor flee. "No one told me about dogs. I thought you said they hardly patrolled the area."

"They don't usually," Norm replied, trying to reassure him. "But now and then the Mounties'll bring a mutt along."

Brody still looked alarmed.

"Lookit," Norm said realistically, "life's a risk, right? I mean, you go out on the street and you can get hit by a truck, and—" He hesitated a moment. "—and we take a risk every time we put up one of you boys." He didn't try to make it sound heroic, merely a statement of fact as he attempted to assuage Brody's anxiety.

"And," Orr said in heartfelt gratitude, "we appreciate what you're doing."

"Yes," Brody added. "Sorry if I sounded—"

"No, no," Norm said. "You boys all set?"

"Yes."

"Then let's go. Back in a while, woman." He saw Orr's surprise and smiled. "I call her 'woman' sometimes. It's an old joke."

The two fugitives shook hands with Helen, thanking her.

CHAPTER FIFTY-NINE

Aussie Lewis was congratulating himself on the JO-TEV's narrow width and its quietness. The only sound it made, of driving through the water, was lost to the much louder sound of water cascading into the canyon. Then, through his infrared night vision goggles, he saw the canyon narrowing again a quarter mile ahead.

"Don't think you'll make this one, Captain," his Navajo guide said.

"We'll see," Lewis replied, not bothering to waste time correcting the Navajo for having promoted him to captain. And he did see. The slot canyon's width at this point, as if in rebuke of Lewis's optimism, was pinched in again, with less than five feet between the two towering cliffs. The JO-TEVs had gone as far as they could.

Brentwood asked the militiaman how far the ruins were, and was told he didn't know, it was the other guy, "who you shot," who knew the way inside the canyon. Brentwood turned to the two Indian guides, who conferred in the Navajo tongue before telling him they hadn't been in this particular canyon for years, but guessed that the ruins of the ancient Pueblo dwellings were probably no more than two or three hundred yards ahead.

"You don't have to come, Place," Brentwood told Montoya.

"Yes, I do," he said simply, his tone not brooking any argument, and the ALERTs understood why. He'd screwed up at the dam. None of this would have been necessary had he been a split second quicker at the dam instead of allowing Hearn and Toro to regain the initiative. Now he saw his opportunity to make amends, not only to the ALERTs and the two women hostages, but to himself.

The two Najavo guides, however, would not go farther. The white men, they said, were now entering the most sacred part of this offshoot, and this "thing" between the federal and militia was a "white man's quarrel" and they wished to have no part of it. Brentwood didn't doubt their sincerity, nor did Salvini or Montoya. For the Navajos to enter this spiritual place with violence in their hearts would be as repugnant to them as the militia's fake surrender at Ship Rock was to Brentwood and the others.

"What side of the canyon are the ruins on?" Lewis asked. Lightning flashed in the narrow defile as one of the guides pointed to his right, the southern wall.

"I think there might be a ledge zigzagging up to the ruins," the other guide said. "But there is always erosion, and its base would be obscured by cottonwoods on the canyon floor." The Indian pointed to Thomas. "We will stay with your dead until you return."

It was said so simply, so directly, that the three ALERTs and Montoya were greatly moved. Brentwood nodded his thanks but told them if the water level got too high, they should leave the JO-TEVs before they were swept away.

"We're not fools," one of the guides replied.

With that, the four white men moved across the slot canyon to the southern wall, the captured militiaman in front. Montoya, taking Thomas's infrared night vision goggles, walked behind Salvini and Brentwood, Lewis a few paces in front of them. The number and species of game, snakes, and other high desert creatures that they saw at night through the NVGs, some wandering about seemingly unperturbed, never ceased to surprise the ALERTs. But tonight, fleeing the cottonwoods, cacti, and giant seven-foot sagebrush that dotted the canyon floor, everything from sage grouse, pronghorns, and badgers to rabbits was seeking refuge on rock ledges or in caves. Where a spring normally gurgled, the four men now waded against a torrent that was thick with the soil, now mud, being washed through the slot canyon.

The infrared ability of the night vision goggles was reduced by the downpour, but Brentwood could still see a thin white trail on the NVG's green background spiraling out from a large cliff cave sixty feet across and no more than a hundred yards ahead. My, my, aren't we comfy? he thought. He put his right hand on the militiaman's shoulder, pushed him down, and told Lewis in a low tone, "Tape and gag him. We'll leave him here till after. He's no use to us."

They sat the militiaman down on a three-foot-high rock only a few feet beneath a six-foot-long sandstone overhang. "Wait here!" Lewis told him, and Salvini had to contain his laughter. Where in hell could the poor bastard go?

Brentwood was looking at the cliff for a way up. "Give me ten minutes," he told the others, then moved forward in water that was now up to his knees, though the canyon was at least a hundred yards wide here. Lewis thought he heard a splash nearby. Probably some animal. Like Brentwood, he was encouraged by the fact that Hearn had lit a fire, obviously thinking he'd gotten clean away, the initial smoke now dissipated in the rain.

Brentwood was looking for the ladder. Only once did he glimpse the fire, when he ventured out from the cliff face, using several cottonwood trees for cover. But he made a mental note that if he moved a hundred feet, thirty paces along the base of the cliff, he should be directly below it and the ruins.

He went sixty paces and there was still no ladder, and he knew he must be well past the fire. It was high up and back a ways. He retraced his path, careful not to wade too quickly for fear of the possibility, albeit a faint one, that the sound could be heard up by the ruins. He came to the point that he knew, from his wrist GPS, was where he'd been when he spotted the fire. He could detect the faint smell of wood smoke, and it triggered youthful memories of going camping with his dad.

The fire was still there, brighter in fact, and he saw in the cave that housed the ruins a giant shadow show, several figures clumped together, probably the four other militiamen with Hearn and Toro, whom the Navajos had seen barreling through Chinle with the two women hostages. One of the huge shadows got up, and through the infrared goggles Brentwood could see it moving against the intensely white heat spot that was the fire. But were two of them Hearn and Toro? There seemed to be only four men. No women.

In fact, there were only four human shapes reflected by the fire. Hearn was in one of the dwellings twenty feet back from the fire. Having taken off his pack earlier, he began to undress, Dana Teer lying tied and gagged on a rough woolen blanket. "You're gonna enjoy this," he said maliciously. "Gets rid of the tension, right?" He could see her trying to say something, the tape across her mouth going in and out, like the chest of a terrified animal.

"Don't worry," he said, reaching down, gently undoing

her skirt, and pulling it down. Her eyes glistening with fear and hatred, she saw that he was genuinely surprised that she had no underwear on. Then he smiled like a pompous schoolboy discovering a cheater. "Ah, yes, of course the good doctor uses her underwear to send messages, right? The good sheriff shows me to win me over, but leaves his own message. You're quite a pair, aren't you?" He squatted astride her and she averted her eyes. "What's up?" he said. "Haven't you seen one before? *Up*, I mean?" He tore her blouse open. "No messages to our good sheriff in your bra, are there?" He reached over, drew his double-edged knife from his pack, and cut the bra open. "That's better," he told her. "And see, I'm not dirty after all this rain. I'm clean as the proverbial whistle, aren't I?"

She was still looking away from him in disgust.

"Aren't I?" he bellowed angrily, and slapped her face, which reddened from the blow. She was bursting to speak, but couldn't.

"Well, I don't give a shit what you think, Doc," Hearn said. "I'm gonna enjoy this. Now we'll see whether you're as tight as Toro says your nurse is." Beverly Malkin was in an adjoining room, sobbing. Hearn turned toward the sound. "Shut up, you whining bitch, or I'll let him do you again."

Brentwood, now back with the others, told them the bad news. "No ladder. Bastard must've hauled it up after him."

"*Shit!*" It was Salvini. "Listen, is it possible the women aren't there?"

"I guess," Brentwood said, "but we have no way of knowing. Why?"

"Well," Salvini said enthusiastically, "if they aren't, maybe we could call for Eliot's party to send a barrage into the cave. Buggers are always telling everybody how damned accurate they are."

Brentwood shook his head. "Canyon here runs roughly east-west. The arty's to our north; the angle of entry down into the canyon is too steep."

"He's right, dammit!" Lewis said as quietly as he could

manage. "Best they could do is use air-burst shells as the round flies over the canyon. Then boom, down comes the shrapnel."

"Yeah, on us," Brentwood said. "Not on the ruins."

"So what're we gonna do?" Salvini asked.

"Gentlemen," Brentwood said, and Aussie knew that what was called a goatfuck of a mission was coming up, "it's time to use our climbing skills."

"In this weather, Dad?" Aussie asked.

"What's the matter, Oz? Can't handle it?"

"And fuck you too."

"As eloquent as ever," Brentwood said good-naturedly. "All right, I'll take the radio. Don't bring anything else but your rope, NVGs, I-COWS—sling them—and a few clips of ammo. Let's try for that ledge the Navajos thought might be above these cottonwoods. Noise of rain and all these water-falls'll help."

"Yeah," Lewis said, "they can *drown* us."

"Sheriff," Brentwood told Montoya, "you stay here with our gear and the militia guy."

Montoya wanted to object, but facts were facts. They were commandos. They were trained for this. He wasn't. "All right," he said.

"If he gives you any trouble," Lewis said, "shoot him."

Montoya said nothing.

"Okay," Brentwood said. "Let's go. I'll lead."

They hoped up onto the overhang above the militiaman and spread out across its six-foot length. Everything would be done by hand signals, now easily seen through the NVGs. They found several good handholds in the sandstone and moved higher, Salvini and Lewis following Brentwood's lead. It was easier than Brentwood had anticipated, and he recalled how one could get a certain rhythm going in rock climbing, a combination of breathing in a relaxed mode even as the feet and hands were straining against gravity.

Montoya heard it, a deep growling, rumbling sound com-ing toward him, but he couldn't see it in the rain. Still, he had the presence of mind to grab the militiaman, undo the cuffs, and hop up on the higher six-foot-long shelf they were under, extending his hand to haul the militiaman up with him. The man's mouth was taped, and as he scrambled onto the sandstone ledge, he breathed so hard through his nose it gave off a low whistling sound. Montoya heard it, then all sound was overwhelmed by the enormous mud slide that thundered down the canyon, sweeping past no more than a foot below them. They could feel the vibration of the mud rapids directly beneath the ledge as the edge of the river of mud swept up and over the rock the militiaman had been sitting on.

With a yelp of pain, the man tore the tape from across his mouth. "Holy shit!" he shouted, but in the rumbling sound of the slide, Montoya could barely hear him. The militiaman took a swing at Montoya, who reflexively used his right hand to block the punch, then smacked the man with his left. The militiaman, leaning the wrong way, was knocked off the ledge and swept away. The ALERT rations, medical supplies, and extra ammunition were gone too, and the rifle Montoya had been given. All he had was the sodden clothes he stood up in, his wallet with the picture of his horse, and his Colt .45.

Brentwood, Lewis, and Salvini had heard the mud slide coming and momentarily stopped, pressed hard into the wall, Brentwood only feet away from a narrow ledge no more than three inches wide, but that looked as if it followed a seam along the cliff face. Through his NVGs, which were giving him a ferocious headache, he could see a huge slab of shimmering white, the heat from the day's sun still being released into the atmosphere, the white slab slashed vertically here and there where waterfalls cascaded. The mud river rushing past them seventy feet below, its temperature colder than that of the still comparatively warm cliffs, showed up in the NVGs as a dark gray mass scratched and dotted as it passed, the dots and scratches temperature anomalies caused by the trees, sage, and other canyon debris being carried away.

* * *

Hearn was sated after his attack on Dana, but on hearing the roar of the mud river, he grabbed his handgun and staggered out of the pueblo, wearing only ragged boxer shorts, none of the four militia daring to tempt his wrath with a remark.

"What in hell's that?" he demanded.

"Big mud slide," one of the men replied. "Don't bother us none, though. We're too high up."

"Jesus, thought the whole friggin' mountain was caving in."

"Was she that good?" One man couldn't resist.

"Yeah!" Hearn said good-naturedly, taking them by surprise with a boyish grin. "Yeah, nice and tight. Any o' you boys want to dip your wick, be my guest. Or the nurse, if you like."

"Nah," one man said, the other three glancing around at one another, casting the giant shadows of their heads into the ruins from which Hearn had come, and then all looking at the fire as if it had the answer.

As Hearn walked back from the fire into the pueblo, he heard sobbing again. Once inside, he had to wait a moment, letting his eyes adjust to the darkness after being in the firelight. At first he thought it was Dana Teer crying, but she was staring at him, unblinking, with hatred and contempt.

"Oh," he said casually, "it's the other one, is it?" and walked into the other room.

Beverly Malkin was cowering in the corner. She was rigid with fear, but her torso was racked by the sobbing.

"Shut up, dammit!" he shouted, and fired above her head. She squealed in terror. "You want Toro to tape you up again, eh? Is that what you want, you whining bitch? Now shut the fuck up!"

He walked back and, pulling on his pants, looked over at Dana. "Now, every time you screw someone, you'll think of me." He laughed. "Oh, you won't want to, I know that, but the harder you try to forget me, the more you'll remember. You hear what I'm sayin'? I'm gonna let you go, you dozy bitch. Soon as we rest up—I'm whacked." He smiled. "And once Toro's dug the rubble out, we're going in there." He pointed to one of the small chocolate-colored adobe houses that made up the ruins in the cave, some with a dozen or more man-made and time-worn earthen steps in front of them. "We're going upstairs." He saw her surprise. "Yeah, Navajos built a kind of stair chimney, a secret way out." He half turned, looking out toward the fire. "Can't go back the way we came in, can we?" He paused. "Hey, Dana, maybe you'd like me to take the tape off your mouth. You'd like that, right?

"Okay," he answered himself. "But I don't want any boo-hooing like that whining bitch in there, otherwise I'll have to see to it. Okay?" He ripped it off.

She would have spat at him, but didn't dare.

Hearn called over to Toro, who was chucking adobe bricks out of the way behind one of the one-room adobes. "Need a hand?"

"No. Only one man can fit in here. Not enough room to swing a cat."

Hearn smiled at Dana. "He's a martyr, is Toro. Wants all the praise himself."

Brentwood, spaced six feet from Salvini, who was six feet from Lewis, was now only thirty feet from the edge of the cave. Through the rain he could make out a faint glimmer of firelight, but a waterfall cascaded from a deep fissure halfway down the cliff face between the three of them and the cave mouth. They'd had to pass through several smaller waterfalls, but this one was a good five feet across and much more powerful. If they tried to breach it, they'd literally be hosed off the cliff into the river of mud and debris.

The only way around it, Brentwood saw, was to climb higher, parallel to the plunging fall of water, then cross the fissure above a deep V-cut channel in the rock that was the conduit for the waterfall. And then, rather than waste time descending from a point just past the waterfall to come level with the cave opening on his left, why not keep climbing across the face of the cliff above the waterfall to a point from which they could rappel in a two- or three-step fall, the last one allowing them to swing right into the cave?

Via hand signals to follow him, Brentwood pointed up to where the waterfall issued from the cliff face and then gave them the sign for "rappel." Both Salvini and Lewis gave him the thumbs-up. Yes, there was the ever-present danger of the noise of rocks and debris falling down over the front of the cave, but in this rain, debris was coming down all the time anyway. Salvini had already been hit hard on his right shoulder by a baseball-sized rock. And unless an inordinate amount of debris fell at any one time, there would be no reason for the militiamen in the cave to think anything of more falling debris.

Brentwood hoped that now all their training endurance missions would pay off.

In the ruin near the edge of the cave, the four militiamen about the fire had by now realized what must have happened to their two comrades who were to have hidden the four-wheel-drive vehicles down in Canyon del Muerto. "Soon as they came through the slot into this canyon," one of the men said, "mud wall must have hit 'em."

"Jesus, what a way to go."

They could not know that one of the two was already dead, shot by Aussie Lewis, when the second one had been swept away by the deluge of mud. The two Navajos, who didn't want to violate the holy place of the ruins, were caught by the mud flow too. Hearing it rumbling down the canyon with the sound of an express train, they turned and tried to climb the rain-polished walls of the slot where the canyon walls were only five feet from one another. The enormous mass of mud hit the slot and immediately filled it up, spilling into Canyon del Muerto, sweeping everything before it, including the two JO-TEVs.

The weatherman was right: Washington State's northern Cascades were in for more precipitation. The edge of the front was far enough east that it began snowing around

Nighthawk and Osoyoos, on both sides of the border. There was only the occasional farmhouse light visible as they neared the line, then Norman pulled off on a side road near a forest of pine and switched off the engine.

"We wait," he said. "It's warm enough in here now, but if you start to get cold, I'll switch the heater on. It's pretty fast."

"I'm fine," Brody said.

"Me too," Orr said, his eyes adjusting to the darkness. The snowfall trailed off, and in another ten minutes they could see the moon bisected by a high pine.

"How much longer?" Brody asked.

"Twenty-five, thirty minutes at most."

"Uh-huh," Brody said. "How far are we from the line?"

"Half a mile."

They heard a dog barking.

"Jesus!" Brody said. "What's that?"

Norman looked over at him. "It's all right. It's the Farquarsons' dog. He's chained."

"Won't they come out, see what he's barking at?" Brody pressed.

"Well," Norm assured him, "he wasn't barking at us. Otherwise he'd've started the racket as soon as we pulled in. Nah, he's doin' his nut over a critter, maybe a skunk. Besides, we're upwind of him, which is just as well if it's a skunk."

After a while, a pair of headlights approached from the Canadian side. They flicked from high to low and back again three times.

"That's the signal," Norm said to Orr and Brody. "But don't walk near the road. Stay at least a hundred yards from it in the pines, and when you cross, you'll see the lights of the customs and immigration building about a quarter mile away on your right. There's only a couple of immigration and customs guys on either side of the border. Bear left onto the highway. There'll be a semi trailer pulled up a mile down. That's your contact." He paused. "You remember the greeting?"

"Yes," Orr said. " 'Are you going to Vancouver?' "

"And," Brody said, "the driver will say, 'No, I'm headed for Toronto.' "

"Good. Best of luck, boys."

They shook hands.

CHAPTER SIXTY

Brentwood, Salvini, and Lewis were eight feet above the cave and working their pitons into the nearest crack they could find. Salvini had been the luckiest, finding a fissure in the rock directly above him into which he could put his piton, pulling hard at it once it was in, testing it for holding the rope he would use to rappel down below the top lip of the cave's mouth.

In another few minutes the three of them were ready to rappel down—one jump, two jumps, and into the cave on the third jump. To say they were ready, however, was merely to say they were now in position. Despite all their endurance training, they were exhausted from the arc-shaped climb they'd made to clear the head of the waterfall. But its thundering noise was to their benefit, covering the sound they made securing their pitons into the rock face.

Salvini was grateful for the momentary rest, and he ruminated on how in the movies such exploits as they were preparing for were always executed with such speed and finesse. In reality, the three of them, though top ALERT commandos, were sodden with rain, their nerves taut, and they were physically tired as well, and would have to draw on the "well of reserve energy," which they all knew was nothing less than pure adrenaline. Salvini could smell the rain, shot through with whiffs of wood smoke that, caught in eddies from the cave, was wafting out above the top lip of the cave directly below them.

Brentwood signaled that they were ready for the next step. All three had their I-COWs slung in front of them, to use the moment their feet touched the cave floor. Each, by virtue of his training, would fire through a sixty-degree arc to cover the full 180. On Brentwood's signal to go, they dropped: one jump, two—loose rock falling under Salvini— and three, into the cave, the fire instantly recognizable in their NVGs as a fluid white blob against the apple-green background.

Brentwood let loose a long burst at the fire, the 25mm armor-piercing rounds dropping two of the four figures that had jumped up. One of the remaining two got off a few wildly aimed rounds before Salvini took him out, and the fourth man managed a burst of M-16 fire in the ALERTs' general direction. Lewis, now on the ground, sprayed his sixty-degree arc to keep down the heads of anyone stupid or brave enough to show himself in the ruins. Salvini, hit in the upper left arm, fell back perilously near the edge of the cliff as Brentwood delivered a full burst into the remaining militiaman, whose body came apart in eruptions of bloody flesh and bone, the ear-rattling gunfire echoing inside the ruin-inhabited cave as if in some vast cathedral.

Lewis glimpsed another melting white figure in his NVGs, swung his I-COW in its direction but held fire, hearing a woman's hysterical voice crying out, "No! No!" as she ran toward them. There was a flash in the ruins, a shotgun, its tremendous boom momentarily drowning the nearby sound of the waterfall, and the woman was blown forward several feet, felled within a yard of the nearest ruin.

Brentwood and Lewis fired at the flash, their bullets chipping stone about an adobe window, several of Lewis's 5.56mm shots ricocheting inside the rock-walled house.

"You all right, Sal?" Lewis asked.

"Yeah," he lied, while Brentwood and Lewis, covering one another, advanced on the ruins.

Brentwood went in first. Nothing. He saw the empty shotgun cartridge, still hot like a molten white sausage in his NVGs. But no one was there.

"Listen!" Lewis yelled as Brentwood exited the ruin, stepping over a ladder, ready to go into the next room. He thought he'd heard someone running on stone stairs. But that was speculation under fire, and they would have to go through the ruins a room at a time, about ten of them, in order to clear them.

It took three minutes—an eternity for them—covering one another, going through each room. They found nothing but a few old Navajo water jars and sticks.

Brentwood had gone back to check on Salvini when Lewis discovered a roughly hewn vertical stairwell leading from one of the rear stone houses up into a kind of rock chimney, barely wide enough for one person. He listened, and could hear no sound from the stairs that disappeared up into darkness. But his NVGs picked up residual body heat bleeding from several spots on the sides of the almost sixty-degree-inclined chimney. Seeing nothing else, he clipped his flashlight to his I-COW's "over" barrel, the slanting rock chimney going on for what looked like several hundred feet, the flashlight beam indicating no end.

"Stairwell," Lewis told Brentwood, returning to the cave room. "One man could hold off an army."

Brentwood, having checked the dead woman, Beverly Malkin, her hospital nameplate still on her, moved on to Salvini, whose axillary vessel was severed. Brentwood applied a tourniquet, but knew that if Salvini didn't get medical attention within a half hour, he'd bleed to death. He got on the radio, but there was nothing but static. He needed to be high, well above the cave, if he was to have any hope of reaching Eliot's force. The problem was, they'd have to get Salvini up the stairs, on the assumption the stairs led to the exit he figured must be atop the cliff face. Lewis didn't need any explanation; he knew the situation as well as Brentwood.

"I'll go on point," he told Brentwood. "Try to get Sal up behind me."

"I can piggyback him," Brentwood said.

"No, the fucking chimney is too narrow. Only way you could do that is to have two of us haul him up on a stretcher. Trouble is, that son of a bitch Nazi only has to fire one shot down the chimney."

"Montoya!" Brentwood said, and going to the cliff edge, he pulled down the ropes while yelling down into the canyon, "Montoya?" hoping the sheriff had escaped the mud flow.

He and Lewis heard a faint response through the rain.

Brentwood cupped his hands and yelled as loudly as he could. "Get on the rope!"

Seconds later he felt the slack rope go taut and heard Montoya, seventy feet below, yelling, "Go!"

"Fucker wants to be hauled up!" Lewis said in mock outrage, but immediately helped Brentwood on the rope.

"You seen anything of the doc?" Brentwood asked between two long hauls.

"Nada," Lewis answered. "He's got her."

"Well, he can't move faster than us once we get on top."

"Yeah," Lewis grunted, "but the prick's got a head start."

As soon as Montoya completed the haul/climb up to the cave, Brentwood told him to grab some of the sticks from the ruins so they could make a stretcher using part of the ladder, belts, and strips of cloth from the dead militiamen's clothes.

"How's our prisoner doing?" Lewis asked as he palmed another 5.56mm mag into his I-COW.

"Gone, in the mud slide," Montoya said. "Where's the doc?"

"Gone with Hearn."

"Dead?" Montoya asked.

"We don't think so. We figure they've gone topside."

Montoya saw Beverly Malkin's body. "The bastard."

"You can say that again," Lewis said.

Unslinging his I-COW, he headed up the chimney, his NVGs back on, the fire in the cave all but extinguished.

CHAPTER SIXTY-ONE

Al Orr and Neil Brody were trudging through the old, deep, wet snow as the dry powder fell about them. Their footsteps made a disconcerting crunching sound as they made their way through the dark pines. Orr was still worried about Brody. Apart from his companion's obvious phobia about dogs, he had for the most part regained his optimism, whispering to Orr as they left the car that he felt it was their "lucky night." Orr found it annoying, as well as unnerving. It was like telling someone that your car was running well— you knew that the next day the wheels would probably fall off. But then Orr had chastised himself for his pessimism. Perhaps that could as easily jinx their venture as Brody's high optimism. What you had to avoid was overdoing it in either direction. Something in between—say cautious optimism. He welcomed that thought and held it in his mind as a talisman.

Now and then they could see a flicker of light from the arc lamps on what Orr kept reminding himself, mantralike, was the "longest undefended border in the world." They heard the hum of an engine in the distance, stopping momentarily, then carrying on. Brody stopped.

"What's wrong?" Orr whispered.

"Nothing," Brody answered softly, "but I just thought

maybe we should keep farther apart. You know, in case one of us is spotted, the other could still get through."

"All right," Orr agreed. "We'll meet at the truck."

Before they separated, staying about fifty yards from one another, putting Orr closer to the lighted crossing a quarter mile away on his right, they heard a heavy, grumbling sound coming from the road, now only three hundred yards in front of them. It was a semi trailer, the glare of its headlights veiled by the falling snow. Then they heard the barking of a dog, but it came from behind them and didn't seem close. Probably the chained-up mutt they'd heard earlier, Orr thought.

"Hey! Hold it right where you are!" A flashlight reached out, and Brody was in its snow-roiling beam. It was the U.S. border patrol. "Put your hands up! Right now!"

Brody did as he was told, then bolted into the pines. The beam followed him off to his left but lost him among the trees.

"Get him, boy!" A dog shot out from the darkness, running hard in Brody's direction, the POW running back the way he'd come. One man, the dog handler, Orr thought, was running also, the flashlight's beam jerking madly up and down among the snow-laden pines.

Orr had remained absolutely still, not daring to breathe, while Brody had drawn them off. He now began to run through the trees in the opposite direction, heading straight for the road. He heard shots.

When he reached the drainage ditch by the road and stopped, he was breathing so fast that the condensation from his mouth came out in what was almost a steady stream. He saw the semi, or rather, the high parking lights that must have been those of the semi, a quarter mile down the road, to his left. Whatever it was—intuition, a gut feeling—Orr was determined not to go to the truck. It had been too easy, the border patrol appearing suddenly, before he and Brody could reach the road.

He heard more shots, then silence.

Orr got out his map and saw that the Canadian town of Osoyoos was only a few miles away. He crossed the road and continued walking.

Back at the truck a furious row was erupting. "Jesus, Warren," the driver of the semi told the two-man-patrol leader. "Why couldn't you just let 'em come to the damn truck like we always done it?"

"Always *do* it," Warren corrected him.

"Don't change the subject, Warren. All you had to *do* was let 'em come to the truck."

"Ah, bullshit. The guy tried to make a run for it."

"So you shot him."

"Hey, Eddie," Warren told the driver, "listen to me. They're escapees. Fugitives. 'Sides, I told him to stop—and then the bastard took off. Isn't that right, Bill?"

"That's right."

"Don't you shit me, Warren," the truck driver told him. "You like runnin' 'em to ground, don't you? The dog and all that shit?"

"Hey, Eddie," Warren told him, "you want to cry about it, go ahead. 'Sides, this gets back to Fairchild, it's gonna make 'em think twice about breakin' out."

"That's right," Bill, the third man, put in.

"Is that right?" Eddie said scornfully.

"Yeah," Bill said, patting the dog.

"Yeah, well, where's the second one? This guy—what was his name—Gore?"

"Orr," Warren said.

"Yeah, where's he?"

"We didn't get him."

"No, and you know why—because you couldn't wait for 'em to get to the truck. You wanted some fun." Eddie paused. "Well, where is he?" he asked, referring now to the one they'd shot.

Warren jerked his thumb back into the trees. "Back there."

"So, bring him out."

Warren scoffed at the idea. "I'm not gonna drag him out through all that shit. Ambulance guys can do that."

"Huh," Eddie said. "You guys are somethin' else."

"Hey, Eddie, if you don't want the money, just say so. Norm and his wife are happy with their cut. You don't want to drive the semi, just say so."

That ended the conversation. It was true there was good money, in U.S. dollars, for everyone concerned, from the informers at the end of the escape pipeline to Eddie, who usually drove them on to Osoyoos, with the promise of taking them to a Canadian militia group, and then handed them over to the Mounties.

CHAPTER SIXTY-TWO

With Brentwood and Aussie hauling, it had taken only minutes for Montoya to reach the cave, but it took a full twenty minutes for the three of them—Lewis on point, with the flashlight, Brentwood and Montoya carrying the stretcher—to reach the top of the chimney. At times the angles were so sharp that had Salvini, already in a great deal of pain and shock, not been securely strapped in the makeshift stretcher by means of the dead militiamen's belts, he would have slid out. By the time Lewis reached the trapdoor—a removable slab of shale opening onto the top of the mesa, one side of which formed the cliff face from which they'd come— Brentwood and Montoya were exhausted. Sweat poured from them, and they itched beneath their flak jackets.

Lewis knelt by the exit hole, his eyes taking several

seconds to adjust to his NVGs. Any residual heat from either Hearn's, Toro's, or Dana Teer's footprints was long gone, washed away by the continuing torrent of rain.

But if the rain had so far aided Hearn's escape, it would in turn aid his pursuers, since there were now myriad fast-flowing streams rushing across the two miles of Little Middle Mesa, which separated Canyon del Muerto, behind them, from Black Rock Canyon, ahead.

Dana Teer had meanwhile kept her head with Hearn and Toro, never refusing outright to do what they ordered, but delaying them in a dozen little ways. Her ankle had given out, she said, and as Toro and Hearn were as much in the dark as she was, they had to go slowly here and there, choosing the least dangerous place to ford the streams. Rocks and other debris had been swept across the mesa with such force that they could be heard rolling and scraping as the flood bullied them across the rock plateau.

Brentwood, Lewis, and Montoya couldn't hope to catch up with Hearn's head start if they couldn't leave Salvini. But then, with the radio static-free atop the mesa, Brentwood had an audacious idea. He radioed Eliot's artillery batteries, quickly giving them his wrist GPS coordinates, allowing for a quarter-mile "overshoot" and asking them to fire "for range."

Within ninety seconds the banshee scream of an artillery round from over seven miles away could be heard streaking through the rain-slashed air. The H.E. detonated two hundred yards ahead, sending a spume of red, fiery shrapnel and rock whistling high in the air. Some of it rained down in dangerous proximity to the ALERTs and Montoya. Following Lewis's shouted warning, Brentwood and Montoya dropped flat next to Salvini's stretcher, Salvini now going into tremors and shouting nonsense.

"Long," Brentwood reported to the arty commander. "Two hundred yards. Fire flare and Savage MRP. I say again, flare and Savage MRP!"

"Stand by, Captain," came the crackling response through Brentwood's radio phone.

Another two whistling projectiles swooshed into the night simultaneously, the first one erupting high above them, a flare round. Its brilliantly incandescent circle spluttered beneath its parachute, immediately followed by the blossoming of the Savage round's drogue chute. Shortly afterward the Savage's main chute deployed. Then canopy release was activated, the medical resupply projectile's canister with morphine, plasma, and plastic-bottled saline IV drip falling away into Canyon del Muerto, behind them.

"Oh, fuck a duck," Lewis exclaimed. "Tell 'em to send another one. We've lost that whore."

Another Savage MRP round, followed by two more, came screaming and deployed their chutes, both descending almost directly overhead.

After Montoya and Lewis retrieved the medical supplies so urgently needed to save Salvini, Brentwood set about administering them, telling his comrades to go after Hearn and Toro.

Propping the stretcher up against a boulder for Brentwood to use as a lean-to to work under, Montoya and Lewis headed off, staying fifty yards apart as the rain eased.

Hearn and Toro, having avoided any sudden undulations where the water would be too deep and swift-flowing to cross, had struck out sensibly across the flattest terrain of the mesa. But in the darkness, Dana Teer had been dropping her watch, a pen, pieces of clothing that she'd ripped up behind her; unseen by Hearn and Toro, but picked up by Montoya's and Lewis's night vision goggles.

Hearn and Toro ran out of flat rock and had to go down a defile and up the other side as lightning cracked above them. It took ten minutes for the three of them to navigate a safe passage, during which Dana Teer tried to jerk away from Toro. He punched her in the face.

By the time the three of them reached the other side of the rocky defile, her nose was bleeding profusely, the drops of fresh, warm blood, like a line of quarter-sized cat's eyes, picked up by both Lewis and Montoya. A flare round burst overhead, flooding the mesa with light.

Hearn and Toro, with Dana Teer in tow, were now nearing the other side of the mesa, the great plunge of Black Box Canyon looming ahead. Lewis and Montoya were approaching, running, to panic Toro and Hearn, who, except for Dana, had run out of hostages. What could they achieve if they killed her? Lewis wondered.

Hearn didn't panic, however. Instead he went down on one knee in the dying flare light and steadied his M-16 against a rock only ten feet from the edge of Black Rock Canyon. As he fired, Dana Teer shoved the rifle to the side. He struck her hard with the butt, and she fell. Lewis fired a three-round burst at Toro, punching him back over the cliff. Then Hearn fired again, the full burst hitting Lewis in the chest, chopping into his Kevlar vest, its fiber weave four to eight times stronger than steel but unable to prevent what would be massive bruising. When Lewis fell, his head hit on the mesa's rock-strewn surface, which knocked him out.

Montoya now began to weave in an erratic course toward Hearn. The Nazi fired another burst—wide. He fired another. Montoya, looking strangely alien in the NVG he wore, kept coming, darkness no hindrance. Hearn knelt down beside Dana Teer, the M-16 at her head. Montoya, he'd assumed, would stop, start talking to him, negotiating for Dana. But Montoya didn't falter, not firing two-handed in the usual police fashion, but from the hip, intuitively. Hearn's M-16 clattered to the rocky edge of the precipice, his hands cupping his neck as he fell to his knees, blood gushing out.

Lewis, now getting up groggily, walked slowly toward the Nazi. Already Dana Teer was trying to stop the bleeding, calling for Montoya to help her stanch it. She and Montoya began tearing their clothes, his shirt, her blouse, for the vitally needed bandages.

Lewis, still "a bit wonky," as he later described it, walked unsteadily like a drunk toward them. "I'll help," he said, and taking Hearn by the collar, began dragging him to the edge of Black Rock Canyon as if he were a bag of garbage. "He'll get a better view from here!"

"What . . . ?" Teer was on her feet, running toward them, unable to see properly in the dark and rain.

"Oh, shit!" she heard Lewis say as he turned to her, his NVGs as grotesquely alien as Montoya's. "Poor fucker slipped," he said.

She was stunned. Suddenly, there was an explosion from halfway down the thousand-foot drop.

"My God," she said, "what was that?"

"Oh, silly bugger," Lewis said, still looking dopey from the concussion. "He must have had a grenade in his pocket."

"You pushed him," she said. It was more an observation than an objection.

"Hey, Sheriff?" Lewis said, his tone ever so friendly. "Did I push him?"

Lewis, through his NVGs, could see Montoya shrug nonchalantly. "I didn't see anything."

"Let's go back," Lewis told her. "Sal needs you more than that fucker."

Teer was confused, but then suddenly, enormously relieved. All she could say was, "Do you always talk like that?"

"Yeah," Lewis riposted. "C'mon, Doc, let's haul ass back to Sal. Soon as this rain wears off a bit more, Davy'll be on the horn for a dust-off." He meant Medevac by helo. Salvini would survive.

In an astonishingly beautiful and quiet dawn, a Huey descended and took them away.

EPILOGUE

The following night in San Diego, shortly after eleven P.M., a perimeter guard at the San Diego Marine Air Base shot and killed a forty-three-year-old man, John Delaney, said to be a long-standing member of the San Diego Sharks Militia, as Delaney tried to penetrate base security near where the Marines' AV-8 Harrier Jump Jet fighters were parked, presumably intent on sabotage.

The significance of the incident, CNN reporter Brian O'Keefe opined, could be seen in the fact that it had happened less than a day after it was learned that Scorpion militiaman Hearn, the most wanted man in the United States, and Wesley Knox, of the Black Brothers of America militia in New York, had been reported killed. "It was," O'Keefe said, "as if the moment one militia group is defeated, another takes up the torch."

Look for this thrilling new novel!

GIDEON
by Russell Andrews

Gideon. An identity shrouded in mystery—the anonymous source who holds the key to an explosive secret.

In a clandestine meeting, writer Carl Granville is hired to take the pieces of a long-hidden past and turn them into compelling fiction. As he is fed information and his work progresses, Granville begins to realize that the book is more than a potential bestseller. It is a revelation of chilling evil and a decades-long cover-up by someone with far-reaching power.

Then someone close to Granville is bludgeoned to death. And another is savagely murdered. Suspicion falls on Granville. He tries to explain the shadowy assignment. No one believes him. He has no proof, no alibis. Framed for two murders he didn't commit, Granville is a man on the run. He knows too much—but not enough to save himself. He has one hope: penetrate the enigma of the name that began his nightmare—unearth the real identity of . . .

GIDEON

DON'T MISS THE MOST AUTHENTIC THRILLER OF THE DECADE!

REMOTE CONTROL
by Andy McNab

A former member of the Special Air Service crack elite force, Andy McNab has seen action on five continents. In January 1991, he commanded the eight-man SAS squad that went behind Iraqi lines to destroy Saddam's scuds. McNab eventually became the British army's most highly decorated serving soldier and remains closely involved with intelligence communities on both sides of the Atlantic.

Now, in his explosive fiction debut, he has drawn on his seventeen years of active service to create a thriller of high-stakes intrigue and relentless action. With chillingly authentic operational detail never before seen in thrillers, REMOTE CONTROL is a novel so real and suspenseful it sets a new standard for the genre.